Alpha's Redemption: My Luna Has a Son

JESSICA HALL

TRIGGER WARNING

However, much like the first book, these girls can survive anything, and everything and come out stronger for it.

They watched, they saw, they realized I'm more.

People remember those who dare to question, not just follow. Others try to brand and break us, but our strength is ours. We're more than they see.

They say not to fight fire with fire, but they misunderstand. Watch it burn, and see it clear the way for new beginnings. In its aftermath, it will prove that destruction paves the way for creation.

Challenge every limit, question every rule. Show them you're more than just skin and bone. Like green grass after a fire, prove that you come back stronger and more alive than ever.

CHAPTER
ONE

E verly
    The adrenaline coursing through me from standing up to my father is short-lived as we drive out of my father's pack territory, Valen following close behind me. Just before we jump on the main road, he flashes his lights and his voice flits briefly through my head.

'Pull over,' he growls. He's angry.

I quickly pull over to the shoulder of the road and away from other traffic. Ava glances at me.

"Wait here," I sigh, climbing out of the car at the same time Valen does. I ready myself for his anger as he stalks toward me. Just as I'm about to defend my actions, he grabs my face and kisses me, pushing me against my car.

"Don't ever do that again," he mumbles against my lips. His fingers tangle in my hair as his tongue invades my mouth, kissing me angrily before he slows with a groan. My face heats, knowing my sister is in the car while he devours my lips.

"Valen!" I squeak against his lips, pushing on his chest. He growls, still trying to maul my lips, while I look around, embarrassed at his public display. With another growl, he grabs my hand and places it in the center of his chest. His heart is racing beneath my hand, thumping so hard I worry he may have a heart attack.

"You just scared the living daylights out of me. Give me a minute," he growls, pressing his face into my neck and inhaling deeply. As if desperate for reassurance, Valen pushes even closer, his entire body flush against me, and I sigh, running my fingers through his thick hair. This man seems almost on the verge of having a nervous breakdown, and he's supposed to be the blood Alpha?

"Don't ever make me do that again. Do you have any idea how hard it was to walk away and leave you there?" Valen says, his voice pleading.

"I didn't mean to scare you; I'm fine. Everything is fine," I assure him. He sighs, nodding his head before cupping my face in his hands as he steps back.

"You challenged your father!" he says, and I'm not quite sure if he wants to kill me or laugh. I can't help the stupid smirk that splits my face at his words, though. He clicks his tongue and shakes his head.

"You better win because if he hurts you, I will kill your father, and you can't blame me for it," he tells me.

"No one is killing anyone," I tell him, and he presses his lips in a line. I know Valen's angry about learning my father knew all along about Valarian being his, but what's done is done. We can't go back and change it, so there's no point in dwelling on it.

In the car, my phone rings loudly and Ava sticks her head out the passenger window.

"What about your sister?" Valen murmurs. "I don't trust her to stay with us. I know she's your sister but…"

"I didn't ask, and I wasn't going to. She can stay at the hotel," I tell him. He nods, looking over my shoulder, and so do I. Ava waves my phone to me.

"Hospital! About some girl named Emily."

My eyes widen, and Valen lets me go. Racing over to take the phone from her, my hand shakes as I hold the phone to my ear. "Hello?"

"Luna Everly?" says a deep baritone voice on the other end of the line.

"Yes, you're speaking with her," I reply.

"I am one of the doctors taking care of Emily. I was wondering if you are available to come to the hospital? You are her only listed contact, and we have no one listed as her family."

"Yes, correct. She has a son, but we still haven't located him, and her only other relative, her mother, died a few years ago," I say.

"I see. Is it possible for you to come to the hospital?" the doctor asks again.

"Yes, I was heading over anyway. Is everything okay?"

"I'm afraid not, Luna, but it is best explained when you get here," he tells me. My heart sinks. Valen grips my shoulder, and I nod.

"I'll be there soon," I tell the doctor before hanging up.

"Emily?" Valen asks, and I nod, dialing Zoe and Macey before merging their calls into a conference call. They both answer at the same time.

"What's up?" Macey asks.

"It's Emily."

"On my way," Macey says, hanging up.

"I'll get Marcus to take Casey," Zoe says before hanging up as well. I swallow the lump forming in my throat and look at Valen.

"I need to go. Can you take Ava back to the hotel for me?"

"Do you want me to come with you?"

"No, Zoe and Macey will meet there, but can you pick up Valarian?" I say, shaking my head.

"Of course." Valen looks over my shoulder. "Ava!"

She sticks her head out the window and looks at him.

"You're coming with me," he tells her, and she looks at me. I nod and she climbs out of the car. As I turn back to Valen, he kisses the side of my mouth. "Call me if you need me to come over," he says, and I nod, unable to form words right now. Swallowing down my worry, I suck in a deep breath before turning back to my car and climbing in.

I don't even remember the drive to the hospital. I'm on autopilot, praying for some miracle that she'll be alright as worry eats at me, yet the doctor wouldn't have called if she was. No news is good news. News always means something to worry about. As I pull up at the pack hospital, I see Macey rushing toward the front door, and I call out to her. She stops and turns, concern etched into her face, her eyes blurring with tears.

Zoe pulls into the parking lot, zooming past us and into a vacant parking spot. She jumps out, still in her pajamas, slams the door, and runs over to us, looking somewhat pained. She looks like crap—but still, she came.

"Emily?" she asks, hitting her key fob and locking her car.

"I just got here," I tell her, and she nods before we all walk toward the front doors. Once inside, we hurry to the elevator and hit the button for the correct floor.

"You sort out the council stuff?" Zoe asks, straightening her pajamas like it will somehow make her look more presentable. Macey pulls a hair tie off her wrist and pulls Zoe's hair into a bun on her head.

"Yep, I challenged my father for my title," I tell them as the door opens to our level.

"You what?" Macey asks, yet I don't really hear her—my eyes are on the room I know is Emily's. Doctors seem to be rushing in and out everywhere. We pick up our pace and walk into the room.

The doctors look like they've just been getting ready to take her bed somewhere. The doctor notices me and walks over, his notepad in hand, and tucks his pen behind his ear.

"Luna, I'm Doctor Porter," he says with a grim smile, offering me his hand before his eyes darted to Zoe and Macey. He offers his hand to each of them. "You are?"

"Family," they both say simultaneously. The doctor's brows

pinch, making a deep crease between his eyes, but he turns his attention back to me.

He sighs, pulling his glasses from his face and rubbing his eyes before looking over at Emily.

"As you know, Emily has been having trouble fighting off the infection, and we had to remove her leg."

I nod, though I already knew that. I glance at Emily and swallow nervously, watching as nurses fuss over her, unplugging machines and looping up cords. Doc pulls the pen from behind his ear and passes the notepad to me. I glance at it, then look at him.

"We need to take Emily back in for surgery," he says slowly, letting that sink in.

"But she will be alright?" Zoe says, and I look at her. Her lips quiver, and the doctor smiles sadly before turning back to me.

"There is a chance she won't survive the surgery; the infection has spread, and her other leg has turned gangrenous." He points to the notepad in my hands. "This is a DNR. We need to know what your wishes are."

"What's that?" Zoe asks.

"Do not resuscitate," Macey tells her, and Zoe makes a strangled noise like a whimper. I glance down at the paperwork I'm holding.

"You want my permission to let her die?" I ask, shaking my head.

"Luna, you need to think of the future."

I shake my head. "I am. Emily has a son to live for. The answer is no. Do the surgery. She'll pull through," I tell him. He sighs and reluctantly nods his head, taking the clipboard back from me.

"Luna?"

"No, she'll pull through." I look over at Emily with tubes hanging out of her—she can live without legs. And she *will* pull through. I have to believe that. I have to hang onto that.

We're ushered out into a waiting room while she's prepped for surgery and taken away. For hours, we waited, desperate for any news about Emily.

All other issues suddenly seem small in comparison. It's hard to believe that just a short time ago, I was fighting publicly with my father, challenging his title. Macey paces frantically, and I'm surprised she hasn't run tracks into the floor. Zoe stares off blankly, biting her fingernails—a terrible nervous habit she has—but I let it go. I just sit still, numb to everything going on around us. After what feels like eons, the doctor comes down the corridor, and we all jump to our feet. He holds out his hands, and we wait to hear what he has to say.

"She is stable. They are moving her to one of the wards soon, but the infection is moving rapidly throughout her body and putting pressure on her heart. We will be running more tests overnight, but she is a fighter," Doctor Porter tells us, and I let out a breath of relief.

"Can we see her?" I ask, and he nods.

"Yes, just let them get her settled first. She is not responsive, as you know, and I don't see that changing anytime soon, but for now, she is stable. I will have a nurse come get you when you go in," he tells us, and we all nod.

Macey grips both of us, tugging us to her. "Thank the Goddess," she whispers, squeezing us tight.

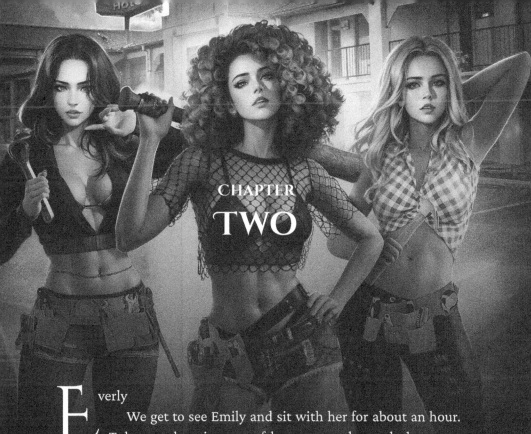

CHAPTER
TWO

E verly
    We get to see Emily and sit with her for about an hour. Tubes are hanging out of her nose and mouth, her arms covered in even more. The room smells heavily of antiseptic, but I can still smell the infection running through her veins, and the IV of antibiotics hooked up to her. Emily doesn't deserve this; nobody does.

She looks so frail, her skin pale, and I find it hard not to break down. Emily was always so bubbly—a real chatterbox. Seeing her like this is heartbreaking. I pray she wakes up soon, pray she will pull through this. I would even drink her terrible coffee. Goddess, I wish I could be drinking that horrible coffee. I wouldn't even complain if it meant she'd come back to us.

Eventually, Zoe has to leave to help Marcus, and Macey wants to go home and check on Taylor. We aren't sure if she can hear us, but they both say goodbye to her anyway. Sitting next to Emily, I hold her hand, rubbing circles on the back of it.

"You hold on, Em. Benny needs you," I tell her. Kissing her hand, I tuck her blankets around her and reluctantly leave as well. It's dark as I climb into my car—it's the middle of the night—and I listen to the radio as I head toward the old commune and to Emily's mobile home on my way to the hotel. I feel mentally and physically drained, and all I want to do is go home, see Valarian, and crawl into bed beside my mate.

The commune is all mud and puddles, the rough terrain a little slippery since the storm, yet I manage to navigate through to the back where Emily's trailer is and get out. Using the key Officer Derrick gave me not long after she went missing, I use it to unlock the flimsy door.

I step inside the tiny little place she shares with her son. Toys and stuffed bears rest on the bed they share, a small TV is perched in the corner, and the walls are littered with Ben's artwork. I see two jars of her special home-made coffee and chuckle.

I also see a blue duffle bag hanging on a hook on the wall and grab it. After going around the little home looking for clothes with her son's scent on them, I carefully bag them, making sure not to taint them with my scent; I hope it will give Emily comfort in her vulnerable state. I also tidy up a little and while doing so, I find a picture of her and Ben taped to her fridge, both smiling as they stand out in the front of the school.

He's only nine years old, and is her entire life, her world; and she's a good mom, quirky, but that's what everyone loves about her. No one loves her more than her son, though. Emily works her ass off, and her only dream is that her son will grow up and one day become part of a pack and have the opportunities the other pack kids have.

We all wish that our kids will be a part of something bigger than us; that they'll achieve more than us. It's what most parents dream of for their kids; to give them more, watch them grow and succeed, knowing we got at least one thing right.

Grabbing the picture, I put it in the bag for her just as my phone starts ringing in my pocket. Valen's name pops up on the screen.

"Where are you?" he says, his voice frantic.

"At Emily's place, grabbing a few things for her room. I'm hoping something with Ben's scent will help her hold on," I tell him.

"Head home now! A forsaken got past the borders! The border patrol has been chasing it for an hour; it keeps going to the commune. Get out now, Everly!" he orders.

"What?" I shriek, looking nervously out the open door of the trailer.

"I'm sending men to your location. Get out now!" he says, and I hurry to grab the bag. Rushing out the door, I lock it before running to my car and tossing the bag onto the passenger seat before quickly starting my car.

"Marcus is on his way!" I hear Valen say as I put the car in reverse and look around into the darkness of the night. The tires spin, yet I'm not moving! The truck only groans as the engine revs, spraying mud everywhere and up the side of my truck. I try to drive forward, but it only makes the hole deeper. I'm stuck!

"Everly?"

"I'm stuck," I tell Valen. My breathing becomes louder as panic sets in.

"Hold on, I'm on my way," Valen says.

"What about Valarian?" I ask, glancing at the phone on the passenger seat, though the sound is coming through the Bluetooth in the car. I don't want my son anywhere near here if a forsaken is on the loose.

"Tatum will watch him till my father gets here," Valen says before hanging up.

"Fuck!" I curse. Just my luck! What's the saying? It happens in threes? Well, I hope this is the last of my bad luck today.

The commune is eerily still—my headlights light up the forest surrounding the commune. As I stare out the windshield, I crack my window just a little to hear howls and wolves in the forest. My heart races, waiting for Marcus or Valen to get here. I refuse to get out of the car; I've watched one too many horror movies and know that's a bad idea.

'*You okay?*' Valen says through the mind-link. I can feel him getting closer, but he's still a fair way out.

'*Yes, fine, just a little freaked out.*' This place is creepy and I don't know how Emily lives out here. Yet, she loves her little spot.

"*I'll be there soon, just keep talking to me,*" Valen says.

I explain about Emily; not that he doesn't already know—he'd been calling me all night, checking in. But rambling is better than panicking. Suddenly, I see a wolf run out of the tree line, two border patrols chasing after it and my eyes widen as I see them tear into the creature. The wolf turns and beelines straight toward my car. Only, it diverts toward the trailer at the last second, clawing at the walls before snarls send it running again. It seems so small for a normal forsaken. It tries to run back toward the tree line to escape, terrified. I watch on in horror.

"*Everly?*" Valen says as I see the two border patrols tear into it. Its howls are horrifying to hear when it's flung across the dirt and suddenly shifts—or tries to. My heart lurches in my chest as I see the figure getting to its feet. Semi-shifted, its body is still covered in fur and its limbs are deformed. He looks like most forsaken, only smaller, until he shifts. It takes me a moment to realize the forsaken is a child. Then it looks at me and I instantly recognize that little face —it's the only recognizable trait he has—and my heart nearly stops.

I don't even remember opening the car door as I see one of the patrols go to rip into him. His petrified eyes, so much like his mother's, widen as I run toward them.

"NO!" I scream. The sound that leaves me is more of a strangled wail as I scream out as one of them tackles him, tearing into his neck and shoulder. He jumps back, looking at me running toward them, waving my arms frantically.

"Please, Goddess, no!" I cry, skidding on the ground as I fall to my knees next to the body. The border patrol try to shove me back, but my claws slip from my fingertips, and slash at them, an angry growl escaping me before I grab him. Sobs wrack my entire body as I smooth back his hair, looking at what has become of him.

He's deformed, and it shouldn't be possible. How is it possible? He's just a boy? He has no wolf yet! One of the patrols shifts back and reaches for me.

"GET A FUCKING AMBULANCE NOW!!" I scream, clutching onto him and trying to protect him from the patrols.

"He's a forsaken," the guard says. I shake my head. The boy's eyes flutter open, bloodshot and rabid, but I only hold him tighter as he thrashes, snarling and growling, trying to attack me. But I know this boy—this isn't him. Someone has done something horrific to him, but that isn't who he is. His wounds are horrific, and he eventually passes out in my arms. His slow heartbeat is the only indicator that he's still alive.

"Call for help!" I wail as tears stream down my face.

"Luna?" the young patrolman questions.

"He isn't forsaken! He's a fucking child!" I scream, baring my canines at them as they slip from my gums.

I hear the mind-link open as the border patrol orders for an ambulance.

"It's okay, it's okay, help is on the way," I whisper to him.

"Luna," the patrolman says, grabbing my arm, but I shake him off.

"Don't touch me," I snap.

"He's dangerous," he tries to reason, but I don't care. I've known this boy since he was in diapers; I've watched him grow. I don't care how dangerous he is, he's family—part of my village.

"He is *not* dangerous. He was trying to come home, trying to come home to his mother," I growl at them.

"Hang on, Ben, hang on for me," I whisper, clutching him closer while my hand presses against his gaping wound, holding it shut, trying to stem the bleeding from his shoulder.

Hearing a car, I see headlights light up the clearing and see Valen jump out of his car frantically. He races toward me. I hear sirens in the distance on their way here and relief washes over me.

"Everly?" Valen screams at me fearfully; probably because I'm so close to the mutated wolf.

"It's Ben, it's Emily's son," I choke out, turning my attention back to the boy in my arm—or half boy.

Valen grabs my arms trying to pull me away, but I shove him off.

"Nobody touches him," I snarl at him. I will not allow them to kill him, I don't care how dangerous he is.

"Everly!" he snarls.

"Tell them to stand down," I growl. Valen growls too, looking at them and nodding for them to back off.

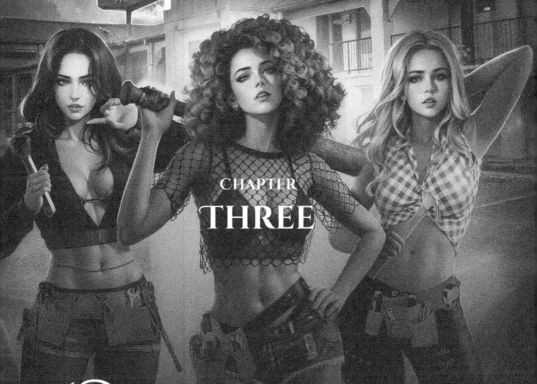

CHAPTER
THREE

One Week Later

Ben has been in the hospital since that night. The doctors have no idea how he was able to shift, but it's becoming clearer that someone is experimenting on not only the forsaken, but also those that were kidnapped from within the city.

This mystery facility that Emily spoke of has become the biggest target on the city's radar. Everyone seems to understand the seriousness of getting to the bottom of it. Ben is not doing well, and every day I've been checking on him and waiting around until the hospital or Valen force me to go home. He's alive, but still in a semi-deformed wolf state. Mostly, he's been unresponsive, just like Emily, and none of the doctor's know how to help him or reverse what was done.

One thing was clear though, Ben had been made into a forsaken. He had turned savage. His little body is ravaged with infections, his heart enlarged, and the few times he's woken, he's tried to attack staff, which has now left him strapped to a bed like a mental patient with a muzzle. A once sweet boy has now been made into some science experiment, and it breaks my heart seeing him like this. The only comfort I have is that he shares a room with Emily.

Her state has not improved either, and the bizarre events are beginning to take a toll on everyone in the city. People are scared—and they should be. Only a monster could do this to a child. This only reignited my fire to ensure the rogues in the city are protected.

Hearing the door open, I look up to see Kalen step inside the room. He's been a great help recently. Valen was busy with pack business, and I've been spending most of the time here or at my hotel, leaving Kalen to watch over Valarian. I never expected him to show up here.

Glancing at the time, I see it's an hour before school pick up; I was about to head over to the school to pick up Valarian . I told Kalen I would today, knowing he needs a break, so I'm surprised when he steps into the hospital room.

Kalen glances down at Ben, brushing his hair from his face. Ben doesn't wake. The entire city has heard and were horrified, despite him being rogue, when they learned what had become of him. Luckily, everyone has found a way to have some heart, probably imagining their own child in the same situation.

"Fucking terrible," Kalen says, smiling sadly.

"What are you doing here?" I ask him and Kalen holds a piece of paper out to me. I take it, noticing the city council emblem on it.

"I pulled a few strings and called in some favors; you get your day to be heard. Your petition will be heard," Kalen says.

"Wait, how? I needed four signatures," I say, confused.

Kalen smiles and I glance at the paperwork to see Kalen has signed as well as a man's name I don't recognize. I look at him questioningly.

"I found a loophole. It said you need four Alpha signatures; nothing stating they can't be from previous Alphas," Kalen says with a sly smile on his face. I glance down at the paperwork to see I have a date and time allotted to be heard by founding council members. One week to prepare. Tears burn my vision as I look back at him.

"Does Valen know?" I ask him and Kalen shakes his head. They are still barely talking unless it has something to do with Valaria—Valen is still upset with his father.

"Thank you," I tell him, and Kalen nods before looking at Emily.

"Any news on how they are doing?" he asks, but I shake my head.

"No. The doctor is due to do his rounds soon, but I need to pick up, Valarian."

"I will wait until the doctor gets here," Kalen tells me, taking a seat in one of the uncomfortable blue chairs.

"Are you sure? The doctor will call me," I tell him.

"Positive. Besides, I have nothing better to do," Kalen tells me. He looks lonely, and I can see this feud with Valen is really starting to take a toll on him. He used to be so involved in his son's life, so it must be hard now that Valen is shutting him out.

I walk over to him, lean down, and give him a hug, pecking his cheek. However, I'm not expecting him to grab a hold of me. He hugs me tight, and it feels good to be hugged by a father figure. Despite Kalen's wrong-doings, Valen doesn't realize how lucky he is to have a father so supportive of him.

"Make Valarie proud. I know you will. Give 'em hell," Kalen whispers to me. With a nod and another peck on the cheek, I quickly leave, heading to the hotel to pick up Ava on the way to the school. I've hardly seen her, and she wants to talk to me about something so she's coming over for dinner tonight. I told her I would pick her up when I did the school run.

My thoughts are plagued lately, and I have trouble keeping my head straight. Now, I have to worry about the upcoming council meeting too. But for the first time all week, I have some hope. Pulling up, I message Ava and wait in the parking lot, staring up at my hotel. I feel like I've neglected it lately. With so much going on, I hardly spend any time here, and when I have a chance, I'm just exhausted. Although I know Zoe and Macey have everything handled or will call if something goes wrong.

Ava takes a few minutes before she appears, coming out of the restaurant doors with her bag slung over her shoulder. She's wearing one of our waitress uniforms. She had wanted to help, and when we were short of staff, she asked Macey if she could. She seems to like it and has been pitching in wherever she's needed.

Opening the car door, she throws her bag over onto the back seat before climbing in and buckling up.

"Any news?" she asks as I start the car and pull out, heading toward the school.

"No, still the same," I tell her and she nods, chewing her nails. She looks nervous, and I glance at her when she remains silent for a bit.

"What is it?" I asked her.

"Mom called me; she said Kalen got your petition pushed through," she says nervously, and I sigh.

"Let me guess, she wants me to pull the petition. Not happening," I tell her.

"She also asked that you rescind the challenge," Ava tells me.

"Also not happening," I tell her, and she nods, looking out the window.

"Are you nervous?" she asks me, but I shake my head.

"Nope. After years of pent-up aggression, it will be good to beat something, or someone; though I wish it wasn't dad," I chuckle, though that's a lie. I didn't want it to come to this, but I feel more than ready for it. Valen has been helping me train late at night when I'm up to it. Not that I'm really worried—I was taught by the best, and you don't suddenly forget.

While I feel like I can handle myself, I am still a little nervous since my wolf isn't nearly as big. I make a mental note to shift soon. Valen has been pestering me about it—he says I have to train in wolf form—yet I never have the time, and I can't exactly shift at home. Training in our living room isn't exactly a good idea in wolf form. That might scare Valarian. Hand to hand, I'll be fine, yet in wolf form...

I'm not sure how I will fair, honestly.

But I know he'll force me sooner or later. Probably sooner when

16

he finds out I have the council meeting in a week, and two days after that is the next full moon and the challenge against my father. So much going on and so little time.

Pulling up in front of the school, I wait for the bell to ring, checking my emails while Ava stares off out the window. Glancing at her, I can tell she wants to say something, and her silence is starting to bother me.

"What is it? Spill. Has this got something to do with what you wanted to speak to me about?" I ask her.

"Kind of." She doesn't elaborate, and I put my phone down to give her my attention.

"Just say it. I won't get angry," I tell her. I could never be angry with Ava, she's my little sister, despite everything.

"Nothing. It's just that being at the hotel and hearing the stories —what everyone puts up with, what you put up with... I should have come with you," she says, wiping a stray tear. "I'm sorry, Everly, I should have done more."

"You have nothing to be sorry for, Ava. You didn't do this. I wouldn't have let you anyway; you were fifteen, what could you have done?" I ask her.

"Been there. I should have been there," she chokes out. I shake my head.

"I'm glad you weren't. And everything turned out alright. I'm alright, Valarian is alright, and you're here now," I tell her, and she nods.

"Mom tried, you know. Her and Dad fought constantly for weeks, but you know how Dad is."

I sigh and nod. The bell rings in the distance and I turn my head to the school, looking for Valarian.

"She still could have called, it's not like I was hiding," I tell her.

"Dad forbade her to go anywhere without her guards or him. Same with me. Damn Nixon ruined everything," Ava says, and my brows furrow.

"What do you mean?" I ask.

"The debt. And I'm pretty sure that's who Dad was planning for you to marry, though I didn't know about that part until the other day, but it makes sense to me now."

"What debt?" I ask, shocked. Ava shrugs.

"It's why he wanted me to marry Valen. If I did, Dad would control half of Valen's assets. Dad wanted Valen to enter into a treaty with our pack. Nixon has been threatening to go to war if Dad's debt isn't cleared soon, so Dad thought if he had Valen on his side, Nixon would back off."

"How much does Dad owe?" I ask.

"I'm not sure, but they had some original deal, which I'm now assuming was you; it's the only thing that makes sense."

"Nixon has a son?" I ask her.

"Yes, he's around Valen's age. His name is Carter. Absolute asshole," says Ava, rolling her eyes.

"How come I've never heard of him before?"

"Nixon hasn't handed the pack down yet. Dad tried to marry me off to him at first, but Carter and I don't get along. The man is a pig."

"So, Dad tried to get you to marry Valen?"

"Yes—told me he had to find the money to pay back the debt he owes Nixon."

"And if he can't?"

"Nixon gets our pack lands. The pack is bankrupt, Everly. It runs off Nixon's finances," Ava explains. Which would explain why Dad backed Nixon over the petition.

Yet, what does Nixon get out of rogues remaining rogue?

CHAPTER
FOUR

Everly

Having Ava over for dinner gave me much to think about. She didn't say anything in front of Valen though, so I ended up waiting patiently for her to leave. Tatum eventually picks her up and runs her back to the hotel, and I realize I should ask Valen about Nixon's son now that Valarian is in bed.

Valen comes walking out of the hall in just a pair of shorts and starts moving the furniture in the living room, pushing it against the windows. I place the last few dishes in the dishwasher and wash my hands before wandering over to him. He points to the couch where he set some yoga pants and my sports bra and I groan.

"Can't we have at least one night off?" I ask him. His only answer is moving the last piece of furniture out of the way. I roll my eyes. I'm exhausted and damn hot. The last thing I want to do is training in the living room and get even more hot and sweaty.

I try to sneak off to shower, yet Valen clearly isn't having that.

"Don't even think about it," Valen growls, and I take off running for the room. I shove the door open and have nearly escaped when his arms wrap around my waist, tugging me back.

"Nice try," he says, turning me and marching me back toward the living room.

"We can have one night off, please. Besides, I want to talk to you, not fucking fight you," I whine.

"We can do both—multitask," he says, and I groan, turning to dead weight in his arms. Valen laughs and continues to drag me toward the living room; I grip the door jamb on the bathroom. I do *not* want to train.

"Everly," he laughs, prying my fingers off the door. "You wanted to challenge your father, therefore, you train or I kill him; which is it?"

"Nope, I'm too tired," I tell him.

"So am I, but you're training."

"Can I bribe you with sexual favors?"

"Hmm, I'm listening? What sort of sexual favors?" he asks, amber eyes narrowing.

"The sort where I can sleep and not have to do anything," I tell him.

"Wait, you want to bribe me with sex, but I gotta do the work?" he chuckles.

"What about an IOU?" I ask.

"Nah, I'll pass. I'll be fucking you anyway. I was thinking you could suck my dick, but since you want to have vanilla sex, I would rather train," Valen says.

"Not vanilla. I was more thinking old man style," I tell him while he tries to get me to stand, but I go all floppy.

"Old man style?" he asks.

"Yeah, where we lay on our sides so I can nap," I laugh.

"Not happening. Now get your ass up and help me drag the mats out," he says, dropping me on my butt beside the TV.

"Run, and I will drag you back," he says while walking off to his little gym at the back of the penthouse.

"Everly!" he calls out when I don't immediately come running after him.

"Yeah, hold your horses. I'm damn well coming," I growl before stalking after him. Valen comes out with a rolled-up blue mat as I pass him in the hall.

"Grab the other one," he says.

I retrieve the other, dragging it down the narrow hallway to the living room. Valen is unrolling the other one before he comes over and helps me undo the strap that holds it together. He unrolls it, and that's already enough exercise for me.

"Everly, hurry," Valen says when I go to lay on the couch. I roll my eyes but snatch up my clothes and quickly run into the bathroom to slip them on before returning to the mats.

"Do you know Al–" The moment I step on it, I'm thrown on my back when he sweeps my feet out from under me. Valen laughs while I glare up at him. He offers me his hand, and I growl at him, slapping it away and getting to my feet.

"As I was saying, do you know Alpha Nixon's son? His name is Carter?" I ask him.

"Why are you asking about him?" Valen asks as he takes his stance. I mirror him, waiting for him to attack. We circle each other looking for an opening.

"Something Ava said to me," I told him.

"What did she say?" he asks, swinging at me, but I duck out of the way, stepping to the side before punching him in the ribs. Valen is bigger, a lot bigger, but I'm quicker.

His foot connects with my thigh a few moments later when he recovers. "You didn't answer," Valen grunts as he blocks me and pins me to the damn floor. I lift my hips, trying to throw him off.

"I don't want to say because it may piss you off," I tell him, trying to get an advantage over him, but I can't really be bothered, and he knows it.

"Come on, it's easy. I've seen you get out of this one," Valen growls at me, but I give up, dropping back on the floor. It's too damn hot for this crap.

"Can you turn the damn AC on at least?" I snap at him. He

growls, pushing off my wrists before moving toward the panel on the wall and fiddling with the air conditioning.

"Better? Now, why are you asking about Carter?"

I chew my lip while he motions for me to get back to my feet, but I refuse, just lying here on the cool mat that's sticking to my back with how much I'm sweating.

"Everly, up now."

I shake my head. Valen growls, reaching down to grab my wrist and haul me to my feet, but as soon as he gets close enough and bends down to grab my hips, I turn on my side and kick his legs out from under him. He lands on his ass and side. I laugh but remain where I am while he rubs the hip he landed on.

"Ava told me Carter was who I was supposed to be married off to," I tell Valen. He sits up abruptly, looking down at me.

"And you're only just telling me this now?" he growls.

I shrug. "So you do know him?"

"Of course I know him. We're the same age, I saw him a few times at meetings. But I wasn't aware he was back in the city."

"What do you mean?"

"He left after high school. Been years since I saw him last. He went looking for his mother," Valen tells me.

"His mother? Wait, Nixon's mate isn't his mother?"

Valen shakes his head. "No, Carter's mother was a forsaken, and the woman you see with Nixon isn't his real mate. He took her as a mate; she was his mistress while he was married to his first wife."

"Wait, if Carter's mother is forsaken, why did he go looking for her?"

"She wasn't always a forsaken, but she was one of the forsaken we kept an eye on. When Nixon met Leah, she was an Omega and he was already married. Leah had Carter and Nixon took him. She stayed in the city for a while until Nixon marked his other mistress after Leah killed his wife."

"Leah killed his wife?"

Valen nods. "Nixon's first wife was an arranged marriage; he never marked her. She found out about Leah and attacked her. Leah stabbed her in self-defense," Valen says, wiping a hand down his face.

"He still chose his mistress over Leah. It sent her over the edge and she left the city. Carter went looking for her not long after graduation; he wanted to find his real mother. Only, when he did, she was a forsaken. She attacked him and bit him."

"And he lived?" I ask.

"Yes, he's an Alpha, plus she was his mother. It's unclear to us why that made a difference, but he was only sick for a bit. Dad said he was never the same afterward though. Then he snapped."

"What do you mean?"

"You think *I'm* a savage? Carter was placed in a mental hospital after he killed eight of his pack members, so I'm surprised his father brought him back to the city. He may have survived being attacked by his mother, but the poison still had some effect on him. He's unhinged," Valen explains.

"Well, Ava said she met him and he was a pig. Why would my father agree to marry me off to him, then, knowing that? Seems extreme to marry your daughter off over a debt—especially to a monster."

"Your father's pack is in debt?" Valen asks, bracing his arms on his knees.

"Yes, I think that's why Dad has been helping Nixon. Ava said Nixon gets Shadow Pack lands if he can't cover the debt."

"How much is the debt?" Valen asks. I shake my head.

"No, idea, but enough that Dad was willing to marry Ava off to you so she could hand over half your territory to Nixon," I tell him.

"I'm surprised your father would agree to that," Valen says, his brows pinching together.

"Yeah. But it explains why Nixon refused to sign my petition about the rogues now, especially since his only child was attacked by one, even if it *was* his fault," I sigh.

"Carter isn't an only child; he's a twin. He has a twin sister, Alisha," Valen says.

"Ava never mentioned her," I tell him.

"Probably because most don't know she exists. I only know because my father told me. Alisha has been in a coma since Carter found her; she lived with their mother. She wasn't a forsaken, though. That's the odd thing. She was able to survive having a forsaken for a mother, but when Carter found them, Leah attacked him. Alisha saved him and her mother turned on her. She's been in a coma since, like Emily. Carter managed to find a way home, but she never woke from the coma, and Carter was sent away to the mental hospital."

My mind is reeling at what he just told me. This is so much information to take in.

"Wait, he only took Carter?"

"Yeah, Nixon has always been a piece of shit. Not only did his mate end up a forsaken, but he also ditched his daughter and only took his son."

"How doesn't the city know about this?"

"Same as no one knew about my mother or you being John's daughter—he made her disappear," Valen tells me. "But I want to know why Carter is suddenly back in the city."

"Maybe he recovered," I tell him.

"No, that's what I'm finding weird. Why would Nixon risk it? Everyone knows about Carter killing his own people. If the city found out he was back, it would cause hysteria."

"What do you mean?"

"Carter didn't just kill his pack members. He ate them and hung their pelts on border fences. The man is sadistic," Valen says.

"Yes, but he's also Nixon's only heir, isn't he? And he can't be too crazy—Ava met him. She said he was a pig but never mentioned him acting insane," I tell him.

"Hmm, I think tomorrow I may have to go see for myself," Valen says.

"You're going to go see Carter?"

"Yes. This is my city, Everly, and I want to know why the fuck Nixon brought a psychotic serial killer back without informing me," Valen says, getting to his feet. He offers me a hand and I grab him, letting him pull me to my feet. He pauses for a second, his hand cupping my face, then smirks, his eyes flashing black.

"What?"

"I suppose I'll be getting that BJ," he purrs.

"Yeah, not likely," I tell him, and he chuckles.

"We'll see," he growls, yanking me toward him and wrapping his arms around my waist.

"You seem so sure of yourself," I growl as he buries his face in my neck and inhales deeply before purring.

"I am, because you're going into heat," he purrs, nipping at my neck.

CHAPTER

FIVE

Valen jinxed me. He said I was going into heat and I am. Here I was, thinking I'm coming down with the flu. If only it was that. The last thing I want is to go into heat. It irks me.

I wake up to his fingers trailing up and down my spine. Valen seems to be enjoying himself, like he's been waiting for it to get so bad that it would wake me. The flare of instant heat rolls over me from head to toe as I roll over and find him smiling at me seductively. He traces his fingertips around my areola, making me look down to find I had stripped in my sleep. I groan when I lift my head to see my clothes have been dumped on the floor. By me? Or by Valen? Either way, Valen just lies here expectantly, like he was simply biding his time until I woke.

"Well, would you look at that? I was right," he purrs. His hand grips my arm and he drags me on top of him. I try to growl, yet I'm surprised to hear a moan escape my lips instead. His skin makes mine tingle and cool as I lie on his chest. His fingers move lazily up my sides and I bury my face in his neck. My tongue rolls over his mark. Coherent thoughts become harder to maintain as his scent consumes me, his gentle touch electrifying. He lies there, teasing the heat that starts to overwhelm me, threatening to set me on fire.

Valen chuckles as I nip and lick his skin. I want to devour the man, climb inside him. I can't get enough of him, can't get close enough as my lips nip and lick my way down his body before wrapping around his cock. Valen laughs. I stare at him, trailing my tongue up the side of his hard length, enjoying the taste of him on my tongue. His eyes flicker black and he smirks mischievously.

"Looks like I don't have to worry about the IOU," he chuckles, confusing me for a second until I take him in my mouth. His cock hits the back of my throat as I take him deeper before it registers. I peek up at him to find him smirking as he places his hands behind his head.

I raise an eyebrow at him and feel my own eyes flicker before dragging my teeth up his length. Valen hisses and his hand moves to my hair like he's worried I may bite it off. Instead, my tongue teases the rim as I wrap my lips around the head, swirling the tip of my tongue around it. He relaxes and sighs. My lips suction around the tip before leaving his aroused flesh with an audible pop.

"Okay, okay, I won't tease," Valen growls. I growl back at him and he puts his hands up in surrender.

My eyes narrow at him, yet my lips return to his cock. He groans as I take his entire length, loving the saltiness of his flesh on my tongue. His fingers tangle in my hair before he fists it, pushing me down on his cock. In response, my hands grip his thighs and my nails dig into his flesh as he brutally thrusts into my mouth, making my eyes water as his cock hits the back of my throat.

The heat craves this rough side of him, relishes the way he forces more of himself in my mouth. The heat soars and my arousal coats the insides of my thighs before he yanks me off him by my hair, pulling me up his body. His lips are demanding and they crash against mine hungrily as he dominates my mouth.

Valen groans, his other hand gripping my hip tightly; so tight I know it will leave bruises as my skin pinches between his fingers. His hold on my hair grows tighter as my heat sucks him in, unleashing the beast that lives within him.

My hips roll against him. His hand gripping my hip moves to my ass, his fingers digging into the flesh there. A whimper escapes my lips, turning to a moan as he squeezes my ass before sitting up with me on his lap and turning.

His movements are too quick to react to as he slams me on my back. Desire writhes through every cell as I stare up at his lust-filled, demonic eyes. His canines jut out between his parted lips. Valen's hands move down my legs, then back up my thighs to my hips before he grabs me again, flipping me over onto my stomach and pulling my ass up into the air.

Sparks rush over my flesh and my pussy clenches in anticipation as he sinks his cock into my depths with one hard thrust. The heat flares to life with a renewed vigor, craving his touch and what it has to offer. His pelvis slaps against my ass, and my walls clench around him like a vice. My legs tremble with need and desire as he drags his cock out slowly, his fingers digging into my ass as he watches himself slipping out of my wet confines before slamming back in.

A moan escapes me as the top half of my body flattens against the bed, my fingers clenching the sheets as he drives himself into me. His hard length scrapes along my inner walls, building friction. My blood ignites like fire in my veins and sparks rush everywhere with each harsh thrust, making me cry out in pleasure.

My insides clench around his large, thick length, my legs shaking and threatening to give out under me, sweat glistening on my skin. My entire body heats as I climb higher into this incredible feeling, my entire body tensing for the exhilarating rush. Valen's hold tightens, his grip almost punishing, yet I relish the pain and pleasure, the line between them blurring as I writhe beneath him, pushing back against him, forcing him in deeper and harder.

Slapping flesh and my cries fill the room beneath Valen's hard breathing. He leans over me, squeezing my breast before yanking me up to him, his hot chest pressing against my back. His grip is painful as he squeezes my breast while he uses his other hand to sweep my hair to one side. The points of his teeth puncture my flesh, breaking the skin as he sinks them in deeply, sending me blissfully over the edge.

The fall into pleasure is violent and tumultuous, and my body convulses in his arms, yet his pace never relents. He drives himself into me and impales me on his cock as his canines slip from my skin and his tongue rolls over my heated flesh, making my toes curl as I ride out the waves of my climax.

My pussy tries to keep its grip on him when he pulls out of me. I gulp when I'm shoved on my back. The intense, animalistic look on his face no doubt mirrors mine as he growls, shoving my thighs apart before sheathing himself inside me. The night slips by without any way to measure time, my heat not abating until I sink my teeth into his flesh.

Valen groans, his cock twitching deep inside me as my walls grip and squeeze him until his hot semen coats my insides. I pull my teeth from his neck, breathing harshly as he drops on top of me. Both of us are sore and exhausted beyond anything I've felt before.

Exhaustion smashes into me once again as my temperature drops, and Valen pulls out of me, rolling onto his back beside me, his breathing heavy. My eyes flutter shut and I welcome sleep.

My brain tries to process the incessant noise that's invading the darkness of my sleep. My eyes feel like sandpaper as I try to force them open. Light filters into the room through closed drapes and I can just make out the sounds of cartoons coming from the living room. My phone starts ringing again, the ringtone loud as it vibrates on the bedside table.

Valen groans beside me, slapping the table, trying to shut the noise off. My body feels heavy as I drag my body over his to reach for my phone. It stops ringing the moment I grab it and I roll back to my side of the bed. With sleepy eyes, I squint at the screen to see thirteen missed calls from Macey and seven from Zoe, and a ton of calls from the hospital. I'm about to unlock my phone to call them back when it vibrates in my hand. Sitting up, I realize instantly that something has to be wrong for there to be so many missed calls.

The fog lifts and fear seeps into me as I watch it ringing in my hand. Macey's face pops up on the screen and the ringtone blares loudly. My hands shake as I swipe my thumb over the screen and answer it.

"Everly!" Macey gasps before she sighs heavily; her breathing is shaky as I listen to her on the other end.

"What is it?" I ask and Macey makes a choking noise. My entire body trembles when she doesn't answer straight away.

"Macey?" I ask, my voice shaking with fear.

"You need to get here," she says, the words sounding so broken. The emotion in her voice as she stammers and cries into the phone has me scrambling to my feet. I jump to the floor and grab whatever my hands land on first.

"What happened?" I ask, frantically dragging a shirt over my head and placing the phone back to my ear.

Macey cries, the sound crushing my soul and twisting my stomach as dread fills me.

"It's Ben," she sobs, and my heart stutters and threatens to stop beating at her words. A cold, sinking feeling settles over me. Valen sits up, looking for danger, and tears burn my eyes as I stare at him, shell shocked. No! Not Ben! My heart and soul screams for the boy, for Emily. It would kill her if something happened to him. Valen gets to his feet, looking alarmed.

"Everly?" he asks.

"I have to go. I need to get to the hospital," I tell him as the cold feeling washes over me again, making me numb and turning my veins to ice. I feel like I'm moving on autopilot as I throw clothes on without seeing them. Valen chases me around the apartment as I grab my handbag and keys, only stopping when I notice Valarian sitting at the coffee table watching cartoons and eating a bowl of cereal. He looks over at me—Ben is his friend, not much older than my son.

"Mom?" Valarian says as I stare at him unblinkingly; a parent's worst fear.

My voice is robotic. "Everything is fine. Eat your breakfast," I tell him.

"I'll head over as soon as Dad gets here," Valen tells me, gripping my arms. He shakes me a little and I blink rapidly, turning to look at him.

"I have to get to him," I gasp before turning on my heel and running toward the door.

CHAPTER
SIX

Walking into the hospital, I find Macey and Zoe pacing outside Emily's and Ben's room. Tears streak both their faces and Macey's eyes are puffy. Whatever is going on is terrible because Macey never cries; she never even gets emotional. She keeps her walls high and takes on the world with a no-fucks-given attitude. My stomach plummets as I approach them, my entire body shaking. The moment I get to them, the door opens and the doctor steps out with a grim expression on his face.

Macey instantly turns to face him. "Well?" she asks, but Doc's shoulders drop.

He looks tired, and I can't imagine having his job—having to deliver bad news to families or parents. Bad news is precisely what we got when he spoke.

"As you know, Ben deteriorated overnight. His blood test when he first came in showed some hope, he wasn't a full-blown forsaken, but now he is. His body is shutting down, his organs are failing; he doesn't have much time left."

I swallow his words down and bite the inside of my lip to stop the quiver. "Emily?" I ask, clearing my throat.

"The only thing keeping her alive is the machines. Without them, she will die," Doc answers. We already knew that, but I had some hope. Doc just killed that hope.

"Is he still conscious?" Zoe asks.

"He keeps coming in and out. One minute he almost seems lucid, the next, he is hurting himself or trying to attack the nurses," Doc says.

"So, what now?" I ask.

"There is nothing else we can do. We did dialysis, but the infection is not just in his blood; it's in his muscles, bones, everything. I'm sorry, Luna, but now we just wait."

"Wait for him to die?" I ask. Doc smiles sadly and nods. I press my lips in a line and gulp before clearing my throat. Zoe sits heavily in the chair by the door.

"He's just a child," she says, putting her head in her hands. Macey grips her shoulder, hugging her against her hip.

"Thank you for everything, Doc," I tell him.

"You're more than welcome to stay with him. I will send some chairs in for you all," he says, wandering down the hall.

I stare at the ceiling, willing the tears to go before pushing the door open and stepping inside. Macey follows me in, sitting beside him and grabbing his hand. Zoe enters too, but remains close to the wall as she stares, not knowing what to do. Doc comes back in with two extra chairs, and I sit between Emily's and Ben's beds, holding Ben's hand and rubbing circles on the back of it. Hours pass.

Ben eventually comes to, thrashing and snarling periodically.

"He didn't deserve this," Macey says, gently brushing his bangs from his deformed face. She sniffles when Valen walks in. He nods to us before hugging Zoe, who is a mess at the back of the room.

"Marcus is on his way," he tells her, and she nods. He kisses her trembling forehead as she stares off vacantly, her eyes glued to Ben and Emily.

Macey falls asleep for a while, and Zoe leaves to get coffee and update the hotel on their wellbeing. She's been gone for about five minutes when the alarms start sounding as the monitors go off. Macey sits upright in a panic just as Ben starts thrashing, his heart rate increasing and blood streaming out of his ears and eyes as he tries to breathe around the tube in his mouth.

Nurses rush in, shutting everything off and I squeeze his hand while Macey whispers to him. Ben's eyes open with a crazed gleam, yet I see him—see the boy he once was, the scared look beyond them. He tries to speak around the tube, and one of the nurses runs out of the room, unable to watch when he gasps.

"Mom," he rasps, the sound barely audible, and Macey breaks, sobbing while clutching his hand. The moment Zoe walks in with the coffees, she shoves the tray at Valen before rushing over, gripping Ben's legs, and rubbing them.

"Can't you give him something to help calm him?" Macey asks the doctor, who lingers helplessly.

"We have already given him everything. Nothing works," he murmurs, holding back his own tears.

Macey and the doctor talk, but I just can't stop staring at Ben's wide eyes looking back at me unblinking. Before I even think about what I'm doing, I undo his handcuff with the key that sits beside the bed and let down the guard rail on the bed. His hand flails, grasping air before I climb on the bed beside him. Ben snaps and snarls at me. He thrashes when I slide my arm under his body and sit beside him, pulling his legs over my lap.

Gently, I guide his head to rest on my shoulder with my hand on his forehead so he can't turn it to bite as he squirms—not that he can do much with the tube in his mouth. Macey reaches over, holding out her hand for the key to unlock the other cuff. Doc protests, but I hand it to her, ignoring him.

"Luna, he is dangerous," Doc says, and Valen goes to reach for me, but I pull away.

"No!" I tell Valen when he tries to pull me off the bed.

"Everly," he whispers, watching Ben grip and claw at my arm with his free hand.

"No, he's scared. Emily can't hold him, so I'll do it for her, as she would for me," I tell him, my voice breaking, knowing she would. No matter the risk to herself, she's part of our village, and when one falls, the rest pick up the slack.

Macey undoes his other hand and moves over, gripping my shoulder. I readjust him on my lap, turning my face into his hair and humming to him as Macey moves beside Valen. He steps out of her way so she can drag the little side table out of the way and drop the side rail on Emily's bed before walking around to the other side of it. Doctors and nurses try to stop her, but they're already dying; what does it matter if cords get tangled?

Macey pushes Emily's bed flush against Ben's, who gasps for air. I stroke his hair before gripping his wrist and moving it to Emily's arm. He whimpers, clutching her forearm tightly, and calms; he stops thrashing completely. He may be forsaken, but he knows his mother's touch.

"She's right there, Ben. Right here with you," I whisper to him. "She loves you so much," I tell him as his breathing slowly evens out. His blood is soaking my shirt, which I realize is inside out anyway, but I simply stare up at the ceiling and just hold him. Macey rubs his back, and Zoe cries while stroking his legs in my lap. The room falls silent, the only sound, his heart rate monitor. I turn my head to look at Emily.

All the things she wanted for her son come to mind: how she worked her ass off to provide for him, never turning down a shift; how she would bring Ben to play with Valarian and Casey if she couldn't get a sitter, just so she didn't miss a shift. She wanted so much for him, and this wasn't it. I look at Valen, who stands there with a hand under his chin, worry etched on his face at how close I am to Ben.

This boy is not a monster. He's a sweet boy. Emily's boy. I kiss Ben's forehead. I can't fix this; our emergency fund can't bail them out; no cure will save him; there's nothing we can do. But I can give her one thing.

I let my claws slide from my fingertips before digging them into my palm; my blood pools in my hand. Macey lifts her head and her lips quiver when I move him, making sure his hand remains on Emily. I pull his other hand from under him, preparing to slice his palm too. The moment I do, Valen reaches over the bed and grips my wrist to stop me. I just stare at him. He looks at Ben and drops his head. He knows what I want.

"You're not doing it. His blood could make you sick," Valen whispers.

"It's all she wanted, and he can't pledge; a blood link is the only way," I tell him, and he looks down at Emily, who he was leaning over. He sighs.

"I'll do it," he murmurs, gripping my wrist. He looks up at me and releases me, his eyes on me as he slashes his palm with his claws. Ben doesn't move or even flinch as I do the same to his free hand that's lying limp on my belly.

Valen reaches over and grips his hand, and I stroke Ben's hair. "I, Alpha Valen of the Nightshade pack–" his words cut off as he looks up. Marcus is standing behind Zoe, his arms wrapped around her waist and his eyes glazed over; he's mind linking.

"You sure?" Valen asks, and I see Marcus nod before Valen turns his gaze back to Ben. "I, Alpha Valen of the Nightshade pack, welcome Ben Steele and declare him the new Beta of the Nightshade Pack," he murmurs. Marcus gasps as his title is stripped, and Zoe reaches up, cupping his cheek with her hand. It will only be temporary, but it probably still stung Marcus.

Suddenly, the mind-link opens up and our pack welcomes Beta Ben, bringing tears to my eyes. I don't know whether he can hear them, but he will not die a rogue. Valen then does the same to Emily and I feel her tether form. Fear courses through me, knowing soon, both their tethers will sever and it will be crippling, but we can grant this wish. Doc stabs a needle in Valen's arm as he stands back up.

"Precaution," Doc murmurs to Valen, who nods. I swallow,

knowing precisely what he risked for them, yet he did, so I didn't have to.

Macey grabs Emily's hand and kisses it as we wait. About an hour later, Emily's machine starts beeping, and Doc checks it, looking at me, and so does Macey. The nurses bring paddles near the bed like they're waiting for the time they'll need them.

Ben's breathing slows, and his heart rate becomes weaker until I suddenly hear him gasp and stop. I clutch him tighter, whispering how much his mother loves him, how much we all love him when his heart rate monitor flat-lines. The newly formed pack tether snaps and pain ricochets through me, ripping at my heart, and my stomach twists. Valen clutches the bed, gasping and sweating until it passes.

I know he is gone.

Zoe sobs and Macey bawls; my entire body shakes as I hold him.

"Luna, we can..." Doc starts to stay, and I stare up at the ceiling.

"Leave her, let her go. Let her be with her son," I croak out.

The nurses move around, fussing with lines and tubes when Macey grips one of their arms.

"If I was in her place, I wouldn't want to wake to my son gone," Macey stammers, choked with emotion. She's right; Emily wouldn't want to be here. Ben was her whole world, just like I couldn't live without my son.

"Turn her machines off," I order Doc. I don't care if they can restabilize her; I know Emily, and life wouldn't be worth living stuck on life support without her son. She held on long enough.

Nurses nod, turning machines off while Doc presses a stethoscope to Ben's chest, calling his time of death, though we know he's gone; his heart no longer beats and his blood pressure bottoms out as blood leaks from his eyes, nose, and mouth. Macey pulls the beds apart so the nurses can clean him up. I continue to sit up with him, letting them remove his tubes and lines before Macey moves his mother over. Emily's body convulses, and unconscious process has her gasping as I lay Ben beside her.

Standing beside her, I brush her hair back while Macey kisses her hand before cupping it to her cheek. She then lays Emily's hand on Ben's shoulder.

"It's okay, Emily. Ben is home," I tell her while patting her hand. "He's safe beside you," I tell her as my tears drip on his little shoulder.

I stroke her hair again, leaning over to kiss her head. "You got your wish. Ben was Beta to Nightshade. He's pack, just like you. You can let go now. You don't need to hold on. We brought Ben home. He's safe with you now," I choke, my voice trembling as her mouth opens, gasping but not actually breathing.

CHAPTER
SEVEN

Valen

My heart breaks for Everly, Zoe, and Macey as they tell Emily it's okay to go—that she doesn't have to hold on any longer. Moments pass and hushed whispers circle the room as they try to soothe their friend. She gasps one last time and I hold my breath, waiting to see if it's a false alarm, yet praying it isn't. She shouldn't suffer anymore, no one deserves to suffer this fate. Everly drops her head on Ben's shoulder and sobs. I feel Emily's pack link sever.

My heart pangs with pain—if only briefly—yet the pain, anguish, and despair that floods from Everly through the bond as she mourns her family breaks my heart further. Marcus hugs Zoe close as she falls apart. Macey just stares vacantly ahead, sitting back down in her chair.

The doctor checks Emily and nods, calling the time of death before saying he'll leave to let them say their goodbyes. The girls tuck the two of them in like they're saying goodnight and not good-bye, and the doctor comes back and tells Everly what will happen next.

"Come on," Marcus whispers to Zoe, pulling her from the room, and Macey quickly follows, closing the door behind them.

Everly kisses the mother and son once again and stands upright. I watch as she swallows down the emotion that threatens to consume her. She tugs her shirt off, pulls it back on the right way, and cleans her face with some water from the sink basin, washing away the tears that stain her face. I move toward her, wanting to comfort her, but she pulls away, looking at me. I drop my hand.

"I'm sorry, but please don't touch me right now," she whispers.

I know if I do, she'll break. I get it, but the urge is still there, the bond calling me to my mate. Her eyes soften as she stares at me and I nod, letting her get herself together. She loved, lost, and mourned, and I am awed by how quickly she slips back into business mode, shuts down everything, and forces her anguish back. Her determination returns, knowing that she has work to do. She broke, if only briefly, before picking herself up and dusting herself off, ready for battle again.

I hate that she instinctively switched and shut down, a coping mechanism from years of taking on everything and everyone else's problems and emotions while ignoring her own. She has me, but Everly has been forced to be independent, endure, and never rely on anyone. She will deal, conquer, and then break when safely alone. But for now, she has to put on a front to do what needs to be done. It makes me realize what sort of leader she is and what sort of Luna she will be—unbreakable to the rest of the world. She's the rogue community's anchor despite the pressure of drowning herself, taking on the persona and getting things done.

The amount of impact she's had on the rogues and how much they look up to her doesn't hit me until I step out the doors after her. I hear Everly gasp before she moves down the corridor. Rogues line the walls, heads down, each one bowing as she passes.

Her village.

That word suddenly takes on a new meaning—what it represents. Everly, Zoe, and Macey were never rogue. The three of them brought hope to the rogues, and they rally for their leaders, and for Emily and Ben. A family built on love and respect. Everly grips my hand as I step beside her and I give it a squeeze.

"You don't have to be strong, you know," I whisper.

"Yeah, I do, for them," she whispers back.

Macey and Zoe wait by the exit doors and Everly lets me go. She walks toward them and they wrap their arms around her waist. The rogues look up to those three. And both girls—Macey, despite being older, and Zoe younger—look to Everly. She is the chief of the village they built. She is their armor, and she wears it proudly. Ava stands outside the doors, looking lost as her sister steps out with Zoe and Macey.

The three girls have a bond, a sisterhood built on their blood, sweat, and tears, and with undying, unconditional love. Ava, for so long, had a strained relationship with her sister and knows she isn't Everly's only sister now. I can see the pain in her eyes as she watches them. But like true queens, they stop, and Macey offers her hand to Ava, who takes it, letting out a shaky breath. Macey tosses an arm over her shoulder, tugging her into their circle, accepting her as one of them.

I look at the overcast sky; storm clouds roll across the horizon. The day is as gloomy as it is depressing. Yet, as the rogues file out after their chiefs, their honorary Lunas, I chuckle and smile as Marcus stops beside me. He leans his shoulder against mine, nodding his head toward them. My mother's words about Everly are so true, and I now understand what she meant.

"Watch her."

I do as she leads her people down to the parking lot. They stand in a circle, hands clasped, the four girls in the middle. Every rogue had come to say goodbye, no matter their state—some still in their work uniforms—having stopped whatever they were doing and running when their family needed them, running to see them off. She calls it her family, her village, but it isn't a village; they are a pack. And as Everly turns her face up to the sky and howls, everyone follows in unison, saying their final goodbyes.

They were never rogue. This is what a pack is. And at the center stands their Alpha. Not by birth, but because she earned the right; she earned their respect and fought for them when no one else would. A true leader. Everly's determination is admirable, and the woman truly is remarkable. A chorus of howls fills the silence, and I offer my own howls as they say goodbye. Mom would be so proud. I am proud.

Everyone thinks she is just a lucky rogue, who an Alpha claimed. Yet, looking at her now, I realize I'm the lucky one. I never claimed her. I thought I did, but a woman as strong as she can't be claimed. She was the one that did the claiming. She didn't need me; she had herself and the village she built. Furthermore, she knows who she is, and she isn't afraid to be it. She will fight, and I know she will win, and I will love watching every second of it as she reclaims the city and changes it.

As she makes Mom proud.

CHAPTER
EIGHT

E verly

Four Days Later

We held the funerals yesterday.

Today, I just can't cope with work, so I've decided to start the mural on either side of the door leading into the old school, now the homeless shelter. I designed the sign and sent it off last night to my manufacturer. When I walk into work to find everything handled and for once, the sky showing no sign of rain, I get a head start on the mural.

I have two days until the council meeting, and two days after that, I have the challenge for my father's pack. I'm a little nervous about exactly what it is I'm getting myself into with his pack, especially if it's bankrupt like Ava believes. Yet, if I can restore a hotel to its former glory, I have no doubt I can dig the pack out of the hole my father dug.

I forgot how much I enjoy drawing and painting, though the old, rendered brickwork is making it a bitch to stencil out the design with my paintbrush. I've done the background white, like a canvas, though standing on a ladder while it's windy isn't ideal. Hearing a car pull up along the road behind me, I glance over my shoulder to see it's Valen's. He hops out, walking over to me.

"Everly, the wind is hectic today. Get down before you fall off," Valen scolds, coming over and holding the ladder. I shake my head but climb down anyway.

"I have a harness," I tell him, unclipping it as I reach each step on the ladder, but he shakes his head.

"A harness won't do much good if that ladder unhooks from up top. It's only hooked to the gutters. That's not the sturdiest thing, especially those old, crumbling ones. It would have been best if you had told me you were doing such a gigantic mural; I would have had a cherry picker brought over. Don't use the ladder. I'll get one sent over tomorrow," Valen scolds, and I shake my head.

He has a point, though, and the site supervisor also gave me a lecture about the same thing, making me wonder if he called Valen.

"The site supervisor called you, didn't he?" I tell Valen. He smirks.

"Of course," he says, and I roll my eyes.

"I thought you had your meeting today with your father over pack business?"

His eyes darken slightly, and he sighs. "I sent my accountant instead," he says while bending down to help pick up my supplies. I pack them into a box and put them in the cleaning closet just inside the school doors.

"You can't just avoid your father," I tell him, following him out to his car.

"Unless it has something to do with Valarian, I don't want to hear it," Valen growls, opening the driver's door.

"Valen, he is your father, and he's a wonderful dad," I tell him.

"He lied to me," Valen states. I sigh, climbing into the car.

"Your mother wouldn't want you to toss your father away. He fucked up, but he's trying to make up for it. The petition got pushed through by him. He drops everything he is doing whenever we need

44

his help with Valarian," I tell him, and he starts the car, nodding his head in reluctant acknowledgement.

We head to school to pick up Valarian. When the bell rings, he comes running out excitedly, jumping up and down to show the painting he had done in class.

"Wow!" Valen says, looking at it. Casey comes over to show us her painting—it's covered with glitter and swirling scribbles, while Valarian's is all straight lines of paint that look like he used a ruler to make sure he didn't go out of the perceived lines. I smile down at him, and he grabs his father's hand as we cross the road to the car. Once in the car, we head home, listening to the radio talking about the upcoming council meeting.

"It appears war is brewing between Alpha Nixon and Alpha Valen. Alpha Nixon was spotted today leaving the council chambers in a rage after learning Alpha Valen's mate, Everly Summers—the infamous disgraced daughter of Alpha John from Shadow Pack—has petitioned to have the laws involving the unfair treatment of rogues changed. Alpha Nixon refused to speak to the media today after he was caught in an argument with Alpha John just in front of the building before reversing into Alpha John's car. It appears tensions among the packs are high, and over the next few weeks, we will either see change within the city or war."

Valen turns the radio off, glancing at me, and I sigh.

Great, the media is going to blow this right up, and if there isn't a war already, they will ensure one starts with the hysteria they'll cause.

"Would the City really go to war over Mom's petition?" Valarian asks, and Valen glances in the mirror at him.

"Hopefully not, but unfortunately, people don't like change. Greed and entitlement start countless issues," Valen tells him.

"But rogues have nothing. They aren't even allowed to own housing," Valarian says.

"And that is why your mother is petitioning to have the laws changed."

"So, Alpha Nixon wants to take more from the rogues when they already have nothing? What's left to take?" Valarian asks.

"Their lives, that's all that's left; and people like Nixon think they deserve to play Goddess and dictate how people should live and what laws they should live by," I answer with a sigh.

"But isn't your dad on his side?"

"He's on the wrong side," I agree

"Does that upset you?" Valarian asks, and I look at him over my shoulder.

"No, because that shows *his* character, not mine," I tell him.

"But you're his daughter?"

"Yes, that's true, but I am not my father or my mother. I am my own person, just like you are your own person," I tell him.

"So I shouldn't be like you or dad when I'm older?" he asks.

"No. Strive to be better, surpass us. One day, be a better Alpha than me," Valen says.

"What if I don't want to be an Alpha?" Valarian asks.

"Then I will find someone else to take over the pack."

"What if I want to be Luna, like Mom?" Valarian asks.

"Then you will be Luna Valarian," Valen chuckles.

"Doesn't sound very cool, no offense, Mom. I think I'll stick with Alpha Valarian," Valarian says, and Valen snickers.

"What? The Luna is more important than the Alpha," Valarian says.

"Is that so?" Valen asks.

"Yep. The Alpha keeps the packs in line, the Luna keeps the Alpha in line." Valarian shrugs, and I laugh, glancing at Valen.

"You think this is funny? Our son just emasculated me," Valen chuckles.

"Alphas—so sensitive," I tell him, patting Valen's shoulder while shaking my head.

We head home, and on the way, I text Kalen to come over for dinner. It's time these two have a chat. Kalen is trying, but Valen has to put in some effort on his end.

Dinner was awkward. Valen and Kalen only spoke about Valarian until Kalen helped Valen do the dishes while I sat on the couch with Valarian; we were watching some kid's show while I tried not to listen.

Around 8 p.m., Valen got a call and walked outside to take it before returning, saying he had to head out. Kalen also said he should head home since it was a school night. Valen was gone for hours, and eventually, Valarian went to bed.

After reading to him, tucking him in, and getting into my own pjs, I only hear my phone ringing in the living room after I close the door; the call is from Zoe—it's unusual for her to call so late.

When I answer and hear her frantic voice, I know instantly something is wrong; the sirens in the background make my heart thump in my chest.

"Everly," she sobs into the phone. All the air is sucked from my lungs at her words and tone.

"Zoe? What is it?"

"Can you hear me?" she asks.

"Zoe?"

"It's gone, Everly! It's gone!"

"What's gone?"

"The hotel! It spread so fast. You need to get here!" she cries before the phone cuts out. I try calling her number again, but all I get is her voicemail. I instantly call Valen's number.

Valen

My father and I stand awkwardly in the elevator together, both staring at the doors in front of us.

"So, where are you heading off to?" he asks.

It was bad enough that I had to sit through an awkward dinner, thanks to Everly. Now he wants to know where I'm going. I know she was only thinking about my and my father's relationship. It's still uncomfortable, yet I can't complain to Everly about my problem, so I tell him.

"Going to see Dion."

"The jeweler?" he asks, and I nod.

"Wait. Are you proposing to Everly?"

"Why else would I be going to see him?"

"Well, it's about bloody time," my father says, and I can't help the tug of my lips. I know that if he had his way, I would have married her the day I met her.

"So the ring is ready? What sort of ring did you get her?"

"One of Mom's rings. Valarian picked out the stone," I tell him, and my father nods and glances away. He swallows.

"So you are picking it up?"

"No, there's an issue, so I'm stopping over there," I tell him. The doors finally open, and I step out, heading for my car.

I pull up in front of the plaza and walk over to Dion's Jewelers. He had called, saying there was something wrong with the engraver. What I'm not expecting is for my father to follow me in his own car. He pulls up behind me.

"What are you doing?" I ask.

"Coming to see if I can help," he says, though I know he's trying to spend more time with me. He was always extra clingy when I was upset with him, and this feud of ours has lasted weeks. Though, I would be lying if I said I didn't enjoy his company a little.

We walked to the jeweler's together, and I knock on the door.

Dion comes over and unlocks it, locking it behind us once we're in, and we follow him to the back of his store.

"What's wrong with the engraving machine?" I ask him. Dion shrugs, picking up a rag and wiping his forehead, which is covered in sweat from the lights in here.

"No idea. I've been pulling the damn thing apart, but I'm a jeweler, not a damn technician, and the ring holder won't spin," he grumbles. My father shrugs his jacket off before pulling a stool over and sitting in front of the laser machine.

They spend hours trying to fix it before deciding it needs some part. Dion then spends a few hours on eBay and various sites trying to find the part for the specific engraver he has. When he finally finds it, he tells me the shipment will take another two weeks on top of the time it will take for the stone to arrive.

"What is with shipments these days?" I growl. I was already impatient to get the ring back before—now it's adding even more time!

Dion shrugs apologetically. I sigh, knowing it isn't his fault when my father speaks.

"I can go pick it up?" he offers.

"It's a four-day drive," I tell him, and he shrugs. "Better than waiting. When does the stone arrive?" he asks Dion.

"Hopefully next week; they were able to ship it off on the next flight, so it's arriving early," Dion says. Well, at least something good came of this.

"It's settled then. I will go pick up the part and bring it back here, so you should have your ring earlier than expected," my father tells me. He looks down at Dion's computer and Dion fills out something about picking it up. My father then jots down the address on a piece of paper.

As I'm leaving, my father follows me out and we walk back to the cars together.

"You didn't have to pick it up. I know you're only sucking up," I tell him.

"Is it working?" he chuckles.

"Kind of," I laugh. We stand there awkwardly until my father hugs me. After I stand there for a second, I finally wrap my arms around him.

"I miss you, son," he says, his voice cracking. I rub his back before he lets go and nods, racing to his car. He leaves before I get in my car. The moment I do, the mind-link opens up and Marcus' voice is in my head.

"Hey, what's up?"

"You need to get to Mountainview Hotel!"

"Why?"

"It's not good, Valen. The whole place is gone. It's just a shell."

"Excuse me?"

"Someone cut off the water and power. We were trying to figure out what was going on when we heard an explosion in the kitchen an hour after closing, and the entire place went up."

"Fuck! I'm on my way," I tell him.

Hearing my phone ringing, I grab it from my jacket pocket. It's Everly. I'm about to answer when I see my father's car come to an abrupt stop at the traffic lights before he turns the car around and drives back toward me on the opposite side of the road. He stops across from me just as I answer Everly's phone call; she's sobbing hysterically.

"I'm on my way there right now," I tell her.

"I can't get a hold of your father."

"He's with me. We're on our way," I tell her before hanging up. Dad winds his window down and I do the same.

"Want me to take Valarian? It's all over the radio," he calls.

"Head to the hotel. Everly is on her way there with him," I call back, and he nods before taking off. I wrench the wheel and do a U-turn, following him.

CHAPTER
NINE

Valen

Pulling up at the Mountainview Hotel, I see fire trucks lining the front of the hotel with police, ambulances, people running everywhere, everything is all flashing lights and shouting; it's a total fiasco. I can see Everly's truck and my father parks beside it, getting Valarian out of the car while Macey stands beside it. My father is quick to get Valarian, then waves Zoe over; she rushes over with Casey and thanks him. Yet, I can't see Everly anywhere. The entire building is on fire, flames spewing out the windows, bursting from the extreme heat that can be felt even from where I'm parked behind my father on the main road.

I glance around, waving to Zoe as I jog over to her and Marcus. Marcus has a tablet in his hand and people are lining the path, standing at the evacuation point as he finishes checking names off.

"Everyone is accounted for. The fire started in the kitchen; thank-fully the alarms still triggered because of the backup batteries, so no loss of life," Marcus tells me. I notice the tablet is a list of who was in the hotel. Ava is handing out bottled water and examining those

Marcus marked off. Everyone is checked off and accounted for but one.

"Where is Everly?" I ask. As my father drives off with Casey and Valarian, he honks the horn and I nod to him. Zoe looks around before pointing between two fire trucks.

"The other buildings?" I ask Macey as she comes over.

"Fine—it was contained in the main building. The apartments out the back and the event room and storage sheds are fine; it's only the main hotel," she answers. At least that's a relief. I nod, glancing around and finally spotting Everly, who stands in her pink and white cloud pajamas with her back to us. Moving across the large lawn, I head over to her.

When I spoke to her earlier, she was hysterical, but now I feel nothing but blistering, fiery anger, so hot it could give the inferno in front of us a run for its money. Yet, the underlying feeling below it is pure devastation. This place was as much her baby as Valarian is. This was *hers*. Coming up behind her, I grip her shoulders, but she's staring at the flames eating away her village—the village she built. I don't know what to say. There's no comfort I can offer to make this right.

"I'll rebuild. This is why we have insurance. This is why I have a failsafe. The main thing is no one is hurt—this place can be restored, but lives can't be replaced," she says as I rest my chin on her shoulder and wrap my arms around her.

"I'm sorry, Love," I tell her, and she nods once in acknowledgment of my words but says nothing else. Media and reporters start lining the streets behind us; murmurs can be heard, police taking statements. I wander off, helping where I can. So does Everly, organizing buses to take everyone that was staying here to my hotel.

The flames are finally gone. The place is nothing but a husk of what it once was. Everly watches the last fire truck leave, but the media linger, taking any last-minute scraps they can for their headlines. Bloody vultures.

"Come on," I tell her, trying to lead her away, but she shakes her head and walks toward the building. I need to get Valarian to school, so I'll have to come back. Yet, I have a feeling Everly isn't leaving anytime soon.

"They warned me," Everly said, staring up at what's left. The structure is sound, but the place is gutted. Yet, despite it all, the building still stands; the brickwork may be tainted black, the render crumbling, and the place hollow, but it's still there, standing against the odds.

"This is because of the petition; because I fought for the rogues, for this city, and this is how they repay me," she growls. "They won't stop, will they?" she asks, glancing at me. I hang my head, knowing this will only be the beginning.

"What's next, Valen? What would your next move be, if you were Nixon?" she asks.

"You think it was Nixon?"

"Who else?" she says.

"Everly? I...." I glance around at the media lingering, watching curiously when she walks off toward the wreck.

Everly

I walk numbly towards the building and stop again. The place is destroyed. As I take it all in, my heart and soul burn to charcoal. I stare at the front door; I can picture that first day like it was yesterday. The night before, it poured, and I had all but given up, until I met the woman who sat on a faded, plastic chair with a smoke hanging between her lips by that very door—the way her eyes looked me up and down with no judgment.

Valen comes over to me while I stare at the spot she sat that day, when I was wet from walking, hopeless, and homeless. He rubs my arms from behind me.

"We should go," he whispers. I point to the spot.

"That's where I met your mother," I tell him. "I thought she was one of the people staying here. She had a cigarette hanging out of her mouth." I chuckle. "She offered me a place to stay, a hot meal, and then a job. But she gave me so much more than that."

"This place," Valen says. I shake my head.

"Hope. She gave me hope. Then she gave me a family, and then a home," I tell him, looking up at what's left.

I point to the room directly above us. "That's where I stayed. The next morning, I came out to her calling up to me, her truck loaded with baby stuff for Valarian. There was so much stuff," I sniffle.

"'It takes a village to raise a child. We are going to build our own village'. Your mother told me that, and we did," I tell him before stepping through the front door. The glass is all shattered and crunches under my feet, the walls are black, and some of the floors are still smoldering. I walk into the back, to my office, which used to be her apartment.

"Everly! It's not safe," Valen calls out to me while rushing in after me. Yet, I don't care; I have to see if it survived. The safe is supposed to be fireproof, but all I can do is hope. It holds something more precious than gold.

It has my letter.

Everything is covered in soot, the room crumbling around me as I fish my keys from my pocket and kneel next to the safe.

"Everly, we shouldn't be in here! They haven't cleared the entire place yet," Valen says, but I'm not really listening. Through my tears, I place the key in and twist, pulling it out and using another key to twist the next lock and the next; the keypad for the digital screen melted, but the manual locks are fine. My heart beats faster when I hear the final lock click.

I close my eyes, gripping the handle, sucking in a shuddering breath before pulling the door open.

The safe is intact—the heat burned the outside hard and it's warm inside, and a few things on top are curled and ruined, but as I dig to the bottom, I burst into tears when I see my envelopes. They're brown from the smoke but intact. I clutch them to my chest and let out a breath.

"Thank you," I whisper to no one in particular. If there was ever a sign that she's still with us, this was it. Goddess only knows how many times I've pulled that damn letter from its envelope when I thought I would break, knowing it would help me carry on again.

Valen rubs my back, letting me fall apart. I can't move as I stare at my safe—I have no idea how long I sit there. Valen goes to grab Valarian's clothes from the apartment, yet I can't bring myself to follow.

I'm leaning against the brown brickwork with my envelope, the one most precious to me. There are so many letters, letters of advice, letters of love. She wrote a new letter every day, each one a detailed report of what we accomplished that day—a reminder of how far we had come—a time capsule of sorts. I find every moment of this place flashing through my mind. Her voice is so clear, her memory still alive within these walls, even though it's now only burned rubble.

Every day, she dropped one in the mailbox out front and sent it to her lawyer to hold on to. But one letter means the most to me—the one I'm clutching in my hand like it's my lifeline, a reminder in case I forget. One thing about Valarie is that she's unforgettable. I close my eyes, leaning my head back against the wall when her voice rings in my ears.

"You don't need them. They aren't wasting tears on you, so don't waste your tears on them. They don't deserve them," Valarie had once told me. Her voice is on replay and I savor the sound of the memories she imprinted on me, and it only makes me angry that someone would

try to take that memory from me—from the rogues. They burned my village and I will *burn* this city to the *ground*. I burn, they will burn with me.

"Hold on to that anger, because sometimes it's the only thing that will keep you going," Valarie had also told me. So I let it fester now, needing something to keep going.

I hear the crunch of somebody walking into the place. I wipe my tears but sigh when I realize it's only Valen. He crouches in front of me, tipping my chin up to meet his gaze.

"Where's my girl gone?" he whispers, his eyes searching my face.

"Sitting in the wreck of her village," I murmur.

"This is not my girl. My girl is a Luna, and chief of her village."

"My village is gone," I tell him.

"Will you rebuild?"

I sigh. I want to punch something, scream and fight, yet at the same time I want to curl into a ball and die along with this place. But he's right. I have a city to burn, and I can't do that here, feeling sorry for myself. I nod, and he stands.

Gently, I open the letter, reading through it for the hundredth time—the one thing that kept me going time and time again. Valen stands back but remains quiet as I skim the page. Valarie's words are unmarred and untainted as I stare at them.

"What's that?" Valen asks.

"A reminder," I tell him. Leaning forward, I grab the others from where they sit and hand them to him. He looks at the hundreds of envelopes.

"These are all from my mother?" he asks, and I nod.

He holds his hand out for the one in my hand, written in her immaculate handwriting, the one letter that means the most to me. It's the shortest of all the letters she wrote. The others are a detailed, day-by-day account of what we had achieved. What we built. But this one is something else. I pull it a little closer and gaze at the words I memorized years ago but still need to see when things get to be too much.

. . .

Just in case no one has told you today!
YOU WILL NEVER DO IT!
I'm watching, always watching, my girl. And I
will be watching when you prove them all wrong!

With that, I tuck the letter back in its envelope and hand it to Valen to hold with the others before walking out of the office.

"Everly? What are you doing?" Valen calls as he follows me through the charred remains.

"Building a village," I tell him. He laughs, and I look at him over my shoulder.

"What?" I ask, and he shrugs and shakes his head. Untucking the envelope I gave him, he opens it and scans it once.

"Build your Village, Love," he says.

"Oh, I am. I built this place from nothing. I will do it again," I tell him, shoving through what's left of the doors and outside.

I stop in tracks as I step into the parking lot. Valen walks up behind me and wraps his arms around my chest, pulling me back against him. The letter in his hand is open, yet my gaze is on the hundreds of rogues and pack members that cover every inch of the lawn, shovels, and supplies in hand as a convoy of trucks and machinery pull into the hotel. I suck in a breath and swallow. Every rogue must be here, and all of Valen's pack. I glance at him over my shoulder.

"Only, this time, it isn't just four rogue-whores and three babies. You built a village and these are your people. You never have to do anything alone again," Valen whispers, and tears fill my eyes as I stare back at everyone who showed up. Macey and Zoe both stand at the front with shovels in hand. My lip quivers. The fact that they would all show up for this place...

Valen kisses my cheek and lets me go. My knees shake as I walk toward my village before they finally give way from under me. Everyone, they all suddenly drop to their knees and bow their heads. The sight of them is just too much.

I break. Tears fall as I place my head in my hands and cry.

Moments later, I feel small hands touch my neck and I look up to see Valarian standing beside me.

"Don't cry, Momma, your village is here to help," he whispers, wiping my tears. He's wearing a neon, HiVis shirt, jeans, and little steel cap boots.

"Hey, Everly!" Valen calls from behind me, and I turn to look at him over my shoulder. Valarian stares at his father when Valen yells out to me:

"You'll never do it!"

I chuckle. I open my mouth to answer him when a chorus of voices rings out through the crowd in unison.

"Watch her!" they all scream back at him.

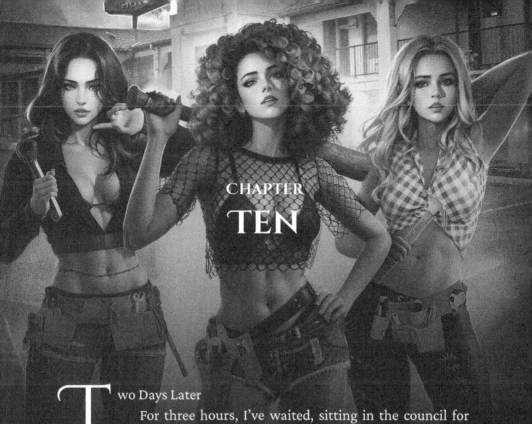

CHAPTER
TEN

Two Days Later

For three hours, I've waited, sitting in the council for my petition meeting. My ass is going numb, and this skirt is so tight it's digging into my hips. The air conditioning in here sucks too, making me feel queasy, and when I see Alpha Nixon walk out of the chambers with a smug smile on his face, my mood sours even more. I stand up, placing my folder on my seat, and move toward him. My appointment was three hours ago. My father comes out and rushes past, heading for the doors before I can even say anything to him—not even a glance in my direction, yet Nixon is all too happy to approach me. He strolls over in his tailored suit, briefcase, and black leather shoes. He stops in front of me, giving me the once-over.

"How lovely to see you, Everly. What brings you here?" he asks with a sly smile. My eyes narrow at him as people push out the doors behind us, leaving the council chambers and heading out past security. They cast us nervous glances, which sets me a little on edge.

"You know exactly why I am here," I growl at him.

"Oh, nobody told you?" he asks, smiling wickedly. He glances at the receptionist. My brows furrow, confused at his words. No one told me or notified me to say it wasn't going ahead, so I have no idea what he's talking about.

"Your meeting was postponed. We postponed it on compassionate grounds after hearing about your tragedy at the hotel. What a shame!" Alpha Nixon says in a mocking tone.

"Compassionate grounds. It was not necessary. I never asked for it to be postponed and nobody notified me that it had been." I look at the foyer desk, and the woman behind it ducks her head when I turn my glare on her. That woman stared at me for three hours and did not say a goddamn word! Just kept saying 'be patient ma'am, someone will be right with you'!

"Not to matter; these things can't be helped. I was coming to see you today, anyway. I wanted to make you an offer," Nixon says, forcing my attention back to him. I purse my lips and fold my arms across my chest, scoffing at his words. This man has done enough, and I won't accept any offer he could ever make.

"How much for what is left of that dump?" he asks.

"It isn't for sale, and if it was, you would never be able to afford it," I tell him.

"Now, don't be rash, Everly. That place is rubble and soot, holds no value."

"Then what do you want with it if it holds no value? I know exactly what that land is worth and what it will be worth once I rebuild. Though I should say thank you for burning it to the ground!"

"I have no idea what you are talking about," he says, fiddling with his cufflinks.

"Sure you don't, but thank you anyway," I smile.

"And why is that?" Nixon chuckles arrogantly, and I lean closer to whisper to him.

"Because I just realized how much larger my pack is. You know numbers; that's all you Alphas care about—the number of members you have, warriors. Well, I outnumber every pack here, so Alpha, I suggest you fall in line before I make you my omega bitch," I tell him.

"You are asking for war, Everly. How will your father feel going to war against his own daughter?"

"That is where you are wrong, Alpha Nixon. In two days' time, I will own his pack. It would be wise to check your alliances because I will own you too," I sneer at him and Nixon laughs.

"I am the mayor of this city, or have you forgotten? I am not going anywhere, Everly. I run this city—you are merely a rogue whore that trapped an Alpha. Don't you read the headlines?" he chuckles.

"Savor your time as mayor, Nixon, because you won't be the city mayor for much longer," I tell him, leaning down and grabbing my handbag and folder.

"And why do you think that?" he asks. I shrug.

"Reputation is everything in this city, Nixon. I can't fall from grace because I apparently already did. As you said, I *am* just a rogue-whore who trapped an Alpha. But don't forget, everyone has skeletons in the closet, and I hear yours is full to the brim with dirty secrets and clingy cobwebs. Be sure to watch the 7 o'clock news tonight; I hear you're starring in those headlines," I laugh before turning on my heel and walking toward the doors. Alpha Nixon grabs my arm and yanks me back, earning some shocked gasps from a few stragglers still leaving.

"What have you done?" he snarls.

"I do not know what you're talking about," I tell him, sending him a wink. I shake his hand off before walking to the doors.

"Sign the petition, Nixon; I'm only just getting started. By the time I am done, your reputation will be lower than any rogue-whore!" I call to him, shoving through the turnstile and out the doors into the blistering hot sun. My father is waiting by his car and starts to walk over to me, but halts his steps when Nixon comes out a few steps behind me.

Ignoring both of them, I climb in my car and send a text to Macey and Zoe to meet me at Zoe's apartment before putting it in reverse. Only, when I glance over my shoulder, I see Nixon's brand-new

Jaguar in the spot across the aisle behind me. I slam my foot on the gas, hitting it so hard it pushes his precious metal baby into the brick barricade in front of it. His horrified face makes me chuckle as I wind the window down and look out my window at his crushed back end.

"Whoops! I'm sure it will buff right out," I tell him before taking off, cackling like a madwoman. I notice him race toward his car and clutch his hair as he looks at the damage. I rub my dash. "Good, Beasty, good girl," I tell my car.

The drive back to the hotel leaves me sweating, and I'm pretty sure I need to get the air-conditioner refilled. By the time I reach the place, I'm drenched in sweat. In two days, with all of Valen's pack and every rogue in the city helping, we stripped the place down to the bare brick and scrubbed it down. The entire site is gutted, and contractors are walking around wearing hard hats and taking things inside to the kitchen and restaurant structure. Giant jacks are holding up some of the floors above while new support beams are put in place.

Pulling into the parking spots out front, I see the safety inspector. With a groan, I shrug off my blazer and climb out of the car. As I walk toward him, he goes to open his mouth, no doubt with some complaint, but I pluck the paper he's holding up from his grip.

"See you in a month," I tell him, not bothering to stop as I flip him the finger above my head; I'm not in the mood to deal with him. I stroll around back and up the steps toward my old apartment. As soon as I unlock the door and step inside, I flick the kettle on, dumping my keys in the fruit bowl. It feels so normal—like home still.

Raiding the fridge and pantry, I grab coffee and milk out, yet the moment I open the coffee canister, my stomach turns violently and has me rushing toward the sink to hurl my guts up. What the heck just came over me? Rinsing my mouth, I quickly clean the sink, wondering if I have heat stroke from sitting in the overheated council lobby all day. Once my stomach settles and the kitchen is clean, I'm about to start making coffee when Macey walks in with Zoe.

"How did it go?" Macey asked, rushing toward the air-conditioning panel on the wall and turning it up full blast. Zoe lifts her hair off the back of her neck and stands under the vent in the living room. "Gosh, it's hot today," she whines, her skin glistening with a sheen of sweat. Macey walks over to the freezer, opening the door and pressing her face inside it, trying to cool down. I move to one of the chairs at the dining table and undo the top button on my shirt.

"It was postponed; waiting for email on a new date. Also, I *may* have accidentally reversed into Nixon's shiny new car," I shrug before catching Macey stealing ice cubes out of the freezer drawer, pulling her shirt open, and dropping them in her bra. Zoe and I stare at her.

"What? Cooling my girls down," she says, like it isn't an odd thing to do. She reaches for more and Zoe snaps at her.

"Nope, you best leave my ice tray alone. I *know* you aren't about to stuff them down your pants!" she shrieks and Macey looks at her, appalled by her words before she pops the cubes of ice in her mouth.

"Not all of us are like you, Miss Hotbox, stuffing frozen vegetables in your pants."

Zoe flashes me an accusing glare for telling Macey and I giggle.

Macey starts making coffee and I tell them about my interaction with Nixon. When Macey sets the steaming mug in front of me and sips her own. I grab it and take a sip before my stomach turns again and I'm rushing for the sink. Coffee comes out of my nose and mouth as I spew. Gagging on the taste, I quickly rinse my mouth and wet my face, trying to cool down.

Once I feel slightly better, I stand up and turn to find them both staring at me. "What? Your damn milk must be off," I tell them.

"Wait, you were in heat, right?"

"Weeks ago!" I tell them, shaking my head and grabbing a Pepsi out of the fridge. I swallow it down to rid the rancid taste from my mouth. Macey clears her throat awkwardly, and I glance at her. "What!"

"Hundred bucks says you're preggo!"

"Nope, we used...." I stop. Did we use protection?

"She's knocked up!" Zoe exclaims and slaps Macey's waiting hand.

No! I can't be; my heat came and went...... In a day! I look at Zoe, horrified.

"How long does a heat last?"

"Three or four days, give or take, and from memory, yours lasted a night? Not that I'm heat cycling you or anything," she says innocently.

"See? All the proof right there, you are preggers—he knocked you up first dive into your coochie because you're definitely pregnant," Macey laughs.

"I can't be pregnant. I have the challenge in two days!" I snap at them, horrified. They glance between each other nervously.

"Shit! I have tests; we can check."

"Maybe your dad will postpone on compassionate grounds for the hotel?" Macey offers while Zoe rushes off toward the bathroom.

Macey eyes her suspiciously when she comes out with four different pregnancy tests. "Why have you got half a pharmacy's worth of pregnancy tests?" she asks.

"No reason," she says, shoving them in my hands.

"Wait, are you and Marcus trying to have another crotch goblin?" Macey asks excitedly.

"No. It's just in case," Zoe says.

Macey pouts. "Fine, at least I get to be this one's cool auntie," Macey says, rubbing my belly like I'm a Buddha and she can rub some good luck out of it.

"Please be triplets, or quadruplets—a whole damn litter!" she whispers. I slap her hand away.

"I am not pregnant!" I tell her, and she folds her arms.

"Well, one way to find out!"

I stalk off to the bathroom. Minutes tick by while I wait for the digital screen to light up along with the other three that I took as a precaution. Chewing my lip, I glare at them, willing them to be negative and crossing my fingers and toes, praying to the Moon Goddess I'm not. I can't afford to be. I have a hotel to rebuild, a war brewing, a challenge to fight, and a Valarian to take care of!

As soon as the screen lights up and the timer beeps, I nearly dive into the sink basin where the tests are perched. I grab them, examining them.

"Wrong!... Wrong!... Wrong!" I cry.

I hear a knock a second before the girls barge their way into the small bathroom as I fling the third one back, hitting Macey in the head with it. She cringes but catches it.

"You jinxed me! Unjinx me! Now!" I demand as she reads the test before fist pumping the air in victory and bouncing on her feet.

"I'm gonna be an auntie again! You owe me— Shit! I forgot to tell you the bet!" she curses. Yet, all I can think about is what fucked up timing this is as I sink onto the edge of the toilet and put my head in my hands.

"Come on, Evie. It's not the end of the world. You won't be alone this time, and Valen is great with Valarian and..." Zoe says, but her words don't help, so I drown her out as memories of my last pregnancy flood me. And what the hell am I going to do about the challenge?

E verly

      Valen is working with Marcus tonight, so after I get Valarian from school, I decide to have dinner with Zoe, Macey, and their girls. The kids have fun, and it reminds me of before our lives got so complicated—when it was just us against the world.

It's comforting knowing that nothing has changed even now with my title. To them, I will always just be Everly—not Luna, not rogue-whore. Here, I'm safe to be my normal self and am free to do as I please without judgment or someone scrutinizing me somehow. When the 7 o'clock news comes on, I send the kids to play with the Lego sets in Casey's room.

"Remote! The news is on," I say, waving my hand at Zoe. She passes it to me and I quickly flip to the channel.

"Since when do you like watching the news?" Macey asks as I race to the sofa and sit in the middle in front of the TV.

"I like the news when I don't star in it. I *may* have handed a list of evidence to the media about Nixon and my father this morning," I tell them.

"What! What'd you give them?" Zoe screeches excitedly and

rushes over to sit on the other side of me. It was petty, but if they want to talk shit about me, I should be able to have fun returning the favor. I'm far from apologetic, even over the one thing that was total bullshit, but then again, it could be true! Either way, it makes for exciting conversations at dinner meetings. I chuckle to myself; he's going to kill me.

"Oh, this I gotta see!" Macey says, snatching the cold bowl of popcorn off the coffee table. Both Zoe and I looked at her questioningly. We all squeeze onto the sofa and get comfortable, Zoe sitting with her legs over my lap and her feet on Macey's.

Macey sits un-blinking, chowing down on cold popcorn from the kid's movie we watched after dinner. She's shoveling handfuls in her mouth in a very un-ladylike but completely Macey-like manner. When the news anchor comes on and Nixon's photo pops up in the corner, we lean forward eagerly.

I purse my lips. They burned my hotel and I will burn their reputations. The newswoman reports on Nixon's first mate and how she became forsaken, how his wife isn't the mother of his child and—the most damning part to him—that he abandoned his daughter to the forsaken. I even managed to find some old photos of Leah, his mate, and a hospital report of a young woman named Kayla, who was Carter's twin sister, which would push the evidence along.

Plus there was an accidental photo that, from the awkward angle, looks like he was picking his nose while sitting in his car outside the pack hospital. Man, it was hard getting a hold of hospital footage, but somehow Valen had managed it. The news anchor even says that they will pay for the DNA test if he wants to prove his innocence. Of course, we all know that won't happen, only making him look more guilty.

The news anchorwoman then goes on to talk about his hate for rogues and speculate that this may be the reason why his daughter is still technically rogue and his mate has turned forsaken. Sitting back, I smile smugly; suck on that, Nixon!

Both Macey's and Zoe's eyes are glued to the TV and Macey is shoveling popcorn in her mouth so fast that she starts coughing and spluttering, choking on her popcorn when my father's turn comes next. I snicker, and Zoe snorts. I smack Macey's back and she sucks in a lungful of air. Instead of his usual portrait photos, Ava and I had managed to find some old pictures on the family link app that he forgot to remove. It was a photo from when we were kids at a dress-up party.

We had sent three photos to them. My father had been wearing one of my mother's mini dresses and fishnet stockings with a wig and high heel boots. One picture was of him in the wig, all glammed up as a woman; another was without the wig, revealing that it was definitely my father, because the photo was of him in our bathroom putting on red lipstick; and the last image was him bending over drunk, his nuts hanging out since he was also wearing my mother's lace panties.

There was absolutely nothing wrong with the photos in general, but I know my father won't see it that way, especially when the news anchor tells the city that he's secretly a crossdresser and that his two daughters confirmed it. We all burst out laughing, knowing how horrified my father will be over this. Though there really is nothing wrong with it, it had all just been for fun, it will definitely taint my father's conservative front he puts up.

"Man, I wish I could wear heels that high. Any more than an inch and I can't walk straight," Macey laughs.

"There is so much I could say to that comment," I tell her, and she glares at me. I snicker at her outraged face.

"Damn! Papa John got some nice legs on him. A bit hairy, but look at them muscular thighs," Zoe says, and I elbow her, a little grossed out she's checking out my father.

"Oh my God! I bet your father had a heart attack seeing this pop up on the news," Macey chuckles.

"You know there will be backlash," Zoe says, and I shrug.

"What are they going to do? Accuse me of lying about who Valarian's father is? It's obvious whose child he is by the eyes, and I am *pretty* sure there isn't *one* article that doesn't taint me poorly. Sticks and stones," I tell them.

Valen starts blowing up my phone. He had no idea what I wanted the footage for; I'm sure he thought I would try to blackmail Nixon with it, not hand it to the media. With a groan, I get up. I know I have to face my mate, and I'm sure he'll have plenty to say about it.

Macey also has to leave, so we both load the kids up in our cars, and I wave as she leaves before driving home myself. I'm still chuckling quietly and Valarian keeps asking why, but I just shake my head. Pulling up in the parking lot, Valarian rushes ahead to the glass doors and is greeted by the doorman. I throw my keys to the valet and retrieve my handbag from the trunk, along with the few groceries I had stopped and grabbed on the way home. Suddenly, I jump as I'm grabbed and yanked away from the door. My bags drop, and I turn to see who it is, only to find myself glaring up at my father.

"What the fuck do you think you are doing?" he growls at me.

"Well, I was getting groceries from my car," I snarl back, picking up the spilled oranges. My father crouches down and starts helping me re-bag everything. While I chase a runaway apple, he picks up my handbag and gasps. I snatch my bag and the pregnancy test out of his hand.

"You're pregnant?" he asks, looming over me.

"Shush! Keep your voice down!" I hiss at him, glancing around.

"You can't fucking shift! The challenge is the day after tomorrow," my father growls, forgetting what he came here for, though I know it has to do with the news.

"Challenge is still going ahead. I am not backing down," I tell him.

"You can't shift, Everly! Why would you challenge me when you're pregnant?" he growls.

"I only just found out today, but it changes nothing,"

"Like fuck it doesn't! I am not fighting a pregnant woman!" he snarls.

"Then stand down!" I tell him.

69

"No! It is *my* pack. I can't, even if I wanted to," he says, making my brows furrow before I shake my head.

"Then I will see you in two days," I tell him, snatching my bags up. Valarian comes out the doors, looking at us.

"Does Valen know?" he asks as I start to head inside.

"No, and you will keep your mouth shut until after the challenge," I tell him. He scoffs and shakes his head.

"It's my birthright! I'm the rightful heir! Do the right thing, Dad. Hand me my title."

He says nothing, and I start walking off when he chases me, stopping me again.

"Mom?" Valerian calls out, looking at me worriedly. Guards start moving in, but I wave them off.

"Your mother will be with you in a second, Val. Wait inside. It's cold," my father tells him, and Valarian looks at me. I nod for him to go in, and he does, standing just inside the doors.

"What?" I asked, turning to look back at my father.

"You fucked up."

"So, it's ok for you to paint me in the media as a whore but don't like the favor returned?" I laugh.

"I don't care about the photos of me. I will deal with that. It's Nixon; he will fucking come for you for what you did. You need to leave the city. Get Valarian and Ava and your two girlfriends and get out while you can."

"What? No! I am not leaving the city."

My father grabs my arms. "You need to get out! Nixon is planning something! Something big!" he says, staring me dead in the face. This is the moment I realize that he knows something he's trying to keep hidden.

"Like what?" I ask. He says nothing and curses.

"This is about your debt?" I ask, and his head snaps back to look at me.

"How– ...bloody Ava," he curses, then sighs. "No. I don't know.

But I have a funny feeling it's to do with the rogues and forsaken going missing," he says, glancing around nervously.

"What do you mean?" I ask him.

"You need to leave the city!"

"Tell me why. What have you done?" I ask him.

"I haven't done anything, but I found documentation on a hard drive Nixon left at the council one morning. He's building an army to take down Valen's pack and the Night Slasher Pack. That's why I tried to marry Ava off to Valen. Not just to absolve my debt, but to ensure Valen holds his reign over the city. If he married Ava, I would have had sway over Valen, but—"

"You want Valen to remain in control?" I ask, a little skeptical.

"We may have our differences, but if Nixon takes down Valen's pack and the Slasher pack, he will hold control."

"We outnumber his pack. You aren't making sense!" I tell him.

"You don't! Think, Everly! The forsaken! Nixon is behind it, and he is building a fucking army out of them!"

I stumble back. "And you're helping him?"

My father shakes his head. "No, it's not like that. I got the pack in debt with Slasher Pack's Alpha. Nixon dug me out, so now I owe him. I will work that out, but...."

"What aren't you telling me?"

My father hangs his head. "He was trying to find a vaccine for his daughter and son. Nixon managed to make the vaccine, but he also stumbled onto something else. He found a way to replicate the venom," Dad says, and my eyes widen in horror.

"And you're helping him kill rogues?" I asked, disgusted.

"No, that's not me. I..... I can't...... Fuck!"

"You want my help, you fucking speak," I snarl, trying to figure out what it is he's wanting. My father sucks in a deep breath.

"It's my fault because I got the pack in debt. I made a stupid bet while drunk."

"You bet the pack land?" I ask, and he nodded.

"Yes, or three million dollars. I'd already gambled everything. Nixon loaned me the money and the pack is collateral. He gave me five years to pay it back or hand my firstborn over. I was going to find the money, but Nixon was pushing for you to marry Carter, and when you said you were pregnant, I knew you wouldn't get rid of your son. So I made you a rogue to cover up the fact I faked your death. If Nixon knew you were pregnant he would have used Valarian against Valen," he explains.

My head is swimming with all this information. I have so many questions, but my father's nervousness and the way he keeps glancing around tells me he can't be seen here.

"So, why are you helping him now?"

"I asked for more time after I met Carter—I couldn't let him have Ava either. When I refused, he kidnapped your mother. It's why I don't let her leave the packhouse. He injected her last year with the venom."

"What?" I exclaim, my heart racing.

"Every month, he gives her the vaccine. It stops it from taking over, but when it does, she's like one of them. The vaccine is the only thing that stops her from turning completely. It's why I went against the petition. He wouldn't give her the vaccine if I signed it," he says just as Valarian calls out.

"Mom!"

My father looks over my shoulder. "I have to go. But I... I'll see you at the challenge," he says, rushing back to his car.

"Come on, Mom!" Valarian whines. I collect the bags and rush to the front door. Moving across the foyer and into the elevator, my father's words replay in my mind, but as we approach the penthouse floor, another worry sets in.

The elevator doors open and Valarian runs ahead, opens the front door, and holds it for me. I drag the groceries to the kitchen and place them on the counter.

"Finally, you're home," Valen says, walking out of the hall with a towel around his waist.

His hair is wet and his skin is glistening, obviously having just stepped out of the shower. Valarian rushes over and hugs him. Valen scoops him up and walks over to me. He pecks my cheek and reaches for the handbag I still have over my shoulder. My heart thumps harder in my chest and I pull away. He gives me a funny look, but Valarian distracts him by talking about Taylor and Casey fighting over her Barbie dolls.

Moving quickly, I put the groceries away before rushing back to the bedroom, needing to hide the damn pregnancy test, at least until after the challenge. I know if Valen finds it, he'll make me back out. But now, even more is at stake, and I'm not about to back down after everything that's happened.

I *need* to do this! Valen wouldn't understand that, especially if he knew I was pregnant—and he can't claim my title for me. Glancing around, I rush into the closet. As soon as I hear him come up the hall toward the room, I panic and jam it inside one of my knee-high boots and set it back on the shoe rack. Just as I finish placing my bag on the small shelf just inside the walk-in closet, Valen walks in, retrieves some shorts from the shelf, and slips them on.

"Why did you rush off in a hurry?"

"I want to shower; I feel gross," I tell him, retrieving my pajamas and walking out to the ensuite. He follows and leans on the door-frame while I get undressed.

"I saw the news. I wonder how they got that information?" he chuckles.

"No idea. But I heard the Blood Alpha has an excellent hacker. I should ask him," I laugh, turning the shower on.

"Valarian said your father was downstairs?" Valen asks me, and I nod. Stepping under the water spray, I tell him what my father told me.

"Your father could be lying. But at the same time, why would he? Can he get evidence of this? It could also be a reason to make you to back out of the challenge. He may be trying to scare you?" he says, and he has a point. However, with the way Dad was and his nervousness, I know he wasn't lying.

"Are you nervous about the challenge?" he asks, and I swallow.

"Nope," I tell him, but I *am* nervous. Not because I don't think I can beat him, but worried Macey or Zoe might tell Valen I'm pregnant. I know I can beat my father in this form, but Valen won't care about that. He'll only care about the risk to our unborn baby.

"You sure you're ok? You feel off," Valen says, and I turn to face him while rinsing the shampoo out.

"Yep, fine, I'm just tired," I lie.

CHAPTER
TWELVE

Everly

Avoiding Valen's watchful eyes in the past 24 hours has been near impossible. It doesn't help that morning sickness decided to rear its ugly head. Now I know I'm pregnant, every pregnancy symptom has suddenly decided to spring forward with an ugly vengeance, trying to screw me out of hiding it.

Zoe and Macey have been at me all day about it. I've been hiding in my makeshift office in the event building—thanks to Alpha Nixon, it used to be a storage room for tables and chairs that's been repurposed to be my new office—but now, just when I thought I finally escaped them, it's nearly time to clock out and head home. Valen knows something is up because I have no doubt he can feel it. Apparently having confused my fear of him finding out with nervousness about the upcoming challenge, he said he would pick me up tonight, worried I would run myself off the road.

But Macey and Zoe aren't giving up so easily. They burst into my office, blocking the door as I switch my desk lamp off—I have to run the damn thing off an extension cord from the main room. I roll my eyes as they stop my exit and glance at the clock above the door, then pin them both with my glare. They know Valen will be here any minute, or maybe that's their plan so they can out me.

"Everly, you aren't leaving us much choice," Macey says as if reading my mind, folding her arms across her chest.

"That's because it isn't your choice. I *have* to challenge my father. The entire city knows about the challenge. I back down now, the rogues will think I'm running. I need to do this," I tell them.

"But the risks! You can't shift!" Zoe says, her hands reaching toward my non-existent bump like she pictures it round and full of limbs.

"I'm durable. I know what I'm doing, I won't let him harm me. Besides, he knows," I tell them, chewing my lip nervously.

"Your father knows, yet you haven't told your mate!" Macey growls at me.

"I didn't tell him, he found out. Listen, Valen reigns over half the city; Slasher pack, Shadow pack, and Crescent pack, which belongs to Nixon, together hold the other half; therefore, all three hold equal votes to Valen within the council. Valen doesn't hold enough to change the laws himself without my father's pack. We only need to tip the scales a little more. This will make it happen."

"Yes, but not at risk to your... child. Think, Everly! If you do this, you are putting yourself at risk," Macey argues.

"I'm already at risk. But this is bigger than me. For all those in the city, my life seems a no-brainer. But don't worry, I'm not planning on losing, so it will mean something. Valen can't challenge for the title, only an heir can. My father holds the land titles to his pack. I need these land titles transferred over to me before Nixon gets his hands on them. This needs to be done. It's the only way to set everything right; back to the way Valarie intended," I retort.

"The city can wait!" Macey says. I shake my head and push past them.

"I won't blow my chance. Every fucking step we take, we get knocked back four. I am sick of playing this yoyo game of cat and mouse. I am done being the mouse! The laws pass when I beat him.

For the first time, I hold power—the fucking rogues hold power for once!" I yell at them.

A couple of the workers in the event hall rush out, thinking we're about to come to blows. We never have and never will, but this shit is getting to me.

"Everly, please," Zoe murmurs.

"I'm tired. I'm so fucking tired of battling. Don't you get it? How many girls have come through our damn doors looking for a place to stay and work? How many?" I ask them. "How many times have we had to scrape them up off the floor when their families abandoned them, their packs shunned them? How many hungry mouths do we have to feed before we suddenly can't anymore?"

"It's not your battle, Everly," Macey says.

"IT IS!" I scream. Everything suddenly becomes too much—everything crashing and smashing relentlessly—and erupts in anger. Something's gotta give! I am drowning here; drowning in grief, responsibility, obligation, and the restraints are so heavy—so, so heavy. And everything is just adding more weight. I can't keep fighting. I am done fighting. I just want to rest, and if this is what I have to do to get it, then so be it.

Tears burn my eyes and Zoe's. Macey purses her lips, looks at the ceiling, and clicks her tongue. I suck in a breath before walking out toward the doors.

"Valarie wouldn't want you to risk yourself like this—risk her grandchild," Macey says, and I stop.

"That's unfair, Macey," I tell her, spinning around, and she shrugs.

"It's true," she says.

"Who do you think I am doing this for?" I tell her as tears slip down my cheeks.

"She gave me everything when I had nothing. She fought for me and all of us when no one else did. This—everything we have done and all those we helped—is for her. She had the vision to make this city free. It was supposed to be free. And they took it from her," I tell them.

"I'm just getting it back and doing what she wanted. Nobody knew sacrifice more than that woman did. So yes, she wouldn't want me to do it, but she would understand why I have to; you don't get to use her against me!" I tell them before turning on my heel and walking out before one of us says something we can't take back.

Her words sting because I know she's right. But Valarie, too, risked her life fighting for the rogues. She could have walked away, hung up the banners and stopped fighting, given in and reformed, but she didn't. She lost her son, her family's reputation, her home, and the city, and I will be damned if I let that keep repeating.

It takes me a few seconds to regain myself and I groan when I feel Valen getting closer at an alarming speed. I wipe my face just as Macey and Zoe come out behind me and Valen runs around the corner of the main building, looking panic-stricken. I'm a deer in headlights, suddenly feeling trapped—caught between my mate and my best friends, the girls I trust more than anyone. Valen grabs my arms.

"What happened? What's wrong?" he asks, his clothes in disarray from running. He looks around frantically for any danger before looking at Macey and Zoe behind me. I wait for it, wait for everything to unravel and fall apart again. We're so close, so close.

"I'm fine. Where is Valarian?" I ask him.

"In the car with Marcus. What's going on?"

"Nothing. We disagreed. I'm fine, everything is fine,"

"You don't feel fine," Valen growls, cupping my face in his hands and looking at the girls.

I swallow, waiting for them to say something. "Why is everyone crying? Answer me, someone!" he snaps, looking at us all, and I look at them. Zoe opens her mouth. I beg her with my eyes not to, and she closes it.

"Nothing. We had a dispute over rosters. We wanted her to take some time off," Macey lies, looking at me. Relief floods me and I hang my head.

"Well, that's a good thing. I agree with them," Valen says, rubbing my arms. "I thought someone died or hurt you. Geez, you nearly gave me a heart attack," he murmurs, hugging me. I keep my mouth shut, unable to speak, but I'm grateful they didn't say anything.

Macey walks over to me and throws her arm over my shoulder. Zoe follows. We walk out to the car and find Marcus leaning against the hood. He moves to the back door and opens it, and Casey climbs out.

"Everything alright?" he asks Zoe, who nods to him. He doesn't look like he believes her either, but we all say our goodbyes. Macey grabs me as Valen climbs in the car.

"Thank you," I whisper to her.

"Please don't ever ask me to lie like this again." She sighs. "But, I get it. Kick his fucking ass! I'll be cheering from the sidelines and ready to hammer him if he hurts you," she whispers, kissing my cheek, and I chuckle.

The drive home is silent, but Valen keeps glancing at me. I can even feel his eyes on me as I stare out the window. He clutches my hand and I look at him before his voice flits through my head. His eyes go to Valarian in the mirror.

'If it's about tomorrow, you can back out. I know it must be hard to challenge your father,' Valen says. I shake my head, and he squeezes my hand.

'It's not that. Just don't be mad afterward,' I tell him, suddenly feeling guilty. We've come so far, and now I'm not only risking myself, but us. But I have a reason. He turns his head to the side to look at me.

'Why would I be mad? I could never be mad at you,' Valen says.

'What's going on?' he asks when I don't answer.

'Nothing, I think Dad just got in my head,' I lie. It's becoming a

thing. Lying shouldn't be a thing, yet I know the rogues need this. *I need this. This will set us free. But why does it have to risk so much?*

'*If you're scared, Everly, you can back out. It's ok to be scared,*' Valen says.

'*I'm not scared,*' I tell him.

'*Good. Because the moment I think you're in trouble, I will be pulling you out. I won't let him hurt you.*'

'*Valen, it's a challenge; that's the whole point. You can't make him submit for me.*'

'*No, but I will. I don't care how many laws it breaks. I know only an heir can challenge, but I will not let your father kill you either, Everly. And before you try, don't ask me not to step in if it comes to that. That's something I won't promise you, so either win or back out now, because if you're on the losing end, I am getting in that arena,*' he says, and I sigh.

'*Ok, I won't ask that, but–*'

'*No. There are no buts. That's how it is. Sorry, but if I have to pull rank, I will if it means keeping you alive, Everly. I don't want to, but don't expect me to just stand there and watch you get hurt or killed. I wouldn't ask that of you if our roles were reversed, so don't ask something of me I know you wouldn't live up to yourself.*'

I swallow down my guilt. His words hit home a little too closely. He knows me too well, which only makes lying to him tear me apart more.

All night, I'm restless and sleep doesn't come easily. Luckily, Valen didn't ask me to train, insisting I need a good night's rest, yet when I wake up the following day, I feel anything but rested.

I'm anxious and my eyes feel like sandpaper. My stomach twists violently and has me running for the bathroom as I retch and gag.

Once I empty my stomach, I rinse my mouth and wet down my face just as Valen walks in and leans on the doorframe.

"Nerves?" he asks and I nod, trying to catch my breath.

"You alright?" he asks.

"Yep, never better," I lie. He nods, walking out, and I stare at my reflection, trying to get myself together. A few more hours and this city is about to have another power player, and for once the ball is in my court, I just have to win the challenge first.

"Everly, breakfast!" Valen calls out to me and I sigh. As long as I can make my father submit before we come to the second round, which requires us to shift, I could win this. If not, it may all be for nothing. That's not an option.

THIRTEEN

Everly

The arena is basically just an old football stadium that no one uses anymore besides for city functions. The building is huge and well looked after, but it's rare for the entire city to participate in the functions; most packs tend to stick to themselves, and besides the annual alpha meeting, you rarely catch everyone in the same place. But this challenge is all through the media, so I'm not shocked to see this place packed to the brim, everyone crammed in like sardines in a can. Nervousness creeps in as we pull in next to the huge entrance.

People are walking in and I feel giddy seeing rogues entering a place that's otherwise forbidden to them; Valen's men made sure they had entry through his tunnel entrance. Macey and Zoe stand by the doors next to Tatum and Marcus. Macey is the only one out of the three of us that's still rogue, and despite the offers, she's refused, saying she's happy with her status. Although, I have a funny feeling with Tatum's infatuation with her it will only be a matter of time.

Valen will take and accept all the rogues without asking, but it's more than that. I may be pack, Zoe may be pack, but we're all rogues. Status may have been given, but at heart, we clawed out from the rubble like the rest of them, bled beside them and took on society exactly the same.

No, my village doesn't need a pack, this city should be a pack; no names, no labels, no designation. One pack is how it should be, how it was supposed to be; everyone free—free to choose and free to live. That's what we want, just our freedoms, nothing more and nothing less.

Valen grips my knee as Valarian undoes his seatbelt when he sees Taylor and Casey. Casey is waving a snow cone in the air for him and he jumps out and runs over to her. His has no color, just ice—the girls know him too well. Valen shakes his head at him and chuckles before looking over at me.

"Are you sure you wouldn't be more comfortable in shorts? You'll ruin those pants shifting in them. I brought you a set in case you change your mind," Valen says while glancing down at my yoga pants. I shake my head. I won't be shifting, it would risk too much, my body would have to change too much.

"No, I'm hoping he submits in the first half."

"You realize how hard that is? We're instinctual. And you know how these things go—after 10 minutes and the horn goes off, everyone shifts. So unless you got some moves I don't know, you are gonna have to shift, Love."

I swallow. He's right. No one likes a challenge going on too long; after ten minutes of hand to hand, the air horn blasts and you have to shift. That was brought in decades before I was born after a challenge lasted three days while both of them circled each other looking for an opening. I laugh at that thought. Screw that, better to get it over with. Then again, I also understand it. What parent wants to fight their child and vice versa?

"Are you afraid to show your wolf?" Valen asks and I stare at him but he looks away. I tilt my head to look at him.

"What is that supposed to mean?"

"Nothing. I just know you're self-conscious about how small yours is. Though when the rogue attack happened, you were a fair bit bigger. Is that why you never want to train in your wolf at home?"

"Well, you would be self conscious too if you looked like someone's pet dog and not a werewolf," I tell him.

"You're not that small," he says and I shrug and open my door. Zoe and Macey are waiting for me by the entrance and I need them to keep me calm right now. We make our way through the dark tunnel and come out the other end, walking along the boundary line. I can see Nixon and his pack watching.

Slasher pack is also here, but Nixon and Dad stand on the other side of the massive ring that's etched into the grass with white paint. We start to make our way over to our place when I feel my head tugged back by my ponytail.

Valen's hand grips it and pulls me to a stop, turning me. His other arm wraps around my waist, pulling me against him, and he tips my head back. The way his lips cover mine in a heated kiss has my cheeks burning with his very public display.

"Valen!" I mumble against his mouth, and he chuckles. He's still laughing when he lets me go and tugs me along as Kalen rushes in quickly.

There's a park at the other end of the arena where he's taking the children to play so they don't have to watch. They could, because I was training at their age, however, a challenge is vastly different. It isn't screwing around, it's blood, claws, teeth, and fur—messy and terrifying. So when Valarian stated he wanted to come, we arranged for Kalen to watch them at the park and bring them over after.

"How are you? Are you still set to leave tomorrow?" Valen asks his father. Kalen stops and pecks my cheek and hugs his son.

"Yep. Leaving at 7 a.m.," Kalen says and Valen nods.

"Where are you going?" I ask him.

"To pick up some supplies that got lost in transit for the hotel,"

Kalen says with a shrug, then quickly hugs me. "Knock his ass out, love. Now, where are these munchkins of mine?" Kalen says, looking around for the kids. He waves toward the girls before rubbing his hands together and heading over to them. "Who wants to race Pop to the park over there?" he says, pointing off toward the other end.

The three kids look where he points before running off and Kalen chases them. Valen laughs at his father who could easily outrun them but lets them win.

Once they're gone, I turn around to face the pit. The place falls silent when my father steps over the barrier and removes his shirt, handing it to my mother. I suck in a breath and Valen grips my shoulders giving them a squeeze.

"Breathe, you got this," he says, yet my eyes are on my father. Images of training with him when I was a kid skip through my head —when I regarded him as my hero. But now, I'm no longer a little girl and he's no longer larger than life. Despite that, though, his size and physique remain the same.

This man is a giant, and powerful. I swallow down the dread, remembering when he accidentally broke my femur in training when he punched me a little too hard. One punch and he snapped it like it was a chicken bone.

I shake the memory away before tugging my shirt off. I have a sports bra underneath—my shirt would only give him something to grab a hold of. My mother stands beside Nixon, looking at us nervously. As I'm about to walk onto the field, I feel a hand grip my arm. I stop when I see it's Ava. She's staring at me.

"Dad's left knee is bad, he's had two surgeries on it. Watch his hooks, but if it comes to his wolf, back out! I'll take your place. I'm not good at hand to hand but," she glances at our father nervously.

It's clear she's terrified of my father, she always hated training and it scared the crap out of her. Ava isn't violent by nature, she wasn't trained the way I was; she was Daddy's Princess while I was his warrior.

"Ava, you don't have to get in there, and you aren't going to," I tell her and she swallows again, though I know she would get in there if I asked and would take a beating happily for me. A beating isn't needed here though—victory is, so I know this is on me.

Ava grabs me and hugs me.

"I know!" she whispers, and I pull away from her to look at her. "I know about the you-know-what. You back out or I'll–" she looks at Valen standing over at the sidelines.

"Who..." I ask, though I already know. "Macey and Zoe."

"You can't shift," Ava continues.

"I don't need to, I can beat him in this form. I was born for this, Ava. Trained in his image for this. I haven't forgotten. I will win," I reassure her.

"You better. If not, stand down. Your people will understand, they won't see it as a failure," she says.

"No, but I will. You haven't been with us as long, you haven't seen the half of it. This will change everything. Now, I am asking you, as a sister, to keep your mouth shut."

She presses her lips in a line and nods. "Left knee. And try to keep on his right side, his vision isn't the best in that eye anymore. Beat him before the shift. If you're in trouble I'm telling," she says, walking off, and I sigh before turning to face my father.

Once inside the circle there's no backing out. My father stands in the center waiting, arms folded, to see if I'll step in.

"Back out, Evie, you don't want to do this," Dad says to me and I shake away the shudder that ripples up my spine as his aura washes over me, then step inside the circle.

He curses and shakes his head but takes a stance. I move closer and further to his right, watching how he shifts a little more in that direction, and I realize Ava was right—his vision on that side isn't the best. He growls and I see his eyes go to her off at the side. She waves to him before he turns back to face me again. Nixon calls out to him but my father ignores him. The whistles go off while we size each other up.

When he doesn't charge at me or make a move, I know I'll have to be the one to initiate the fight.

So I do.

He blocks my punch easily and ducks under my arm which leaves him an opening to my ribs, but he doesn't take it. Nixon yells at him to fight, but Dad goes on the defensive. After a few minutes it's starting to irritate me. I catch his left knee three times but he never swings back. When I try to kick him again, he catches my foot, putting me in a bad position, and growls angrily at me.

"Submit!" he snarls at me before punching me in the thigh. I groan, feeling it bruise, and stagger back when he lets me go. My eyes go to the huge, digital display—4 minutes before we will be forced to shift.

"No!" I growl.

Dad growls back before rushing at me and tackling me. The air catches in my lungs as I'm flung airborne in his grip . I'm waiting for his substantial weight to smash me into the ground, but at the last second, he twists and I crash on top of him instead of being crushed under him. I sit up, shocked, and punch him even as he pulls me closer in a headlock that leaves me struggling to get out of it. My fists connect with his ribs and the side of his head, yet Dad is only holding me.

"Fight back! I am not a little girl!" I tell him.

"Wrong! You're my little girl! My *pregnant* little girl!" he snarls before rolling me off him.

I get to my hands and knees, then push to my feet.

"What are you doing John?!" Nixon roars from the sidelines. My father ignores him and gets to his feet, glancing at the clock.

"Stand down! Submit!" Dad says and I clutch my knees while he tries to catch his breath.

"I can't!" I tell him, looking at the crowd of rogues.

"John! Stop playing with her and take her the fuck out!" Nixon booms across the field and I glance over my shoulder at him. My mother is standing beside him, her face pale as a ghost and I turn my attention back to my father. He looks torn.

"Please, Evie," he whispers.

I take my stance and he growls, taking his before we start fighting again—or I do while he continues playing this stupid game of just blocking and dodging.

CHAPTER
FOURTEEN

Valen

This is not what I expected. Everly is on the attack the entire time, yet the longer I watch, the more I realize John isn't even fighting. He could have landed multiple blows on her, and she even left herself open a couple of times when he could have taken her out, but he didn't. Ava stands beside me chewing her nails nervously, her eyes glued to the match. Macey and Zoe are rigid beside her with the same frightened expressions on their faces.

Something is going on. It's almost like John is deliberately throwing the challenge. *I've* put up more of a fight when training with her, yet John almost seems scared of hurting her, and Everly is also holding back. He hit her once, but it was only in the thigh—he's had ample opportunity for body and headshots, but never took one of them. But Everly is becoming tired, and she only has two minutes left before they have to shift.

"Why isn't he fighting back?" Marcus whispers and I shrug. Nixon is screaming at John to take her out—screaming like a damn banshee and distracting both of them.

The siren blares, signaling it's time to shift, and I notice Everly glance at Ava nervously. I could see John talking to her while they were fighting, but now that horn has gone off, he has no choice but to shift.

However, Everly doesn't.

"WHAT ARE YOU DOING! SHIFT!" I scream at her and I see Ava take a step forward to the pit. Macey grips her arm and shakes her head. Ava's body trembles like she was about to shift herself and run in there if Macey hadn't stopped her.

'Everly, shift!' I Command through the mindlink. She tenses and looks at me over her shoulder, fighting my Command. When Ava notices my Command over her, she yells at me.

"She can't! Drop your Command! You're distracting her!" she snaps at me. My brows furrowed in confusion and I'm about to ask what she's talking about when John's huge wolf stalks toward Everly. She backs up, turning to her side, making herself a smaller target, but still, she doesn't shift.

Ava walks the sideline with me.

"Everly, back out!" she snarls at her sister, but Everly shakes her head, not turning her gaze away from the fight.

John charges at her and I hold my breath. Everly jumps back and pivots, her foot connecting with him under the ribs only for him to turn and slash her thigh. She staggers back and he pounces on her at the same time her fist connects with the side of his head. He shakes his head and backs up, snarling and snapping his huge teeth at her.

"EVERLY, WHAT ARE YOU DOING? FUCKING SHIFT!" I yell at her as her pants become soaked with her blood from his claws slashing her outer thigh.

Nixon screams at him, distracting him for a second. She seizes the moment and jumps on him, wrapping her arms around his neck and her legs around his torso, but he rears up, trying to throw her off. Once again, he nearly lands on top of her but twists at the last second, bouncing lightly off her before his weight can crush her. She rolls out of his way before he can snap his teeth at her face but he makes no move to, and doesn't attack when she tries to get to her feet which leaves her wide open.

"Fucking take her out, John!" Nixon snarls angrily on the other side. He's so furious his canines slip from his gums, and I glare at him. John looks in Nixon's direction and hangs his head when I notice Claire beside the other man. Tears stream down her face as she watches her daughter and her mate.

"It's ok, love," she yells at him.

Everly circles around him but he hangs his head, then finally charges at her. My breath lodges in my throat as she runs at him too and I wait for them to collide—claws, teeth, and skin don't mix. Ava screams out and runs toward the circle just as Marcus snags his arm around Ava's waist, hauling her back.

My heart races. Suddenly, John jumps clean over her. Everly spins, her feet losing traction on the grass and she falls on her hip. Get up! Get up!

John turns around and moves toward her, snarling and snapping his teeth. Everly backs up on her hands and feet in a strange crab-walk. As he stalks toward her, she raises her foot to get ready to kick him just as he pounces on her. My breath lodges in my throat and I move to run onto the arena but stop when John suddenly drops on his belly and she halts.

John tilts his head and bares his neck to her in submission while I try to figure out what just happened. I look at Marcus to see if he just witnessed the same thing.

John submitted.

Nixon curses and yells before storming out, shoving past his people, while Claire rushes onto the field with shorts and a towel. Everly reaches forward and brushes John's fur. He whimpers and Claire throws a towel over him while I gape. What the fuck just happened? Once the towel is over him, he shifts back and is on his knees in front of her. Everly gets to her feet.

When it's clear it's over, I walk into the center of the arena, wanting to know what happened and why he suddenly caved to his daughter. Confusion is evident in the crowd as murmurs break out in a chorus—this wasn't what anyone was expecting, especially after all the fighting between packs. Everly's mother is talking in a hushed voice, and as I approach Everly, I catch the end of her mothers words to John. I halt my steps.

"You did the right thing, love. We lost one grandchild and daughter, we don't need to make the same mistakes again. You did the right thing; she's carrying our grandchild," Claire whispers and Everly tenses as I stop beside her. Claire is trying to console John, yet I can't take my eyes from my mate. They drift over her briefly before going to hers.

"Pardon?" I ask Claire and she gasps, taking a step away from me.

"You're pregnant?" I ask, looking at Everly, shocked. Everly looks at me and clarity hits; what Ava meant when she told me to drop the Command, why Everly wouldn't shift, why she asked me not to be angry after the challenge. I look at John on his knees, then at Ava.

"They knew?" I ask Everly and tears shine in her eyes as she takes a step toward me, but I take a step back.

"Valen, I–"

"That's what you were arguing with Macey and Zoe about, isn't it?" I ask her and she reaches for me but I take another step back from her. I feel betrayed. I can't believe she would go through with the challenge and risk our unborn child.

"Don't!" I warn her when she reaches for me again.

"Valen–"

"No, Everly. That wasn't just your secret to keep from me," I told her before turning on my heel and walking away from her. Never have I been so angry at her, betrayed by her. I'm furious she would keep that from me. Needing to get away from her before I do something I regret, I go looking for Valarian. Marcus rushes over to me and grabs my shoulder but I shove him off.

"Did you know too?" I snarl at him. He puts his hands up in surrender but shakes his head. I growl at Zoe and Macey as they pass me; I feel betrayed by all of them.

My father walks over to me when he sees me walking in his direction but I don't stop, instead, heading for my son, who's on the swings.

"Valen? What happened? Did she win?" Dad calls out to me when I walk past him. I growl.

"John submitted," I fume, too pissed off to form proper words.

"That's a good thing, why are you upset?" he asks, trying to keep pace with me as I move toward my son.

"She lied to me!" I snarl, my entire body trembling with rage.

"Who did?"

"Everly. She's pregnant!" I tell him and he grabs my arm, pulling me to a stop. I glance in Everly's direction to see her chasing after me.

"What?" he asks, before holding his hand up at Everly, telling her to back off. I'm glad he did because I want to slap her for what she did. She stops, looking torn between ignoring him and obeying. He shakes his head and I growl at her.

"Valen, please. Let me—"

"I don't want to hear it! Just get out of my face!" I snap at her.

Valarian rushes over, looking between his mother and I. He stops a couple of yards away from me.

"Can Valarian and I stay at your place tonight? I can't be near her right now," I ask my father.

"Yes. Of course," he says. I stalk off, grabbing my son and picking him up. Everly rushes over, trying to take him from me. Tears streak down her face and my canines slip out as I push her hands away from him.

"Mom!" Valarian screams while twisting in my arms.

"Valen, give him to me." she says, reaching for him. Dad gets between us. Valarian cries out for her when I start walking away, heading for my car. My father, I can hear, is talking to her and trying to calm her down, but I ignore her and make my way to the exit.

"What about Mom?" Valarian cries, still twisting in my arms.

"Stop it. You'll see her later," I tell him and lift him higher, hugging him closer.

"Are we going home?" he asks. I fiddle with the key fob and unlock my car as I step into the parking lot.

"Dad! We can't leave Mom!" Valarian sobs, pushing on my shoulders and kicking his legs, forcing me to put him down. I growl when he takes off running back toward the entry.

"Valarian!" I growl while turning around, only to see Everly grab him. She scoops him up in her arms and my father messes his hair as I approach them to take him back again.

"I want to stay with you!" Valarian cries, clinging to her neck as she sets him down.

"I'm not going anywhere, you're just staying at Pop's for the night with Daddy," she says, wiping his tears. At least she isn't fighting me on this. She pries his fingers from her neck and steers him toward the car with me following closely behind her.

"It's just for tonight?" she asks me as she opens the back door.

Valarian climbs in and I quickly move to buckle him in, making Everly step aside. She touches my back and I look at her over my shoulder—she removes it quickly at the angered look on my face.

After I shut the door, she tries to grab my hand and I fight the urge to shift, instead, growling at her as my aura slips out. She takes a step back, her ass hitting the side of my car.

"You lied to me! Kept it from me!"

"You wouldn't have let me go through with it!" she snaps back as I step closer to her.

"With good reason, too! You didn't just risk *your* life!" I tell her, barely holding myself together.

She goes to defend herself or explain, but I cut her off before she can. "Enough! You're causing a scene and scaring our son," I tell her and she peers down at the window beside her. She swallows and looks back at me.

"You'll bring him back tomorrow?" she says and I clench my jaw. "Valen?"

"I need to go," I tell her, walking off to the driver's side. My father rummages in his pockets and pulls out his keys. He passes them to her.

"I'll talk to him, it will be alright," I hear him tell her and she nods, taking them from him. I climb in my car and Dad jumps in the passenger side before I tear out of the parking lot.

Valen

Dad's place Is like a shrine of my childhood. Even today, he still has my artwork framed on his walls and photos hung or in frames on all the furniture. Growing up, his entire life revolved around raising me, and his house shows that clearly.

Despite having done some horrible things in the past; he loved me, and that much shows.

One thing I love, though, is seeing that some of Valarian's artwork and school stuff also displayed like treasured possessions alongside mine. It's embarrassing that he kept some of this crap, yet I know it means something to him, despite how crappy my art skills were.

Dad cooked dinner for us, and we watched movies on DVD. Every channel is displaying scenes from the challenge and Valarian doesn't need to see that or become involved in adult issues, so after the fourth headline, Dad decided to put a movie on.

Later that night, Valarian wouldn't sleep without talking to his mother, so I let him call her. Still, he was restless, tossing and turning on the couch as I rested his head in my lap. I let my head fall back onto the back of the couch, trying to rest. My father had muted the TV, and we were watching it with captions.

"Everly alright?" he asks, and I nod.

"I have Tatum staying with her. He's outside the door," I tell him, and he nods.

Our argument was broadcast across every TV station. Luckily, no one knew what it was about, and John and Claire were tight-lipped and said 'no comment' when interviewed. John even slapped one of the reporters for coming too near.

It was all on display, and assumptions were made, so it will only be a matter of time before they figure it out.

Dad has been quiet most of the night and let me be, though I can tell he's itching to say something. Turning my head, I look over at him to find him watching Valarian.

"Just say it. I can see it's eating you up, so out with it," I tell him. Dad sighs and I turn my attention to him.

"Don't make my mistakes," he says, and I roll my eyes.

"I'm not abandoning her as you did Mom," I tell him, and he takes a deep breath. He shakes his head.

"Your mother was a spitfire. When my father met her, he told her she would never be good enough for an Alpha—that her status was as low as a dog," he says before laughing and shaking his head.

"You find that funny?" I ask him, shocked he would laugh over that.

"No, Valen. I don't. I always regretted not standing up to him, but what she did next is what makes me laugh," he chuckles.

"What did she do?"

"She slapped him and said 'No, your son isn't good enough for me. And the only fleabag is the ass-hat standing in front of me'," he says, then laughs.

"Bet Grandpa didn't take that well," I tell him, remembering the old prick. He was nasty right up until he died. Dad looked after him in his old age; he only lasted a year after my grandmother died.

"No, of course not. Yet, I kept sneaking off to see her. And she did whatever she could to make sure he found out about it," Dad chuckles. "She was right, though. I wasn't good enough for her. Your mother was tougher than I was. It wasn't about titles with her. She didn't care I was Alpha, she didn't care who my father was, and she sure as shit didn't care that she pissed him off. She and her pack of rogues turned up to every council meeting, causing havoc. Yet, no matter what she did, she never admitted to anyone that I was her mate," he tells me.

"What do you mean?" I ask.

"She knew it would cost my reputation, and she didn't want to ruin it. Once my father stood down and handed the title over, she hoped I would help her, back her, and claim her."

"Why didn't you?"

"Because I was an idiot. I feared my father. Scared he would do something to her or her parents; and he did. I knew if I claimed her, he would kill her like he did her parents," Dad says, looking down at his hands.

"Did she know it was him?" I ask him.

"I think she suspected it. I never told her, but I don't think I had to. When my father found out she was pregnant, he asked her to get rid of you. He wanted me to marry Stacey Langford, his Beta's daughter." Dad swallows and clears his throat.

"When you were born, she had you at that hotel. She didn't even tell me. I snuck over to see her and found you. Dad had me on a tight leash, even froze all my trust funds, and I hadn't seen her in months. I assumed she got rid of you, but there you were in your crib.

"I couldn't bear to leave and hid there for a few days. Dad came looking for me, of course. I always regretted that—wished I never went there—because he wanted to kill you and her when he found us. He said no rogue would marry his son and taint his reputation. I convinced him to let me take you and say she died," he said.

I've never seen him cry, but reliving whatever memory he's stuck in, I can tell that destroyed him.

"When you took Valarian today, Everly had that same look on her face—sheer panic. I get you're upset, but never keep your son from her. Nothing killed me more than prying you from your mother's arms and seeing that look on her face, hearing her beg for you back." He shakes his head and wipes his face on the sleeve of his shirt.

"But Dad would have made good on his threat. I knew that, and so did she. So she handed you over. She stopped fighting to protect you. I should have protected you both, but I failed her, and after that, she wouldn't forgive me. She even asked me to kill her and put her out of her misery," he whispers the last part.

"I snuck you to her for visits, but when you started asking for her, I knew I had to stop, and even she said it was too risky. If the media found out, she would be destroyed by my father, and so would I."

"I'm not taking Valarian from Everly, Dad. I would never do that!" I tell him.

"I know. You're better than me, you're a better man, I know that. And I know you won't give up your mate or your kids."

"Then why tell me this?"

"Because you're angry because she didn't tell you, but what would you have done if you knew?" he asks me.

"Not let her enter the challenge for one," I tell him and he nods.

"Exactly. She should have told you, but I get why she didn't. She reminds me of your mother."

"How so?"

"The fire in her, her will to fight for what's right, no matter the sacrifice to herself. She would sacrifice herself for her people, and that is what a good Luna does; that is what your mother did for you and me and all the rogues when she rallied for them. I burned that fire out of your mother because I wouldn't stand beside her and fight for her. Don't make that mistake, don't extinguish the flames that make her brilliant," he says. Leaning forward, he smoothes Valarian's hair with his hand.

"She didn't raise him on her own because she wanted to. She did it because she had to. The rogues, to Everly, were all she had, and yet you expect her to give them up and tell you? Knowing she would be forced to stand down? I know you, son. You wouldn't have let her enter, and Everly knew that too."

"Yes, because she is pregnant!" I growled.

"And so is every other rogue that is relying on her to change those laws. If the Blood Alpha's mate can't change them, what hope do they have of it ever changing? It wasn't about telling you or about her being reckless; it was about saving those who have no voice, all those other babies that will have it hard in winter while their mothers are scraping pennies for formula so they can leave them in someone else's hands all day and try to find whatever pitiful work they can," he retorts. I sigh and scratch the back of my neck. This is so fucked up!

"Everly sees the bigger picture, just like your mother did. She sees society for what it is and doesn't sugarcoat it. She knew the risks, but she did it anyway because one, she knew you wouldn't let her get hurt, and two, because even if she lost, she would still have fought, and it would still cause change. People would remember the Blood Alpha's mate taking on her own father for the rogues, fighting for change, and change only happens when people start questioning their beliefs."

"So you want me to forgive her just like that?" I ask in disbelief.

"No, son. I want you to stand beside her and fight for her like I wish I'd fought for your mother," he says, leaning back.

"You know I will. As I said before, I'm not leaving her or taking Valarian from her," I tell him, looking down at my son.

"Then why are you here and not with her like you're supposed to be?" he asks, and my brows furrow.

"It's okay to be angry, but don't walk away like a coward. She will test you, but don't you think you tested her enough? Five years is a long time to be on your own raising a kid and building an empire, yet she forgave you," he says with a shrug. I sigh, yet I'm not sure I can face her, and I'm still angry, no matter her reasoning.

"I am not saying you don't have the right to be angry, Valen. I'm just saying to be there. Everly has been on her own for so long and is used to doing everything independently. It will be hard for her to rely on anyone other than herself. You don't have to forgive her, but go home. At least let her know you're still there, and despite being angry, you love her and are still fighting alongside her."

CHAPTER
SIXTEEN

Everly

All night, I can't sleep. Valen won't answer any of my texts and shoves me out whenever I try to mind-link him. His silence is driving me insane, and I'm worried about Valarian. He sounded upset on the phone and wanted to come home, but I managed to calm him down enough and told him I would pick him up from school. Valen didn't object, so I figure he's okay with that, or at least I hope he is.

Throughout the night, I obsess over the horrible shit that was portrayed on the news, saying Valen and I were fighting because he was cheating on me, that he finally realized Valarian isn't his son. It's all bullshit. I know it, they know it, but they will do whatever they can to sell a story.

The bed feels too big without Valen in it—cold and empty—the house too quiet without him snoring beside me and making me want to smother him while he sleeps.

Many times I get up and check the locks and windows and check Valarian's bed. That was something Zoe and I both did when we lived together, almost like we took it in turns during the night when it was just us. We were always scared because it was only us in the house, knowing that rogue-whores aren't much of a fight if someone broke in, especially with my tiny wolf and hers.

It's a habit I thought I outgrew, however, now I'm alone, I find myself reverting to old habits and nearly have a panic attack when I realize Valarian isn't in his bed when I check. I keep reminding myself he's safe with his father, yet *knowing* that and *seeing* it for myself are two different things. Maybe if he wasn't angry with me, I would be fine, because I never had this issue when Valarian would sleep at Kalen's. I know it's because I'm entirely alone in a huge, empty penthouse, and without having anything to distract me, it reminds me of being on my own in my car. The feeling is still the same.

Having just closed my eyes again, I hear the front door lock twist and click, which has me sitting upright, panic coursing through me, and my hand instantly searches for Valen in the bed before remembering he isn't here. My heart thumps in my chest as I creep toward the hall. Then Valen's voice flits through my head.

'Calm down. It's just me. Don't hit me with anything; I'm carrying our son,' he mind-links, and I let out a breath of relief.

Walking down the hall, I see him step out of the entryway and into the dim lighting—I left the stove light on—and as I step into the living area, I see Valen is carrying Valarian, who's asleep in his arms. It's a little after midnight, and I move closer, wanting to take him, but Valen turns away.

"Get his bed ready. I'll carry him," Valen whispers, and I nod, rushing off down the hall and pulling his sheets back.

I step aside, flicking on his nightlight and lighting up the ceiling with his solar system projection. Valen sets him in his bed, tucks him in, and relief floods me that our son is home. Although, when I lean down to kiss Valarian's head, Valen walks out without a word to me. I hear him walk into the bathroom down the hall before the shower starts.

After checking the front door is locked, I climb back into bed;

Valen comes in a few minutes later in his towel. Once again, he says nothing as he gets dressed, but when he grabs his pillow, I know he isn't coming to bed.

Instead, he walks out of the room, and my stomach twists, knowing he's still so angry with me that he won't even sleep in the bed beside me. At least he's home. Maybe now I can get some form of sleep.

No such luck. It takes hours to sleep and I end up staring at the ceiling most of the night.

The following morning, I'm awoken by morning sickness. It sends me running for the bathroom as I heave and throw up the contents of my stomach, splattering the front of my pajamas with my vomit. It's the first time I've woken up needing to be sick.

My stomach turns violently, but suddenly I feel Valen's fingertips brush the back of my neck and pull my hair away from my face. Catching my breath, I feel him sweep my hair over my shoulder before he wets a face cloth and hands it to me.

"Are you alright?"

I nod my head, feeling breathless. My throat is raw and burning and I wipe my mouth as he walks out.

I'm climbing in the shower when Valen walks back in. He's already dressed, and he places a towel on the sink basin. I watch him scoop up my dirty laundry, and when he starts to walk out, I call out to him.

"Are you leaving early?" I ask.

"I'm going with Dad. I already packed Valarian's lunch. It's on the counter," he says, walking out and shutting the door. So I guess unless it's to do with Valarian, we aren't on speaking terms. It saddens me, but right now, I'll take anything. It's better than nothing. When I finish showering, I hop out, and hear that Valen is getting Valarian up and ready for school. When I walk into the room, I sigh when I see Valen has set my clothes out on the bed for me.

As quickly as I can, I change into my work clothes; I want to try to speak to him before he leaves, but Valarian is animatedly telling him about something while he eats his Cocoa Krispies. Valen watches me as I walk into the kitchen before sliding a cup of tea and my breakfast in front of me. I scrunch my face up at the tea. I hate tea. What I really want is coffee, yet when I go to look for it, he clears his throat.

"I tossed it out. You shouldn't drink so much caffeine. Also, there are prenatal vitamins above the microwave. Make sure you take them. And you have a doctor's appointment tomorrow at 2 p.m. and an ultrasound," he says, and I nod, wanting to speak to him, but he turns his attention to Valarian.

"Why is Mom going to the doctor's?" Valarian asks, looking at me.

"Because Mommy is having a baby," Valen tells him, kissing his head and grabbing his suit jacket. "Behave for your mother. I'll see you in the morning," he tells him before walking off.

"Wait, you're not picking me up from school?" Valarian asks, twisting in his seat to look at his father.

"No, I'm going with Pop and won't be back until late tonight."

"Where are you going?" I ask him.

"To pick up that part with Dad. I have to go; I need to pick him up because you have his car," Valen tells me.

I turn around to retrieve his father's keys out of my bag, but by the time I do, Valen has already left. I sigh before pouring the tea down the sink; I can't wait to get to work to make some coffee, though honestly, I'm not sure my belly will handle it with how my stomach has been lately. The smell alone has made me sick a few times, yet I still crave my morning hit of caffeine.

The day goes by slowly, time really dragging out. I spent all morning at the hotel talking to contractors—they're slowly getting everything done, but it will be a few months before we'll be able to reopen—so after lunch, I go to the homeless shelter and continue painting my mural. It's coming along nicely, and I meet with the sign manufacturer to approve the final sign design before picking Valarian up from school. I wanted Valen to come with me to see the sign, but I suppose he'll see it when it's set atop the old school.

Pulling up in front of the school, I receive a text message from him.

'*Don't forget to pick up Valarian from school.*'

'*I'm outside the school already. Roughly what time will you be home?*'

He doesn't reply.

With a sigh, I toss my phone into my handbag and wait for the bell. Everything is very routine; once home, I cook dinner while Valarian does his homework, then he has a bath, I shower, then put Valarian to bed. Once he's tucked in bed, I make a coffee—I managed to sneak a small jar home from the hotel, hiding it in the back of the pantry—intending to wait up for Valen. I go over the hotel accounts and pay some of the bills that are outstanding, watching our funds slowly dwindle away. But we'll grow again, that much I'm certain of. When I finish, I message my father.

'*Can you send me the pack's accounting details, and the accounts and assets inventory?*'

'*If you want, I can meet you for lunch tomorrow and go over everything. I will have to sign the deed to the pack house over to you.*'

'*No, keep it in your name. I am not taking your house. Just make sure you leave it to Ava in yours and Mom's last will and testament.*'

'*You're not kicking us out?*'

'*No, of course not. It's your home. You're still my parents and part of my pack now. I just need to clean up the pack finances, you can still run things on your end.*'

'*Where do you want to meet tomorrow?*'

'*Can you meet me at the homeless shelter? I'll be there most of the day.*'

'*Can you bring Valarian? Your mother and I would like to see him?*'

His message shocks me, and I chew my lip, debating what to reply.

'*If Valen says it's ok.*'

'*Okay. I'm sorry he found out the way he did. Hope you are both doing well, we haven't spoken to the media or told them. See you tomorrow.*'

'*Night dad.*'

'*Goodnight, Evie. See you tomorrow. I will text when I am on my way.*'

Well, that went better than I thought. Dad and I managed to have a civil conversation, something I wasn't expecting after the challenge.

It's hours later and early morning before I hear the key in the door. I glance at the hall leading to the front door to see Valen quietly walk in before noticing the lamp on beside me. He pauses for a moment, then drops his keys into the bowl on the hall stand.

"How was your day?" I ask him.

"Long," is all he answers before he heads down the hall, retrieves a towel from the linen closet, and walks into the bathroom. Packing up my laptop, I walk to the bathroom door and grip the door handle, but he locked it. I sigh and knock on the door, yet he ignores me. I know he heard me because I can feel his annoyance.

"I'm having lunch with my father tomorrow and I wanted to take Valarian. Mom and Dad want to see him," I call out to him through the door. Yet Valen chooses to ignore me and I hear the water shut off.

Sighing, I move back to the couch and wait for him to come out. He does, walking off toward the bedroom before returning with his pillow and blanket.

"Did you hear me?" I ask him, though I know he did because I felt his annoyance earlier.

"Do what you want, you do anyway," is all he says, tossing his pillow and blanket on the couch.

"Are you seriously just going to keep ignoring me?" I ask him.

"I have nothing to say, Everly. It's late, I want to go to bed," he says and I press my lips in a line before getting up.

"Don't forget, you have the ultrasound tomorrow at 2 p.m.," he says as I start walking off.

"I'm not sure what time I'm meeting Dad," I tell him.

"Well, you *won't* be meeting him at 2 p.m., will you!" he says before shutting the lamp off and sending the living room into total darkness.

"Are you coming to it?" I ask him, wondering if I'm doing this alone. My last experience wasn't the best and I couldn't even afford to go to ultrasound appointments; I had to choose between eating for the next week or not eating and going to the appointment.

The only one I had besides my initial one was at twenty weeks, and the only reason I got to go to that one was that I slipped over at the Chinese restaurant. My boss was worried I would try to sue, so he took me to the hospital and they did one because I started bleeding. That was when I found out Valarian was a boy. They put me on bed rest, like that was actually a possibility. Instead, I was back to scrubbing dishes mere hours later.

I try to remind myself this time is different, but though things may have changed, this one bad experience is enough to ruin this pregnancy for me already.

I dread being pregnant. It terrifies me, and I shudder when I think of giving birth—how the midwives sneered and taunted me while I cried in agony, the hunger from trying to produce milk to breastfeed only for it to dry up quickly from not getting enough food. If it wasn't for Macey, I would have starved those first few days. Who would have thought the offer of a granola bar would start a lifelong friendship.

Yet, the worst was seeing everyone's families come to meet their new family member while not one person from my previous life remembered I existed.

"Yes, Everly, so don't be late," Valen says, pulling me from my thoughts. He moves around on the couch trying to make himself comfortable.

"You can sleep in the bed," I offer suddenly, not wanting to be alone. He says nothing. I want to climb on the couch with him, just so I can shake the dread away. I take a step toward him to see if he'll let me until he speaks.

"Go to bed, Everly," he says, and tears prick my eyes as I turn around and head for bed. I don't know what's worse: being alone or having a mate and feeling alone. Another night of restless sleep and checking the damn locks. Fine. It's not like I haven't been on my own before. I'm no stranger to loneliness. Loneliness is something ingrained and woven through me.

Yet, why does it hurt so much more now?

CHAPTER
SEVENTEEN

Valen

I'm woken by noise up the hall. Rolling over on the couch, I rub my eyes and can feel that Everly is awake, hear her at the back of the place, rummaging around and doing something. I try to go back to sleep, but when I hear tiptoed footsteps in the hall, I crack an eye open to see her go to the front door, whispering under her breath to herself. I sit up, wondering where she's going so late at night. I hear the door unlock, then relock before hearing her footsteps again.

"What are you doing?" I grumble and she jumps, startled.

"Nothing. I was making sure we locked the door," she answers before padding off back down the hall. Now awake, I go to get a drink, yet she feels off through the bond; it makes me wonder why she feels scared? The scariest thing in this damn place is lying on the couch. Does she really think I would let someone in to get to them?

Lying back down, I try to go back to sleep. Just as I'm in that part of sleep when you're asleep, yet also not, my ears prick at soft footsteps, only this time checking the balcony doors. What is she expecting? Someone to scale up the side of the hotel? I watch her, trying to ignore the nagging of the bond when she goes to the front door again.

"You already checked it," I say and she stops. I can just see her from where I'm standing in the hall. She rubs her temples and goes to walk back to our room when she pauses and walks back to the front door.

"Everly I said you already checked it," I growl at her.

"I just need to be sure," she mutters, and I listen to her twist the locks and relock them again. I click my tongue and sigh, listening to her walk off again before Marcus tugs on the mind-link.

"You just got home? I thought the company driver was meeting you halfway. Why are you up?" Marcus asks.

"They did meet us halfway; Dad and I took turns driving. And to answer your other question; because Everly keeps checking the damn locks."

"You two still not talking?" he asks.

"I don't want to upset her, I have nothing nice to say right now," I admit, feeling like a damn asshole. But I don't know what else to feel. I'm angry, and the words would sting, so I don't want to throw them out in anger and upset her.

"Try to get some sleep. I'll be by at 7 a.m. to pick you up," he says, cutting the link.

The last thing I want to do is go see Nixon, but after what we found out from John, I need to investigate, though I don't see him being cooperative, so I try to sleep.

I catch a couple of hours when I hear the damn lock on the front door twist again. Though I'm trying to ignore her, I listen as she checks the balcony doors, then the kitchen window. She's driving me up the damn wall, but when I hear her check the kitchen window, I sit up. Valarian would struggle to fit through it, let alone any ninja that managed to scale up the building. She rushes back off to the bedroom and I shake my head, lying back down and closing my damn eyes, only to feel eyes on me a few minutes later. Unease rolls over me and I know she's awake. What I'm not expecting is to open my eyes as I roll over, only to find her next to me. I nearly shit my pants and jump out of my skin. She jumps in fright when I do and I groan, clutching my hair.

"What?!" I snap, annoyed. I've spent all damn day and night in a fucking car and now all night with her waking me up every Goddess damn second! I growl at her and sit up, only to notice her blanket and pillow on the floor next to the couch. The look on her face makes me feel like a prick for snapping at her when I realize it was her staring at me in the dark.

She says nothing, but I don't miss the way her lip quivers as she stands up to go back to the room. As she reaches to grab her blanket, I grip her wrist and feel the tremble in her hand. With a sigh, I lift the blanket and tug her on the couch with me.

The stupid bond!

She rolls into me and I slide my arm under her head so she can bury her face in my neck. She says nothing and falls asleep almost instantly. Her breathing evens out, her heart rate slows, falling in sync with mine. However, I find myself now unable to sleep, trying to understand her strange actions and the weird look of fright, but also humiliation on her face, like she was caught doing something she shouldn't. Eventually, her scent calms me as I tuck her closer and finally fall asleep.

The following morning, however, I wonder if I dreamed it because I'm on the couch alone and Valarian and Everly are nowhere to be seen. I reach for my phone to find missed calls from Marcus; it's 10 a.m.!

I open the mind link and feel for Marcus' tether. He answers immediately. *'Why didn't you wake me?'* I snarl at him.

'I tried, but Everly said she kept you up last night and to let you sleep.'

'Fuck! I'm getting ready now.'

'All good, I canceled with Nixon until tomorrow. He said he had to leave the city anyway.'

I sit up and rub my face. *'What time tomorrow?'* I ask and yawn.

'11 a.m. tomorrow, go back to bed,' Marcus says, but I shake my head before remembering he can't see me.

'"No, I need to check the homeless shelter anyway. Make sure you wake me tomorrow. I don't care if I'm tired or she keeps me up, we need to get this meeting out of the way and see his reaction,' I tell him.

'Okay, well, John just got to Zoe's place with Everly, so I should go,' Marcus says.

'Wait, Everly is with you? Where's Valarian?'

'At school. She dropped Valarian here at 5 a.m. this morning and asked us to run him to school so she could get an early start on her mural. Zoe and I dropped him off for her.'

'So, she didn't take him to see John and Claire?' I asked him.

'No, Everly didn't want to upset you and bring him, though Claire looks pretty upset he isn't here.'

'Is Everly ok?' I ask him, slightly worried since she didn't wake me. I didn't even hear her leave.

'Yes, why wouldn't she be?'

'Because she kept checking the damn locks all night. She seemed frightened.'

'Ah, yeah, Zoe does that. Drives me nuts. Anxiety. Zoe takes medication for hers, but isn't so bad when I'm here. Old habits die hard," Marcus says with a sigh.

'What do you mean?'

'The girls. Zoe said they hated living at the back of the hotel because it was so close to the reserve, paranoid about forsaken breaking in and taking the kids. Apparently they had a few scares there. Everly must have been scared last night. Anyway, I know she said she's going to the homeless shelter later; her sign is finished, so she's going to watch them set it up at 1 p.m.. Maybe you'll catch her there."

'Okay, thanks. Mind-link me if John tries anything,' I tell him before I cut the link.

In an effort to wake myself up, I walk to the bathroom and shower, pondering what Marcus said about the girls. Does that mean

Everly doesn't feel safe here with me? I don't understand it; she was fine before and it's the first time I've seen her do it.

My shower is quick and I dress equally quickly. I can't believe I wasted an entire morning! I know Everly is going to be at the homeless shelter, so I'll make sure to meet her there so I can take her to her appointment. After having lunch at my father's place, I drive over to the homeless shelter just in time to see a crane lifting a huge sign on top of the building, but my eyes are drawn to the mural on the front of the building.

Climbing out of the car and approaching the building, I can see she's finished it, but as I get closer, my footsteps halt at the front gates and I find myself staring up at my mother. Everly, I can see, is guiding the men on the cherry picker, telling them the sign isn't straight as they attach it above the mural and front doors leading in.

My eyes go back to roaming over the huge mural; last time I saw it was a blank canvas. On one side of the doors is the woman I remember from the pictures Everly had shown me. She used the photo layout, but instead of Everly, Zoe, and Macey beside her like in the original, my mother's arm is tossed over the shoulder of Emily, and her son stands between them both.

I suddenly feel like an asshole; she got up this morning to finish this despite us arguing. Emotion clogs my throat as I stare up at the women who influenced my mate the most and made her into who she is today. Dad's words come back to me about how the rogues were all she had, and seeing my mother up on the wall, I now know what he meant. Valarie was my mother but also Everly's, and now I understand why Everly went ahead with her challenge; it wasn't just for the rogues—it was for Mom! She wanted to fix the one thing my mother couldn't.

Walking over to Everly where she's staring up at the sign the men are placing in the brackets, I find her covered in paint and sweaty from the hot day. I wrap my arms around her waist and she jumps.

"Thank you," I whisper, kissing her cheek. She sighs in relief and points to the sign. I look up and watch as the men peel away the white film covering it, revealing the sign beneath.

'Valerie's Place'—Where your village begins.

"Now, no one will forget her name," Everly whispers.

E verly

    I worked on the mural all morning, only stopping when my parents arrived for lunch. The meeting with them went well, but the pack's finances are destroyed. Dad has been using loans to pay off loans, which only put him into more debt, and I have to think of a way to absolve all of that.

    I don't have millions packed away. What savings I do have aren't enough to cover the debt *and* the hotel, and I'm not about to ask Valen for the money. Then there's the contract between my father and Nixon, who holds the pack as collateral for the debt my father owes. Dad has kept up with his repayments, but all those repayments are loans from the bank too.

    I'm in over my head, I know it, and with Valen not speaking to me, I don't know anyone that can help without selling off the pack assets. All the pack businesses are in the red as well. A few of the loans taken out are through two of the banks owned by Valen's pack, so maybe I could at least have the interest rate lowered or relinquish those businesses back to the bank to remove those debts without filing bankruptcy.

I paid most of the others off completely today, but the larger sums I have no way to cover. As for the debt to Nixon, I called Kalen and asked him about it, since he handles most of Valen's accounting, and he said there was no way around the contract—that now that debt is mine because it was put on the pack's finances, not on my father's personal finances. The pack still owes Nixon 1.6 million.

Which leaves me with two options: sell what remaining assets my father's pack has or try to get a loan, which I don't want to do because it will just get us into more debt. We have six months left to pay off Nixon, or the pack—and all its assets and land—belong to him.

I know my hotel's land alone is worth more than that, but I'm not willing to give it up; this place isn't just mine. So now, I'm debating whether to see if, once fixed up again, Valen's pack would buy it. Then I wouldn't be losing it and neither would the rogues. But with how angry he is, I'm not sure if he would help, even if it was his mothers.

I get the text message saying the sign is ready to be placed just as Dad and Mom left after lunch. Before heading outside, I quickly check on Macey and Zoe, who left a little while ago to pick up the kids. They're inside the rec room, putting up the finishing touches. It looks great, and I quickly kiss Valarian before rushing back out.

I pause to check that the paint is dry on my way through the door, and it is. Seeing Valarie up on the wall makes tears spring to my eyes. Out of every mural I've done, this is my favorite; maybe because of its meaning. I just hope Valen likes it and the one I did inside the rec room.

I watch as they put the sign up and instruct them to move the bracket a little higher on the left, as it's a little crooked and I know it will set off Valen's OCD that he believes he doesn't have. They're setting it in the brackets when I feel arms circle around my waist and I'm tugged backward against a hard chest. His scent envelopes me. I was so preoccupied, I hadn't even realized he was here.

"Thank you," Valen whispers, kissing my cheek.

I look up and point to the sign. Valen tilts his head up to see, and I watch as the men peel off the white film covering the sign.

'Valerie's Place'—Where your village begins.

"Now, no one will forget her name," I whisper.

"Is that Mom's handwriting?" he asks, choking a little on emotion.

"Yep, I used the letters and blew it up so I could transfer her handwriting," I tell him.

Turning my head to look at him, he rests his chin on my shoulder.

"I'm sorry I didn't tell you," I tell him.

"I'm sorry, you felt you needed to hide it from me," he says, kissing the side of my mouth.

"Do you like it?"

"Love it."

"Then come on, I want to show you something else," I tell him excitedly.

"There's more?" he asks, and I nod, grabbing his hand that's around my waist and walking to the front doors. I grab two hard hats and drop one on his head. Valarian's, Casey's, and Taylor's voices reach our ears, and Valen squeezes my hand.

"Valarian is here?"

"Yep, the girls picked the kids up on the way over after Dad left. We promised they could help with this part. Valarian asked me last night. They helped me pick out the frames last week," I tell him, tugging him down the hall.

We stop in the old cafeteria that's been done up as a huge living area for those that come here. It's the first place that Valen had done up. It has a kids' play area, three huge dining tables, and on the other side is a huge TV and couches. But the walls had looked bare, so I wanted to do something so it felt more homey.

Valen stops at the double door leading in and gasps. Valarian spins on his heel, noticing his father, and squeals, rushing over excitedly. Valen stares around the enormous room and scoops Valarian up when he rushes over.

"What's wrong, Dad? Don't you like it?" Valarian asks when seeing his father become teary-eyed.

"No, I love it," he chokes out.

All of Valarie's banners from her protesting days are framed on the walls, along with the blown-up and framed newspaper articles about her efforts to change the city.

On the far wall is another painting I did of Valarie, using the photo of her standing on the cop car, a banner raised above her head which reads, "No Packs, One people". It takes up an entire wall. This is who Valarie was, and despite Valen not knowing her, he'll know how many lives his mother changed.

Valen sets Valarian down, and Valarian tugs him over to the wall that's full of handprints—rogue handprints. Everyone who knew Valarie had put their handprints on the wall and written something about her on each one. Hundreds, showing how many lives she had touched over the years.

Macey and Zoe come over. Macey rests her head on my shoulder and Zoe leans against me.

"She would love this," Zoe says, and I nod as I watch Valarian point out his handprint; his reads 'My Nana'.

"No, she would ask why we're dredging up the past and tell us to get back to work," Macey chuckles, and so do I. She's right; Valarie was a tough cookie to crack, yet when she did, she crumbled.

Valen stands by the wall reading each one, and I move away from the girls to go over to him. When I touch his back, he looks down at me, tears trekking down his face.

"It's dusty in here," he grumbles, wiping his cheeks.

"Pretty sure I saw someone cutting onions back there," Macey states, coming up on his other side and gripping his shoulder. He laughs and tugs me closer, hugging me and kissing the top of my head. Reaching over, he grabs Macey and Zoe to embrace us all.

"Thank you," he says to all of us.

"You should be proud, Valen. She was an amazing woman. I wish you got to know her as we did, but we'll always remind you of who she was, and there is no bigger reminder of her than the woman who carries your mark," Zoe says, and I smile sadly. I feel him nod against my shoulder.

"Fuck, the dust is terrible in here," Macey mutters, and Valen laughs.

"Fucking terrible," he agrees. He lets us go and wipes his face, looking around. "This is amazing."

I couldn't agree more.

My phone beeps in my pocket—the reminder to go to the ultrasound. I pull it out and sigh.

"Want me to take Valarian?" Zoe asks, but I shake my head.

"No, he can come with me," I tell her. She nods before rushing off to wrangle the kids, and I look at Valen nervously.

"You're still coming with me?" I ask, and he gives me a funny look.

"Of course. You aren't alone this time, Everly. I'll be right beside you every step of the way," he says, draping his arm across my shoulders. He tips my chin up to look at him.

"Mine," he whispers, leaning down and kissing my lips before his hand drops to my stomach. "Ours," he adds, rubbing my belly. "Don't ever doubt that. I will never leave you to do this on your own, not again, no matter what," he says, kissing my temple.

I sigh, relieved; I don't think I could do it again by myself. The last time, I had Valarie; she was a godsend. But I would have if I had to.

"Come on," he whispers, holding his hand out to Valarian, who waves to the girls, and we head to the doctor in Valen's car.

Nerves kick in as we pull up and Valarian asks why we're here.

"Because Mom has to get a check-up, and then we get to see the baby," Valen tells him.

"Will we find out if the boy wrestling worked?" Valarian asks.

"No, not for a while, and it will probably look like a jelly bean," Valen laughs.

Valarian scrunches his face up, looking confused.

This time around, it's different. My father isn't here to demand I abort; there's no judgment, no worry as I wait for the urine test to come back. Once it's confirmed, the doc takes blood samples before leading us down the hall to where they do ultrasounds.

"You can lie down," Doc says while motioning toward the gurney. I lie on it, lifting my shirt, and Valarian watches with avid fascination as the doctor squirts the jelly on my belly.

He fiddles with the device, and after a few minutes, we hear the heartbeat. I sigh, not realizing just how worried I was about the fetus until now. During the challenge, I was so concerned with protecting my stomach that I could hardly fight. I was making sure to pick my moves and keep my abdomen out of reach. I would hate to see a video replay, because not much action happened in it. Dad was worried about hurting me, and I was concerned about hurting myself, so it probably looked more like a synchronized dance than an actual fight.

Doc takes some measurements, then announces, "There we are."

I peer up at the screen, then squint when he moves to the next view.

"Wait!" I gasp, and Doc chuckles.

"I wondered when you would notice the other one," he laughs, and Valen looks between the doctor and me.

"What's wrong?" he asks, sounding frantic.

"Nothing, Alpha; both heartbeats are strong," Doc says, and Valen sighs, leaning back.

"Wait! Both?" Valen suddenly shrieks, leaning forward to look at the screen and making Valarian fall off his lap.

"Yep, you're having twins," Doc tells him, and his eyes widen. He looks horrified, and I laugh at his face. He looks like he's calculating some math equations.

"Two. There are two in there? Are you sure?" he asks, looking at my stomach.

"Yep, definitely two," Doc says, pointing at the screen to show him.

"That is so many diapers. We're never gonna sleep again," Valen whispers, shaking his head and trying to wrap his head around it.

"Twins? Mom is having twins?" Valarian gushes.

"Yep, you are going to have two—"

"Two brothers! This is awesome. Can they sleep in my room?" Valarian says, cutting me off. I laugh, and Doc chuckles.

"What if they're girls?" Doc asks.

"Na, Mom and Dad promised to wrestle in the boy way, right, Dad?" Valarian says, tapping his father's shoulder, while Valen appears in shock.

"Uh, yeah, right, in the boy's way," Valen mumbles, staring at the screen.

"See, I'm gonna have two brothers," Valarian declares.

"If you say so," Doc laughs.

CHAPTER
NINETEEN

Valen

Valarian is bouncing excitedly on the balls of his feet as the doctor points to the two beating hearts. Not even I can sit still. This is too much information to process. I expected one. Is it hot in here?

Everly reaches for my hand when I stand up and tug at my tie; I'm overheating. Doc falls silent again and squirts more jelly on her belly. After turning the screen away for a second, he clears his throat and tugs on the collar of his shirt.

I stop my pacing and notice him becoming a little nervous as he moves the device. Valarian is babbling happily about the twin brothers he thinks he'll have. Doc's nervousness has me uncomfortable. Why did he turn the screen away?

"Doc, is everything alright?" I asked, suddenly frightened that something is wrong with the twins I wasn't expecting.

"Maybe you should take a seat, Alpha," Doc says, and I freeze. Something is wrong. I glance at Everly; her fear is just as bad. She leans up on her elbows to look at Doc.

"Take a seat," Doc repeats and he motions toward the chair. Yet, now he has me panicking. I didn't necessarily *want* twins, but the thought of something being wrong with them makes my heart race faster and my stomach drop. I shake my head.

"Just spit it out, Doc," I snap, becoming annoyed.

"It appears I was wrong about there being twins."

I clutch my hair and let out a breath. "Oh, thank the Goddess," I sigh.

"It's not twins?" Valarian asks, pouting.

"No, I found another heartbeat!"

I nod along at his words. Thank Goddess; I wasn't looking forward to never sleeping again.

"What!" Everly shrieks, "but I saw two."

Doc holds his hands out in an apologetic gesture. I know she's outraged, but this is a good thing; I only planned for one.

"I was wrong; I found another, so you're having triplets," Doc says, and I blink. I must have heard that wrong.

"Triplets?" I murmur, looking at Doc as he turns the screen.

"Yep, Everly is five weeks along. Here's babies A and B, and this one, Baby C, was hiding behind the other. I thought it was a shadow." Doc says while pointing at the screen.

My vision tunnels and his words fade away along with the room.

My head pounds as I open my eyes only to see Everly's worried face hovering *above* me. She taps my face with her hand before sighing. Oh Goddess, I fainted!

"Thank the Goddess, and why are *you* fainting? You don't have to carry them!" she laughs.

"Please tell me that was a dream. Are we having a litter?" I mumble incoherently.

"Uh, no, there are definitely three. We finished the scan while you were... uh... napping," Everly says, holding up the printed picture. I snatch it from her and peer up at it.

"I'll give you both a moment," Doc says, leaving the room.

"We're having triplets!" I repeat, trying to wrap my head around that information. I have some super sperm. I should be selling that shit! This is a damn nightmare. She's getting her damn tubes tied afterward.

"Valen?" Everly says, staring at me worriedly. Man, how embarrassing.

"You didn't tell anyone I fainted, did you?"

Everly presses her lips in a line and shakes her head.

"Nope," she says, but I can feel her lie.

"Who did you tell?"

"Marcus. You were out for about ten minutes. I thought I was going to have to carry you back to the car," she says and I huff. Great, he'll never let me live it down.

"Did you tell him why?"

"No, Doc said it was too early. Best not to announce it until I hit twelve weeks."

That makes sense, but I know Valarian will blab to the girls. His excitement is kind of annoying, yet also contagious. I look at the small ultrasound printout in my hand before getting to my feet.

"Give me your keys. I am driving," Everly says, holding her hands out for them. I reluctantly give them to her before following her out to the car.

Triplets. What the heck am I going to do with triplets? I pictured one baby, and I ended up with a damn litter! Well, almost. My head is spinning the entire way home. Valarian is chatting away happily about his baby brothers.

Please, Moon Goddess, be boys; he'll be on the warpath otherwise. Valarian is already picking out names and they haven't even got a brain yet! Literally, a heartbeat, and that's it. She's only five weeks pregnant, so we still have thirty-five weeks left.

"Are you alright?" Everly asks me. I swallow. Mentally, I prepared myself for one, but now there will be three. *Three!*

"Yep, fine," I tell her, a little embarrassed that I fainted on her. Thankfully, the drive home is uneventful, but I have so much to do tomorrow. Marcus and I are going to visit Nixon tomorrow. Everly tells me her plans over dinner—she's meeting with her father's accountant and checking over some business accounts; both of us are going to be busy.

I've just put Valarian to bed when I hear Everly curse from the living room. When I walk out to check on her, she turns the news up.

"What is it?" I ask, but she holds a finger to her lips when I see Nixon is in some sort of conference meeting with one of the news channels.

I move toward the couch and sit beside her. She turns it up a little more. So this is why Nixon didn't want to meet today. He was doing damage control. I growl as I watch him give some sob story, which I know is a lie. My father told me the real story. Nixon handed himself in, knowing we were onto him.

He tells the news reporter he was trying to find a cure for his sick daughter, leaving out the part where he abandoned her to her mother. Instead, claiming she had been sick all her life, and he was trying to find a cure—that he has top leading scientists working on a vaccine. He knew we were going to uncover everything, and we blew our chance. He painted himself a saint, so when this came out, he already had an explanation.

He made it look like Leah, his mate, dumped her kids on him, including a sick baby, before running off with another man.

"What is he doing? He's admitting everything!" Everly exclaims.

"Damage control. He knew he was about to be busted. Nixon covered his tracks and got those in the city on his side."

He then says he tried to offer me the vaccine for Emily and Ben but I refused. We listen a little more and it's clear to me this is his way of covering up. He's trying to save his reputation while destroying mine.

Everly's phone starts ringing, and so does mine. Pulling it out of my pocket, I see it's Marcus calling. I quickly answer it.

"Are you seeing the news? Nixon is being broadcast across every station," Marcus tells me.

"Yep, I'm watching it now," I tell him and I hear Everly on her phone talking to someone. It only takes me a moment before I realize it's her father.

"Dad, slow down, let me think. You need to calm down. I'll think of something," I hear Everly tell him. The mind-link also opens up and my father's voice rushes through my head just before utter chaos ensues when every pack member suddenly starts trying to alert us through the pack link. Everly screams, clutching her head, and my own spins as voices flit through the open link.

Dropping my phone, I race to her before booming through the link, *'Don't use the mind-link. We are aware!'* I order my pack before shoving them out. They'll give one of us an aneurysm!

I help Everly to sit on the couch before flicking the damn TV off. John, I can hear, is calling out to her. I look around for her phone and find it on the floor. John's voice screeches in my ear when I pick it up.

"Everly, what's going on? Do you need me to come over?" John says, sounding rather panicked.

"She's fine. The pack link overwhelmed her," I tell him, moving into the kitchen. "What is it you want? We already know of Nixon's bullshit interview."

"I called for the same reason, and also to warn her that Nixon has told me if I don't verify this to the media, he's stopping Claire's treatment."

"Fuck!" I curse under my breath. I fill a glass with water, take it back to Everly, and pass it to her, watching as she sips it.

"What happens if she doesn't get the vaccine?" I ask.

"She will eventually turn forsaken," John says. "I have one more dose, but it will only hold it off for another month. She needs that vaccine every month. I'm sorry, but I have no choice, Valen."

I growl—he gets up there and states Nixon's claims are valid, it's going to cause a rift between all the packs and the rogues.

"Wait! You have one vaccine left?" I ask.

"Yes, so?" John says.

"Give me the vaccine. I'll see if any of our doctors can replicate it. If we can't, then go public as he wants."

"I haven't got the money to fund a science team. Everly has seen my pack's accounts," John tells me.

"I'll pay for it, but if you have to, go public. You out Nixon, you tell them everything. Even if you are involved in any of it, you go public. It will force him to hand the vaccine over to Claire and buy us some more time to prove a case against him," I tell him, and I see Everly's head turn to look at me as she listens in on the conversation.

"Or better yet, we beat him at his own game—tell them about Claire, paint him as the hero and tell the city he promised to give her the vaccine free of charge. If he backs out, it will backfire on him. I know he won't, and it gives us time to work out a cure while she receives treatment," I tell John. I could hear him talking to Claire in a calm voice before returning to the discussion.

"I get seen going over there, Nixon will know we're talking," John says, and I look at Everly. We go over there, Nixon will definitely know—yet one of the rogues might be able to meet John somewhere.

"I'll send Macey to the gas station near your place; give it to her," I tell him and we discuss details of the time, etcetera. Everly uses my phone to call and gives Macey her father's number. Once we hang up, we wait.

CHAPTER
TWENTY

Everly

Macey drops the vial off later that night. However, when I hear the knock and open the door, I'm stunned to see Tatum with her. I knew they were close, but to see him with her so late at night makes me wonder if more is going on than them than just being friends with benefits. Macey, noticing my shock at seeing him, speaks.

"Oh, we weren't... Tatum just came with me... just in case."

"You woke Tatum up at one in the morning to see my dad? You sure he wasn't already at your place?" I laugh, raising an eyebrow. I don't understand why she's being so secretive about it. No one will care, but I know Macey still hates packs, so I wonder if it's because he's one of Valen's pack members. I let them in and walk into the kitchen to make coffee.

"Hey, Mace," Valen says as he comes into the kitchen to help. Only then do I realize that by getting my hidden coffee out, Valen would see it. He snatches it off the counter.

"No caffeine. You're pregnant," Valen growls, and I try to take it from him, but he holds it above his head.

"It's basically morning. I'm tired, and I have to be up soon. So there is no point in me going to bed now," I growl at him.

"You'll make them come out with six heads," he snarls. I shake my head at his logic. Caffeine is fine. Macey, taller than me, snatches it from him and sticks her tongue out at him, handing it to me.

"It won't hurt her. But why aren't you going to bed?" she asks. I point to all the files on the coffee table.

"Have a meeting with Dad's accountant tomorrow. I'm going over everything first to figure some shit out," I tell her, and she sighs.

"Make me one; I can help."

"Don't you have to get home to Taylor?"

"Nah, Mom has her," Tatum says. I look at him and smirk before eyeing Macey, and her face heats.

"Just friends, huh? But his mom now has Taylor?" I ask, knowing Macey doesn't trust anyone with Taylor other than her own mother, brother, Zoe, and me.

"Oh, for Goddess' sake, babe! Just tell her already," Tatum says with a shake of his head. I look at Macey expectantly.

"Nothing! There is nothing to tell at all. Crystal is just babysitting because I had dinner with her," Macey says, and Tatum growls.

"Macey is moving in with me. Mom has Taylor for a sleepover while I move all her crap. I filled a damn trailer with toys. Toys!" Tatum says, shaking his head. "I swear if there's a Troll or Smurf toy on this earth Taylor doesn't have, I will eat my left kidney! Fucking crazy the amount of toys that girl has. We could use a break so we can move the rest tomorrow."

"She doesn't have that many toys," Macey says, rolling her eyes at him.

"We fit an entire living room in and bedroom in that trailer, Macey. She has too many toys. My house only has three bedrooms. One room will be just for all of her toys!"

I snicker at their quarrel. I know Macey spoils the crap out of Taylor. I do the same with Valarian, although he never asks for anything. That kid is limited in what he likes, so his toy hoard isn't even a quarter of what the girls have. He wants order, and regularly cleans out his toys to make room for new ones. However, when he does want something, he always gets it; same with Zoe.

I understand it. For so long, we scraped coins to make ends meet, and often that meant no toys and buying only the staples. So after the hotel kicked off, once we had money, we made up for lost time; we spent it on the kids, giving them what we couldn't before. I get it.

"So you're moving in with Tatum?" I ask, pouring the hot water into the mug. Valen growls and reaches for my cup, but I glare at him.

"Oh, here," Macey says, distracting him by giving him the vial. Valen holds it up to the light and I can see the metallic silver liquid inside.

"By the way, how did your ultrasound go? I forgot to ask earlier," Macey says, looking at Valen. It's Macey, and I know she wouldn't blab to the world, and neither would Zoe; and Valen told his father already.

"You jinxed me," I tell her with a giggle.

"Jinxed you?" she says, her eyes sparkling with mischief. "Twins?"

"Triplets," Valen says behind her, and her lips part as she looks at my nonexistent stomach.

"Girl, you gonna be huge! Like beach ball huge!" she laughs.

"Wow, bet that was a shock," Tatum says before coming up behind Macey. His arms encircle her waist as he buries his face in her neck.

"Yep, you can say that again. Everly will get her tubes tied after."

"Oh really," I scoff.

"Yes, I am not being neutered," Valen says.

"Yeah, I'm with Valen. No man wants someone cutting into their junk," Tatum agrees.

"But someone should cut into mine?"

"They will already have to. How many triplets have you heard of being born vaginally?" Valen asks. I suppose he has a point, but why do I have to get it done?

"Nope; if I'm carrying them, you can sacrifice your balls. Your balls caused it," I tell him, sipping my coffee.

"No way."

"Why?" Macey demands, just as outraged.

"Because I don't want my balls cut off!"

"They don't cut off your balls," Macey says, shaking her head.

"I am not losing my manhood." Typical male response.

"Idiot. And I am not getting my tubes tied. You will either get the snip or wear condoms."

Valen pulls a face. "It doesn't feel the same."

I shrug, uncaring. He's getting it done if he doesn't want any more after these ones.

"Bloody damn litter."

"Bet Valarian was excited," Macey teases.

I sigh. "Let's just hope they're boys," I tell her, and she laughs.

"I hope you have three girls."

"Hey, don't say that! You jinxed me last time, so close your damn swallow hole."

"I can assure you, she doesn't swallow," Tatum says, and Macey elbows him.

"Prick, will you shut up! Go annoy Valen and compare dicks, or whatever it is you men do," she snaps at him.

Tatum chuckles but doesn't leave her, and Valen grabs a beer out of the fridge and passes one to him.

"Maybe you can convince Macey to let me put a baby in her," Tatum says, wiggling his eyebrows at me.

"Fat chance. I like the babies I can hand back to their mothers. Taylor is enough for me," she says, and Tatum pouts.

"Just one."

Macey shakes her head.

"Two," Tatum says.

"How did we go from one to none and now two?" she says,

shaking her head. "Just get. You want kids, go find someone else. When I agreed to move in with you, I told you that I didn't want any more children," she tells him.

I know why that is, which makes me wonder if Macey told him. She can't have children; she had a hysterectomy with Taylor because she bled out and nearly died.

"Macey?" I whisper once he wanders over to Valen in the living room.

"I know, I have to tell him, but..." She looks over her shoulder at him. "He'll leave when he finds out," she sighs.

"Is that why you didn't want anyone to know you moved in with him?"

She shrugs. "Just enjoying it while it lasts. Once he finds out, he'll run for the hills. They always do."

I smile sadly. In the last five years, Macey has had two serious relationships. She even got engaged once, but both left her once they found out she couldn't have children. She told the first one just before they moved in together, and he walked out as quickly as he came into her life. The other she told the day after they got engaged —same thing.

"I don't think Tatum is like that, but you need to tell him before he gets his hopes up."

She chews her lip nervously as I tell her. I pray I'm right. Finally, Macey nods and sighs before running her fingers through her hair and grabbing her mug. "Come on, let's sort these papers out," she says, wandering over to the coffee table.

Valen is on the phone with Doc, who's waiting for the vial. They speak for a few minutes before he stands and looks at Tatum.

"Want to come for a drive with me to the hospital to drop this off?" Valen asks, and Tatum gets up off the couch.

"You've been drinking," Macey scolds.

"I've had one mouthful," he says, passing his almost full bottle to Macey. She takes it and looks at it.

"Fine, go then. Can you bring me some Pringles back?"

Tatum laughs and leans down as she looks up at him, then pecks her lips.

"Yes. Be back soon," he tells her.

Valen kisses me before walking out with Tatum, leaving us alone. Macey and I go over the paperwork for the pack, and I sigh, finding it getting worse the more we dig.

"This one here," Macey says, holding out a slip of paper. I take it from her and glance at it. It's an old arcade that's in the red.

"Yeah, what about it?"

"Want to sell it?" she asks, and I glance at it.

"You want to buy an arcade?" she shrugs.

"Zoe and I were discussing pooling our savings and buying something to fix up and invest in," she says.

"But we have the hotel?" I ask her.

"No, *you* have the hotel, Zoe has her apartment out the back of it, and I have nothing. Not that I'm complaining—I know we've always split the hotel income—but I want something to leave to Taylor; same with Zoe. So we've been looking into it."

I chew my lip, feeling bad now she's said it like that. I was initially planning to cut the girls in before I got my father's pack. Maybe I still can, though.

"You can have it if you clear the electricity bill on it. Just pay what's outstanding on it. It just shut down, but hold off buying anything with Zoe for a bit. I want to speak to Valen first."

"You're giving it to me?" she asks, glancing down at the arcade. It's owned outright by the pack, but it's rundown and the electricity bill is nearly ten thousand. The machines needed work, so Dad just shut it down and it's been sitting vacant since.

"Ten thousand and it's mine?" she asks, checking the electricity. I don't know how much she has exactly, but I know she can cover it easily. One thing all of us are good at is saving. The only time we really splurge is with the kids.

"If you want it, you can keep all the crap in it, too," I tell her. I have no use for an arcade and have no idea what state it's in, but it would be one less bill for me to figure out how to pay.

"Valen won't have a problem with that?" she asks.

"No. I may have something else if you want it, but I need to speak to Valen first."

"Are you sure? The building is worth a lot more than that. It has a bowling alley in it and it's on the main drag," she asks.

"Macey, if you and Zoe want it—or even just you—cover the electricity bill and it's yours," I tell her. It will only help me out if she takes it off my hands. I have no time or funds to fix it up. If she wants to put her time and money into it and save me the headache, that's fine by me.

"Thank you," she whispers, looking at its portfolio. Now, I just need to speak to Valen about the hotel. Maybe I won't have to sell it to Valen if he lets the girls chip in as partners. They know what it holds in value, and it could help cover the rebuild cost. Besides, they helped fix the place; it seems only fair they also own it along with me.

But the rest of this crap, I'm in way over my head with.

CHAPTER
TWENTY-ONE

Valen

Tatum and I dropped off the vial last night and Doc split it into samples before sending it off to the labs. Hopefully we hear some good news soon.

I'm taking Everly to the accountant; after last night I don't want her on her own anywhere. She's been nervous all morning, and I can tell she wants to ask me something. Even when I got home last night, she was weird, making me wonder if she argued with her father or something.

Glancing at her as I drive, I decide to ask her because her weird mood is freaking me out.

"What's wrong?" I ask as we pull up at a set of traffic lights.

"I'm worried about the accountant," she admits.

"Why?"

"Because I wasn't expecting you to come with me."

My brows pinch together, wondering what she means. "It's that bad?"

"No. I did something when I inherited everything, and I was hoping it would remain hidden, but now you'll find out," she says.

"What did you do?"

"I got even. I was angry at you, so just don't be mad. It was a lot of money, and I had this stupid idea, but it may piss you off." She shakes her head.

"You won't tell me?"

She shakes her head again.

"And you told no one? How much money did my mother leave you?"

"Zoe and Macey know. We had a good laugh about it, but I wasn't expecting you or anyone to find out."

I'm about to ask her what it is when she speaks again.

"I also wanted to ask you about the hotel. Macey said something to me last night, but I worry it might upset you too," she says.

"Why would it upset me? It's your hotel," I tell her.

"Well, legally, yes. But it was your mother's."

"You don't want to continue the rebuild or sell it?" I ask, wondering what she's getting at. I would never interfere with the hotel. My mother left it to Everly; she wanted her to have it—therefore Everly is free to do as she pleases with it. Though I hope she won't sell it off.

"No. Not *sell* it-sell it, I'll still own it, but..."

My brows furrow and I accelerate as the light turns green.

"Just say it, Everly," I tell her, and she sighs.

"I was planning on doing it anyway before you came back into the picture. But now you are, I thought I should ask," she says.

"It's your hotel. That won't change regardless, so tell me what you want to do."

"I'm running out of funds for the rebuild. The insurance didn't cover everything, and the savings set aside for emergencies are running out. Everything else is locked down in term deposits and trust funds, which I don't want to touch unless necessary. I know you offered to help, but–"

"But you refuse to take money from me," I growl. We have a kid and live together, yet she never lets me pay for everything for her or

Valarian; she's always contributing, even though I don't want or need her money. But hearing all this makes me wonder how much she *does* have.

"I don't want a handout, and I don't want to owe anyone," she says.

"I'm your mate," I tell her.

"I've never needed help, and I don't want it, but Macey and Zoe have been pooling their money to invest..."

"You want to split the place three ways? Change ownership into three titles?" I ask, and she nods, glancing at me before she starts nervously defending herself.

"I know it was your mother's, and I'll still own it. But Macey was telling me last night, she and Zoe are looking into buying something investment-wise to leave to their kids, and I was already going–"

"I think it's a good idea," I cut her off, and she turns in her seat to look at me.

"You do?" She actually seemed shocked.

"It may have been my mother's, but you three girls built that place. I do have one condition if you go ahead, though," I tell her, and she clicks her tongue.

"I'm not losing ownership, just partnering up–" she starts to say.

"Give it to them," I interrupt her, and she gapes at me.

"I think you're missing the point, Valen. I kind of can't afford to unless I touch Valarian's money, which I don't want to do. I don't know how much they have, but anything will help with the rebuild, and the money will only be going back into the hotel until we can open, and then I would hand it back."

"I know that, but my condition is either I buy it off you, or you give it to them and let me cover the rest of the cost," I tell her.

"No. I don't want your money, and Macey and Zoe wouldn't agree to that anyway. They would think they owe you."

What is with these girls and settling debts—even gifts?

"Then split it four ways. We don't need their money, Everly, and they're like your sisters. You three built it. I can get contracts drawn up so they know I can't interfere with the hotel. I'll merely be an investor; I'll hold no control," I tell her. "Once Valarian comes of age, I can transfer any title I have to his name."

"Just let me ask the girls first," she says, and I nod.

I would rather she take the money, but she's too headstrong. Maybe I can speak to the girls and get them to convince her. The way I see it, they helped build it to the way it is, they should have equal shares. Besides, they may not believe or think it, but I owe them for being there when I wasn't. So if this helps them and clears my guilty conscience, it's a win-win.

When we pull up at her father's accountant's building, my father is already there, waiting. Everly climbs out of the car and waves to him. While I grab the box of files off the backseat, Everly opens the back door and snatches a pink folder from next to it.

"I can take it," I tell her, eyeing the folder. She shakes her head, making me confused. What has she done that she doesn't want me to see? She almost looks embarrassed.

When she closes the door, my father hugs her. I can tell he's tickled pink about her pregnancy. John also meets us and we all walk into the accountant's office, along with my own accountant that arrived at the same time. Not that I don't trust John's accountant, but I want to be sure.

Once through the doors, we move into a room with a huge oval mahogany desk and I take a seat next to Everly, who's clutching the pink folder.

The accountants start chatting amongst themselves and going over paperwork, but my father has a silly smirk on his face as he stares at Everly. Turning slightly in my chair, I see Everly's eyes go to his and her lips part.

"You know?" she asks, and he nods once.

"Honestly, it is something Valarie would have done," he chuckles, and the room falls silent as everyone looks between my father and Everly. The door swings open, and Everly shrinks down in her seat as her accountant walks in.

"Joseph," my father says in acknowledgment. My eyes narrow at my father, and Joseph smiles and sits next to Everly. He squeezes her hand. I have no idea who he is, but she said he would be here.

"Joseph, this is Valen," Everly says.

He nods. "Nice to meet you. Your mother was a wonderful woman," he says.

"You knew my mother?"

"Yes. I was her lawyer. Everly kept me on after she passed," he says, and I swallow, trying to figure out what's going on.

All the accountants start talking, trying to find the best approach to deal with Alpha John's pack. It's now technically mine and Everly's, but Everly doesn't want to take control form him completely, which shocks me. Instead, her father will continue running things.

"You still want me to run the pack?" John asks.

"Yes. You're Nightshade pack; you know them. I have my hotel and Luna stuff. I may be their Alpha now, but it's still your home."

"What's the catch?" John asks.

"For starters, no gambling. And you don't handle finances; Joseph will. And you answer to Valen now," she says, and my eyebrows raise. The room falls silent—you could hear a pin drop it's so quiet. Everyone looks at John, waiting to see what he says. Our packs have been rivals for decades and I don't expect him to agree.

"Okay, but can we please see Valarian? Claire has been asking every day, and Everly won't bring him to see us unless you say so," John tells me, and Everly looks at me.

I know she's trying to make up for not telling me about the pregnancy by letting me decide that, but I know she secretly wants her parents in her life. Despite having their differences, she still loves them. Everly is just no longer a child and has no problem cutting people out of her life now—she doesn't have time for bullshit.

"You want this?" I ask her, and she nods.

'Valen, they are her parents,' Dad mind-links. I sigh and nod.

"Fine. But, if Valarian doesn't want anything to do with you, you won't force a relationship with my son or our babies," I tell him, and he nods and lets out a breath, then gasps.

"Wait! Babies?! As in more than one?!" John blurts, and I pale. We were trying to keep that on the down-low for now.

"Yes, Dad. I'm having triplets," Everly admits. John gapes at her before gathering himself like he's doing the math in his head on the diaper changes.

"Can I tell your mother? She's going to love this. More grandbabies—she'll be so excited," John says, seemingly quite happy about this information. "Yes! Yes. I agree to your terms," John says.

I raise an eyebrow at his enthusiasm and my father mind-links me again a second later; he probably saw the look on my face—I was about to demand the reason for his sudden change of heart toward his daughter.

'Valen, leave it,' Dad says.

'What?! He wants to pick and choose whose kid's lives he'll be in? Where was the bastard when Valarian was born?' I tell my father, watching John.

'No. I get it.' Dad says.

'Get what?!' I snap through the link. Everly looks over at me, probably feeling my sudden anger.

'He is trying to make up for his mistakes. He can't go back in time to fix things with his daughter, but he can try to fix things with your kids— just like I am doing with you and Everly. That is what I get, Valen. That's all I get. You don't have to trust him straight off, but let him try. Everly is a smart girl; she isn't the kind of person that will let someone hurt her twice," Dad says.

I feel Everly squeeze my hand under the table. I nod to my father and he turns his attention back to the accountants.

Dad bought a few of the businesses himself—those he thought would be suitable investments—to get rid of some of the debts, and a bunch are going to be put up for sale. But Everly makes it clear they're not to be pack bought, and will only sell to individual pack members or any of the rogues. Yet that still leaves the debt to Nixon and also a backlog of debt from pack loans. Some I will sort out, but John really buried the pack deep and was stupid enough to take out loans from human banks out of state, which will be the biggest issue.

"You should have enough to cover those debts without touching the trust fund if you sell the land off," Joseph whispers to her. My father snickers to himself, and Everly glances at me nervously.

"What trust fund? And what land? She was a Rogue. She couldn't have purchased land within the city; only inherited it. She owns the hotel and its land," I ask, confused. Rogues couldn't own anything in this city once the packs took over and put the laws in place, so my mother wouldn't have been able to purchase anything.

"The trust fund is Valarian's. Half the money your mother gave her is in that trust—Everly set it aside for him. Everything else went into the hotel and on the land Everly bought. But you are correct; she couldn't buy more land *within* the city..." Joseph says, and now everyone in the room is looking at her. Joseph wears the same smirk my father has, and Everly looks like she wants to run from the room.

"I was mad at you," she turns from me to her father, "and you!" Okay, now I'm intrigued.

"Spill. What have you done?" I ask her, but she presses her lips in a line.

"It is actually pretty funny. Checkmate," Dad laughs.

"It *is* kind of funny. Well, Macey, Zoe, and I thought it was anyway," Everly laughs.

"Okay, can someone tell me what is going on?" I ask, and John also leans forward. Funnily enough, my father is the one that answers.

"Since she was rogue, she couldn't purchase within city limits," he says.

"I know that," I tell my father.

"Nothing says she couldn't purchase the land outside of the city," Dad laughs. John and I look at each other.

"I own all the forsaken lands," she chuckles, and Dad laughs.

"You what?" I ask.

"Remember initially, when we were all looking for a treaty agreement and were looking at purchasing outside the city limits to start mining by the mountains?" Dad asks.

"Yes. None of the packs could purchase the land. The werewolf council said it was a forsaken habitat," I answer. What a complete waste of time that was, months of planning only to not be able to purchase the land.

"I checked into that, and it was already bought," Dad says.

"Wait! You knew the land couldn't be bought and didn't tell me?"

"At the time, I knew it would lead you back to Everly and your mother, so no, I never said anything," Dad admits.

"So you own all the vacant land at the back of my pack up to the mountains?" I ask her, and she snickers.

"No," she answers.

"She owns *all* the land outside the city borders—behind *every* pack," Joseph laughs.

"Wait, how much land is that?" I ask.

"Enough to build an entire city on. Your mother was a very wealthy woman. Before her father started selling it off, they owned nearly all the state, and Everly bought a sizable chunk back," Dad laughs.

"But why would you *want* all the land?" John asks her.

"So no one could grow their packs," I grind out and Everly laughs.

"Not one of the packs could extend their border limits because I owned it. So technically, when you all did your border patrols, you were all trespassing on my land," she chuckles.

"You cunning little...." I growl and shake my head.

"As I said, I was angry. So I purchased all the vacant land outside the city, spanning all around the city limits. All that empty farmland is mine and Valerians. With the city becoming overcrowded, I knew the packs would want to buy into that land; I made sure they couldn't," she laughs.

"*You* are why we couldn't purchase the land for mining," I growl at her. That was a big deal three years ago.

"So that is why Nixon couldn't build that mall," her father laughs, and she nods.

"Every pack looked into why the werewolf council wouldn't sell the land. We were told it had an anonymous buyer and was for the preservation of the forsaken habitat. We thought they were being jerks, since they weren't part of the city," John laughs.

"Wait! You stopped my skate rink idea," her father growls, pointing an accusing finger at her.

"Yeah, and the subdivision I was planning out behind the reserve."

"I said I was angry," Everly says with a shrug.

"Angry? You plotted behind every pack and bought out their land!" I tell her.

"Smart," my father says.

"Or stupid. What if the packs found out?" I ask her.

"They would have killed me. But at the time, I didn't care. I just wanted to hit back at the packs. They owned the city—I just made sure they couldn't extend it," she says, folding her arms across her chest.

No wonder she refused to let me pay. After going over her books, in assets alone, she trumps everyone here. She owns more land than all of us—has more money and net worth than anyone in the room. It astounds me and, quite frankly, is a little intimidating. Every one of us was played by one little rogue who outsmarted us all. Dad was right; checkmate! She had us all by the balls and not one of us knew it!

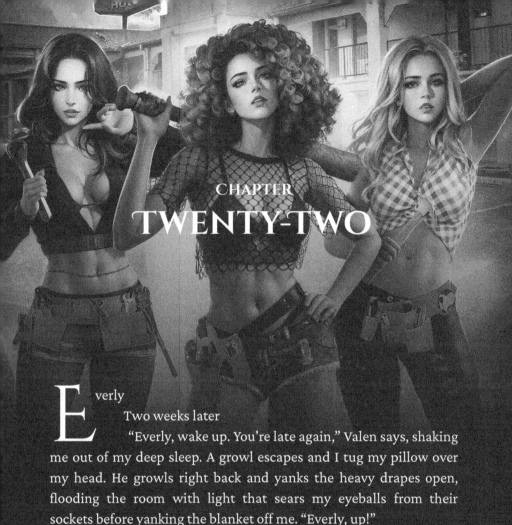

CHAPTER
TWENTY-TWO

Everly

Two weeks later

"Everly, wake up. You're late again," Valen says, shaking me out of my deep sleep. A growl escapes and I tug my pillow over my head. He growls right back and yanks the heavy drapes open, flooding the room with light that sears my eyeballs from their sockets before yanking the blanket off me. "Everly, up!"

My eyes feel like sandpaper, and I'm so damn exhausted. No matter how early I go to bed, I always wake up feeling like crap. And it doesn't help that he watches me like a damn hawk and won't allow me any coffee, making me question if it's an addiction. I usually have two before I even do the school run. Now, no caffeine has resulted in me becoming a zombie.

"No. Leave me," I whine.

"Valarian was ten minutes late yesterday and today. You were supposed to do the school runs the last two days, and on both days, he couldn't wake you and I had to come home! The tantrum I just dealt with was insane! Now up!"

"I'm tired," I tell him, reaching blindly for the blanket that he tugged away.

"Up!" he says, slapping my backside and earning another growl.

"Why?" I whine.

"Because it is time to get up!" he snaps.

"Time for *you* to get up. I don't have to be anywhere," I growl. It's my day off. I want to sleep!

Valen growls and storms out of the room, and I snuggle beneath my blanket. A moment later, I wrinkle my nose at the smell of coffee. Damn, do I miss the taste and the energy buzz, but the smell I can't stand sends me running for the bathroom. I growl as his scent wafts in from behind me and the pungent aroma of caffeine goodness grows more potent.

"I swear, if you made that just to make me get up to puke, I will provide the damn vasectomy myself," I gasp, my throat burning. In general, once I throw up, I'm okay drinking it—it's just the initial smell that always gets to me. It's such an odd reaction to the one thing I love.

After flushing the toilet, I glare at him in the mirror as I watch him take a sip while I quickly rinse my mouth. He's pushing my limits. I snarl as I stand up while he simply smiles tauntingly.

"Ahh. Be nice, and I may let you drink it," he says.

"Hand the coffee over, Hun, or I feel this mining deal may not go through,"

I tell him. "I hear the owner is a real bitch without her morning coffee."

His smile falls. Maybe him knowing now will play to my advantage. When I originally bought it, I knew if the packs knew, they would hunt me down and probably kill me. But with Valen and my Dad behind me, no one would dare touch me now.

"You can't blackmail me—and that was *my* land you bought," Valen tells me.

"No claims, therefore, no-man's-land and now my land," I tell him, putting my hands on my hips.

"I still can't believe you did that. You nearly started a war between me and the Slasher pack Alpha."

I reach for the mug, but he pulls his hand away.

"That land would make a nice protected reserve," I muse, folding my arms across my chest. He glares at me before cocking his eyebrow at me and sipping the coffee without taking his eyes from mine.

I purse my lips. "Maybe I'll sell the land directly behind your territory. Slater, I hear, is looking to extend. I am *sure* he would offer a good amount for the spot right at the back. Do you know where I'm talking about? Where your packhouse is," I told him.

"You wouldn't dare. Then you'd get yourself in trouble!" he says and smirks.

"It was kind of the intention when I bought it. You know, to cause trouble. And I hear it was quite the headache for the Blood Alpha," I tell him, and he clicks his tongue.

"Fine, one coffee. One, Everly. And once that jar is gone, no more. It should last you a while," he says.

"The whole jar?" I ask excitedly, and he nods.

"Deal?" he asks, holding out his hand.

"Two a day?" I retort.

"One!" he says.

"Three!"

"One!"

"Three, and you have a deal," I tell him, and he growls.

"Two, then," he says, and I smile, shake his hand, and he gives me the cup. I take it excitedly and have a sip before it comes spraying out my mouth as I spit it back in the cup. Valen laughs.

"What the fuck, Valen! That is *not* coffee," I snarl.

"We had a deal," he laughs. "And you shook on it."

"Yes, a deal for *coffee*! Not whatever the heck that is!"

"Decaf!" he says, and I growl. "Well, I know never to let you go over a contract. Always verify what you're making a deal on, Luna," Valen laughs. I pull a face at him and flip him the finger behind his back as he walks out. I get dressed, pouting about my coffee fix that is not coffee.

Valen tells me he's going to see his father, who's meeting him at the homeless shelter, so once dressed, I text Zoe and Macey to see what they're doing, since the hotel is under renovations. We have so much spare time on our hands now, but it was like the moment we stopped working, all of us crashed and burned. Working seven days a week for months on end, you don't realize how tired you've become until you have one day off.

The girls agree to meet up with me for lunch, and before I know it, I'm driving over to the hotel to check it's all still on schedule.

Everything seems to be happening so fast, but it's a drama free day, which I like. Valen took care of most of the debts while I'm waiting for my accountant and some agents to sell off some of the land. I'm parceling off everything except the land behind Shadow Moon and Nightshade packs, and out of spite, I'm also keeping the land behind Crescent pack. It might come in handy later on when dealing with Nixon.

Valen seemed rather shocked about everything to do with my old scheme, as one would be, but, though I knew I had it, I never actually thought of doing anything with it. I only bought it out of spite, but it may just be what saves us from going under. Valarian's money is locked in a trust until he comes of age. I could get it out, but the hoops to jump through would be a pain in the ass. Plus, the thought of touching it sickens me.

Somehow, the morning seemed to slip by slowly. The girls and I meet for lunch in the city center, but it feels odd being served and not doing the serving. We all look and feel out of place. People stare and mutter, mainly at Macey because she still smells like a rogue.

The waitress places our food down in front of us along with a tea. I glance up at her.

"I think you gave me the wrong one."

She smiles apologetically. "I'm sorry, Luna, but—"

"Valen!" I growl and she whisks away quickly. I know it must be

Valen's doing, seeing as it's one of his pack cafés we're sitting at. Macey glances around before sliding her cappuccino in front of me with a wink.

"I saw nothing. And I think he is being ridiculous over the caffeine thing," she declares.

"And cheese," I tell them, glaring at my salad.

"Cheese?" Zoe asks.

"Yep, listeria. Oh, and fish—mercury levels apparently. And since he can't be bothered looking up which fish specifically to steer clear of, he has banned all fish. Oh yeah, and mayonnaise, too. I'll kill him by the end of this pregnancy. Every night he has his nose in a baby book," I say with a roll of the eyes.

"Yeah, fuck that," Macey says, and Zoe glances around like she's waiting for him to pounce on me over the coffee Macey gave me.

"Have you told Tatum yet?" I ask Macey—she keeps avoiding it, although she has admitted that he's been hounding her since he found out about my pregnancy, especially now that they've officially moved in with each other.

"I will," she sighs, picking at her Caesar salad. Zoe smiles at her sadly. I feel terrible because I'm pregnant with not one baby but three, and Macey can't even have one.

"What about you? What's going on with you and Valen?" Macey asks, spearing a piece of lettuce and popping it in her mouth. I know she's trying to change the subject away from not telling Tatum, but I'll let it slide this once.

"Fine. He's super annoying and clingy now, but I was thinking..."

"Thinking about what?" Zoe asks, biting into her wrap and watching me curiously.

When I signed the titles the other day, it bothered me that I was using my last name because, technically, the packs on the paperwork are separate packs.

"Do you think it would be strange if I proposed to Valen? I know it's usually the other way around, but—" My cheeks flush. It's been nagging at me, and even though we've marked each other and I'm

Luna of his pack, the confusion of who is Alpha of which pack still makes me wary.

Macey stops mid-chew to stare at me, her eyes narrowed.

"Wait, you want to get married? I thought you were against the whole marriage thing? Aren't you always saying it's just a piece of paper and blah blah blah?" Macey says, and she has a point; for so long, I've believed that. However, now it bothers me.

"Well, I am, but even though Valen is handling Dad's pack for me, he still has to run everything past me because technically, I'm Alpha," I tell her.

Zoe snickers. "Valen is your Luna," she laughs. I nudge her, but technically, whoever holds the title is Alpha, so I'm his Luna, and he is mine.

"And Valarian has Valen's name now and—" I pause, chewing my lip, waiting for the reactions. Macey rolls her eyes.

"Oh my gosh, Everly, if you want to marry him, marry him, damn. You don't need to give us a list of reasons why you should; it isn't a business deal. Just admit you want to marry him!" Macey says.

"So, when are you going to do it?" Zoe asks, and I shrug.

"I don't know. I would have to get him a ring first." I shake my head. "Just saying that sounds so backward."

"Why?" Zoe asks and I shrug. It just does, and my face falls. What if he says no?

"What?" Macey says.

"What if he says no?" That would be mortifying, yet they both look at me like I'm absurd.

"He's your mate; there's nothing more permanent than the mark on your neck, but you think he won't marry you?" Zoe laughs, shaking her head.

"I told you, ladies, we can become nonsexual lesbians if necessary. I will gladly marry you if Valen says no. And the same goes for you," Macey states, nodding to Zoe, and I laugh.

"But I ain't eating pussy. I don't even like the look of my own vagina, let alone getting up-close and personal with either of yours.

Valen says no, I'll ditch Tatum and marry ya. I gotcha, baby girl, I'll let ya put a ring on it," she says, holding up her finger and blowing me a kiss. I laugh. It does sound rather silly that he would say no.

"I say do it. Besides, you've got options! Macey is your backup plan if he says no," Zoey says, snickering before going back to eating her food. We all go back to our peaceful lunch and make small talk before deciding to check out some jewelers. As we wander around downtown, we come across one hidden up some side alley.

"I didn't even know this place was here," Zoe says, glancing up at the sign. *'Dion's Jewelers'.* I shrug, opening the door and stepping inside to find some rough-looking biker man sitting behind a glass cabinet with his glasses perched on the end of his nose as he reads something. Tattoos cover his arms and neck, and from what I can see poking out from his button-down shirt, his chest, too.

He glances at us while we look around. "Luna. Ladies. What a surprise. What can I do for you today?" he asks.

"She's looking for an engagement ring for her mate," Zoe answers him, peering into the glass displays. He nods, sipping his can of coke and stepping into the main area where we are before turning to look at Macey.

"Oh, not me, her. She's going to propose to Alpha Valen," Macey tells him, and my cheeks heat. The man coughs on his drink before punching his chest.

My eyes widen and I move to pat him on the back while he gasps for air.

"Are you alright?" Macey asks, looking at him worriedly.

"Went down the wrong hole," Dion gasps, sucking in a breath. I step away from him as he clears his throat. The man is a giant—not what I expected a jeweler to look like.

"How about I show you a few things, then?" he says awkwardly.

CHAPTER
TWENTY-THREE

Everly

"When are you going to do it?" Zoe asks as we wait for Dion to polish it; he's taking forever. Macey drums her fingers on the counter impatiently. How long does it take to polish a ring? I think to myself.

"I don't know. Kalen said he can take Valarian tonight. Maybe I can try to make us dinner and do it then?"

I say *try* because the smell of food really makes me gag; he may be eating Chinese from a container. How romantic. Not. Although, I should probably buy Chinese after I drop Valarian off at Kalen's because the more I think about it, the less it seems possible I'll be cooking.

"Yeah, do it tonight before you chicken out. You do that and I will tell Tatum about my broken baby maker," Macey says, peering through the door out the back of the jewelers.

"Really? You're going to tell him?" I ask.

Macey sighs but nods her head. "Yes. If you have the guts to propose, I should woman up and tell him," she says.

"So much going on today! So exciting!" Zoe gushes.

"Exciting? I am about to possibly ruin my relationship while she gets married!" Macey says, nodding toward me. Zoe rolls her eyes at Macey.

"So dramatic, but I'm here for it!" Zoe chuckles and Macey raises an eyebrow at her.

"Tatum won't leave you over something you can't control," Zoe says, and I agree. He doesn't seem the sort to run just because he can't have kids. He loves Macey.

"We'll see, but I am about to jump this counter and polish the damn ring myself if Dion doesn't hurry up," Macey growls.

"Kalen is alright with taking him at short notice? I can take him for the night if you want me to?" Zoe offers.

"No, he seemed excited when I messaged him earlier," I tell her.

"What did you tell him?" Macey asks.

"Told him I wanted to have dinner with Valen," I shrug.

Dion finally returns, looking extremely sweaty and nervous.

"Are you ok?" I ask him.

"Yeah, just not feeling well, Luna," he replies.

"Ah well, then that is our cue to leave before you give us whatever scourge you got. I don't need my ass sealed to the toilet, and I'm pretty sure Everly is puking enough for all of us, so I'll pass on the disease thanks!" Macey growls, stepping back from him like he has the plague. Dion chuckles, handing me the small jewelry bag and my receipt.

"Yeah, I agree. Sharing is caring, except when it comes to STDs and the flu," Zoe says, stepping closer to Macey.

"Thanks," I tell him as we all leave. We have to race to the school because the time we spent at Dion's jewelers took way longer than we thought.

Macey purchased another cappuccino as we left the restaurant, sneaking it to me when I hopped in the car. After taking a sip, I sigh in relief before reaching into the tote bag in the back for the canister of decaf coffee. Macey takes the jar and empties the dreadful contents into a bin near my car before Zoe fills it with real coffee that she snuck from home.

"I did not give that to you, and if he finds out, I will totally deny it and blame Macey," Zoe states with a soft laugh.

"Wait, why blame me?" Macey asks.

"You're scarier than Marcus—Valen won't fight you. He would fight Marcus though," Zoe says. Macey clicks her tongue and folds her arms.

"Is that so?" she asks.

"Marcus thinks so. Besides, Valen is his Alpha. I can't get him into trouble," Zoe tells her.

"Oh, I see. Choosing cock over your sister. I will remember that," Macey tells her.

"No, I am not! I just know you would protect me better than Marcus," Zoe says, batting her lashes at Macey. "Yeah, yeah. Whatever you say," Macey says.

"He won't know; it's the same jar. Besides, I'm a werewolf, not a damn human, and doc said caffeine has no effects on werebabies. He's just being anal," I growl, screwing the jar lid back on. I place it back in my tote bag on the seat and follow the girls to the school.

We wait in front of the school for the bell to ring, leaning against the brick wall.

"Geez, my hands are sweaty. I am so nervous," Macey says.

"Yeah, I feel a little nauseous myself. Should I get down on one knee? I have no idea what I'm going to say," I admit.

"I say go all Alpha on his ass and toss it at him and say 'we're getting married'," Zoe says, aggressively.

"Gosh, calm down, Mighty Mouse, why so aggressive?" Macey says.

"Channel your inner Alpha Female," Zoe states, and I raise an eyebrow at her.

"She *is* an Alpha female, Zo," Macey laughs.

"I guess you're right, so yeah. Do that! Why not? They mark away without asking. Just shove it on his finger and say 'pick a date'!" Zoe states.

"Yeah, don't listen to her. But I probably wouldn't get down on one knee. I just can't picture that," Macey says with a shudder

"You two are not making me feel any better. What will you say to Tatum?" I ask Macey.

"No idea, but I'll wait until Taylor is in bed, then I'll bring it up."

"Want me to take her?" Zoe asks.

"Really? That would be good. Then I can try to tell him—no, I *will* tell him at dinner—he's always in a good mood at dinnertime."

"I would be too if my future mate is a chef," Zoe says.

"Fill-in chef! I am not a chef; but yeah, I am a pretty good cook, even if I do say so myself," Macey says proudly.

"Make him that crème brûlée he likes; that will soften the topic," Zoe tells her.

"I don't know!" she groans. "Yes, I'll make him something nice, but Tatum *really* wants more kids," Macey stresses.

"It will be fine, Macey," I tell her.

She bites her lip nervously. I have never seen her so anxious about telling someone something. Macey has no filter and at times her words can be brutal, so to see her so nervous tells me she really likes Tatum.

The bell rings and the kids come racing out. Macey makes arrangements with Zoe to drop Taylor off to her while I buckle Valarian in.

"Call me if you need me," I tell Macey, and she nods.

"Good luck," Zoe calls to both of us. "And I will see you at 4:30, Mace," Zoe calls out.

Macey waves to her and nods once, then climbs in her car with Taylor. Jumping in my own driver's seat, I head home and get a bag ready for Valarian with some clothes for the night.

However, when I get to Kalen's, he doesn't seem to want me to leave. He keeps wanting to show me stuff and talk. Man, he can talk the leg off an iron pot. I try to remind him I'm going to cook Valen dinner tonight, but still, he insists I stay, dragging me off to show me some old record collection.

"Definitely Chinese food," I declare by the time I'm about to leave. Valen mind-links me just as I sit in the driver's seat.

"Having fun with Dad?" Valen laughs.

"Did you set me up?" I ask him, and he laughs through the link.

"Yep, Dad said you were dropping Valarian over and you were going to make me dinner?"

"Well, it looks like Chinese now. It's almost dinnertime already," I say with a sigh.

"Good thing I organized dinner, then," Valen says.

"It better not be your sausage; I intended to cook actual food," I growl.

"It is real food, but you will definitely have a feed on my sausage later," Valen laughs.

"What are you making?"

"Hurry home and find out," Valen purrs through the mind link. I laugh, then cut the connection.

Driving home, I park underground before grabbing the small, velvet box and slipping it into my handbag. It feels like it weighs a ton; I can't believe I am actually going to do this. My palms become sweaty as I wait for the elevator to take me to the top floor. By the time I reach our floor, nerves twist my stomach as I push open the penthouse door while giving myself a mental pep talk; Zoe's idea is sounding better and better.

Yep, I am going to do what she said or I will chicken out. I wander down the entryway, flicking the hall light on and shaking my head, wondering why it's so damn dark. I know he's home—I can smell something cooking.

"Valen?" I call out, but get no answer. I mutter to myself. Dropping my bag on the hall stand,I rummage through it and grab the small box out, gulping. I turn the corner into the living room and kitchen area to find the whole place lit with candles on every surface and rose petals scattered across the floor.

Stunned, I stop and gape, wondering how long I was gone—this must have taken some time to set up! It's only 5:30 p.m. and when I left here at 4:30, the place was normal. Now there are hundreds of candles. I consider the fire risk briefly until Valen clears his throat, making me realize he's right in front of me on one knee.

"I intended to do this next week. But Dion called, so I had to improvise," Valen says.

"How?" I ask; This would have taken more than an hour!

"Marcus and Tatum, while I cooked and screamed like a banshee for them to light them and rip roses apart," Valen chuckles and I peer down at him.

"You don't get to take this from me," he whispers, turning his palm over, and opening a velvet box, revealing a ring.

"I watched, I saw, and I loved you more, so Everly Summers, will you marry me?" Valen asks. Thank the Goddess he asked, because I was about to chicken out.

I can't stop the stupid grin that splits my face or the tears that roll down my cheeks as I nod my head.

"Yes," I reply, and he lets out a breath before taking my hand and slipping the ring on my finger. I peer down at it. I recognize this ring! Only, now it's shiny and the stone is replaced.

"Is this..." I'm about to ask, recognizing it as one of Valarie's rings, and he stands up.

"My mother's, yes. Valarian helped choose the stone, but," he slips the ring off again, showing the inscription inside it is what he said.

'I watched, I saw & loved you more.'

"I will spend the rest of my life loving and watching you," he whispers before slipping the ring back onto my finger, lifting my chin, and kissing me.

E verly

I kiss him back before remembering his ring in my hand and pulling away. He growls, gripping the back of my neck; his lips cover mine again as he kisses me deeply, his tongue dominating my mouth.

Oh, well, I guess I'll give it to him later, I think as he pushes me against the entryway hall stand.

My ass hits it, making everything on the top rattle, and my handbag falls off with a thud. I put the ring box in the small bowl that rocks precariously on the edge just as he grips my thighs, making me shriek as he sits me on top of it.

He chuckles, his lips moving to my neck, but I grip the collar of his shirt and yank his head toward me. I bite down on his lip with a growl and kiss him while my fingers work down his buttons, trying to undo them as desire burns through me, searing my veins and making my skin warm. As soon as I finish undoing his shirt, he pushes himself between my legs and my fingers trail down the hard ridges of his chest and abs before I tug on his belt.

Valen's tongue tangles with mine in a fight for control that I am on the verge of losing when I push him back, trying to undo his damn belt. His fingers wrap around my wrists, prying my hands away before one arm goes around my waist and the other to my thigh. With strong fingers, he hoists me higher and nearly stumbles into the dining room table. I wrap my legs around his waist and he growls, about to press me against the dining room table when I pull away and shriek.

"Candles, candles!" I tell him—he nearly lifted and cooked my ass on a bunch of them.

"Whoops," he laughs, turning and heading for the bedroom.

"No! Put them out first," I gasp, and he groans, moving toward the table and blowing them out quickly before he turns toward the hall leading toward our room.

What about the rest? Now that I've pointed out the candles, I keep thinking of the fire hazard in the living room, dining room, and kitchen. Valen doesn't seem to care—his lips leave mine and nip at my chin and neck before his teeth graze over my mark, making me grip his hair to tug his head back. His hands squeeze my ass and I moan into his mouth.

But again, what about the candles!

"Valen, the candles," I murmur around his lips that assault mine as he pushes me against the bed and presses himself between my legs. He keeps his weight off me with his arm beside my head as he rocks his hips against me, making me moan softly.

"Valen, the candles. Candles!" I shriek, and he groans, pulling away and looking down at me.

"They're fine," he growls, nipping at my lips, but I shake my head. "Everly, I will smell them if they set anything on fire," he says, and I purse my lips.

"Geez, woman, you're a pain in my ass," he purrs, pushing off me and walking out, muttering about having to blow out the candles. I hear him groan and I laugh as he blows them out.

"Fuck! Whose stupid idea was this?!" I hear him curse, and I laugh again as I move toward the edge of the bed and remove my shirt and bra. When he walks back in, tugging his belt from his black slacks, I reach for him the moment he's close enough, gripping the waistband of his pants and yanking him toward me.

Desperately, I unzip his pants, shoving them down his legs, making him laugh as he steps out of them. Almost immediately, I grab his hard cock in my hand, wrapping my lips around the end and licking up the pre-cum, making him groan.

Valen's hips jerk and he sighs. His fingers run through my hair as I run my tongue up the side of his shaft, sucking on the tip. My hands move between his legs, cupping his balls before tugging down on them. He groans as I take him in my mouth, sucking every inch of his aroused flesh, bobbing my head as I find my rhythm while enjoying the noises he makes. I know it's hard for him not to thrust into my mouth as he wants—his legs are shaking when I grip his hips, pulling him onto the bed.

"I'm not sure how I feel about you manhandling me," he laughs as I shove him onto his back and move to kneel between his legs. My fingers wrap around his shaft again and I stroke his hard length, dipping my head and wrapping my lips around him once more.

"Fuck!" he curses, his hand fisting my hair as his cock glides over my tongue. Lifting my eyes, I watch his reactions as I suck harder, enjoying the way his hand trembles in my hair as he tries not to force me down on him but then fails. I gag and growl, and he lifts his hands in mock surrender, placing them behind his head.

"I won't touch, promise," he smirks. I return my lips to his cock, swirling my tongue around the tip.

"But I'm glad I was right," he chuckles, and I look at him, taking more of him in my mouth and his lips part.

'Right about what?' I mind-link, since my mouth is full of his girth.

"That you would be eating my sausage," he laughs. I graze my teeth up his cock and raise an eyebrow at him.

'Hmm, I should probably chew my food before swallowing,' I mind-link back.

160

"I'll be quiet, just keep sucking, I'll be quiet," he says, winking at me. I cover my teeth with my lips again and continue sucking his cock while running my tongue along his length.

"Just eat your sausage," he chuckles, and my lips leave his cock with an audible pop. I'm about to go off on him, but he suddenly sits up, pinning my arms and yanking me against his chest before quickly rolling so our positions are reversed.

He kisses me softly, cutting off the profanities I was going to spit at him. His hips roll against mine suggestively and I gasp before he sits back on his knees and grips my leggings, pulling them down my legs. After tossing them aside, he grips my knees and pushes them apart before running his hands up my thighs, exposing me to him. His gaze makes me hot. I never feel self-conscious with him, the complete opposite, so I don't feel the need to cover up or close my legs as his eyes trail over my naked body.

With his gaze between my legs, his hand moves down my thigh to the apex of my legs so he can brush his thumb against my clit. Fingers splayed across my lower abdomen, he rubs his thumb over it, making me moan softly as he teases me. I rock my hips against him, but his other hand pushes on my thigh harder, holding me still.

His hand moves again and he runs his fingertips over my lower lips before twisting his hand and slipping his index finger inside me, making me gasp as he slides it out, then watches as he corkscrews it back in.

He adds a second finger, and I throw my head back, lifting my hips for him. He fucks me with his fingers, sliding them in out, watching my reactions as he forces them in deeper with his thumb pressed against my clit. I squeeze my eyes shut as I feel my orgasm building, getting nearer as he builds up friction.

The bed dips as he leans over, sucking on my nipple before tugging it with his teeth. After a moment, he sits back, watching his fingers plunge inside me before placing his other hand on my chest and squeezing my breast. His fingers move harder and faster while he squeezes my breast with the other, rolling my nipple between his fingers, watching me squirm. The entire room smells of lust and my arousal.

Once again, Valen leans down and kisses me. There's an urgency and heat to the kiss as our tongues tangle. His tongue is hot as it dominates my mouth. Without pulling away, he pushes my leg higher, trapping it between his arm and body as he positions himself at my entrance before sinking his hard cock into my depths and our bodies come together, his hips flush against mine.

Valen holds himself up before dragging his cock out and sliding it around my opening, then farther up towards my clit, coating himself in my arousal. He groans before pushing the head of his cock inside again.

Slowly, inch by inch, he pushes in until he's sheathed deep inside me. His lips move to my neck and up my jaw before kissing me once again. Equally slowly, he starts to pump in and out, his cock brushing all the right places and driving me wild with the slow pace. I rock my hips against him, wanting him to move faster.

He squeezes my thigh harder before grabbing my hips and pounding into me. My muscles squeeze around him with each thrust. My skin heats and my breath turns to pants as I roll my hips against him, trying to take more of him. Enjoying the friction he's building up, I feel my walls grip his cock as my orgasm rolls over me, making me cry out. His lips cover mine, swallowing my moans as he slows, letting me ride the orgasm out while I tremble beneath him.

Abruptly, Valen pulls out.

And I sit up on my elbows and watch him climb off the bed, knowing he hasn't finished. He wanders into the closet before returning with a bottle of lube and something else tucked in the palm of his hand. Kneeling on the bed, he watches me as he drops the bottle on the blanket beside him, but not whatever is in his hand.

Instead, he grips my ankles and drags me toward him, making my head hit the mattress. Immediately, his hands grip my hips, and just as I wonder what he's doing, he flips me over and tugs my hips up in the air. I groan when his cock pushes inside me with one thrust before he drags it out slowly.

After pulling my cheeks apart so he can watch himself slip in and out of me, I feel his hand move over my ass, his thumb pressing against my back entrance. I squirm when he probes it with his thumb and I pull away slightly, only for him to pull me back, slamming me back on his cock. I groan, relenting, and he pumps himself into me a few times before slowing again, his thumb still pressing against the one place he hasn't gone.

"Valen, you are not sticking anything in my ass," I growl at him, and he chuckles.

"Really?" he purrs, pressing his thumb down harder and making me squirm.

"I won't hurt you, and I'll stop if you don't like it," he says and I roll my eyes as he thrusts into me slower. Won't hurt? Yeah, right! Has he seen the size of his cock? It isn't going anywhere near my ass.

"Nope! Not happening!" I tell him.

"It's happening. I'm locking in the hubs and going up the mud track," he says.

"Don't be crude! And no, we are not!" I screech.

"We're going to brown town!" he states with a laugh.

"Fuck, you suck at the dirty talk," I snarl, but also can't help but laugh at his vulgar words.

"I'm fucking that ass," he purrs before slapping my butt and making me hiss. He rubs away the sting, and I jump when I feel the cold sensation of the lube as it trickles between my cheeks. Valen thrusts into my pussy, his thumb returning to my ass, and I growl, but I figure I'll entertain his silly little obsession with my butt.

Valen groans as his hips slap against my ass, and I push back against him, meeting his thrusts. The hand on my hip moves, his rhythm remaining steady, and I moan as his cock hits my cervix. This position is deeper and so much more thrilling when he grips my shoulder, shoving it down to the mattress.

Pushing the top half of me entirely on the bed, he picks up his pace, pounding into me and making me scream as my walls grip him, fluttering around him. Then I feel his thumb slide into me. It isn't painful, just an odd sensation, an odd but good sensation, making me push back against him.

"See?" he murmurs, drawing his cock out slower and slamming back into my pussy. His hand fisted on my hip suddenly starts vibrating, and he reaches around, pressing something small against my clit. The sensation makes me gasp as it sends shock waves through me.

It takes everything not to sink into the bed at the feeling. Valen leaves his fingers with the vibrator there, and I move my hips against them. Suddenly, he moves them away, making me growl at the loss of the new sensation. He leans forward, gripping my wrist and tugging it behind me, then drops the bullet-shaped thing in my hand.

"Touch yourself with it. Just don't press the button until I tell you to," he says, drawing my hand back toward my hip. He doesn't have to tell me twice. I'm not a prude and I've spent a reasonable amount of time searching adult toy stores with the girls.

My hand moves between my legs and I moan as I run the device between my swollen pussy lips while Valen rams into me, his thumb still inside my back entrance. When he pulls out of me, I miss the fullness of him stretching me

His hand locks around my wrist, placing my hand back between my thighs and I moan at the vibration of the small toy and his hot breath sweeping over my pussy.

His hands on the back of my thighs push my legs open more before he forces his tongue inside me, licking up my arousal as it spills from me, teasing more out of me. As he moves between my folds and back to my opening, hungrily tasting every part of me, his hand on my ass moves between my cheeks; I feel him ease his lubricated finger inside my back entrance.

I moan at the sensation when he slides his finger out, adding another, stretching me while I play with the toy in my hand. As his fingers push in deeper and harder, my walls clench. There's something thrilling and very sordid about it, but erotic. Valen sucks on my swollen lower lips, dipping his tongue inside before standing and lining himself up with my back passage. The tip presses against my back entrance and I tense.

"Press the button on the top of it," Valen purrs, and I do. The vibration grows stronger and I moan, my body relaxing as he rubs my ass. But when he begins pressing further inside me, I choke, my hand clutching the sheets as I hold my breath. He stills, pulling my hand back between my legs.

"Don't move your hand," he says, kissing my shoulder and pressing the button on top again. The thing feels like it will explode in my hand as the vibration intensifies, and I quickly place my hand back between my legs. Valen remains still until I feel him coat himself in more lube and work his cock into me slowly.

"That's it," he whispers, leaning down and kissing the side of my ribs, his stubble making me shiver as it brushes my sensitive skin. I moan as the small device vibrates against my clit, and Valen increases his speed before I finally feel his hips meet mine and he groans. He stills for a second when I rock back against him, letting me move against him for a few minutes until I'm a moaning mess and slow my pace. Then he grips my hips, slamming into me; I'm so close and am pushing back against him, taking what he gives me.

Valen's grip tightens on me and he pumps into me harder. I cry out as my skin tingles when he grips my shoulder and yanks me back against him, his chest pressed against my back as he thrusts into me. The hand flat on my stomach moves to my hand between my legs, and he takes the device I'm holding in place. As he slides it between my soaking wet folds and rubs it against my clit, his lips travel down my neck and he sucks on my mark, his other hand squeezing my breast.

"Cum for me," he purrs, licking my mark before grazing his teeth over it. I come apart with a scream, his arms the only thing holding me upright as my legs tremble, wanting to give out from under me.

Suddenly, he sinks his teeth into my neck, remarking me and extending my orgasm. Valen groans against my neck and I feel him still inside me. He clutches me tighter and pulls his teeth from my neck before trailing his tongue up my neck and sucking on my ear.

"I love you," he whispers.

"I love you too," I tell him, exhausted when he pulls out of me.

"I'll run you a bath," he chuckles behind me before kissing my shoulder. I nod breathlessly and collapse on the bed before he speaks again.

"And I should probably reheat dinner, even though you just had a meal of sausage," he laughs, and I reach for my pillow before lobbing it at him. He ducks and laughs while walking into the bathroom.

It's the incessant noise of my phone ringing that wakes me the next morning and has me untangling myself from Valen; it's still dark outside, so it must be early. He growls, trying to tug me back to him while I lean over him, reaching for my phone. Valen's hands trail up my sides before he purrs and his lips lock around my nipple as I snatch my phone from the bedside table.

Peering at the screen, I see Macey's picture pop up on the screen. I sit up, but Valen tries tugging me back to him and successfully pulls me on top of him. I push off his chest, straddling his waist as I answer it. Valen's hand rubs my thighs as he mutters under his breath.

"Macey?" I ask, answering the call and holding it to my ear. "Macey?" I say again when I hear a choked whimper.

"I didn't know who else to call. I can't go home. My brother moved back in with my mother when I moved out. Zoe's place is too small, and you know we clash when living with each other," she says before sobbing.

"Mace, what's wrong?"

"Can Taylor and I come stay the night? I know it's terrible timing, but I told him, Evie. I told him and he stormed out. I don't want to be here when he gets back," Macey cries.

"Of course, come over. I'll set up the spare room," I tell her, and she quickly says goodbye. Valen stares up at me, his amber eyes glowing in the dark.

"What's going on?" he says.

"I think Tatum just broke up with Macey," I murmur, and he sits up.

"What?" Valen says, shocked, but I don't want to say anything more because I'm not sure what's going on myself. I climb off him and retrieve some clothes.

"I need to set up the spare room," I tell him and he gets up, grabbing some shorts.

"I'll help," he says and I nod as he pulls his pants on.

CHAPTER
TWENTY-FIVE

Macey

I feel like an idiot calling Everly, but I can't sit at Zoe's and try to hold myself together in front of her; she's too emotional, and seeing her cry will make me fucking cry; the woman is a damn onion. Zoe wears her emotions for the world to see and tends to have an effect on people. I love that about her, but I just want silence right now.

Everly is the opposite. I swear she's made of steel. It takes a lot to break that woman. Everly is our rock—the glue that holds us all together; she never judges, or questions, and is just there when you need her, no matter what.

So that's why I chose her. I would have gone home to Mom, but even she isn't an option. She would blame me, and rightfully so. Mom loves Tatum, and so does Taylor. Now Tatum is just another person ripped away from her right as she got used to them—another way I've failed her.

Taylor is at Zoe's. I had been going to go over and pick her up, but I decide against it as I climb into my car; I would feel terrible knowing I ruined her night. I know Tatum will come home eventually, and I can't face him.

I should have known better. Werewolf men are all the same. They want heirs—something I can't provide. Is it too much to ask for somebody to want me and not what I can give them?

My phone vibrates as I'm about to pull out of the driveway. I stop, my shaking hands racing to dig it out of my handbag. Tatum's name pops up. It's only a text message, and I open it.

'Can you leave the back door open? I've lost my keys.'

'I'm still home. I haven't left.'

'I'll grab some clothes tomorrow while you're at work.'

'Want me to bring some clothes over to you? Where are you?'

'No, and I'm at Creed's place. I don't want to see you right now. Just leave me be. You and Taylor can stay there until we figure something else out.'

'I'll leave my keys in the mailbox for you. I'm not staying in your house while you sleep on your friend's couch,' I reply before tossing my phone back into my bag.

It rings and I ignore it. I don't want a handout, and I am not living in a house that belongs to someone who wants nothing to do with me.

Turning my car off, I twist the house key off the ring before heading inside. I grab one of the moving boxes from the shed and load up some of Taylor's toys I know she won't leave without, then grab her school clothes, my work uniforms, and our documentation. The rest, I'll organize to pick up later. If not, I'll just dip into my savings to replace it. I know how this works; it isn't the first time I let myself get my hopes up.

Once I have my bag packed and a box full of Taylor's stuff under my arm, I flick off the lights and lock the door.

After dropping the key in the mailbox, I pop the trunk and drop everything in before climbing back into my car. My mind is a mess as I drive to Everly's, angry with myself. If I had told him from the start,

I could have avoided all this. We would still be perfect strangers that fucked once on a desk—how it should have remained.

Yet, as I pull up at Valen's and Everly's place, I can't bring myself to get out of the car. My mind is plagued with what I'll tell Taylor. She really likes Tatum, and he was good to her—the first real father figure she had. Her own father was a dropkick.

Taylor's father, Preston, beat me when I told him I was pregnant; he hoped I would lose her. My mother warned me not to get involved with him. She was right. He was no good. Mom patched me up, and we waited to see if I would miscarry. But my girl was a fighter.

My next encounter with Preston was at the shopping center when I was with Valarie. I lost sight of Valarie as I wandered down an aisle with Taylor in her stroller. The panic I felt when he walked into the same aisle with his pregnant sister nearly made my heart stop. He'd looked into the stroller and snarled when he realized he didn't successfully abort his child.

I had left the aisle, searching for Valarie, but when she couldn't be found, I went to the parking garage. I had just gotten Taylor into her car seat when he attacked me from behind. He slammed my head into the door frame, splitting my forehead open. Luckily, the keys were still clutched in my hand, and all I kept thinking was that I needed to lock the car. I needed to protect her from him. So I hit the lock button on the key fob and got to my feet as he tried to rip the car door open.

Me or her.

And I chose her.

I will always choose her, even if it costs my life. That's what being a parent is. You give your last breath so they can take another. I was a rogue, and Preston was Slasher pack's Gamma's son. His reputation was on the line, and Taylor could destroy it.

So I did the only thing I could at the time: I hit the speed dial on my phone, which was Valarie's number. I dropped the phone when he smashed the windows, trying to get to Taylor. Until Valarie could get to her, I needed to keep him distracted. And that's what I did.

Taylor was screaming her head off in the car, but I just kept thinking I couldn't let him touch her, so I kept getting back up, no matter how much he hurt me.

As he reached through the driver's seat window to unlock her door, I picked up a broken piece of glass and plunged it into his neck. Valarie came out moments later, frantic, with a stolen bat she grabbed from one of the display stands. Yet, it was too late, Preston was bleeding out at my feet, and I was looking at prison time.

Or so I thought.

Valarie had grabbed my arms and shook me because all I could do was stare at his dying body, choking and gasping for air as he stared at me helplessly.

"You didn't kill him," Valarie said to me. "I did!" I remember staring at her when she raised the bat and hit him in the head.

One.

Two.

Three.

"Now get in the car while I clean this up," she'd said.

However, I couldn't function and she ended up putting me in the car, as she made a call. At the time, I was in too much shock for it to register who she called, yet he came.

"Get home. I'll take care of it," Kalen told her, and that was the end. Kalen took the rap and said it was self-defense. The camera footage miraculously disappeared, and it was splashed over every newspaper about how Slasher pack's Gamma's son attacked the Blood Alpha's father.

Only four people really knew what happened. Valarie, Kalen, me, and Everly, because when Valarie brought me back to the hotel, she called her to help clean me up and we never spoke of it again. After that, she put me in self-defense classes and watched Taylor for me while I went to every class, determined not to feel helpless again. I still have the bat—the bat Valarie gave me.

Yet right now, as I sit in the parking lot of Valen's hotel—one so similar to that mall lot—I'm reminded of that helplessness, only this time, it's my fault.

My phone vibrates in my bag and Everly's ringtone plays. Reaching over, I grab it out and answer it.

"Where are you? Did you pick up Taylor?"

"No, I didn't want to wake her or Zoe," I answer.

"Okay, where are you?" she asks.

"In the parking lot," I admit. I just can't make myself move and destroy their good night while mine falls apart. *So stupid! So, so stupid!* I think when the phone hangs up. I can't remember if I said goodbye or not, or even if I hung up on her. I feel numb, stuck in memories of so many men's worst and the one good one I just drove away.

The driver's side door opens.

"Move over," she says, and I undo my seatbelt and slide into the passenger seat. She climbs in, starting my car and leaving the underground lot, winding her way up the ramps to the rooftop lot. She parks up top and swings her door open.

"Get out," she says. Walking to the front of the car, she climbs on the hood and rests her head against the window.

"Everly, it's freezing! And you're pregnant," I tell her, but she pats the hood and I roll my eyes.

"Better warm me up then," she says, and I laugh, climbing up beside her. She wiggles closer, the metal creaking under our weight. Everly rests her head on my shoulder and I wrap my arms around her. When she asks what happened, I explain as we watch the sunrise together.

"Where's Valen?"

"Dunno. Probably still inside," she says.

"I'm sorry for ruining your night."

"Nah, you're good. Valen knows us girls are a package deal."

I laugh because she's right. No one will ever come between us three—we have a sisterhood stronger than any bond.

"He'll come around, Mace," Everly says.

"And if he doesn't?" I ask.

"Plan B! And Valen gets an extra wife," she laughs. I sigh. Everly can always switch a situation around.

"I'm dreading telling Taylor," I admit, and she nods.

"It'll be alright. She has you, Zoe, and me."

I nod, again knowing she's right. We have each other. Always each other.

We lie there in silence, watching the colors of the sky change until someone clears their throat. I turn my head to find Valen holding a blanket and a tray of coffee.

"Room for one more? Or will we break this rice bubble car?"

I chuckle. We've definitely dented the hood already, yet we shimmy over and he climbs on next to Everly, passing us our coffees. Everly raises an eyebrow at him cautiously.

"Don't think I don't know that it was Macey or Zoe swapping out the coffee in that jar," he says, kissing her cheek.

"It was me," I lie for Zoe, and Everly laughs. Valen clicks his tongue.

"You three are terrible, but I'll let it slide," he laughs while tossing the blanket over the three of us.

"Did Evie tell ya, you may have an extra wife?" I chuckle, messing around with him.

"Really? Sounds like a bad reality show," he says, kissing her head and rubbing her arms to warm her freezing skin.

"I'll have the hotel set up one of the apartments for you until you and Tatum sort everything out. If you don't, you know you're always welcome here. Until your hotel opens up, then I'm sure you'll want to move back there," Valen says.

"Yeah, true. I could stay with Zoe if it puts you out too much," I tell them.

"Or you could stay in one of the apartments there, since you own it," Everly says and Valen moves, digging in his pocket. He hands me some rolled-up documents.

"What's this?" I ask.

"We wanted to give it to you and Zoe when we opened back up," Everly tells me.

I unroll it and look at it to find the title to the hotel. It's been changed. Mine and Zoe's names are now on it, as equal partners with Everly.

"I can't accept this! Zoe won't accept this!" I tell them, shaking my head.

"You can and will. Everly wanted to cut you girls in anyway, but I don't want her taking your money. Save it for the arcade. But you all built that place—made it what it was—and you looked after my mate and son when I didn't, so I will foot the bill as my way of saying thank you. And you will accept and sign it," Valen says.

"And you're okay with this? It was your mother's," I ask him.

"Of course! Besides, you just said I have an extra wife, so I'm not losing anything," he laughs.

"Guys, I can't–"

"If not for you, accept it for Taylor," Everly says, cutting me off. I nod. Zoe is going to lose her shit.

"Thank you," I tell them, not knowing what else to say.

They both nod, and Everly lifts my arm and places her head back on my shoulder.

CHAPTER
TWENTY-SIX

Everly

We helped Macey settle in. Valen is pissed off with Tatum and even called him. When they finished speaking, Valen assured me that it wasn't that she can't have kids, it's because she didn't tell him from the start and to give him space. I tried to tell Macey this, but she wouldn't listen, saying she's done and that it's for the best.

This morning, Macey heads out to get Taylor from Zoe's—they'll be staying on the floor below us. I know everything will work out in the end, but Macey is stubborn, and once you hurt her, she walks. She always says she doesn't have time for drama, and she's right. None of us do, yet somehow we always find ourselves stuck in it.

"I'll go grab Valarian from your father," I tell Valen as I scoop up my handbag from the floor by the hall stand. I rummage for my keys before spotting the ring box—with everything going on, I had forgotten to give it to him. I grab it just as his arms wrap around me from behind and he kisses my shoulder.

As I start to open it, I suddenly realize why Dion was so insistent on this particular ring—because it actually matches and has similar patterns etched around the outside. Valen's hand clamps over my mine, closing the box before I can open it properly.

"Put it in the safe. Save it for when I marry you," he purrs.

"You don't want to see?" I ask him, and he confirms my thoughts.

"Nope. I assume Dion helped you pick it out, so I know it will match," he chuckles. I sigh, closing it, though I want to show him the engraving it has inside. I guess it can wait.

"Go get Valarian," he says, turning me around to face him.

"Then you can put this away then," I tell him, handing him the box, and he pockets it with a nod.

Three weeks later

Nixon is really pushing my father to go to the media to back him up, but after his claims, the city is divided. Valen's pack scientists have been trying to replicate the vaccine and have so far been unsuccessful.

Despite Nixon saying he was doing it to help the city and the forsaken, he's refused access to this so-called facility, even when Valen mentioned it at the Alpha conference meeting. Nixon claimed he didn't want the pack becoming involved and the vaccine slipping into the wrong hands.

In other words, he doesn't want the vaccine replicated, knowing he would have nothing to use over my father. And with the debt hanging over my head, he uses it to get his way in the council. Nixon is also still fighting me about the Rogue laws.

We're still fighting for the change, but until the debt is paid, Nixon still has partial ownership; therefore, my vote doesn't count. And if I marry Valen before it's paid, then we're one pack with Nixon still holding partial ownership and Valen's vote won't matter either, leaving the Slasher pack in a precarious position if he goes against Nixon, seeing as they have business dealings together.

Nixon has the people of the city wrapped around his demented finger, and now he claims that my father handed the pack over after threats from Valen. He also claims that removing the restrictions against the Rogues would endanger the city, since they're only one step away from becoming forsaken. His logic makes no sense, yet the media eats it up. Ballots go out and the city is given a voice, yet most are too scared to go against Nixon, and our packs aren't even allowed to vote on it.

The Slasher pack Alpha has confided in Valen that he's also worried about Nixon, and how the constant media attention is dividing the city. Like us, he believes Nixon is doing something that will sway the city to get rid of the rogues completely. We just have to figure out what.

And just to add extra protection for himself, Nixon has reporters with him constantly, so no one can get to him and his every move is watched, suggesting he's being completely open and honest.

The rogues are being painted as villains. Nixon claims that the missing rogues are *choosing* to turn forsaken, and that it will only be a matter of time before the rest follow to take down the city. He looks like the city's hero and has caused hysteria within the packs, including ours, who have been questioning everything now, so we're at a standstill.

I'm headed to the hotel after dropping Valarian off at school when sirens go off behind me and I'm pulled over by one of Nixon's officers. This is becoming a daily thing, and before the officer even reaches my car, I wind down my window and hold up my license and registration.

"What is it today, Cleo? Bald tires? No, you claimed that yesterday. Tail light? Nah, it can't be that—that was the day before. You're gonna have to be crafty this time," I tell him.

"And why is that?" he asks, peering in the window. He looks in the back at the empty car seat.

"I'm sure you're running out of bullshit to fine me for," I tell him.

This is a waste of time, and it's starting to irritate me. I rest my head back on the headrest, rubbing my hands over my huge swollen belly. I'm only nine weeks pregnant, but my stomach is already looking quite round. Macey was right; I'll be the size of a house!

He examines my truck, writing more tickets and passing them to me—I stuff them in the glove box with the rest. Officer Cleo follows me all the way to the hotel, so I drive extra slowly, earning honks from drivers behind him.

Pulling into the lot, I see the place is nearly halfway to being finished, and I'm more and more excited to open it again. Yet, the bigger I get, the harder it's getting to move around, and I'm constantly hungry and horny. Damn, am I horny! Poor Valen has his stamina tested frequently, that's for sure.

I speak with the project manager while waiting for my mother. She called yesterday, asking if she could go baby shopping with me. It's such a bizarre situation for me to see her so supportive of this pregnancy, and I have to keep reminding myself things are different this time around. Yet, the same fears remain. Even with Valen's reassurance, I'm constantly waiting to be thrown out and cast away like last time.

I know a lot of it has to do with pregnancy hormones, but my anxiety levels are constantly through the roof. Sleep has become troublesome, not only for me but for Valen. As much as he tries to understand, I know he doesn't get the lock thing. Anxiety is making me paranoid, hormones are making me overly sensitive to everything, and the stress is getting to me.

I'm still talking to the manager when I see my mother's car pull into the parking space beside mine; we're going in her car. I smile and wave when I see her. Quickly, I finish my conversation with the project manager before wandering over to her.

I climb into her car, placing my handbag between my feet before pulling my belt on, while she reaches into the back to retrieve something from the back seat.

She drops a bag on my lap. "I made them something," she tells me, and I open it to find matching yellow crocheted booties and beanies. I smile and thank her, looking at how small they are. They look so tiny in my hands—it's hard to remember Valarian being that little.

"We can go to Baby Bunting first if you like?" she suggests, and I nod.

"Yes. Valen said he would meet us for lunch, though," I tell her. Every weekend now, my parents come over on Saturdays for dinner to spend time with Valarian. At first, Valarian was wary of them, although recently he asked me if he could go to training with my father. It's a little odd and took some convincing for Valen. Valen has been taking Valarian along with him, but only to watch. He thinks Valarian is too little to train, but I was training from the moment I could walk, and I know my father won't allow him to get hurt.

We've merged pack training, so both packs now train in the arena every Sunday together. Any rogues that wish to attend also train with them. I attended the last one, and it was odd seeing my father training my son, so similar to the way he taught me.

For the most part, life is good. Even Ava is even training, and I can tell it means a lot to Mom that everyone is getting along again. However, pulling up at the baby shop, my mother is just staring out the window as she stops the car.

"I should have done this with you last time," she murmurs, gazing blankly up at the store decorations. I swallow but say nothing.

"We failed you," she adds, and I nod, not knowing what to say. They did, big time. I accepted it and moved on from that, or so I thought. My anxiety says otherwise. For the most part, though, I've come to terms with everything and don't see the point of dwelling on things I can't change—it's in the past.

"You're here now. Let's focus on that," I tell her, but she shakes her head.

"Nixon would have made you keep Valarian just to use him

against you and your father. We knew that was no place for a child to be raised, amid war. We should have told you, protected you properly, and gone to Valen. We messed up. We thought we were protecting you, but instead, we destroyed you."

"You think you destroyed me? You didn't," I tell her.

"How can you say that? When your father came home and told me you were going to let us be a part of your life, I almost didn't believe him. After everything we did, we didn't deserve a second chance," she says, staring off vacantly.

"No, you didn't deserve a second chance."

She looks at me and nods, her lip quivering.

"But hating you won't hurt you, only me, and I haven't got time to hate, Mom. I haven't got time to harbor the sort of energy that would take. You say you destroyed me—yes, you did. And I'm not sure if I will ever fully forgive that, but at least some good came of it," I tell her.

"Valarie?" she asks, and I nod. Valarie was a massive part of it. Mom knows Valarie took her place in my life, and I'm not afraid of hurting her feelings by her knowing that. Valarie's influence in my life is greater than any passage of time I endured, but that isn't all.

"Yes, but also, through everything, I found myself. I grew up too soon, but finding my place came with finding my purpose—a purpose that was more than just being the Alpha's daughter. I found my identity, who I am, the person I was born to be. And that isn't in the shadows of another. With that comes acceptance, Mother. I am not some little girl anymore. I am not frightened of the world, because I saw it at its worst, lived and endured it, and it didn't break me. It stoked an inferno inside me to prove everyone wrong. It showed me I was more than an Alpha."

Mom chews her lip. They think I hate them. I don't. I hate the things they have done, hate the feelings they invoked, but not them.

"I don't know if I would feel the same if our roles were reversed," she admits.

"I used to put you and Dad on a pedestal, higher than life. I tried to live up to that ideal. Then it fell apart. I went from future Alpha to rogue. But there was one title that meant more than that—the title of being Valarian's mother," I tell her and she smiles sadly and nods.

"And I was yours. I always regretted not fighting harder for you. I should have, as your mother. We wouldn't be here like this now, wouldn't feel awkward."

So I wasn't the only one that felt odd. My family had become strangers to me over the years, but still, I love them.

"I gained so much more because of it, though. So for that, I don't hate you, because I found I was more than that title. More than your daughter. I just needed to climb my own pedestal and hold myself higher. Doing that made me see everything clearer than when I was just the Alpha's daughter. Now, I am a mother, a friend, a Luna, an Alpha, and I am *me*. So you don't get to claim that you destroyed me, because I wasn't born yet. I wasn't built. And only I can destroy what I built. Only I can destroy my value. Because it isn't up to you to give it to me. Yes, at first, you destroyed me in a way, but I rebuilt myself —in *my* image and not that of others," I tell her, reaching over to grip her hand. "And you're here now." I squeeze it.

"So don't reminisce about a past that no longer exists. That was just the foundation of a better future," I tell her, and my hands go to my belly—my future, Valen's, and my kids'.

"So come on, let's shop before I need to pee again. I know that is definitely in my near future," I laugh, and so does she. We climb out of the car and head inside.

We pick out a few things but, not knowing the genders, we opt for neutral colors. However, on the way to the next store, I notice my mother is becoming fatigued and irritable, not at me but at herself as she tries to keep up. I'm looking at crib sheets and mobiles when she makes a strange noise down the aisle. I glance over my shoulder and see her clutch a rack, her body trembling, making the stand shake under her grip.

"Mom?" I wander back over to her and touch her arm. Her head whips up, canines protruding, and bloodshot eyes stare back at me as she snarls. I stagger back a step and she takes one toward me before shaking her head.

"What did you ask?" she says, looking at me expectantly, like I asked something of her. "Oh, this is cute," she gushes, holding up a onesie against my belly. Did I imagine it?

"I'm kind of tired. I was thinking of heading home soon," I lie. Seeing that frightened me.

"What? We just got here. Didn't you want to go to Baby Bunting?" she asks me, and my eyebrows almost rise into my hairline. We just left there!

"We went there first," I tell her, and she seems confused.

"We bought the bassinets," I remind her, and her brows furrow.

"I must be tired," she murmurs, so softly I almost miss it.

I need to speak to Dad and Valen. It's like a switch had flipped within her, and so suddenly.

"Come on, we'll get you home," I tell her, leaving my basket. I text Dad to come get her, not wanting her driving.

He meets us in the parking lot, and despite me telling her he was coming to get her, she seemed surprised to see him. Dad places her in his car and hands me Mom's keys so I can get back to my car.

"Is she always like that?" I asked worriedly.

Dad sighs. "Yes. When she's due for another dose," he says, looking in the window at her.

"It shouldn't be coming on so quickly," he said, his eyes darkening to black.

"Nixon hasn't stopped treatment?" I asked.

"No, he wouldn't risk it. But the vaccine is not lasting as long now. Wearing off faster, like she's becoming immune to it."

"I'll speak to Valen and see what the scientists have come up with. If need be, go to the media and declare the vaccine isn't working. Maybe we double the dosage?" I ask.

"Nixon would kill me," Dad says.

"Not with everyone watching, he won't. He'll have no choice but to agree or admit his vaccine doesn't work and let other pack scientists in to help. If he does that, he'll lose his sponsors from the other cities. Big pharma won't back him if he can't disprove that it doesn't work," I tell him, and Dad nods.

"It will buy us time to find a cure," I tell him. Dad nods again before turning to me.

"Have you sold that land yet? Nixon said the other day he was going to file against the pack soon if it isn't paid," he says guiltily. I shake my head. Valen said he would sell some of his shares and help cover it until we can sell off the land, but it looks like I may need to dip into Valerian's trust. I'll have to put it back though.

Valen could pay it, but a lot of his money is also the pack's money, not just his to blow how he likes. As it is, our pack is already questioning his authority, what with all the media attention; we don't need tensions to rise more. It could make everything fall apart if he did.

"I'll speak with Valen and try to call a pack meeting. We need to get this taken care of before it's too late," I tell him, and he nods, giving me a quick hug before climbing in the car to take care of my mother.

E verly

Another four weeks later.

Life is hectic. I've just hit my second trimester, and the hotel is only a few weeks from being finished. Macey and Zoe are doing everything at the moment, from school runs to managing the renovations, now that the structure is fully fixed. Kalen is running the homeless shelter, while Dad works for my pack and Valen his.

Valen's scientists have managed to replicate the inhibitor that Nixon created and have started working on finding a cure. Mom is getting blood tests but the vaccine needs to be administered every few days now; as we suspected, she's becoming immune to the vaccine. The disease has also brought on early onset dementia; she's losing her grip on reality. Dad is beside himself, and Ava is devastated.

Ava and I are tasked with watching over Mom, which means taking her to these appointments. We're also forced to carry tranquilizers everywhere we go with her, just in case, but she seems to have been able to pull herself out of her episodes each time before anything bad happens.

Mom thanks the nurse who takes her blood before the doctor administers the next dose, shivering when the needle stabs into her arm. Because of the inhibitor, her hair is beginning to gray and she's aging quickly.

Valen hates that I offered to help watch over her, said I was putting myself at risk, and he's right, but she's my mother. The woman taught me to walk, speak, and use a damn spoon; I know if our roles were reversed and it was his father, he would be by his father's side too.

My mother is deteriorating fast, and the scientists who are working on the cure are working around the clock. More rogues have gone missing, turning up along the borders as forsaken, which only amps up Nixon's claims that they were deliberately turning forsaken to overrun the city.

Speculation and theories over whose claims to believe hang over the entire city like a dark cloud.

Valen sold most of his shares in businesses outside the city to pay half the debt owed to Nixon. Still, Nixon presses for more, and we've had enough. We've filed against Nixon to have his pack dismantled. My father even went to the media two nights ago and outed everything, including the debt and how Nixon was the one who injected my mother.

Now, we're waiting for the repercussions. Nixon is officially under investigation, and the werewolf council is now involved. Everyone is on edge since Dad went to live across the city.

Unfortunately, that means my father is also under investigation and forced to remain in his pack territory, the same as Nixon; another reason why I have to help Ava with Mom. Dad can't leave pack borders, and until I marry Valen, he has to stay on the opposite side of town because our packs are still separated. However, the forsaken enzyme inhibitor, now that Nixon won't administer it, can only be given on Valen's territory. The investigation is a slow process that will buy us time, though maybe not much with tensions on the rise.

Riots have started in the streets already, and the city wants answers. Nixon's pack has gone quiet—they don't leave their borders, and only trucks with supplies have entered since he found himself in hot water.

Mom is in a cheery mood as we leave the doctor's office, almost childlike and giddy as she climbs in the car. Ava sits next to her. As I clip my seatbelt, my phone starts ringing and I quickly answer it after seeing Zoe's name pop up on the screen.

"Hey, what's up?"

"I need you to pick up the kids for me. We've sprung a leak. And the fire alarms, for some reason, turned on and have yet to turn off. Macey is also locked in the basement because it tripped the locks and I'm currently standing in water to my knees." She sighs heavily, sounding frustrated.

Great, this is all we need. This new tech system is becoming a pain in the ass—so many sensors—and I'm starting to second-guess the entire thing.

"Is Macey alright? Is it flooding down there?"

"Yeah, she's fine. Currently eating all the chocolate and drinking all the wine. At least we know the basement is waterproof," Zoe laughs. I chuckle. More bad news, but we'll live.

"The damage?"

"Expensive," she answers, and I groan.

"Okay, I'll grab the kids." I glance at my phone screen, seeing I have to get them now, and curse.

"I may need to drop Mom home first. I only have five seats in this car and I have Mom and Ava with me," I tell her, which means I'll be late. Just then, I see Tatum outside, walking directly toward us. Shit! He must have followed us out. He's on security at the clinic and had tried to stop me on the way in but got called away.

"Never mind, I have a solution," I tell her, hanging up just as Tatum taps on my window. I push the door open and climb out.

"I thought I missed you," he says, tugging on the tie around his neck to loosen it.

"Nope, still here. And I kinda need to ask you a favor," I tell him.

"Great! Then maybe you could do me a favor in return?" he asks. I know what he wants; we've all been at Macey for weeks about it, but she refuses to listen; the woman is stubborn. But this is the first time I've spoken directly with Tatum about the situation. Usually, all messages come through Valen to me, then through me to Macey. It's driving me insane!

"You first," I tell him.

"Macey hasn't answered a single call from me. She refuses to speak to me and I can't even mind-link with her since she isn't pack-linked."

"Well, since you are about to solve my problem, I have a solution to yours, too," I chuckle.

"I'm all ears," he says.

"Macey is stuck in the basement, but it has an intercom. Zoe is held up and I need to get the kids from school, including Taylor. Come with me and help pick them up. I don't really want them in the car with Mom," I whisper, and he glances behind me and nods his head.

"Now, *that* I can do. I haven't seen Tay in ages. Wait! Will Macey be okay with that?" he asks, and I shrug. Either that or I'll be twenty minutes late getting them by the time I drive Mom back home.

"Well, I'm out of options, so she'll get over it."

"Are you sure?" he asks, looking worried.

"She has no choice. Besides, you should both talk. I'm sick of passing notes for you both," I tell him, opening my door.

"I'll meet you at the school," he says, and I nod. We drive over and pull up out front, and I quickly race in and get the kids from their classes. Valen's pack school is under heavy security at the moment— all children are required to be signed out. With the growing missing reports of the rogues, better to be safe than sorry.

Walking back out to the car, my phone rings and I pull it from my pocket and answer it. My father is on the other end.

"I'm just about to drop her home," I tell him.

"No, don't. Investigators just showed up. I'm calling to see if you could hang onto her a bit longer. She doesn't do well with strangers in the house and I currently have seven with warrants," he tells me.

Fuck! Could anything else go wrong today?

I pinch the bridge of my nose in frustration. "That's fine. I'll figure it out."

"Why? What happened?"

"Nothing; I have the kids, is all,"

"She won't hurt them."

Yet I can hear the worry in his voice.

"It's fine. Tatum will drop the girls off and I'll ask Kalen to get Valarian. Valen doesn't want Valarian around her when it's only Ava and me, since I can't shift," I explain and Dad sighs.

"As soon as they leave, I'll send someone to come get her."

"Okay," I tell him, hanging up. The kids look up at me, but I shake my head. Walking out of the school, Taylor spots Tatum and squeals, running ahead of me.

"Hey, Tay!" he says, scooping her up, and she wraps her arms around his neck before showing him her pasta necklace around her neck. She takes it off and wraps it around his neck.

"Aw, thanks," he says, pecking her cheek.

"Are we coming back home soon?" she asks. I know she must be confused. Tatum has been part of her life for months now, only for her to wake up and not see him again.

"I'm working on it. And I'm hoping to see your mother this afternoon," he says before looking at me. "I only have two car seats in the car. Her old one and my sister's daughter's one."

"On it!" Ava calls out, pulling Valarian's car seat from out of Valen's car I'm driving. We spend a few minutes anchoring it before buckling the kids in.

"Change of plans," I tell Tatum. "Mom is staying with me for a few more hours, so can you swing by my place before you drop the girls off? Ava texted Zoe on the way over to tell her you were dropping the kids off. She also assured me that Macey is still locked in the basement." I chuckle, knowing it's already been fixed and Zoe is just keeping her locked in there so Tatum can talk to her.

"I feel like a dick." Tatum sighs heavily.

"Yeah, well, she thinks you left because she can't have kids."

"Well, if she would let me explain, that wasn't the reason I left."

"Then why *did* you leave?" Ava asks, her tone coming off as defensive. He looks back in the windows, ensuring the kids aren't listening.

"Macey said she never wanted kids. She made that clear. I thought I could change her mind. When she finally told me, I felt a little angry that she didn't tell me right away, but more because I had been bugging her about kids for weeks and hurting her the whole time!" He groans.

"I even went and bought baby stuff. I wondered why she got so angry and tossed it out. Then the next day, she told me, and I haven't heard from her since," he says.

"It'll work out," I tell him.

"Yeah, but I feel like shit! My sister went through IVF for years before having Sam. Had I known, I wouldn't have pushed so hard, or at all. My sister hated when people mentioned anything baby-related or asked when she would have kids. I became one of those people. That's why I left," Tatum growls, shaking his head.

"I was angry, but more embarrassed than anything. I'm happy just having Taylor; even though her toy collection takes up half our house!" he chuckles.

"Well, Zoe locked her in the basement. So now she has no choice but to hear you out," I tell him, and he nods his head, then turns to the driver's door.

"And Tatum?" I call, and he stops, looking at me.

"Every person she has dated walked the same day she told them. She held off with you, hoping you would stay. The only reason she didn't tell you is that she was worried about losing you."

"I know that. But I wasn't going anywhere," Tatum states.

"She didn't know that, though. Before you, she went on dates, and all of them walked out once they learned she couldn't provide them an heir," I tell him, and Tatum frowns, then nods his head before easing himself into the car. I go back to mine and climb into the driver's seat, and Ava gets in the back with Mom.

I get Ava to text Kalen on the drive home; he says he'll be there in half an hour. We are just down the street from home when static crackles over the radio. I flip through the stations to find them all the same. Suddenly, the traffic lights go out up ahead. I peer up at the sky. Is a storm brewing? Yet the overcast day is the same; the sky hasn't darkened more. I glance at Ava, whose face is scrunched up as she peers at her phone. She's been playing some game on it.

"I have no cell service," she says, and I reach over and pass my phone to her; she unlocks it.

"Neither do you," she replies, just as the tornado sirens blare. However, the sirens aren't used for tornado warnings; we never get tornadoes here. I haven't heard that noise since I was a kid—and I only ever heard it once.

My eyes widen and I peer at Tatum's car behind me when Valen's voice and my father's boom through the mind-link.

'*All warriors to the borders! Everyone else, get inside and lock your doors!*'

I swallow. My mother is blissfully unaware as she speaks to herself, looking at me and smiling.

"What's that noise?" she asks. Neither of us answers her and I glance at Ava. She stares back, looking petrified when Valen mind-links me.

'*Get home and lock the doors!*' he repeats.

'*How many? And where?*' I ask, opening the link to Marcus, Zoe, and Tatum.

'*Get home and lock the door, Everly!*' Valen orders.

'*Valen, how many?!*' I snarl.

'*Hundreds!*' he says.

'*The girls?!*' Zoe screeches through the link.

'*I have them and Valarian. I'm behind Everly now,*' Tatum chimes in as we pull into the hotel parking lot. The shutters are sealed on the lower-level windows and doors. I roll my window down, waving Tatum toward the underground car park and he gives me a thumbs up.

'Zoe, get to the basement! I'll get to Casey!' Marcus orders her, and she whimpers before being shoved out of the link.

'Where are they coming in?' Tatum asks.

'Everywhere!' Marcus and Valen say. The mind-link turns to chaos and I nearly run into a pillar before I manage to force everyone out of my head. We pull up and start yanking the kids from the cars when my mother finally comes back to her senses.

"We're under attack," she gasps as she shoves them toward the elevators. "That's...?" she starts, looking at Ava, who nods to her.

Valarian hits the button, but the doors don't open. The emergency generators don't operate them, leaving only the stairs.

"Fuck!"

The roller shutters start dropping to the underground parking lot as we rush the kids to the fire exit. The bells sound as I throw the door open and we usher the kids inside the stairwell when snarling growls echo through the underground parking lot.

Tatum pivots just as a group of forsaken rush inside the parking garage. He rips his shirt off before looking at me over his shoulder.

"Get inside, Luna!"

My heart races as I stare at the forsaken stalking into the place.

"Tatum!" I call out. Tatum's eyes are on the forsaken, and he is too focused on them circling him.

"Inside, Luna! Now!" he roars before shifting as they run at him. My eyes widen, and I rush through the door, slamming it shut and locking it. Turning around, I see the kid's frightened faces peering back at me.

"Tatum?" Taylor says, her eyes on the door, where vicious growls and banging come through.

"He's okay. He'll be okay," I tell Taylor while turning her and pushing her up the stairs. Ava stares at me. I nod to her and her eyes turn glassy, but she nods once, pushing Mom up the stairs. We're locked in the stairwell, all the doors are locked as we climb the levels.

'Valen, we can't get inside!' I call through the link. I get no answer, meaning he's blocking me out of whatever is happening outside. We're halfway up the stairwell when we hear desperate banging on the door below.

"Tatum!" Taylor squeals, rushing back down. I just manage to grab her before she gets past me when I hear the door burst open below. Ava looks over the side of the railing and the blood drains from her face. I follow her gaze over to see forsaken rushing up the steps.

"Run!" I scream. Ava grabs Valarian and Mom, who's struggling to climb the stairs—she's exhausted after being given the inhibitor.

"Get to the roof!" I scream while grabbing Casey and Taylor.

Mom rips her hand from Ava.

"I'm slowing you down. Get the kids up!" she growls at Ava, who looks at me. I place Taylor on the ground and Ava's hand locks around her wrist.

"Valarian, like we practiced at training," I tell him. "Don't look back. Don't stop."

"Mom," Valarian stammers with tear-filled eyes, and his lip quivers.

"Don't look back. Don't stop," I repeat, and he nods. Seeing the fear on his face makes me want to hug him, but he listens and takes off running up the steps while Ava hauls the girls up behind him.

"Three more flights, Mom," I tell her. She keeps trying to pull my hand from hers, but I snarl at her before Commanding her.

"Move faster! Now!" I order. I hear my sister and the kids make it to the roof while vicious snarls come from below, but the Command works, and she's forced to move quickly. Only, they're gaining ground fast. We're one set of steps away from the roof when I hear a snarl behind me.

Mom freezes and so do I. Turning, I find the two forsaken on the steps prowling, stalking up the steps toward us. My mother's hand grips the back of my shirt.

"You're gonna run for me now, baby girl," she murmurs as we both walk backward up the stairs as they hunt us. Their fur is falling out and what's left is matted; blood drips from their muzzles as they snap their teeth and snarl while creeping ever closer up the steps.

I shake my head.

"I'm proud of you, baby. But I need you to do this for me," she says. I hear her bones start snapping just as she whips me backward behind her, and I only just catch myself.

"Tell your father and sister I love them," she says just before shifting completely. I scream as she leaps at them and they begin tearing her apart.

I go to take a step toward her when I look down at my stomach. Tears burn my eyes, but I tear my gaze from the bloodshed and run for safety.

CHAPTER
TWENTY-EIGHT

Everly

My hands hit the door, jarring them with the force as I burst onto the roof. Ava screams and shoves the kids behind her body, using herself as a shield, and I twist, slamming the door shut. The racket coming from the stairwell is deafening and I stare at the door where I had just abandoned my mother. Ava rushes over, jamming a piece of a broken pipe she ripped off from somewhere through the handle and pipeline that runs to the vents on the roof above it, and I finally pull my gaze from the door.

All I can think is, *I left her in there. I ran and left her behind.*

Ava whimpers as she secures the bar; I don't have to tell her. She knows because Mom didn't come out behind me. As she turns to look at me, I can see her heartbreak.

My entire body shakes with adrenaline and shock.

I left her.

My thoughts are consumed with that thought when a tiny hand slips into mine. Looking down, I find Valarian looking at me.

"Grandma will be okay," he says, only I know she won't be. I swallow and blink back tears before turning to him and picking him up.

"Yep. She found another open door," I tell him while walking over to the girls. I place him beside them where they're huddled on the ground by the air-conditioner vent.

Ava moves to the ledge of the building and I follow her, checking over my shoulder to make sure the kids don't follow. Together, we look over.

The city is in utter chaos and ruins. Buildings in the distance are on fire, screams ring out loudly, and a frenzied battle can be seen on the main street even from here. Warriors are trying to hold the forsaken back from their borders.

Valen is right—there are hundreds of them. They just keep coming. The street directly below us is a scene from a horror movie as our men try to keep them back. Two forsaken are dragging another wolf off, and I don't want to think about what they're doing to him as he yelps loudly.

"Her tether?" Ava asks me, and I swallow.

"Not broken yet. She's fighting," I whisper, staring out blankly. I notice from up here that not one of those forsaken are trying to get into Nixon's pack directly across from us. They're targeting ours and Slasher pack.

"How is the city outnumbered?" Ava gasps when an explosion goes off down by the café on the main street.

Carnage.

There is no other way to describe it, and the pack warriors are outnumbered. Slasher pack's men are trying to stop them from getting in, but a few slip through, and just like our men, they can't hold them back—they just keep coming. It should be impossible that so many could go unnoticed!

One of the high-rise apartments across from us catches on fire and more screams ring out from the apartment building as forsaken get inside. I just hope our roller shutters and the locked stairway doors hold.

The mind-link opens up, and I hear Zoe.

'Is Casey alright?'

'We're on the roof,' I answer while peering over my shoulder to look at the children. She sighs before sobbing through the link.

'And Marcus? Is he there yet? I'm being blocked out. I can't get a hold of anyone,' she asks, but I can't lie to her.

'Not yet, but…. Zoe, the city…' I don't finish. The place looks like a battlefield.

'As long as Casey is safe,' she says.

'Are you safe?' I ask her.

'I'm in the basement with some of the younger workers. But Macey, she…'

'Macey what, Zoe?' I ask, panicked.

'She heard the sirens when I opened the doors and bolted out. We tried to stop her," Zoe says. *'She has no phone. We have no service in here, and–'*

'She has no pack link,' I finish for her. My heart beats faster at her words.

'We think she went to warn the rogues at the reserve and homeless shelter. This side hasn't been hit yet," Zoe tells me.

Yes, because they're all over here trying to access our pack and Slasher's, while Nixon's remains untouched. That isn't a coincidence.

The mind-link is stretched when I feel Valen force it open and Zoe is shoved out.

'We're trying to get to you. You just need to hold tight a little longer,' he tells me, though pain radiates through the bond and I know he's hurt.

'What about Marcus? Zoe is trying to get a hold of him.'

'No idea. Everyone is blocking the pack link so we don't become distracted. We–"

The mind-link cuts off abruptly, only for Zoe to reopen it, having felt the connection from Valen override hers.

'Marcus?'

'They lost sight of each other. Marcus is fine, Zoe. Valen would have

felt the tether break,' I tell her, though I have no idea if that will remain true. I feel helpless as I watch our pack getting slaughtered on the streets below while I'm holed up on a roof, unable to help them.

T atum

Teeth, claws, blood, fur.

Everything is a blur as I try to hold them back. I'm screaming through the link for Valen to get here as a few slip past me. Men call through the link that they're on the way, yet as one forsaken falls, another replaces it. They seem to just keep coming and I'm taking a beating.

The venom in my system is starting to make my muscles ache and lock. The only thing keeping me on my feet is adrenaline and knowing that Taylor, Valarian, and Casey are in that stairwell. I just hope they get inside the building and aren't sitting ducks in that stairwell.

My back leg is ripped into as two attack simultaneously, snarling. I pivot and twist, nearly ripping my leg off in the process.

Yelps and snarls echo from the stairwell, causing me to become distracted as I try to double back, only to be jumped on. His claws rip through my fur, making my back arch, and his teeth are like a serrated knife as they tear into the back of my neck.

The stairwell. The stairwell, I keep thinking, trying to toss him off as more flood into the stairs, escaping past me while I'm being ripped to shreds. My teeth sink into its front paw and I feel the crunch as its bones break under the pressure of my teeth, forcing him to release me long enough to fling him off. I turn, running for the stairwell, my vision blurring as I go, just as forsaken are suddenly running back out of the stairwell.

My heart jolts at seeing the rabid creatures running from something. One drops as a huge, molten-colored wolf tears into its neck. It takes me a second to realize it's Claire. Yet, she doesn't look like a pack wolf—she looks like one of the forsaken. Her blood-red eyes are savage, and venom is oozing and dripping from her teeth. Panic courses through me, knowing if she turns on me, I'll have to kill Everly's mother. Her head twists in my direction and her lips pull back as she drops her head, snarling and stalking towards me—then she runs at me.

I snarl back when she lunges, but she misses. I jump aside, skidding on the slick, blood-soaked floor, only to see her rip into a forsaken that must have been coming up behind me. Four more rush through the barrier and I leap over her, jumping into the fray.

She's a full-blown forsaken. However, she's fighting on our side, not theirs, which gives her an advantage, as they keep recognizing her as their own. With the savage gleam and the way she fights, I can tell John trained her himself—she's just as lethal, but with a vicious edge.

She tears into them, locking her jaws each time and ripping them to shreds, not even flinching as they tear into her back. Relentlessly, she fights, saving my ass twice, and I hers, as we fight tail to tail, trying to hold them back.

My back leg is useless—I'm running on three, the other hanging behind me.

'We're in the street!' Valen calls, but I can't reply. I'm too focused on the wolves in front of me. We need to try to push them back to the street through the broken roller shutters.

Claire is taking on three, but even she is on the losing end this time. I rip off one on her that's tearing into her flank, while her jaws lock around another one's neck.

My paw swipes at the other and together, we push them back, herding them up the ramp. Daylight breaks as we keep forcing them further. Suddenly, she lets out a whimper just as we make it out the front of the hotel. Pivoting, I run towards her when a deafening howl rips through the air as she sways on her feet.

Forsaken are swarming her; her throat is torn out. Her front legs buckle. A giant black and gray wolf starts wrenching them off her as another forsaken tackles me. I break the wolf's neck and I turn my head to find the black and gray wolf is John. The three forsaken that had attacked Claire are lying dead around him, and John now stands naked, petting her wolf. Her chest rises and she wheezes as blood pools around her—then her chest appears to deflate. The agonized howl that turns to a wail shakes me to the core when I hear Everly's keening scream ring out above as she feels her mother's link disintegrate.

Everyone stops at the noise—even the forsaken, who are flooding into the street. Valen's wolf is huge and the one beside him is equally big; I recognize the wolf as the Slasher pack Alpha. Marcus' gray wolf rushes past me toward the forsaken, his coat tainted red, and the chaos starts again.

John's angered roar makes my fur stand on end. He seems to erupt as he shifts and barrels towards the forsaken with blind fury, ripping them apart as the bloodshed starts again.

Now an observer, I realize something. The forsaken are only heading here and for the Alpha's homes, making this obviously targeted and well-thought-out. The information I hear coming through the link says the side of the city where the rogue's live and Everly's hotel stands remain untouched. The carnage is only happening on one side.

Nixon has to be behind it. And he's casting the rogues as the ones starting it.

He's trying to divide the city.

Pandemonium ensues as we battle. Our men are falling, yet the forsaken keep coming. The four Alphas—new and old—work together, getting right in the middle of the battle. Valen and the Slasher pack Alpha, even John and Kalen, are lethal beasts. They are huge, towering beasts compared to the forsaken. Their coats are dripping in blood, both theirs and the forsaken; there's not a speck of fur left untainted.

This is what makes them Alphas—pure, lethal muscle, and precision like no other. Despite their massive sizes, they're fast, running through forsaken like bowling balls knocking down pins. The street's gutters run with rivers of blood, and it stains everything.

They don't stop, but neither do the forsaken. These numbers should not exist! How can they outnumber us? Three packs are fighting, and we are *still* somehow outnumbered.

Suddenly, a tidal wave of snarls shakes the windows. The deafening force of pure rage reverberates around the street and everyone stops to stare down the road, searching for the source of the rumbling noise.

Macey appears.

My heart stops as she runs down the street straight at us with a huge bat in her hands. Fear courses through me and I run toward her. Forsaken take off in her direction, only to start skidding across the ground, trying to stop and double back. What could scare so many forsaken so badly? I stare up ahead of them in shock.

Hundreds of rogues are racing up the street toward us. I stop as she leads her army of rogues to the battle. They are a sight to be seen.

Our men are given some relief as rogues jump into battle without hesitation, saving the very people who shunned them, and cast them out. Pack members and rogues are fighting alongside each other—fighting as one—painting the street red with the blood of the forsaken and proving their innocence in their own desperate need to fight for our city.

Teeth sink into my neck and I'm flung across the road. My head smashes into the gutter, and I can hear screaming in the distance before I feel a violent breeze rustle the fur on my face as her bat smashes into the wolf's skull with a thud.

My eyes blur as I open them to see her bashing its head into the earth with brute force. Her clothes are stained with blood, her arm bleeding from where she's been bitten. But even covered in blood, she is beautiful as she fights. I catch sight of Zoe's small, white wolf protecting Marcus, who is trying to protect her.

My heart thumps and feels like it's left my body as I try to get to my feet, staggering as the venom takes hold. Macey screams. Only, it isn't a scream of pain, but a war cry as she flings her bat at the wolf ripping into Alpha John. A grunt is knocked out of her when she's tackled from behind, only for Kalen to rip the wolf off her. I'm delirious from the venom. As I try to find my footing and get to her, I feel my surroundings flip and turn on their axis before I succumb to the nothingness.

CHAPTER
TWENTY-NINE

E verly

There are no winners in war. Either way, somebody loses. Even the winners lose; they lose friends, family, humanity, and themselves. We may have won the battle, but no one truly wins the war because no one walks away the same after witnessing such carnage, such loss, and it always ends in grief.

Grief shows you how valuable life is, but also how cruel; how precious life is, but also how short; the darkness of loss and how torturous it can be when you lose someone you can't imagine living without.

Yet, somehow you do. Somehow, you're still breathing, even when the pain of grief is so intense you believe it will kill you—sometimes wishing it would, just so you don't have to know the pain of losing them. Nothing will kill your soul more than losing a loved one. Nothing will break you down more than realizing you will never hold them again, never hear their voices, never see them.

Standing in this hall with hundreds of faces staring back at us, you can see their grief as if they wear it like armor; as if it's branded into their very being like a tattoo, screaming their anguish. You can hear their gut-wrenching wails as they realize the pain they are feeling isn't hurt loved ones but broken bonds, broken families.

Just broken.

We stand on a podium while Valen calls out the names of loved ones, needing them to come forward to claim their dead sons, dead mates, and dead parents. He does this while trying to mask my grief, trying to keep the bond blocked. I witness theirs, feel theirs, with each broken tether.

The way Valen calls out the names, it's almost as if he's desensitized to death, expressionless, emotionless. Yet, through the bond, I know he's barely holding it together as their screams and pain ripple through him like a stone tossed in the lake, that rippling tide on repeat. I don't know how he bears it. He's doing his best to block it all, but those emotions that sift through, I feel those. I feel *them*—our pack—and I feel *him*.

We won the battle, but we lost too. One hundred seventy-six lives were lost, and ninety-one bonds were broken. Most of those deaths were men, and she-wolves rarely live without their mates, meaning a possible ninety-one more lives will wither away until either they die slowly or their bond does. Seeing my father sitting staring vacantly ahead, I know he wishes it had killed him instantly.

It feels surreal, like a nightmare, a loop of horror that we are desperately trying to wake up from. When Valen finishes, we make our way out and meet with the council investigators. They were raiding my father's house when the war started and were quick to jump in to help. Then, while we were cleaning up, they raided Nixon's pack.

A vast majority of the forsaken turned out to be from his pack, his own people, unbonded males that apparently volunteered in the name of science—they put up their hands for their own suicide. Half his pack gone, and for what? The other half is shocked.

Nixon used the attack as a distraction to escape from the city, while his pack was left abandoned. As each forsaken shifted back after their death, we were left with their true identities. He killed his people.

Those that weren't from his pack were the missing rogues. They were promised money, a cure, and a pack for their sacrifice. A sacrifice that ended in their deaths. Some thought it was worth the risk.

We were shocked to find that his daughter is dead. He had apparently switched off her life support before fleeing the city, leaving his son behind in a padded room—the man that holds the cure in his veins. His blood is the key needed to save them.

The investigators told us that Carter is shocked by his father's plans, that he had nothing to do with it or knew anything of it. That he, too, is a victim of his father's cruelty.

Nixon had moved all his money and taken every cent the pack had—the pack that is now left to Carter to deal with—before killing Carter's sister and running away like a coward, leaving behind his mate and son. I thought I knew evil, but Nixon proved he's more than evil. There isn't an accurate word to describe what he's done to this city, to his people and his family.

Carter handed his blood samples to Slasher and Valen's packs for testing. He's a miracle. Nixon had accomplished something, at least. He managed to find a cure for the incurable. Of course, we also learned that he had intended to infect the world and then sell the cure to them.

Zoe is standing by the car with the kids and Kalen. I touch Valen's arm and he looks over at me. I nod toward Zoe, and he gives a swift nod before I make my way over to them. Valarian and the girls are sitting in the back of the car with the heat going; the night has turned terribly cold.

Cold. Just like the emptiness we all feel. I check on them before leaning against the hood next to Zoe when my father wanders out, looking rather lost. I'm about to go to him when Kalen grips my arm.

"I'll go check on him," Kalen says, and I nod gratefully.

"Macey is still with Tatum. He's gone in for surgery to try to save his leg," Zoe whispers to me.

"And Macey? She was bitten, wasn't she?"

Zoe shakes her head. "She isn't infected. She called me before; her blood tests came back clear. Tatum is riddled with venom though, and they aren't sure if he'll make it."

"Marcus?"

She nods toward him where he's walking over to Valen, who is still talking to the council investigators.

"He's fine. Beta blood. He's stronger than most, but so many are infected. Hopefully, Carter's blood really is the cure that's needed," Zoe says, and I swallow.

"Have you seen Ava?" I ask her.

"I gave her your spare house keys."

I nod. Ava had said she wanted to stay with us for the night. Dad, too, is staying at our place, not wanting to go home without Mom.

We wait. Neither of us knows what to do, so I leave it to Valen and the Slasher Pack Alpha. They seem to be in their element dealing with all the aftermath, and I don't know the first thing about dealing with the werewolf council or what we do from here.

When they're finished talking and everyone eventually leaves, Valen comes over with Marcus and rubs his hands up my arms. His touch is warm, making me realize how cold my skin is.

"You should be in the car. It's too cold out here," he murmurs.

"Where did our fathers go?"

"Your father is staying with mine. Yours was apparently pretty drunk by the time Dad finished talking to him."

"I could go for a damn drink myself," Marcus says, sounding exhausted as he nudges Valen. Zoe shoots him a look, knowing I don't like Valen drinking. He's been drinking again over the last few weeks and I don't want him to fall back into old habits.

"Come on, I should get you home," Valen says, pulling me closer to use himself as a shield to protect me from the wind. He moves to the back of Zoe's little car where Valarian has fallen asleep with the girls.

"Am I taking Taylor, or are you?" I ask Zoe.

"Marcus and I will take her," Zoe answers, and I nod, grabbing Valarian's blanket after Valen grabs him.

I kiss both the girls, who are sleeping soundly, before following Valen to our car. He puts Valarian in the back and I place his blanket over him while clipping him in. We drive home in devastating silence.

I'm glad it's dark because I know the roads are still painted in blood. A storm is brewing above and I'm hoping most of it is washed away by morning. Yet, we still have plenty of clean-up to do, and plenty of people still missing because it was dark before we found the vast majority of bodies.

Valen parks out in front of the hotel instead of underground. I stare at the front by the hedges where my mother's body was before Valen grips my hand, pulling my gaze away. Those were the most harrowing hours of my life, sitting on the rooftop watching, trying to keep the kids distracted from witnessing the horrifying scene below us, trying not to scare them. When it was all said and done, Valen's desperation to check on us sent him to the roof, which was not ideal, considering there wasn't a speck of skin that wasn't covered in blood.

Luckily, the kids were half asleep, so hopefully, the girls won't remember seeing him, though I know our son saw him. He didn't stop trembling until after Valen stepped out of the shower clean and Valarian realized it wasn't his father's blood, though he's remained silent ever since.

It had been impossible to convince the kids to keep their eyes closed while we left the roof, but Marcus brought blankets up to toss over their heads so they wouldn't see the forsaken my mother killed in the stairwell while we carried them to the first accessible floor.

When we finally get home, I unlock the door and Valen immediately goes to put Valarian in bed. The sound of crying I can hear up the hall makes me move to the guest bedroom. I nudge the door open to find Ava in bed, huddled under the blankets, her body shaking as she sobs.

Quietly, I move toward the bed before climbing in behind her and wrapping my arms around her, hugging her as close as my belly will allow. I hold her as she cries, the sound breaking me into a million fractured pieces with sharp edges that pierce my soul.

"She's gone," Ava whispers. I nod my head against her back and sniffle.

"I know," I whisper, not knowing what else to say. I can't take her pain; it's mine, too, though I wish I could at least stop her from feeling it.

She cries herself to sleep, and I hold her until then. Slipping out of bed, I move toward my room and push the door open to find Valarian in our bed, Valen wrapped around him. I slip my pajamas on, and Valen lifts his head.

"He came in about twenty minutes ago," he whispers. I nod my head before quickly slipping into bed on Valarian's other side. Valen drapes his arm across both of us and his hand rubs the side of my belly.

"I was worried you would try fighting," Valen murmurs, propping his head on his hand to look at me. I shake my head, place my hand over his on my belly, and lean forward, kissing Valarian's head.

"No. I wanted to, but it wasn't worth the risk, and I would have been no help anyway; I was where I needed to be and where Mom wanted me to be—safe with Val," I tell him.

We've had an entire week of funeral services. Everything feels wrong, though.

Tatum is in a medically induced coma. They saved his leg, but the infection has spread everywhere and Macey has been sick with worry, barely leaving his bedside. Zoe and I have been alternating taking Taylor.

Ava has busied herself with work and so have I. Anything to take my mind off how quickly everything has spiraled out of control.

All morning, I was holed up in my office—which is finally finished—going over documents from both packs and the accounting from the hotel, leaving me scraping money left and right to pay bills. Then I spent all afternoon helping Ava move her stuff back home from the apartment out behind my hotel, which Macey will now take over.

When I finally get home from work and walk in the door, Valen looks over the back of the couch; the beer in his hand doesn't escape my eyes as he quickly places it down to turn to look at me.

"I put your dinner in the microwave, and Valarian asked for you at bedtime."

I nod while dumping my handbag on the hall stand.

"Why didn't you answer your phone? I've been calling all afternoon. And you shoved me out of the mind-link," he says, his tone clipped at the end.

"I was with my father and Ava. I helped her move back in with Dad," I answer while moving to the kitchen. I put my dinner on to heat and finally sit down to wait. I'm exhausted, and even eating seems like a major task.

Valen strolls in and I eye the bottle in his hand. He quickly tips it up and drains it, then tosses it in the recycling. He catches me watching him when he turns around and arches an eyebrow.

"What?" he demands.

"You know how I feel about you drinking, and I definitely don't want you drinking around Valarian," I tell him, and he scoffs.

"Right. Because I'm an alcoholic?" He clicks his tongue and shakes his head. I lean back from the counter and fold my arms across my chest.

"Don't put words in my mouth, Valen; I never said that. I just said I don't like you drinking, but hey, if you say you are, you must be." I sigh; I would rather not argue tonight. He growls but moves closer, his hands going to my bump as he caresses it.

"I only had one, and Valarian is asleep. I am not an alcoholic. Geez, Everly, I don't obliterate myself," he says, leaning closer. He dips his face closer, his lips brushing mine softly, before biting my bottom lip playfully. I roll my eyes, pushing on his shoulders, and he chuckles, stepping back and opening the microwave when it dings. He grabs the plate out, setting it on the kitchen counter.

"Did you sort out the finances for the hotel and find out how much is owed to the contractors?" he asks, and I nod.

"And you paid it?" he asks. I growl before walking over to my handbag and grabbing his card out. I hand it to him, but he pushes my hand away.

"Keep it," he says, and I shake my head but place it back while he fetches me a knife and fork.

"The real estate agent called today. She said Alpha Daxon from Slasher pack wants to repurchase the land from behind his pack," I tell him, and he nods.

"Yes, he wants to build some training grounds. He even mentioned wanting to train with our pack for a bit."

"Sounds like a plan. Also I got a weird message from Carter today," I admit. Valen points to the table, and I sit down while he brings my plate over, setting it in front of me.

"How did he get your number?" Valen asks, and I shrug. It wouldn't be hard, probably from his father's files.

"What did he want?"

"Asked if we had settled the debt. Carter said he found the paperwork and bank statements."

"What did you say?"

"I told him the truth, then offered him the titles for the back of his pack, but he said no."

"Yeah, his father wiped every cent from the pack's accounts. I'd say the pack will be dismantled if he doesn't do something soon."

"So, what should I do?"

"I'll talk to him tomorrow and handle it. From what the investigators said, we owe Carter nothing. As soon as Nixon's found, he'll stand before the council and probably be executed, anyway, and Carter isn't a part of that agreement, so has no warrant to claim it."

"Have they seen any sign of Nixon?" I ask, moaning as I spear a piece of ravioli and pop it into my mouth—the sauce tastes heavenly. Valen chuckles, leaning down and licking it off my lips.

"I have something you can moan around that tastes better."

"Somehow, I think this tastes better," I tease, spearing another piece. He laughs, pecking my lips before walking off into the bathroom. I hear the water turn on a few seconds later while I turn back to my food.

E verly
Several Weeks Later
Valen sits nervously beside me, his foot tapping as Doc squirts the lubricant over my huge belly; the coldness of it makes me want to pee. It's my twenty week ultrasound already.

I glance at the clock above the door. Macey said she wanted to come. Maybe she got caught up at the hospital. Tatum is getting better with the infection gone, but because of the nerve and tissue damage left behind from his leg being nearly completely torn off, he has to go through physical therapy to learn how to use it again. He could shift to heal himself, but they aren't sure if his leg would shift with the rest of him, so until he's healed completely, it isn't worth the risk.

Doc starts the scan, taking measurements, when we hear a knock. He leans over on his stool, opening the door, and Macey walks in, tiptoeing as if making noise will somehow disturb the doctor. She bends over and pecks my cheek before deliberately messing Valen's hair, earning a growl from him as he swats her hands away. She laughs and stares at the screen before squinting.

"So, you all placed your bets?" Doc asks. He knows from previous scans that Macey and Valen have a bet on the genders; hence why she's here.

"Yep! Two boys and a girl," Valen says.

"Nope! I say three girls," Macey says.

"Well, for your sake, I hope there's at least one boy. Valarian said last time you promised to wrestle the boy way, and you'll break that boy's heart," Doc laughs. Valerian came to my last ultrasound with Valen. I will give Valen one thing. He has never missed an appointment. He's even had to remind me to attend a couple.

"Well, Mom, what do you think?" Doc asks.

"Two girls and a boy," I tell him, crossing my fingers. He laughs and moves the device across my belly. I close my eyes when he declares Baby A to be a girl.

"The next one is a boy," Valen says.

"Sorry, Alpha, Baby B is a girl, too," Doc says.

"Ha! It's a girl, and you owe me three foot rubs, and you have to refer to me as 'oh favorite one' for a full week!" Macey says. She rubs her fingers together, then rubs the side of my belly. Doc chuckles and shakes his head, moving the device over my belly again.

"Stop with your karma voodoo!" Valen snaps at her, having already lost his bet.

"And what do you win?" Doc asks, since it's down to us girls.

"A jar of coffee," I say, and he turns his head to look at Valen.

"She isn't human, Valen. I told you to stop reading those baby books. She can drink as much coffee as she wants," Doc says, and I purse my lips.

"We don't know that for sure."

"Do you have a doctor's degree?" Macey asks.

"Just because you want to risk our kids coming out with three heads—" he retorts.

"I would hope so! *Only* two heads would be an issue, since there are three of them," Macey taunts.

"You know what I mean," Valen growls at her, and Doc laughs at their banter as he moves the device over my belly; it takes a while because the little bubba is hiding behind the others, but he's finally able to get a good enough view.

"Baby C is....."

Valen and Macey lean forward eagerly.

"A girl!" Doc says, and Macey squeals and jumps in victory while Valen deflates like a balloon.

"Looks like you wrestled in a girl way, Alpha."

"Apparently so," Valen mutters.

"Oh! That is so much pink!" Macey squeals excitedly.

"Maybe we can dress one in blue and hope Valarian doesn't notice?" Valen says thoughtfully.

"He'll notice," I deadpan, and Valen sighs.

"I don't know what to do with girls," he pouts before glaring down at his crotch as if it wronged him in some way. "You had one job! And you give me three girls! You couldn't have shot *one* boy out?!" he growls at his dick.

"I think he's just trying to hide his excitement for the three foot rubs he owes me," Macey says, and Valen pulls a face.

"I am not touching those Neanderthal feet!"

"A deal is a deal. Oh, and I'll let my toenails grow just for you before I claim my first one."

Valen pales and looks like he'll puke.

"Tell you what? I'll take one foot rub off if you give Everly her jar of coffee."

"Wipe all three and I will."

"She can drink coffee, and no, I'll get rid of *one*," Macey says, holding up one finger. He growls and scrunches his face up.

"Fine, and you better scrub those damn feet raw. And I'm wearing gloves," he snarls when Doc leans down and whispers to me.

"Do they always fight like this?" he asks.

"No, this is their love language, and Macey will win," I tell him. He laughs, finishing the scan.

THIRTY-ONE

V alen

Ten weeks later

Everly has been put on bed rest. She's made it to thirty weeks and Doc already said there's a high chance she won't carry the pregnancy to term. He also told us at her last appointment that she'll need to have a c-section. But with everything going on, we haven't even started setting up the nursery.

Valarian and I stop by the hotel on the way to the baby store to pick up Macey and Zoe, who are coming to help pick out the baby stuff. Everly wanted to come, but she can barely walk a few yards without having to pee, and her feet are swollen. However, she doesn't trust my 'vanilla taste', as she calls it, so the girls are coming to advise.

She insisted Valarian go to spend some time with me after we learned he's received detention twice for hitting two boys at school and has been playing up. We spoke to him about it and all he said was the boy deserved it. He refuses to tell us what it was about, despite us trying to talk to him about it.

Though I'm glad the girls are coming because I know Valarian will have a meltdown when he learns the genders. We didn't have the heart to tell him when we got home after the ultrasound. When we picked him up from school that day, he was holding balloons he'd painted blue, so today will be his revelation that he's getting three sisters instead of brothers. I nervously chew my nails as I wait for Zoe and Macey to come out.

Zoe is first out of the hotel, skipping excitedly over just as I see Macey come out the side doors of the restaurant. Zoe spots her, and for a second, they stand there staring at each other. My brows furrow at the reason until they both start racing toward the car, shoving and pushing each other.

"Shotgun!" Macey screams.

"I called it first!" Zoe snarls, shoving her, only to be yanked back as she reaches for the door handle. Macey sticks her tongue out at her when Zoe falls on her butt. She hops in the car and I raise an eyebrow at her. Zoe huffs and climbs in the back with Valarian.

"You two are idiots. I can't believe you just fought over the front seat like damn children," I tell them, shaking my head while they place their seatbelts on.

"I shotgun the front on the way home!"

"If you can get to it first, small fry," Macey taunts.

"Enough. Zoe gets the front on the way back. Stop your bickering, or both of you will sit in the back," I tell them. Geez, they're like Everly's annoying sisters. *I need to keep my daughters away from these two crazies*, I think to myself.

"Well, looks like I'll be claiming that foot rub today," Macey says.

"Macey gets the front seat on the way back," I quickly declare. No way am I rubbing her feet.

"Ew! Dad won't rub your feet," Valarian says. Macey snickers.

"Your father has to. He lost a bet," Macey tells him.

"What sort of bet?" Valerian asks, and Zoe answers.

"Oh, you'll see soon," Zoe says, messing his hair. "Are you excited about going baby shopping?"

"Yep! I want to find the babies some dinosaur plushies!"

"And other plushies, remember. And we're mainly going to find cribs," I tell him.

"What girl–" Macey starts to say.

"Shh!" I hiss at her, not wanting Valarian to have a meltdown in the car.

"Huh?" Valarian asks.

"Nothing. I was saying dinosaur plushies sound great. Taylor used to love dinosaurs."

"She still does, but only T. rexes. She likes their little arms," Valarian says.

When we reach the store, I can't believe how terrified I am of entering, knowing my son will find out the genders today. Alphas fear nothing, yet here I am, scared to tell my child I wrestled in a girl way because my pecker decided it was throwing girls this time around.

Valarian wanders around the store, finding stuff with Zoe and looking at crib blankets, while I find the cribs Everly showed me on the store's website. They're white, and I checked to see if they had them in stock; they do, and for half price, too. Once I have them set aside, I wander around the aisles looking at baby clothes and blankets. Just as I pick up some pink stuff, Zoe and Valarian come over with some dinosaur plushies.

"Can I pick a mobile?" Valarian asks before his eyes go to the pink onesie in my hands. Macey wanders around the store with a cart that has a blue blanket over it.

"One's a girl?" Valarian asks, and I chew my lip, about to put it back when Zoe leans down beside him.

"Girls aren't so bad. You like Taylor and Casey," Zoe tells him, and Valarian nods, looking at me.

"I found the bottle sterilizer Everly was looking at online, and the breast pump. Oh, and I found the breastfeeding pillow," Macey says, showing us.

"I got blue plushies," Valarian says happily.

"Aw, that's great. They'll love them."

"Yeah, but now I need to find a pink one," Valarian says.

"Why? Girls like blue," Macey says, batting her lashes at him. She points to her eyes.

"See? Blue eyeshadow," she says.

"Hmm, I guess you're right," Valarian says. We buy a few more things—he picks out some colorful mobiles for their cribs—and the rest we'll order. He seems to be taking the news of one girl alright, but I know we have to tell him there won't be a brother. Macey and Zoe want to see Everly, so we head home afterward. The store is delivering the cribs and the rest of the furniture tomorrow.

When we get home, Valarian is questioning names. We haven't picked any names yet, though I have a couple in mind, and so does Everly, but deciding names is hard because the kid has to live with whatever we choose. The stress it's causing me is shocking.

We show Everly the few things we have with us, and Macey and Everly start pulling out the sterilizer and bottles, wanting to try them out. Valarian watches with eager eyes, drinking it all in. He talks of wanting to help with bottles, and Everly explains she's going to try breastfeeding, but he can help when she expresses milk, which launches us into a conversation about how she has milk. I think the boy will need counseling after that conversation—he seems to think she's going to grow teats like a cow.

"So, are you going to pick the girl's name and dad picks the boys' names?" he asks while testing the bottle brush viciously. Everly looks at me.

You didn't tell him? she mouths. I smile at her awkwardly and hold my hands out apologetically.

"Well, you know how your father has to rub Auntie Macey's feet because she won the bet?" Everly shoots me a look as she's about to break the news to him and break his heart. He shudders.

"That is so gross," Valarian chuckles.

"Hey! My feet aren't gross," Macey tells him.

I shudder at the thought.

"Yep. Dad won't tell me what the bet was, though," Valarian pouts.

"Well, Auntie Macey bet that the babies would be three girls," Everly tells him, and his brows furrow. He looks at me and I swear I feel the blood drain from my face.

"You said you would wrestle in a boy way!" he growls, stunning me. Astonished by the sound, I stare at Everly, who also seems startled by it.

"Now they won't like my plushies!" he sobs, placing the bottle down and burying his face in his arms as he leans on the counter. Everly brushes her fingers through his hair and glares at me.

"Now we have to take them back, all because you wrestled in Mom's butt!" Valarian cries. Macey snorts and chokes at his words, while Everly gapes at him and Zoe snickers.

"It's not funny! I told Dad to wrestle in a boy way and he got it wrong," Valarian pouts. He snatches the plushies off the counter, putting them back in the bag.

"Valarian, there is no way to wrestle in a boy or girl way," Everly tells him.

"Yeah! Casey said she came out her mom's hoo-ha, but I came out your butt. And Dad promised he wouldn't wrestle your butt!"

"Vagina," Everly corrects and laughs, and Zoe's face heats.

"Babies don't come out of the butt," I tell him.

"But Casey said–"

"Casey came out of my vagina, Valarian. Not my butt," Zoe states.

"And Taylor came out of my belly. They cut me open, but she's still a girl," Macey tells him, and he seems confused.

"Girls aren't so bad," Zoe tells him.

"I know, but now I will have to fight all the boys to protect them," he says, glaring at the plushies in his hands.

"Huh?" Everly says.

"Like I do for Taylor and Casey. The boys pick on them. I had to punch Blake in the nose the other day. He tugged on Casey's hair and made her cry and called Taylor a rogue whore," he says.

"So that's why you got detention at school the other day?" I ask him.

"He called Taylor that?" Macey asks, and Valarian nods his head.

"Did you tell the teacher?" Zoe asks, yet Macey's eyes water, knowing the title bestowed on her is now on her daughter by default. I despise that name. It sickens me, and to know children of my pack are referring to other children by it angers me.

"No. I punched him on his big nose."

"You shouldn't have hit him—you should have told me. I'll speak with Blake's father. Violence isn't the answer," I tell him.

"I don't want them to call my sisters names," he says.

"They won't. Besides, they'll be tough, like your momma. And they'll have you to protect them," Zoe tells him. Valarian nods.

"So, do I still have to apologize to Blake?" Valarian asks. In my eyes, no, but the principal asked for an apology when he returns from his two-day suspension.

"You still need to apologize for hitting him, but I'll be making sure Blake also has to apologize," I tell him, looking at Macey. She folds her arms across her chest and nods once, clearly not happy that her daughter is being picked on.

"I'll handle it," I tell her, and she nods, yet, the look on her face says she wants to go deliver the boy the spanking his mother never gave him.

The girls stay for coffee and cake that Zoe made me stop at the bakery for on the way home, then I drive them back to the hotel so they can get the girls from school in an hour. Around 3:30, Everly's phone rings and she reaches for it on the coffee table where Valarian is drawing.

"It's Auntie Macey," Valarian says, passing the phone to her. She quickly answers it, and a moment later, I feel the mind link open up.

Marcus's voice frantically echoes in my head.

'Have you seen Ava and Zoe?' he asks.

'Not since I dropped Zoe back at the hotel. What's up?'

'Ava and Zoe went to pick up a few things from the hardware store and

219

were supposed to pick Casey and Taylor up. The school just called me because they weren't picked up. I'm on my way there now to get them.'

'Where's Macey?'

'With Tatum. He had a physical therapy appointment this afternoon. She's meeting me at the school,' Marcus says.

'Have you tried mind-linking her?'

'Of course! But the bond is blocked. I can't feel her, Valen!' he says more frantically. I can hear the fear in his voice.

'What? Where are you?' I ask, confused. Everly is talking frantically as she stands up and moves to the landline.

"Driving to get Casey, I... I feel off, and I can't feel her. Why is she blocking me out?"

"Yeah, I'm trying her cell now," I hear Everly say as she dials a number into the house phone.

'Hang on, Everly's calling someone.'

"I'm trying Ava's phone," she says. I listen to it ring out.

"I'll try my father," I hear her say as she starts dialing more numbers with shaking hands. I make my way over to her when Marcus suddenly screams through the mind-link before it cuts off. My heart races at the agony in his voice. I instantly try to reopen it, but I get nothing but howling through the link—he's shifted.

Zoe

Half an hour earlier

"Did you grab the paint thinners?" I ask Ava as we line up at the hardware store. She rummages through her basket and holds up the tin, and I nod. We're revamping some outdoor furniture and stopped on our way to the school to grab a few things before picking up the kids.

"You think it'll get it off?" Ava asks, reading the instructions on the back.

"Yeah, it'll work. Just don't get it on your skin, it burns like a bitch," I tell her while we go through the self–checkout. I take the tins from her and quickly scan them, then pay for our items before walking back out to my little car.

We're loading everything into the trunk when I hear the screech of tires on the road and we look over our shoulders to see a red van race past at alarming speeds. Both of us watch the commotion on the main street before the car leaves our sight.

"Geez! Asshole. It's school time," Ava says, shaking her head. I sigh, quickly closing the trunk before climbing into the driver's side.

I've just started the car and Ava is climbing into the passenger seat when my phone rings—it's Marcus checking if I'm still set to grab the kids. I tell him we're on our way to the school, he promises to meet me at home, then we quickly hang up.

Ava and I buckle up and pull out onto the road. We're driving past the reserve toward Valen's pack school when we hear the roar of an engine coming up fast behind us. Ava looks behind me and groans.

"It's the dickhead from the hardware store," she says, turning back to the front. Must be the day for idiot drivers. Just as I'm going around a slight bend, I'm jolted forward in my seat and my head hits the steering wheel. I vaguely hear Ava scream and the sound of creaking metal before everything goes black.

My head pounds when my vision returns and pain slithers up my spine. The smell of oil and rubber reaches my nose, along with the scent of blood. Dazedly, I blink, but my eyes blur and throb to the same beat as my head. Smoke and dust fill the car from the smashed windows.

My hands hang above my head and I slowly realize I'm upside-down—we've crashed. I try to remember what happened, but I groan, dazed and pained. Looking over at Ava, she also groans before tugging at her belt. I try to warn her and reach for her, but it's too late; she undoes her seatbelt and crashes onto the roof of my upturned vehicle.

I try to put my hand on the roof to support my weight when shooting pain races through my hand. I shriek, looking at it to find my thumb dislocated. Ava unclips my seat belt without warning and I immediately land on my busted hand.

"Zoe, what happened?" Ava murmurs, clutching her head. My surroundings spin as I roll onto my back and glance out the window. We're in the reserve. How long have we been out for?

"The truck," I groan. As I roll back onto my side, and through the broken window, I see feet racing toward us. A gasp escapes me and my eyes widen when I see a man reach in through the broken window and grip Ava's hair just before she can turn to see what I'm looking at. He starts yanking her through the smashed, mangled window and she screams and thrashes. I grip her legs, trying to hold her, but she's torn from my grip.

Her screams ring out loudly until a man I've never seen before punches her and knocks her out—her body goes limp and he lifts her over his shoulder. I crawl out the window of my wrecked vehicle to try to stop him somehow, only I've forgotten about the other two sets of feet I saw.

As I scream for them to let her go, arms wrap around my torso. Twisting, I attempt to turn in the man's grip, trying to get loose before I sink my teeth into his bicep. He growls and lets go, allowing me to escape his clutches. The man with Ava is walking up the steep incline and I chase after. Before I can reach her, I'm tackled and the air is expelled from my lungs with an *oomph*.

"What do you want to do with this one?" a deep baritone voice calls out above me as I thrash, trying to get out from under him—his knee presses into the center of my back, crushing my lungs further.

"Bring her. The boss may let us keep her," I hear another voice call out. The man above rolls me over, his hand wraps around my throat, and he smiles cruelly, his dark hair falling into his eyes. I wheeze, trying to catch my breath. Suddenly, I feel the mind-link open up and Marcus' voice flits through the mind-link.

'Babe?' Marcus says before he screams. *'Babe!'*

'Marcus!' I shriek.

"Oh, we'll have fun with you, alright," the man growls, flashing his teeth as I try to free myself. I scream when I feel his tongue roll across the side of my face and he groans lewdly. His friend behind him is laughing. I try to alert Marcus, but a fist connects with the side of my head. I gaze dizzily up at the sky, my eyes losing focus before I'm hit again and see nothing but darkness.

Ava

Motion and bumps wake me. We're in the back of a van and my hands are tied behind my back. My fingers feel like they're losing circulation and I hit the side wall before hearing a chuckle.

I look up only to be kicked in the stomach by the man sitting along the side wall; his legs are what I slid into. I grunt at the impact and a whimper escapes me as I roll on my trapped arms. I can't even catch my breath before I'm winded again when the van stops, causing me to roll onto the other side. The double back doors are swung open and I suck in a harsh breath as pain rattles through all of me. I can taste my own blood and smell... smell...

Turning my head, I search for Zoe to find her also tied up and another man with ash blonde hair pawing at her and squeezing her breasts. Her chest is littered with bite marks, her shirt has been torn off her, and she's only left in her bra and black pants. Zoe is unconscious and completely limp. Fear coils and slivers through me. *No!* I gasp. I struggle against my restraints and growl at him.

"Don't touch her, you sick fucks!" I scream at him when I see the man push his hand down her pants. At the same time, I feel a pinch in my neck and the dark-haired man waves a syringe in front of my face.

"That'll do bitch. Now quiet, or you'll get a taste of what she gets," the man who kicked me says. He sweeps his dark hair from his eyes before gripping my arm and dragging me from the back of the van. I feel funny. My vision tunnels, though I remain conscious. However, I'm helpless as I feel the drug take effect; I can feel the wolfsbane burning through my system, stunning my wolf and muting the mind-link. I curse at myself—I should have played dead and alerted my father.

I'm tossed onto the cold, concrete floor. My head bounces off it painfully when Zoe falls beside me.

"Zoe?" I groan. She's drenched in blood. I know I am too, but she has a deep gash across her forehead and blood is dribbling out of the corner of her mouth.

"Zoe!" I cry when I see the man who stabbed me in the neck also stab a needle into hers. She doesn't respond. When I hear more footsteps, my eyes try to glance around, but my body is paralyzed, and it isn't until the footsteps draw close enough that I can see his face.

Carter.

A growl vibrates and dies in my chest. He's wearing a dark blue suit and looks like his father, only more unhinged. His eyes are half red and half green like snake eyes, the aftermath of being forsaken. His scent is also off—not rogue but also not like a pack wolf either. His hair is styled messily, like he's run his fingers through his gelled hair. Tattoos on his chest poke out from under the open buttons on his white dress shirt and on his arms where his sleeves are rolled to the elbows.

"Who is that?" Carter asks, motioning toward Zoe with his hand.

"Some whore she was with. I think Ava called her Zoe?" the dark-haired man says while looking over at his buddy, who shrugs.

"Uh... just a rogue whore," the blonde man says.

She isn't. She's Beta Marcus' mate, I try to rasp out, but my tongue thickens, swelling in my mouth and my words are not even audible with the way they are slurred. My heart races in my chest when I see him bend down and grip her face, turning it to look at her.

"She's marked," Carter sneers.

I watch as Carter stands up and nudges her onto her back with his foot. He sighs, looking at his men before his eyes roam over her half-undressed body.

"Do what you want with that one. No one touches John's daughter, though; I need her alive for now," Carter says, and the two men chuckle darkly. The blonde man licks his lips as he bends down to grab her.

My heart sinks into my stomach, a pit forming as I watch her get tossed over his shoulder before I'm also grabbed. We appear to be in some sort of warehouse, but as they move toward a door, we're suddenly descending stairs. I try to take everything in, looking for an escape and trying to remember my way through the tunnels as they navigate the twists and turns.

We seem to be in the old emergency evacuation tunnels that run beneath the city. They were all supposed to have been closed up years ago. But it's obvious Nixon's pack has been opening them, because after about 10 minutes of walking, I'm deposited onto the cold floor in a part that opens up wider, creating a large space. Zoe is dumped beside me and when she hits the hard ground, she grunts as she comes to. She blinks rapidly as she wheezes, trying to catch her breath.

Her eyes fall on me. Tears burn my eyes and she opens her mouth, but like me, she can't get her tongue to work. Yet, it doesn't stop her blood-curdling scream when one of the men starts ripping her pants off. I want to help her, yet I'm powerless to do anything but watch and listen to her screams. I sob when Carter wanders into the room, his shoes loud on the concrete as he saunters over to me and crouches beside me. He peers over his shoulder as his men fight over who will get her first, then smirks and taps my face in his hand.

"Don't worry, Ava. I will make sure you get to watch," he purrs, sweeping my hair away from my eyes. "Should have taken me up on the marriage proposal. Oh well." He clucks his tongue.

"Your sister and father made an enemy of the wrong person. But," he pauses and laughs when Zoe screams again and I watch one of the men run a blade between her breasts, cutting her bra away. All she can do is lie there and watch what they do to her—*feel* what they do to her. A whimper escapes me.

"Now, if Valen and your father don't meet my demands, that will be you next," he says before rising.

The dark-haired man shoves her legs open and pushes inside her. Zoe cries and pleads for a while before her screams die out and she just stares off vacantly, her eyes fixed on the ceiling, like she suddenly becomes an empty shell.

I scream and cry, clenching my eyes shut, unable to watch as they rape her, praying someone will get to us before they kill her. But as the hours drag on, I lose track of time. At regular intervals, I'm jabbed, just like Zoe, with a needle.

I have no idea how much time has passed. We must have dozed off when I hear footsteps of the two men and Carter returning, along with another man. Carter nods toward his men, who then drag a screaming Zoe from the room, down the tunnel, and around the corner into the next room. Once again, her screams ring out loudly, and I throw up, choking on my vomit as it suffocates me.

I pray it will kill me. I can't handle her screams, her cries, or what I've seen. I want to tear my eyes from my head to unsee the horrible things they did to her, the horrible things I was forced to watch, and the vile things she's enduring.

Only, death doesn't come.

Carter swiftly walks over, turning my head enough that I don't aspirate on my own vomit.

"There, that's better. Can you see? Don't want you to miss the show," he taunts, wiping my wet eyes before he grabs my hair and drags me through my vomit so I have a better view of the new man raping my friend. Anger burns through me and I roar, my fury forcing words out.

"I hope Marcus rips you to shreds, you fucking pig!" I scream and Carter laughs and drops me on the floor. The back of my head smashes the pavement just before I see his foot come toward my face and everything goes black.

Time is lost to me when I come to. I have feeling in my limbs, yet my mind feels stunted. Warmth presses against my back and a body shakes, which makes me turn my head to find Zoe huddled beside me, her knees clutched to her chest—the dead look in her gaze is agonizing. Sluggishly, I pull myself up to a sitting position and lean against the wall she's leaning against. I press closer to her, trying to warm her naked form; she looks like she's been bathed in blood.

"Zoe?" I murmur, but she just stares vacantly ahead. I turn my head to find Carter on the phone.

"I'll hand the little one back; send the rogue to get her. But Ava stays until you stand down and hand the city back over to Valen. And don't forget my money," he snarls into the phone before hanging it up.

"What's going on?" one of the men asks, glancing over at us.

"Grab her. Her friend is going to do the exchange at the bridge."

"And if she doesn't bring the money with her?"

"Then we toss her over, but Everly won't risk her sister. You, watch Ava," he says to the ash-blonde one.

"Grab the bitch. She's coming with us."

"What about Valen?" the dark-haired man says.

"Not an issue. He knows if he follows the woman, I kill Ava. He wants her back? He stands down as Alpha and relinquishes his pack to me," Carter says and I gasp.

"And John?" the man asks.

"He wants to swap places with his daughter. We'll let him sweat it for a bit, maybe send him some pictures. But I think our only chance is keeping her. John will die for his girls, and Valen knows that. We aren't doing the swap. Besides, I want John to live with the knowledge he's the reason his family is dead."

"Well, obviously. But what next?"

"Once Valen stands down, the city is ours. Then I'll get revenge on Alpha John when I kill his daughters and grandson," Carter says, confusing me.

"And her?" he motions toward me.

"We kill her. But first, we'll play with her," he cackles loudly while walking out. The dark-haired man moves toward us and reaches for Zoe, who spits on him. He backhands her and I launch forward only to be kicked in the face by the other man as she's dragged out kicking and screaming by her hair.

THIRTY-THREE

V alen

We find Marcus when we locate the car down a ravine by the reserve. He's furious, and I can't get a coherent thought out of him—whatever he's feeling through the bond is making him want blood. He's more crazed than any forsaken I've come across; it takes 12 of my men with me to take him down. We have to sedate him, which only causes fear to twist in my stomach.

Zoe's car is on its roof—tire tracks in the mud tell us they were run off the road—but there's no sign of the girls. We have the entire city out looking for them. None of us can locate them via the mind-link. Slasher pack is also out searching further away. John is beside himself and Everly is a frantic mess. In a matter of minutes, our worlds were once again turned upside down. I had sent men out looking for Carter and he was located quickly. He gave the council the all-clear to search his pack but they found nothing. Everly is convinced Nixon has come back and taken them, but makes no sense.

They've been missing for two days when the first ransom call comes in.

A growl tears out of me when I hear Everly answer the call and Carter's voice is on the other end.

"Now that I have your attention, and you have been unable to locate them, you will meet my demands," Carter states.

Everly stares at the phone, checking the number—it's definitely Carter's. She puts him on the loudspeaker and my brows furrow. The bastard even helped us search his pack territory! Is this some sick game to him?

"Carter?" I ask.

"Hello, Valen," Carter drawls through the phone.

"Done wasting resources? Though I'm shocked at how hard you searched for... Zoe, is it?"

"You vile bastard! Marcus will kill you when he gets his hands on you," I growl at him while opening the mind-link.

"I never touched her," he claims.

'Find Carter! He has them,' I call to my pack through the link.

"Well, that was fast," he says, confusing me.

"Excuse me?"

"Two seconds. You didn't waste any time. I haven't even asked for anything yet, and you've already called across the mind-link. You won't find me," he adds, then laughs.

I look at Everly. I knew he was crazy, but this is a whole other level.

"You have a mole," he states. "Don't be surprised—you have plenty of enemies in this city. It shouldn't come as a shock to know one lives in your pack."

Fuck! That renders the mind-link useless.

"Where are Ava and Zoe?" I demand.

"With me, of course. Now call off your men or I'll send Zoe back in pieces."

Everly whimpers beside me and I glance at her, the blood draining from her face. Macey bursts into the living room and rushes to Everly's side, then helps her sit down when she sees the look on her friend's face; Macey's been staying here while we organize search parties.

"What do you want? I swear if you've hurt them–" Though I know he already has, by the fact my Beta has had to be sedated for two days.

"You'll do nothing, Valen. I am calling the shots. Now, I have two requests. One, I want the money John owes. Two, you stand down as Alpha, hand your pack over to me, and leave the city, leaving your mate and son behind until I know you are far enough away for me to escape."

"Like fuck, I will! Hand them over and we can talk this out," I tell him.

"Uh, uh, uh, you're not in a position to compromise. As I said, *I'm* calling the shots, not you. As a sign of goodwill, I want the money by 5:00 p.m.—I will select the meeting spot—and send Everly to drop the money–"

"No!" I snarl, cutting him off.

"I don't think you understand the position you're in, Valen."

"I'll do it," Macey says. I glance at her and Everly shakes her head, trying to get out of her seat, but I growl, telling her to sit down.

"See, you have a volunteer. May I know who the brave lady is?" Carter asks and Macey growls. "Oh, she sounds feisty," he chuckles.

"You're a sadistic prick!"

"Oh, you have no idea how sadistic. But nonetheless, money at 5:00 p.m.. I will call with the drop-off point and tell her where to go. In return, I will give her Zoe. Once you see I made good on this, then we move on to the next part."

"You want me out of the city? That's fine, but I am taking my mate and son with me."

"That isn't what I agreed to, but for now, I need the money. If anyone follows her, I will get one of my men to slit Ava's throat."

Everly gasps at his words, making my eyes dart to her briefly.

"Why are you doing this?"

"I don't know. Why *am* I doing this? Maybe I'm just a sadistic prick," he laughs.

"Do as he says, Valen, please," Everly begs with tears in her eyes, though her rage is evident through the bond.

"Take the deal. I'll meet him," Macey growls.

"So the girl, what's her name?"

"Her name is Macey."

"Ah, the rogue whore. I heard about her—quite the brute."

Macey growls, snatching up the phone. She gives Carter her number, and Everly starts calling banks to empty accounts to come up with the money.

It just makes no sense. And who is the mole in my pack? There is only one way for him to know I used the mind-link—one of my men is with him.

"One person follows her, and I kill Ava," Carter snarls as Macey hands the phone to me.

"Yeah, yeah. I fucking heard you." I'm about to hang up when he speaks again.

"I'll hand the little one back; send the rogue to get her. But Ava stays until you stand down and hand the city back over to Valen. And don't forget my money," he snarls into the phone before hanging it up.

"He had them all this time," Everly says, her hands shaking as she rubs her face with them, wiping the tears away. "I have to tell my father" she murmurs, getting to her feet and passing me the phone that she was on the bank with.

I send Officer Derrick to retrieve the cash and bring it here while I have Doc sent over to give Macey a dose of the cure in case Carter tries anything. Then we wait by the phone for it to ring.

John comes over with my father, and the moment the phone rings, he pounces on it and begs to swap places with Ava. According to my father, John had called Carter on the way here, but Carter refused.

This whole scenario is bizarre, and I can't figure it out—none of us can. We thought Carter was a victim in this. That's how he portrayed himself when his father fled. We found him in a padded room for fuck's sake. Was it all an act?

"Put the girl on," Carter snarls, obviously getting sick of John's begging. John hands the phone to Macey.

"Get in your car. I will tell you the directions. One person follows and Ava is dead, so don't try anything," he snarls. Macey swallows and looks at us.

Taylor comes out from up the hall, tears brimming in her eyes. My father instantly tends to her, escorting her off.

"Do as I say and no one gets hurt," Carter says, and Macey lets out a shaky breath.

Everly goes to pick up the duffle bag, but I take it from her and place it over Macey's shoulder. Officer Derrick stops Macey as she passes him and holds a finger to his lips. He pulls his gun from his holster and turns the safety off and on to show her. She nods before he tucks it down the back of her pants.

Macey's also wearing a tracking device and voice recorder tucked in her bra and the council is already alerted—there is no way he's leaving this city once I stand down. But what's the point of that if he intends to leave? All it would do is sever my ability to mind-link, and I know my people won't bow for any other Alpha. Except, of course, whoever the traitor in my pack is.

It just makes no sense. I watch helplessly as she walks out the doors, knowing he's watching from somewhere outside. I want to go with her, but it isn't worth the risk; I know Ava would be killed. For now, I'll play his game until the council returns.

Then I will kill him.

M acey

My stomach is in knots.

The gun digs into my lower back as I follow Carter's directions—he has me driving around the city for ages like he's wasting my time.

"Turn at the next roundabout and double back."

This is the sixth loop of the city. I know he's making sure I'm not followed, but Valen won't risk Ava and Zoe, I know that much. Carter's an idiot if he thinks Valen won't come after him for this, though. And Marcus will kill whoever hurt Zoe when he wakes. Even the rogues will hunt the bastard down for what he did.

"Pull over by the post office sorting facility."

I do as he says, yet I see no one, not even any cars.

"Get out of the car, walk up the alley, and place the bag by the bin."

"Where is Zoe?" I growl.

"Dump the bag first."

"Not until I have Zoe!" I snarl.

"Little stupid making demands, don't you think? Very well, Zoe is with me."

"And where are you?" I ask.

"Close. Now dump the bag."

"No! Not until I have Zoe!"

Carter snarls. "Foolish woman," he sneers, and Zoe shrieks in the background.

"Okay! Okay!" I yell, shoving the door open. We're close to the old meat factory. This part of town is dead, but I have a sneaky suspicion he's in one of these warehouses.

I grab the bag from the back seat, glancing around.

"There is a dumpster and one of my men is up there. Once you hand the bag over, I will tell you where to find your friend."

I growl but do as he says. A man with dark hair smiles and waves as I draw closer.

"That's close enough, drop the bag," he calls.

"Do as he says," Carter adds.

I do. I hear a car pull up behind me and my heart rate picks up.

"Back up, slowly," the man says, leveling his gun at me. I raise my hands in the air, backing up like he asked, the phone clutched in my hand; I'm aware a car has pulled up down by mine at the end of the alley. The man backs away, before rushing off.

I hear a car door open and hear a grunt behind me and a whimper.

"You can turn around. Tell Valen this is a warning. If he doesn't heed the warning, what happens next is on him," Carter says and I turn around.

I notice Zoe first, wearing only a man's shirt and covered in blood. I scream, dropping the phone and rushing toward her just as his scent hits me. A man shoves her forward to her knees and I stop in my tracks as I peer at him—no doubt that is Carter. He appears just as shocked and I stagger, my heart nearly stopping.

No! No! Not him! Anyone but him!

Yet, my entire body screams *mate*!

"Macey!" Zoe screams, pulling us both out of our stunned stand-off. He shakes his head, racing back toward his car while I race toward Zoe. She screams again and the sound tears my soul apart. Her entire body shakes as I fall to my knees to clutch her, grazing them as I fall.

"He still has Ava!" she cries. "You have to help her!"

Three male scents are all over her. Not Carter's, yet he let them do this to her. The stink of the man from the alleyway is all over her, along with another man's, but the third is the most disturbing when I pick up that scent. I know it. I'm about to say the name when she does.

"Micah! Micah is helping Carter!" she chokes out and sobs.

"Micah did this?" I ask and Zoe whimpers. Wait, does Derrick know his son is in on this?

"Where's Marcus? I want Marcus!" She whimpers as I haul her to her feet.

"I'll take you to him. Come, we need to get you to the hospital."

My stomach turns. How can I be mates to a monster? A monster that hurt Zoe! Hurt my sister! My blood boils in my veins, yet I contain it. He'll get what he deserves, and he absolutely deserves what's coming for him.

"My Casey? Oh my Goddess, Macey, where is Casey?"

Zoe is unbelievable. After whatever she endured, all she cares about is her mate and daughter. Her hands clutch me tightly, and I open the passenger side of my car, then help her in.

"She's with Everly. She's safe. But for now, I need to get you out of here and alert Valen about Officer Derrick's *son*." I snarl the last word.

THIRTY-FOUR

Everly

Macey calls me as soon as she gets Zoe, and I demand Valen take me to the hospital to meet them. Macey also said to bring Officer Derrick along with us, so we leave the kids with Kalen and my father while we go off to meet them.

My anxiety is through the roof as we wait. We're sitting in the room with Marcus, who's coming out of sedation. Valen is trying to calm him down because as soon as his eyes opened he was trying to climb out of bed.

My phone starts ringing; I pull it from my pocket and answer it to find it's Macey.

"I'm in a room a few doors down from Marcus. Hold off on letting him see her for a second. And come here. He shouldn't see her like this," she tells me. I glance at Valen, who's trying to hold Marcus in place. Officer Derrick whips out his handcuffs the moment Valen tells him and cuffs Marcus to the bed.

'Macey has asked me to go see Zoe. Are you alright with him for a second?' I mind-link Valen and he nods, looking at officer Derrick, who also nods. Officer Derrick follows me a few doors down and I

suck in a breath before opening the door and stepping in. What I could never have expected was the scene in front of me. Zoe is frantically fighting Macey, who's trying to restrain her and calm her down.

Nurses stand around her and a doctor with a syringe looks like he was about to try to sedate her. I growl at him. He drops the needle, stepping away from her, and Zoe's eyes snap to me; so does Macey's, though the snarl that leaves her when officer Derrick walks in behind me is thunderous. The next second, she's pulled his gun on him.

"Macey!" I hiss in shock, rushing to Zoe, who clutches my arms. Macey refuses to lower the gun, but I'm more focused on Zoe, who won't let go of me, begging and pleading to be able to see Marcus and Casey.

"Shhh. Breathe, Zoe. Deep breaths. Marcus is fine. You can see him in a minute," I whisper. Tears burn my eyes at seeing her so frantic. She reeks of multiple wolves' scents, but I pick up one familiar scent. One that has my head turning toward Officer Derrick.

"Out!" Macey snarls, pointing the gun at him. He holds his hands up and does as she asks, stepping out of the room while she follows after him.

'Valen, get to Derrick before Macey shoots him. She's in the hall,' I mind link, turning my attention back to Zoe.

"I just want my baby! I want my Casey!" Zoe sobs, her nails digging into my arms.

My eyes run over her. She's a mess, covered in blood, and I swallow against the pain in her voice, the desperation. I don't even think she registered Macey has left—her mind only has one focus, and that is to get to her family.

"Okay. But you don't want to scare Casey, do you?" I ask her and she appears to be confused. I grip her hands, prying them off my arms where she drew blood with her nails.

"You don't want to scare Casey, Zoe," I tell her, holding her hands up in front of her face. She blinks at me before noticing the blood on her hands.

"I promise I will take you to them. But you need to let the nurses check you over and..." I swallow, looking at them. "They need to take some swabs, so we can get those that hurt you. So they don't hurt anyone else," I tell her and she blinks, staring at her hands that tremble violently.

"I don't want to scare Casey," she murmurs.

"That's right, we don't want to scare Casey. I am right here, okay. But I need you to lie down so we can make sure you're okay." I feel stupid saying that. I know she isn't okay.

"I'm right here," I tell her, nudging her toward the bed before turning to the doctor.

"Get a female doctor. You're not touching her," I tell him, and he rushes out.

Casey mutters to herself as she lies down. I can see she's in shock, and she appears to remain in that state while doctors and nurses clean her up and run their tests. Suddenly, she lurches upright.

"Ava!" she gasps with wide eyes. "They still have Ava! You have to help her!"

Tears prick my eyes at her words, some escaping and slipping down my face.

"I know. But for now, my focus is on you," I tell her.

Doc comes in. I'm about to tell him to get out because we have the female doctor here and that he isn't really needed, but Zoe sits up.

"Marcus?" she asks, her voice pleading.

"He is down the hall. I can take you to him. But first, I have some officers who want to take a statement from you," Doc tells her. He smiles at me sadly.

"No! I want my mate." she says, shaking her head.

"Can you do this one thing first? Just this one thing and then he'll take you to Marcus," I tell her a moment before I hear a howling wail from outside. Zoe, understandably in shock, doesn't seem to notice it as she lies back down when a female officer comes in. I bite my lip, wondering what's going on out in the hall when Macey comes in.

I glance at her and she walks over to me.

"Micah was one of them," she whispers to me, and my stomach drops. He would do that to his daughter's mother? My blood boils, but it explains his scent and Derrick's reaction from down the hall.

Zoe gives her statement and we help her out of bed. She's wearing a hospital gown, and though she's been cleaned up, the nurses help us shower her to get rid of the scents that still linger on her. She's jumpy, but she also knows we're trying to help her—Zoe knows Macey and I would never hurt her. I nod for Doc to get Marcus.

The moment Marcus steps in the room, something snaps within her and she tears out of our grip. Her body crashes against his, sending him backward as he clutches her.

Valen walks in behind him and steps around them. The nurses quickly leave while we stay with the couple, watching all the broken parts of both of them shatter more as Marcus comes to the realization of what happened to her. No one told him, but he knows. That much is obvious when he sniffs her and his eyes go to Valen.

The murderous look on his face is evident. He wants blood. Valen nods to him in a silent message. *You will get it.*

"You're okay," Marcus whispers to her, tears slipping down his face as he rocks her.

"We're gonna be okay," he whispers repeatedly to her, using his mate bond to soothe her as she sobs against him.

'Derrick?' I mind-link Valen.

"Hunting his son."

'He had no idea?' I ask.

'No. I Commanded him—he had no idea. Apparently, Amber left Micah and took another as a mate. He's hardly seen his son since. Said he hasn't been of sound mind.'

I nod, clenching my teeth.

He will pay for what he's done, and so will Carter for allowing it.

240

We know he didn't touch her because his scent wasn't on her, but there were two more. I just pray Ava isn't being subjected to the same thing.

"I need to go. Can you watch Zoe? I'll be back soon," Macey whispers to me. My brows furrow but I nod to her—she probably wants to get changed out of her blood-soaked clothes.

"Are you heading home?" I ask and she nods.

"I just want to change and I need to check on Tatum. He's been blowing up my phone."

I nod, but I can't help feeling something is up with her, too. Or maybe it's the shock of everything. She leans down and touches Zoe's hair where she's sitting on the floor with Marcus.

Zoe looks up at her.

"I'll be back soon, okay," Macey tells her.

"Casey?" Zoe asks.

"I will check on her, okay? You'll see her soon," Macey tells her, and she nods.

Macey leaves when Doc comes in with a medicine cup in his hands and a bottle of water. He silently stands there, reading the room, and his eyes fall on Marcus as he watches for any reaction. Marcus is deadly calm as Doc explains what the tablets are; morning-after pills. Zoe stares at the little cup before she breaks down, putting her head in her hands.

"I can't. It's so wrong," she sobs.

"I will leave these over here for her if she wants them," Doc says, placing them on the little table and walking out.

Marcus talks to her.

I hate this. Zoe reflects my own thoughts of when I found out I was pregnant and my father demanded I get an abortion. However, seeing her struggle puts it into perspective. Our situations are so different. It seems silly that Zoe is worried she would be going against the Goddess; no goddess would condone this—condone someone's will being taken from them.

"If you want to take them, Zoe, no one is judging," Valen tells her.

"But the Goddess," Zoe whimpers.

"The Goddess will understand. The Goddess would give you the right to choose. And no choice is wrong. Everyone's situation is different and no one is judging. This isn't a judgment. You won't be judged for doing what you want to do," I tell her. Zoe seems unsure, yet I can tell she doesn't want to potentially carry her rapist's child.

"Choice. There is a reason the Goddess grants it. The only ones getting condemnation are those taking another's choice. Your body, your life. No one gets to tell you what you do with it. And no one has a right to judge your choice. They aren't the ones that have to live with it," I tell her, and Zoe nods.

"I don't want to—... I can't carry—..." She shakes her head.

My judgment and beliefs suddenly shift.

This is one of many circumstances where one should have the right to choose. This is not the work of any goddess, nor would any goddess punish someone for aborting a few cells. Now I understand why she gave us a choice. Why we get to choose. If all our stories were the same, why would our opinions on it be so different? If she wanted us all the same, why would situations be so different? Why are our fates different?

No one chooses this for themselves. Just like no one chooses poverty. Those that can't bear to bring a child into the world due to life circumstances—like poverty or rape—aren't heartless, they want to stop any future child from having to live with the torments or consequences of whatever existence they may face.

Options and choice.

Not all choices are made the same. And no one's choices should be judged when it comes to their own life or a life they would have to bring into the world—especially a life that would only know pain or judgment. No child should be forced into a world this way.

I hold the pills out for her and she looks at Marcus. He adds no input, letting her decide—the decision is her and hers alone.

She chooses.

She chooses to let the suffering end.

There is no right or wrong decision—it's not my life and not my place to judge, though it's the same decision I would have made.

Marcus hugs her tight as she hands the little cup back to me empty. I set it down and she lets out a breath. Marcus rests his head against the wall and Zoe looks at Valen.

"Micah is helping Carter," she whispers and Marcus growls. Valen crouches down next to her.

"I know. We'll get him," he promises her and she nods, wiping a stray tear before she looks at me just as Doc walks in. He nods his head, tossing the small cup in the bin.

"Can you tell us anything about where you were kept?" Valen asks her. She sniffles but answers.

"The old tunnels under the city. He was talking about getting vengeance for–" She looks at me. "He wants revenge on your father. I overheard him. He wants Valen to stand down as Alpha," she shakes her head like she's trying to remember something.

"He needs Valen to leave the city, so he can get–" Her eyes widen and she looks at me. "To kill you and Valarian! To get revenge on your father, he... I can't remember," she rubs her temples and Valen growls.

"The council will be here by tomorrow, but I bet Carter has moved. He wouldn't have stayed there after handing Zoe back," he says, looking at me.

I'm still stuck on what this had to do with my father. "My father? That's who said he wants to get revenge on?"

Zoe nods.

"So not Valen and me? But my father?" I ask. Hadn't Carter's father caused my family enough pain?

"Might have something to do with Rachel?" Doc says. I turn to look at him and so does Valen.

"Why does that name ring a bell for me?" Valen mutters.

"Nixon's first wife, the one Carter's mother killed. Rachel was close with your mother, Alpha," Doc says with a shrug.

"But what's that got to do with my father? She turned forsaken," I told him.

"No idea. But there was a lot of speculation around that time."

"What do you mean?"

"I knew Leah, I was her doctor when she was pregnant with her twins—I was sworn to keep quiet. So many conspiracies around that time and everything was swept under the rug, but even I heard about the rumors when Leah disappeared."

"No. She left," Valen says.

"That's what everyone thinks, but rumors still went around that your father banished Leah from the city. Though I can't be sure they were just rumors," Doc tells me.

"Wait. Why would my father banish her?"

"Because she was Nixon's mate and was from the Shadow pack. She was one of your father's pack members," Doc answers. "They are just rumors, of course. I suppose the only people who really know what happened are Nixon and Leah," he shrugs.

"But Nixon admitted to abandoning her and forcing her forsaken."

"Doesn't mean it is the truth," Doc says. "I knew Leah and there was no way she would have left Carter. And Nixon loved her. He was forced to marry Rachel for the pack alliance."

"Pack Alliance?"

"I'm not sure, but maybe you should ask your fathers; that was their time ruling. Or maybe check the council files. There has to be some record of what happened. It's no secret that the Alphas have a way of covering their tracks, yet that doesn't stop the rumors."

CHAPTER
THIRTY-FIVE

A^{va}

Carter had me moved, and I appear to be in some basement. I must have been asleep for a few hours when I finally hear the door open and the man I hadn't recognized in my dazed state comes down the stairs. He has a blue cap on his head and a handkerchief tied around his face like last time. But his scent is familiar, not just from the last time I saw him, and I cant figure out why at first. Yet as my sense of smell and taste returns, my eyes widen when I finally recognize the scent—a scent I used to smell around Amber.

Micah!

He walks over to me where I sit in the corner with my wrist handcuffed to a drainpipe. He produces a needle and stabs it into my thigh, and I yank on my restraints. Snarling at him as he simply turns and walks back toward the stairs. My eyes begin to blur again, yet I fight to keep them open.

"Micah," I try to call. My voice is barely a murmur, yet it's enough to make him freeze on the bottom step, his entire body tense as he grips the handrail. Slowly, he turns and his eyes roam over me, and I know undoubtedly it's him. Something shrivels inside me and dies as it dawns on me that he raped the mother of his child.

"When they kill you, I hope it's slow," I growl at him, though the words are hard to get out.

He growls and stalks back toward me. "They will never know, and you won't be alive to tell them," he sneers, gripping the back of my hair. I glare at him.

"No woman forgets the face of the man who fathered her child, just like they never forget the face of their rapist," I sneer at him, and he shoves me back. My head bangs on the pipe and he rips his hat off, clutches his hair, and screams in frustration.

"Fuck!" he curses, kicking a wooden chair. "I had no fucking choice. Do you think I could just stand there and watch? They would have fucking killed me!"

"You deserve far worse for what you did, and I can't wait for Marcus to give it to you," I spit at him through clenched teeth.

"She won't remember. They drugged her," he says, shaking his head. I don't know if he's trying to convince himself of that or me. Either way, he's wrong. Zoe was out of it, but she wasn't that far gone. She wouldn't have missed a scent she was accustomed to through her daughter.

My head spins and throbs where I hit it. Micah scratches his chin, then snarls and starts wandering around the basement, looking at the shelves before snatching a piece of timber.

"I am not going to jail because of you," he sneers, tapping the timber on the palm of his hand. My eyes open frantically as he stalks toward me and I yank on the cuffs in a last-ditch effort to free myself.

"They don't need to know, and Carter was planning on killing you anyway," he says slowly, trying to convince himself this would work. He lifts the piece of timber, and I gasp when he swings it, clenching my eyes shut in preparation for the hit, only I hear a crash instead. My eyes open and I sag against the wall in a huffed wheeze when I see Carter shove him. I didn't even hear him come in.

"WHAT THE FUCK DO YOU THINKG YOU'RE DOING?" Carter

bellows, gripping the front of his shirt. Micah is on his back, hands up in surrender. Carter snarls at him before shoving him. Yet, the tension rolling off Carter is palpable; his Alpha aura is menacing as he straightens his suit, picks up the knocked-over wooden chair, places it upright, and takes a seat with his head in his hands.

"Zoe?" I murmur. My lip quivers. Carter's head lifts and his eyes go to me before flicking away.

"Your friend is alive. The rogue girl, Macey, got her," he says, staring off blankly at the concrete wall behind me. He mutters, but my ears can't pick up the sound, and I let out a breath of relief. At least Zoe is alright. Micah sits up and tries to get to his feet.

Carter watches him, and his lips press in a line when the two thugs from before come down the stairs. My muscles start to go numb and tears burn my eyes when they move toward me.

"Don't touch her," Carter snaps at them, and they pause, looking at him. "No one touches her," Carter repeats, looking at each of them.

"But you said—" the dark-haired man begins.

"I said no one touches her."

"Geez, bro, what crawled up your ass?"

"Nothing, I just need to think," Carter says, rubbing his temples before running his fingers through his thick, blonde hair. The two thugs look at each other before looking at me. Micah also appears confused as he glances between the three men.

Carter's phone rings. He looks at the screen, and a silly smile splits his face before he looks up, noticing everyone watching him. Quickly rejecting the call, he looks back at his men before his eyes fall on Micah briefly. He nods to the other two, who instantly snarl and start stalking Micah while he backs up.

"Wait, what's the meaning of this? Carter, we had a deal," Micah says.

"Deal changed because now my plans have changed. Throw him in the trunk while I figure out what to do next," Carter says. Micah fights but is no match for the two men, who quickly overpower him.

"Wait, why have our plans changed? I thought we were killing the bitch and kid?" the blonde-haired man asks while holding a struggling Micah.

"I need to think of something else first. Something has come up."

"So, what do you want us to do?"

Carters ponders for a second and bites his lip, looking at the ceiling.

"We hand over a peace offering. And get me everything you have on that rogue girl, Macey," he says, and the men look at each other, confused; my brows furrow.

The dark-haired man licks his lips. "The feisty bitch? I wouldn't mind taking a bite out of h–"

His words cut off when Carter launches out of the chair and punches him. The man staggers back and Micah uses that chance to escape up the steps. The blonde man gives chase, yet I can't tear my eyes from Carter. His face is barely recognizable and he's pummeling his man bloody before he stomps his head into the ground, spilling blood and brain matter everywhere as he kills the man right in front of me. Horrified at the display of violence, I remain quiet and still.

The blonde man returns, stomping down the steps, but stops when he sees his dead friend. When Carter stands upright, he shrugs his suit jacket off and tosses it on the broken chair before slowly undoing the buttons on what was a white shirt, now stained red. I watch the blonde man's Adam's Apple bob in his throat as he swallows.

"Find Brendan, clean this piece of shit up, and get me another shirt," Carter snaps at him without so much as a stutter, like killing his pack member means nothing to him.

"Uh, Boss, Micah–"

"Fuck Micah! He can get himself out of his shit. I have bigger issues. Now get me everything on that Macey girl and get this place cleaned up. And fucking feed her, and get her a drink," he says, pointing to me. The man nods swiftly, rushing off up the steps to do his bidding.

Carter removes his shirt and moves to a rusty sink basin in the far corner, washing his bloody hands before drying them on a rag. When he's finished, he pulls his phone from his pocket, types in a message, and smiles to himself.

I watch him—his entire demeanor changes when his phone rings. He answers it.

"Hello, little mate," Carter purrs and a gasp leaves me. Who is he speaking to?

Macey

My head is swimming. I can't bring myself to tell them about Carter being my mate. I want nothing to do with the vile man that would allow the woman I consider to be my sister to be violated the way she was. Shame courses through me.

I feel like I don't deserve to be around her after what my mate has done to her. Am I cursed when it comes to men? Am I a bad omen for my girls? I'm seriously considering it. My mate ruined Zoe's life and kidnapped Everly's sister, and his father is responsible for killing Everly's mother.

Carter being my mate leaves multiple additional issues because unless Tatum marks me, I'm as good as dead once I reject Carter—and I *will* be rejecting him. But then what will happen to Taylor? Who will look after her and love her the way I do? My Mom is getting old, plus she has my brother and his mate living with her, and as much as I love my brother, he isn't exactly a good role model.

After showering and checking in with Kalen and the kids, I head over to see Tatum. At the moment, he's the only good thing in my life other than Taylor. Everything feels like it's falling into tatters, and I have no idea how to come back from this. I saw the hell Everly went through without Valen—saw how Kalen's rejection killed Valarie—so what will me rejecting Carter do? What will be the consequence of that?

Walking down the corridor to his ward, I stop and speak with his physical therapist. Her name is Tracey and she's the one helping us get him back on his feet. She warns me he's in a mood before I leave her to head to find his room. I know something is wrong before I even open the door. I can hear him cursing and hear glass break as he tosses something.

Pushing the door open, I find Tatum on the ground, his crutches by the bed.

"Stupid fucking leg!" he curses with a growl. Immediately, I rush to his side, gripping under his arms to help pull him.

"Why didn't you use the crutches?" I ask him when he pushes me away, forcing me to drop him. He grunts, and I move to help him again when he snarls at me.

"Just fucking leave me, Macey! Stop fucking mothering me!" he snaps. I roll my eyes. I've put up with his pity parties before, only this time, I ignore him and retrieve the wheelchair, pushing it beside him. He growls angrily at me and punches it.

"Just fuck off! For once in your Goddess damn life, Macey, stop trying to fix everything!" he snaps. I start to reply when he holds up a hand, cutting me off. "Don't! I am fucking sick of it! I am useless! And I don't want you feeling sorry for me."

"I don't feel sorry for you. You'll be fine. Tracey said you did great today. It's only a matter of time, and soon you'll be walking around," I tell him, trying to lift his mood. "Want the crutches instead?" I ask him, moving to retrieve them.

"Get out!" Tatum snarls at me, and I freeze, glancing at him over my shoulder.

"Pardon?"

"You just can't help yourself. Always gotta try to fix everything. My leg is fucked, Macey. It ain't getting any better, and I am sick of you telling me it will! So just get out! This isn't going to work," he says, turning to look away.

"Tatum? You're just having a bad day, you'll see. I can help you shower, then how about we go outside?" I tell him, leaning down and offering him my hand. He slaps it away.

"I said leave! I don't want you here! Are you fucking deaf?" he snaps, yet his words piss me off and before I realize it, I've slapped him.

"You dare speak to me like this after everything? Where the fuck is your family? Huh? Who has been here every fucking day? You don't get to speak to me that way. You think you're the only one having a shitty day?" I snap at him while he rubs his cheek. I know he's upset about his leg and needing help and relying on people, but that is no reason to take it out on me.

"I am fucking useless, don't you see that? I couldn't even help you today to get Zoe back. I had to hear about it through the damn mind-link!" Tatum yells.

"No one expected your help, Tatum. We had it handled. And I am not here to visit your damn fucking leg. I am here because for once, I need you," I tell him.

"Well, I don't want you here. I am sick of you babying me, so just leave."

I growl that he's trying to kick me out and click my tongue. Fine, Tracey can deal with his stupid ass and I'll see him tomorrow.

"I get you're upset, so I'll just leave you and come see you tomorrow," I tell him, heading toward the door before I end up beating him senselessly or breaking his other damn leg. I so do not need this drama right now. I just wanted to spend time with him, maybe get a hug, so I could pretend for a few moments everything is okay.

As I grip the door handle, Tatum speaks, making me stop.

"Macey?" he says, and I look at him just as he pulls himself up to sit on the edge of the bed.

"Don't come back tomorrow. I've been thinking about it all day, and I can see it isn't going to work. So please don't make this harder than it needs to be for once. Just do as I ask."

I swallow, my throat suddenly clogged, and my eyes burn with the urge to break down. He's seriously going to break up with me? Over a leg? Or is he using it as an excuse since I can't give him a kid? I start to ask, needing to know, when he shakes his head.

"Just go, Macey. We're done," he says, and my eyebrows raise.

I really am cursed. Suddenly, I find myself speechless. I don't know how to answer, so I just nod my head before walking out.

Yet another thing was just taken from me. I just needed to pretend, if only briefly, that I would find a solution where there was none. I needed to pretend someone other than a monster would want me. Clearly, I'm not even allowed that moment's grace.

I can't stop the tears when I climb back into the car. Everything is so fucked up! It feels stupid crying—pointless, and a waste of time—yet I can't seem to stop as I head toward the hotel. I can't go back to Everly and Zoe like this. They have enough stress at the moment, so instead, I go to work. I need the distraction.

When I pull up, I see the project manager out front talking to someone in a suit before realizing it's Everly's lawyer. He must be here to drop off the new deeds to the place. Getting out of my car, I learn that is precisely what he's here for.

He hands me the paperwork and goes over it with me on the hood of my car. When he's done, he bids me farewell. I watch him walk back to his car when I call out to him.

"Uh, Joseph? I don't suppose I can ask for your help with something?"

He stops. "Of course. What is it you need?" he asks.

"Everything I tell you is confidential, right?" I ask him.

"Yes. If you are my client, it is. Why do you ask?"

"Because I need to do something, but I don't want Everly and Zoe finding out."

His brows furrow. "May I ask what it is?"

"Last will and testament, and also some custody documents."

"A will and guardian for Taylor, I assume?"

I nod.

"Well, the first step is the guardian must agree. You can't just leave her to a family member, though that is usually where they are placed."

I sigh. I thought he would say that.

"How about I draw up some documents for you to look over and I can have them set for you to go over at the end of the week?"

I shake my head.

"Can you have them done by, say," I pull my phone out, checking the time. "8:00 p.m. tonight?"

He glances at his watch and scratches his neck but nods. "I assume all assets, like your share of this place, go to Taylor?"

I nod.

"And Taylor?"

"I want to leave her in the care of Everly or Zoe, or both?"

He nods. "I will see you at 8 o'clock tonight. If you could meet me at my office at that time?" Joseph says.

I nod my head and let him leave, feeling like I accomplished at least something.

Now I just have to hope Everly and Zoe don't question me wanting to sign guardianship to them if I die, because one thing I know is, once I reject Carter, I'm as good as dead.

Getting in my car, I pull out my phone and message Carter, asking if I can see him. The phone rings a few minutes later.

"Hello, little mate," he purrs and tears burn my eyes.

"We need to talk," I tell him.

"Correct. And I have a proposition for you," he says. I pause. Can I use this to get Ava home?

"I'm listening," I tell him.

"You need me."

"Definitely not."

"Hmm, that is what you think, but I have a peace offering. Tell

Officer Derrick to check the mine entrance tunnels. I hear he has been looking for his son, Micah?" Carter tells me.

"A peace offering? You had my best friend raped!" I snapped at him.

"No. She fought back; she wasn't part of the plan. But I give you Micah as payment for that."

"Payment? She isn't a fucking whore!"

"I am trying here, Macey. I offered to barter, and–"

"I want Ava back," I tell him

"And I want my mate," he growls. "Wouldn't want anything to happen to little Taylor, would you? Or Tatum? I hear he is in a bad way. I doubt he would put up much of a fight. And seeing as I have eyes on Kalen and eyes in the hospital, I don't think it would be too hard to get to them," Carter says, and I swallow.

"What do you propose, then?" I ask him. Fuck, how many traitors do we have among us? I don't doubt his words, though. I've seen firsthand what this man's father is capable of, and clearly, the apple doesn't fall far from the tree.

"I want immunity to leave with you. I have my money. My pack will handle John. I wanted to handle Everly and Valarian myself, but seeing as you have come into the picture, I am willing to renegotiate."

"What is this bullshit vendetta you have against the Shadow pack's Alpha?" I demand, and Carter laughs.

"John started it when he tossed my mother from the city and told my father she left."

"No, your mother left because of your father's infidelity. Everly told me this story before."

"Wrong. That is what everyone was told. John forced my mother forsaken for killing Rachel."

"And this has something to do with Everly, how? Because of who fathered her?" I scoff. It sounds ridiculous.

"Her family started it, I am just finishing it," Carter states.

"STARTED WHAT?" I scream at him.

"Rachel was Claire Summer's cousin. She tried to kill my mother, and my mother killed her in self-defense. And now he will know what it's like to lose everything, just like my mother did."

I glance around nervously, looking out the windows.

"Now, I will give you a chance to deal with whatever you were speaking with good old Joseph about, and take Micah as proof my word is good," Carter says, and I say nothing, though he confirmed my suspicions that he has more people working for him.

"Think about it, Macey. You have until tomorrow to decide—or I kill Ava, Everly, and everyone you love and hold dear. Their fates now rest on your decision, so choose wisely, Love. Because either way, you will be mine."

"And if I agree, you leave them alone?" I ask him, cogs starting to turn in my head as I navigate this new proposition.

"You have my word," Carter says, and I chew the inside of my lip.

"We will speak soon," I tell him, hanging up before he can say anything else.

CHAPTER
THIRTY-SEVEN

Valen

Relief floods me when I finally get Everly home. She didn't want to leave Zoe, and I even had to get Doc Darnel in to tell her to go home. She's supposed to be on bed rest, but I knew she wouldn't rest at all until she saw with her own eyes that Zoe is alive. Everly has been quiet most of the trip, and I know she's worried about Ava. We had people scour the entire city, including the tunnels, but found nothing. My hands rub over Everly's huge bump.

"Any news yet?" she asks as I lean down to kiss her belly. I shake my head, and she pushes my face away, trying to tug the shirt she's wearing down.

I growl at her and she sighs, but I can tell she's too tired to argue with me. She hates her body. She believes she looks stretched out and ugly, but I love the stretch marks lining her skin. I love each one, love that she's the vessel that currently carries thirty little fingers, thirty little toes, and three extra beating hearts—hearts that are mine to protect and love. Yet to me, none are more important than hers, the one that beats so they can.

257

"We'll find them. The council–" My words cut off as my phone starts ringing and I reach for it. I told everyone to not use the mind-link; Everly doesn't need the extra stress, and I know she'll find no rest with everyone chatting away in our heads. Plus, now I have no idea whom to trust.

Macey's name pops up on the screen and I glance at Everly as she rolls to reach for her water bottle. Sitting up, I grab it and hand it to her before kissing her head and walking out, just in case it's about Zoe.

"Hey, everything okay?"

"Uh, yeah, it's fine, but can you send someone out to the old mine road?" she asks. I pull the phone from my ear to make sure it's her. It's an odd request, and she sounds strange through the phone.

"Why?"

"I just drove past the hotel and reserve and saw a suspicious car head out that way. Just seemed odd."

"Okay, I'll send Derrick out that way with Dion. He's filling in tonight," I tell her.

"Where are you anyway? Everly was expecting you back by now."

"Just sorting a few things out at work. I'll grab Chinese on the way home for everyone. Saves your dads from cooking," Macey says.

"Okay, can you–"

"Yes, I'll make sure to remember to get the dumplings that the kids love," Macey laughs.

"Great, see you soon," I tell her. We have a whole houseful at the moment—both our fathers are with us, as well as Macey and Taylor, plus Casey, and probably Zoe and Marcus soon, depending on how comfortable they are with going home. I text Derrick and Dion, who say they'll head out now, then wander into the kitchen where my father is preparing food for dinner.

"Macey is grabbing Chinese," I tell him, and he sighs.

"Thank the Goddess! I was trying to think of what to make and was about to send John grocery shopping."

I try to picture that. I'm sure he's shopped before, but to shop for this many would be a nightmare.

"What's up? Everly okay?"

"Yeah, just tired. I've been thinking of moving everyone to the main packhouse. It's been sitting empty for months and it has more space than here," I tell him.

"If it's too much, I can take John, Macey, and Taylor with me."

"No, it's fine. I think Everly likes everyone in one place at the moment, and I know she's worried about her father, even though she won't admit it."

"Yeah, he feels guilty about Claire, Ava, and Zoe," Dad tells me.

"Where is he anyway?"

"I think he's doing puzzles with the kids," Dad says with a shrug. "I know you don't like him, but he's her father, and we've all done some shit that we wish we could take back, son."

"I know, and I don't hate him. I'm just worried that if something happens to him it might be Everly's tipping point."

"Ah," he murmurs, turning the kettle on.

"Anyway, I was talking to John. He confessed something to me earlier," Dad tells me, and I raise an eyebrow, leaning on the counter.

"John banished Carter's mother from the city. She didn't leave because of Nixon."

"What?"

Dad nods. "Yeah. Claire threatened to leave him if he didn't because they were close; Rachel was her cousin. So he banished Leah, but when he banished her and ordered her out, she had Nixon's daughter with her. John let Nixon believe she ran off with his daughter, but she didn't. He said he felt guilty about it, but he couldn't find her once she was gone. He and Nixon had a rocky relationship as it was, with business dealings falling through, so he didn't tell him," my father tells me.

So Doc was right, there was more to the story.

"Anything else?"

"No, that's all," he says when my phone rings. I pull it from my pocket and see it's Derrick.

I answer it quickly, turning and leaning against the counter. Except, it's Dion's voice that comes through the other end.

"We got him."

"Got who?"

"Micah," Dion tells me just as I hear a crash in the background.

"I'll be down soon," I tell him, getting ready to hang up.

"Hold on, Derrick wants to speak to you," Dion says, and I wait for Derrick to beg for his son as I hear the phone exchange hands.

"Pick up Marcus on the way," Derrick says before hanging up.

That wasn't what I was expecting. "I need to go."

"I heard. I'll keep an eye on Everly," Dad says, and I nod my head.

As I walk down the hall, I stick my head into one of the rooms to see the kids playing with John.

"Can you come with me?" I ask him, and he nods, getting up from where he's sitting on the floor.

"Everything okay?" he whispers, following me down the hall.

"Yeah. I need you to sit with Zoe. I need to take Marcus somewhere, and I know he won't leave her with anyone she doesn't know."

John nods and doesn't ask questions. He knows there's only one reason I would be pulling Marcus away from Zoe's side.

I stop by the hospital on the way to find Zoe asleep and Marcus sitting in a chair, staring at her. As I step inside the room, I motion to him and he gets up from his seat to join me in the hall.

He looks exhausted. Huge bags hang under his eyes and his hair looks like he's been running his fingers through it. John steps past him into the room.

"What's going on?"

"I need you to come with me. John will wait with Zoe in case she wakes up," I tell him, and he glances into the room at his mate and John, who has taken his seat by her bed.

"Is it Casey?" he asks worriedly. I shake my head.

"Come on," I tell him.

Marcus sighs and runs a hand down his face. "Valen, I'm not–"

"We found Micah," I whisper to him.

The look on his face turns to pure feral rage. His eyes flicker and he looks back in the room at John, who nods.

"She wakes, tell her I went to take a shower," Marcus tells him before pushing past me.

We leave the hospital and head to the police station. As soon as we're buzzed in, I can hear arguing and fighting in the back before we even step into where the cells are. The crashing of furniture comes from one of the interrogation rooms; on the screen on the wall, I can see Derrick pummeling the living shit out of his son, who's bloody and trying to block his father's punches.

Dion hits the intercom and it buzzes inside, making Derrick rise. Micah is sobbing uncontrollably, and blood coats his swollen face. Marcus tries to rip the door open as soon as he notices the viewing screen. Dion and I have to grab him—his entire body is trembling with the urge to shift.

The door opens and Officer Derrick grabs the front of his son's shirt, tossing Micah out the door. Micah sprawls onto the floor in the center of the room. Tears trek down Officer Derrick's face, and his lips quiver.

"Dad, please," Micah pleads. Marcus slams against me, wanting to get to the boy.

"You are *not* my son; I didn't raise a *rapist*," Derrick spits at him before looking at Marcus.

"He's all yours," Derrick says to Marcus before walking out. I nod to Dion to check on Derrick as he leaves through the doors. As soon as they're out of earshot, I let Marcus go. Micah backs up in terror, trying to scramble away as Marcus strips his shirt off, stalking toward him.

"You can't kill me! I'm Casey's father!" Micah cries desperately.

"No, Casey is *mine*," Marcus snarles. There's a crazed look on his

261

face before he shifts, and a growl grows in his throat, the noise so feral it makes the forsaken seem tame.

Marcus attacks.

I step back, sitting quietly on the edge of the desk while Marcus rips the man apart limb by limb, coating the police station with his blood and filling every ear with his dying screams.

THIRTY-EIGHT

E verly

When Macey returns home, she brings dinner with her, and tucked inside her handbag is a folder of documents. She sets the Chinese containers on the counter and I pull down some plates and start serving, only to be scolded by Kalen.

"Everly, you are supposed to be in bed. Do you not know what bed rest is?" he says, clicking his tongue.

"I've been sitting in bed all afternoon, Kal. I'm fine."

He shakes his head, helping me to serve dinner to the kids, who are perched in their chairs around the table.

Zoe is getting released from the hospital tomorrow. She video-called earlier, and thankfully the nurse had given her some makeup, so she didn't freak Casey out. My father has been waiting with her until Marcus returned, but I wasn't willing to tell her where it was that Marcus went and why. Though I think she knows because there's only one reason that would make Marcus leave her side, and that's revenge.

"Are you okay?" I ask Macey, touching her arm, but she pulls away from me, smiling the fakest smile I have ever seen on her face. I narrow my eyes at her and she sighs.

"Sorry, I'm on edge. All this rogue stuff, the hotel, Zoe."

I swallow nodding and turning to flick the kettle on.

"Tea only, Everly," Kalen scolds. Geez, now I know where Valen gets it from.

"Yes, Dad!" Macey and I say simultaneously, and he chuckles.

"I'll eat in the room with you. I need to speak to you about something anyway. Something not for kids' ears," she says, and I nod just as Kalen chimes in.

"Great idea! You girls get settled, and I will bring some trays in and make your tea!" he says, looking at me before pushing us out of the kitchen.

"Hold on—"

"No. Shoo, shoo! Make her sit down. I caught her trying to bleach the damn bathroom! Watch her," Kalen scolds.

"She's nesting, leave her. Besides, she cleans when she's nervous," Macey defends me. Besides, this sitting around nonsense is annoying, and I don't like how everyone fusses. I get they're concerned, but I'm damn near going insane from it.

"Not with my three grandbabies, she doesn't. She is supposed to be on bed rest. We want them babies to stay in as long as possible," Kalen tells Macey.

"Fine. Just let me get some Tylenol, these cramps have been the worst. Stupid monthlies!" she curses, and I blink at her in confusion.

"Wait. You still get your period?" I ask her.

"Uh, yeah. I *am* a female," Macey says. "What did you think? The hysterectomy turned me into a man?" she curses, shaking her head.

Kalen looks at her funny, and I look at him. Macey retrieves her Tylenol from above the stove and downs two pills with a glass of water. As she turns, she notices us staring at her.

"What?" she asks.

"You said you had a full hysterectomy?"

"No, a partial. They took all the baby carrying bits out," Macey says as if she's tired of this conversation already.

"But you have ovaries?" I ask.

"Well, duh! I get a period, so I assume so," she shrugs.

"Then you're not infertile," Kalen says. She pops her hip and puts her hand on her waist.

"What part of 'I haven't got the baby carrying bits' did you not understand?" she says sarcastically. Kalen says one word.

"Surrogate!"

She seems taken aback. "Because someone would want to carry my baby? Yeah, right. Besides, I kind of need a man to fertilize the egg and all. Unless your old dust sperm is volunteering?" she says.

Kalen pulls a face. "Pass! I am too old for babies! But this news will make Tatum happy."

"*Would* have made him happy. He dumped me," she says, rubbing her temples. "We're werewolves—we all know how impossible it would be to find a surrogate. Can't have a human carry them, and we're pack animals; it doesn't matter if it's not a blood child, you know what that would do to a she-wolf."

She does have a point. I've never heard of someone becoming a surrogate. I would do it if I wasn't already pregnant, though Valen probably wouldn't let me. And Zoe is in no state to be asked, though I'm pretty sure she and Marcus were trying before all this happened.

"Now, come on, I want to ask you something," Macey says, grabbing her handbag and tugging me toward my room. I get comfortable on my bed, propping myself up with pillows and settling under the blankets. Kalen comes in a few minutes later with dinner trays for us. Once he's left, she retrieves the documents from her bag.

"Are you okay?" I ask her.

"Yeah, why wouldn't I be?"

I let out a breath. "I'm talking about Tatum."

"It is what it is," she says, trying to deflect the conversation as she sets some papers on my legs.

"Last will and testament?" I ask, looking at her.

"I just– In case something happens to me, I want to ensure Taylor will have a place to go," she says.

"And you want to do this now?" I ask her. She shrugs.

"Just, with all the rogue stuff, I just want to be sure. So I wanted to ask if you and Valen would be willing to take her. You know, cuz I can't leave her to Mom or my brother," she says.

"That isn't even a question. I would move heaven and hell to keep her. You know that."

She nods. "I know, and you and Zoe are the only ones I would trust my baby with. The only ones I know love her just as much as I do."

I sign the document, and when Kalen comes in, I ask him to sign the witness part. He quickly does, though he gives Macey the same odd look I gave her.

"Planning on going somewhere?" he asks.

"What? No! Of course not! I just want to ensure Zoe's future, is all."

He looks at me and I shrug. It's the first time she's ever brought anything like this up. But she does have a point; we all should have it. I'll have to speak to Valen about it later. Though I have a will, and everything goes to Valarian, I never even thought of what would happen to him if something were to happen to Valen and me. It gives me much to think about.

We eat our dinner, and Macey goes to help Kalen shower and bathe the kids while I get ready for bed before we tuck them in. When Valen calls, I answer my phone quickly.

"Hey, when will you be home?"

"I am home. Where are the kids?"

"In their beds, why?"

"Make sure they don't come out of their rooms," he says.

With a groan, I climb back out of bed, shuffling over to the door and up the hall. I stand between their doors, but they're all asleep.

"Yeah, they're fine," I tell him when I hear the door click open. I glance toward it, hearing movement. When Valen appears down the hall, I gasp, glancing back at the kids' rooms to ensure they're asleep.

Valen is drenched in blood from head to toe. Not a patch of skin isn't coated in the coppery substance.

He rushes into our room and I hear the shower turn on in the ensuite. Following him slowly back to the room, I close and lock the door in time to see Valen step into the shower. I scoop up his clothes, tossing them in the hamper—they're soaking wet. The shower water turns red as it swirls down the drain.

"Micah?" I whisper, recognizing the scent, and he nods, turning to face me and rinsing the blood off his face. He says nothing, just reaches for the soap.

"Marcus?"

"Wants the other two."

"I thought you were leaving Micah to Marcus?"

"Marcus revived him and wanted my help. He's my best friend. And Goddess help them when we get our hands on the other two," he says, his eyes darkening, and a growl escapes him. I swallow before having to leave the bathroom from the pungent smell.

When he finally comes out, he's clean and retrieves his pajamas. "My father?"

"Went to the bar. Don't worry, I sent Dad to get him. And... that would be them," Valen says, and I nod, hearing the front door open and my father muttering down the hall. The smell of vodka reaches my nose from under the gap in the door and makes it wrinkle. Dad is drinking far too much, not that I expected anything else. His daughter is missing and his mate is dead. I wouldn't want to live either if our circumstances were reversed.

"Any news from Carter or any sight of them?"

Valen shakes his head when there's a knock on the door. He tugs his shirt on before opening it. It's Macey.

She tells us about the link she found between Rachel and my father. So that's what she was doing all afternoon. Kalen leans against the door, listening but adding nothing. It suddenly makes sense why Carter is so hellbent on ruining us.

"How do you know all this?" Kalen asks her, and her brows furrow.

"I went to the council chambers and dug through the old archives," Macey says, though something is off about her.

"I sent men there and found nothing," Valen says.

"I also checked myself and couldn't find the link on the online records," Kalen adds, and I look at Macey.

"There were some files buried. They were in the wrong box," Macey says.

"What box?" Kalen asks. I don't understand the look on his face as he scrutinizes everything she says, wanting to know how she knows.

"Some old newspaper clipping box, buried right up the back," she says dismissively.

"Thanks. Well, I'll call Officer Derrick and let him know, and also the council."

"The council is still here?" Macey asks.

"Yeah, they aren't leaving until we catch him," Valen says, and she nods.

"At least for once, they've stepped in. But just be careful what you tell them, I feel like Micah isn't the only mole we have."

"What makes you think that?" Kalen asks.

"Dad, leave her be. She's tired," Valen defends Macey.

Kalen puts his hands up in mock surrender, yet doesn't take his eyes off Macey, who's chewing her fingernail.

"Well, I'm off to bed. I'm beat. Wake me if anything happens, anything at all," Macey says, making a quick escape. I watch her leave, and Kalen follows after her.

CHAPTER
THIRTY-NINE

C arter

The bastard is cocky, and it's pissing me off that he thinks he's calling the shots. I watch as John's Beta slinks around his office as we review the plans. Little does he know...

"I'm changing the plans," I tell him.

He rocks back on his heels as he passes me my drink where I sit in the armchair.

"Excuse me?"

"Are you hard of hearing, Beta? I said I am changing the plans."

"We can't. It's too late. I already have everything set in motion," Clarke says. I raise an eyebrow at his words, watching him over my glass as I take a sip of the cheap whiskey.

"Plans change, Beta. You will heed my demands. Comply and you still get your revenge. If not, you will find yourself disposable," I tell him, watching as the idiot swallows. I would have thought John's Beta would have been more loyal. Turns out he was a snake, just like his daughter—jumped at the opportunity when my father offered to take down John. His price is the pack, and he can have it.

269

"These new plans you speak of?" he asks, leaning on the edge of his desk.

"Everything is set in motion. Did you speak to your brother? Is he keeping the council away?" I ask him. Clarke nods when Amber waltzes into the room and pecks her father on the cheek; the girl has her father wrapped around her finger.

Clarke didn't take too kindly to Everly and Ava calling her out when Everly challenged her father, even if what they spoke was true —and it was true, Amber was willing to bed anyone to remain high on the totem pole. It damaged her and her family's minuscule reputation, yet appearances are everything to these bastards. Fools. Though I'll use it if it helps me to keep gaining the advantage.

"Amber, out; we're discussing business," her father says, and she pouts, batting her lashes at him.

"Can I go see my mate?"

Clarke waves his daughter off. Amber escapes quickly, sending me a wink as she sashays out of the room.

"So, what has changed?"

"Nothing for you. You will have your pack once Everly and John are dead—my father will grant the pack to you upon his return. As for me, I have found my mate, so I will bargain Ava in exchange for her and leave the city," I tell him.

"So I don't have to do anything?"

"No, just stick to the plans as originally said, and I am leaving you in charge of making sure my father gets back into the city to challenge Valen once the council leaves."

"Your father wants to challenge Valen?"

"Yes, because if I go through with my original plans, my mate won't submit to me—unfortunately, she is close to them. I promised I would back down for her."

"And you intend to?" he asks incredulously.

"She is my mate," I tell him simply.

"But what of John?"

"The evidence the council has for the forsaken facility, and all records, are in his name. So as long as your brother keeps up his part of the deal, John will be executed either way by the council when they realize it was Claire's DNA that my father used to morph the forsaken. Rest assured, this has been in the planning for nearly a decade now. I know what I am doing. They will have no doubts my father was forced, especially when handed the information about my mother."

"So we frame John, you leave with your rogue mate, where does that leave me? Valen will kill me," Clarke growls.

"Not if my father kills him first."

"He's the blood Alpha," Clarke states, as if I didn't know that already.

"My father only has to get close enough. One bite and it's all over for him. Valen will kill his own family once he turns rabid. Then the city is yours and my father's to do what you wish with. And I will be far away from here with my mate and her daughter," I tell him.

"You're keeping the brat too?"

"Mind your tongue, Beta! I can easily change the plans again and cut out you and that whore daughter you have, too. I wonder how your rep will fare if I release the footage of the gang bang she was involved in?"

Clarke growls. "And you'll hand that footage over when it's all said and done?"

I nod to him. We have a deal. He just needs to help my father get back into the city.

After finishing our little meeting, I head home—well, what I'm calling home for the moment. Pulling up outside, I see Amber's little hatchback and groan. I can't stand the bitch. If she wasn't mated to one of my men now, I would tell her to fuck off. The first thing I do after walking inside is check if Ava is okay. She's still tied up and gagged. I untie her so she can use the restroom in the corner of the room when Porter comes in.

"Got that information you wanted, boss?"

I hold my hand out for the folder, and he places it in my hand.

"I sent some men to kill the kid for you. They plan on taking her out during the drive to school."

"You what!" I bellow, spinning on him. He flinches, taking a step back.

"I thought that's what you wanted," he stammers. I growl, stalking toward him.

"Did I ask you to do that?" I snarl. He shakes his head as Amber comes in, and I sneer at her.

"Call it off, now!" I snap at him. He nods his head, quickly ripping his phone from his pocket and nudging Amber out of the room.

"She stays!"

"I'm sorry, boss, I'll sort it out. I thought–"

"You thought wrong! You dare make decisions on my behalf? Now you'll know what it feels like."

"Amber!" I growl, pointing to my feet. He has to learn there are consequences for not obeying me—and he will learn. Amber, the whore, is all too willing to comply. Porter quickly dials.

"I'll take care of it," he gushes.

Amber looks up at me as I look down at her. The woman disgusts me. She really is a whore—willing to do anything to remain at the top, even with her mate watching behind her.

Porter makes the call, and I nod to Amber as Ava moves back to her spot near the wall. "Sit!" I tell her and she does, rolling her eyes before cuffing herself, knowing I would send Porter over to do it if she didn't anyway. I nod to Amber, who fumbles with my belt before pulling my cock out.

Porter whimpers, clutching his stomach, and I focus on the wall. Vile thing—she's like a leech. If she wasn't the Beta's daughter, I would have killed her by now.

No matter how much she sucks my dick, it will never go hard for her. But this is merely a punishment for her mate, who eventually begs for me to stop, and I'm glad once he does. Shoving her away, I tuck myself back in, and she wipes her mouth before I grip her face.

My phone starts ringing in my pocket, and I know it will be Macey. She definitely would have felt that, which only angers me more, and I grip Amber's face harder.

"Disgusting whore! And you're not even good at it!" I sneer, shoving her away.

"Fuck you, Carter!" Amber snarls.

"Been there, done that. You were even worse at that than you are sucking cock, Amber. Now, get out of my face. Both of you!" I tell them, pulling the phone from my pocket.

"YOU FUCKING PRICK!" Macey shrieks at me the moment I answer.

CHAPTER
FORTY

M acey

Leaving Everly and Valen, I escape to the roof, slip-ping through the doors and up the stairwell. I can't afford to be overheard as I make the call to Carter.

I'm furious. It's bad enough I have to bargain with him for Ava.

"YOU FUCKING PRICK!" I scream at him the moment he answers.

"Well, hello to you too," he purrs.

"You think I can't feel your infidelity, you asshole? And you expect me to run off into the sunset with you!" I snarl through the phone.

"I was teaching one of my men a lesson. The whore means noth-ing. And don't pretend you haven't got up to mischief today, love. I know you visited your internet boyfriend," he says.

I scrub a hand down my face and stare at the night sky, chewing my lip.

"Macey, are you there?" he asks, almost sounding concerned.

"Yes, I'm still here."

"Good. So, have you thought about what I said? Have you gotten all your ducks in a row and are ready to leave with me?"

"How do I know you'll stick to your end of the deal? I don't trust you."

"I gave Micah back, didn't I? Don't doubt my love now. But for insurance purposes, we can leave her at the borders before we head to the cabin."

"A cabin? I'm supposed to leave my daughter, my life behind for a cabin?" I chuckle.

"No, you can bring Taylor," he says.

Yeah, definitely not! I would never allow her near this monster. Though, he would be suspicious if I left her behind.

"No. Not until I know you stick to your word. I'm leaving Taylor here. I want to ensure you're safe first."

"I would never harm your daughter, Macey. Why do you think I was punishing one of my men? He wanted to have your daughter killed. I stopped it and made him watch as his whore of a mate sucked my dick. Vile woman!" he says.

"Where is Ava?" I ask, ignoring his words.

"Beside me, safe and sound. And she will remain that way as long as you abide by the plans," Carter tells me.

"And no harm will come to anyone here?" I ask him.

"None, you have my word. I just want you."

I chew my lip, leaning on the wall and looking over at the city.

"Fine, we have a deal. Send me the details," I tell him before hanging up on him. I don't want to talk to him more than I need to. I sigh heavily.

I can do this! I just hope the bond doesn't get in the way when it's time to kill him. He will die for what he did! I'm about to head back inside when I spot John sitting in one of the fold-up chairs.

"Interesting conversation you just had, Macey," he says quietly, drawing back on his cigarette.

"Yes, indeed, it was. So I assume you have a plan and reason for keeping this from my son?" Kalen murmurs as he comes to stand by John.

"And my daughter?" John adds.

How I was stupid enough not to realize I was being followed and that John was up here the entire time is beyond me. I let my anger get the better of me and became solely focused on Carter's infidelity that I wasn't paying attention to my surroundings.

"You lied to Everly and me earlier, though I knew it was a lie. You don't get periods after a hysterectomy," Kalen says. I admit, I panicked when put on the spot. But it wasn't actually a lie; I still get cramps.

"Technically, I still get the occasional cycle, and monthly cramps, though they're more of a dull ache."

"So you did only have a partial hysterectomy?" he asks, and I nod.

"Yes, I still have ovaries. The way Doc explained it is that besides eventually going into early menopause, my body will still have a form of a cycle, though the body absorbs any egg."

"But you still lied?"

"Do you think I want to? How would Zoe feel knowing the man responsible for letting what happened to her is my mate? Carter needs to die and they won't risk my life by killing my mate, so I have no choice."

Kalen and John look at each other.

"So Carter is your mate? You're certain?" John asks.

I nod and bite the inside of my cheek. "You can't tell them. I know the girls and they won't risk my life. Killing Carter is the only way!"

"And you could really kill your mate?" Kalen asks.

"I have no choice. Besides, if I do as Carter says, he'll give me Ava back. It's a trade."

John leans forward, clasping his hands together. "And you're the trade?"

"Let us help you. I get why you don't want to tell the girls, but you don't have to do this alone. Let us help," Kalen says.

"It can only be you, no one else. Carter has people on the inside helping. He knows things he shouldn't know," I tell them.

"Okay. Say we let you go along with his demands, you ambush and kill him, so then what, you die? You have a daughter, Macey. You and Tatum split. What happens to her then?" Kalen asks.

I've thought of it plenty, which is exactly why I had Everly sign those papers. My baby will be safe.

"I have plans for her in place. Everly and Zoe will take her," I tell them, and John looks at Kalen.

"I'll talk to Tatum after we sort out this mess. Killing your mate —we have no idea what effect that will have. It's different from Valarie and me, and you're rogue," Kalen points out.

I know exactly what will happen; I'll deteriorate faster. It's one thing breaking a bond, and quite another slaughtering it.

"No, Tatum was clear. We're over. I don't want to be pity marked." I growl at the thought. No one wants a sympathy mark.

John and Kalen seem to think before John sits back in his chair and gazes at me.

"Okay, what about—and don't take this the wrong way—what if Kalen or I mark you? You, not us, just to keep you alive?"

I gape at him. "Dude, you're old enough to be my father! Ew! Gross!"

"Not like that! Just–"

"Nope! The bond will still have effects, grandpa! Keep your wrinkly, dusty old balls to yourself! I'll let you help, but neither of you is marking me!" I shriek and pull a face. Yeah, I have no desire to be Valen or Everly's stepmother by default.

"Okay, we'll figure out that bridge as we cross it," Kalen says.

"No! I will figure out that bridge. Neither of you is taking a bite out of me. I would rather die than be attracted to your old asses!"

"I am not that old! What is it with this generation thinking we're old? I have plenty left in the tank! Not that I would–... You're not the only one grossed out by the idea, okay? But at least we have one!" Kalen snaps.

"Did you have a black-and-white TV? You're fucking old then!"

He curses.

"Damn stubborn woman! Fine! But tell us the plan and let's work something out," Kalen says, reaching over and snatching John's smokes. He puts one in his mouth.

"Since when do you smoke?" John asks him.

"When I am anxious. So shut up and hand me a lighter!" Kalen snaps, clicking his fingers at John. John offers me the packet and I take it, leaning against the wall.

"So, what is this plan?" John asks, lighting his own smoke before passing me the lighter.

"We kill Carter and take back the city. But first, I need to get close enough to him and get Ava out," I shrug.

"And the *plan*?" Kalen asks.

"Uh, that's all I got so far," I admit and Kalen curses.

CHAPTER
FORTY-ONE

Everly

Two Days Later

Something is going on with Macey and Kalen; they've been joined at each other's hip for the last two days. And it's always the same excuse, too—they're dealing with the hotel renovations. Yet as Kalen left this morning, I couldn't help but wonder because of the way Macey hung up abruptly on whomever she was talking to when I came out to make something to eat.

"Where are the kids?" I ask her as she starts putting her belongings into her bag. And why is she so dressed up? She's even wearing makeup.

"Kalen and John dropped them off at school," she answers with a shrug, trying to push me back toward the room.

"Go lay down, you're on bed rest. I'll bring your breakfast in."

"And Valen?" I ask her. I didn't hear him get up this morning; usually he wakes me.

"Uh, something about meeting the council elders with Marcus before they pick up Zoe," Macey answers as she shuffles me down the hall to my room. Their constant fussing is driving me insane.

"Zoe is coming home?" I ask, feeling relieved. She could have come home yesterday, but they kept her an extra night so she could meet with a counselor this morning.

"Yep, and I think everyone is moving to the main packhouse today. Valen said something about organizing it," Macey says as I climb back into bed. I stare at her as I pull my blankets back up,, still wondering why she's all dressed up. It's odd.

"Where are you going? To see Tatum?" I ask her. She chews her lip.

"Um, yeah, I was going to try to patch things up with him. Hopefully he's in a better mood today," she says, yet her jitteriness makes me nervous.

I can't explain why I feel that way, but she seems off; she has for the last two days. With everything going on, it's understandable, but for her to suddenly hang around Kalen and my father has me rattled —two men, who for years she despised and are now acting like they're all best buddies.

She walks off, returning with a tray of tea and toast. "Sorry. Valen," she sighs.

It's fine, I'll wait for her to leave and hunt for my own coffee so she doesn't get in trouble. She leans down and gives me a kiss on the cheek as I pluck a piece of toast off the tray.

"You know I love you, right? You and Zoe," Macey says with a shake of her head. "I would do anything for you, without question or fear of consequence. You girls are my family—always have been, always will be. Taylor and I wouldn't be where we are if it wasn't for you both."

I smile sadly, feeling the same way about her. Yet, my brows furrow in confusion. It strikes me as odd; Macey isn't one to declare her love or show her emotions. She gives me a quick kiss before stopping by the door.

"I love you," she says.

"I love you too. Are you sure everything is okay?" I ask her around my mouthful of jelly toast.

"Yes, I'm fine. I'll see you later," she says, then walks off. Taking another bite of my toast, I shake my head at her strange behavior. I'll be sitting her down when she gets home to find out what is going on with her. Maybe I'll call Tatum later and tell him to pull his head out of his ass, or get Valen to do it.

For the most part, my day is as boring as every other day I've spent in this place. By lunchtime I'm starving again and decide after dragging myself out of the shower that I'll make something to eat. I'm craving cucumbers and peanut butter. My mouth waters.

I slip my robe on, deciding against clothes, knowing I'll just be uncomfortable and itchy. Besides, no one's home yet, though that has me confused. Kalen or Dad are usually back by now. Valen would be fuming if he knew I was home by myself, but I'm not going to call him and snitch on them; I'm enjoying the peace and quiet.

I don't feel like being stared at or criticized for my weird food cravings, and that means I can sneak more coffee. Just as I wander out to the living room, however, the devil himself calls, his ringtone blaring loudly from the bedroom. I waddle my fat ass back to the room, puffing and panting, and barely make it to my phone before it rings out. Snatching it off the dresser, I put it to my ear.

"Hello?" I gasp out.

"Hey, just checking in," Valen says while I sit on the edge of the bed and try to catch my breath. My lower back is killing me from the fast pace I made back to the room and my hips throb.

"Everly?" Valen asks.

"Yeah, I'm fine, just had a shower and had to race to the phone," I tell him while tugging off the towel that's wrapped around my hair. I toss it at the basket by the door but miss and internally groan, knowing I'm not going to be able to pick the damn thing up easily.

"I may be a little while longer. I'm just visiting Tatum."

"Good, maybe you can find out what's going on with Macey. She was odd this morning. Did she say anything to Tatum?"

I hear Valen ask Tatum about Macey before answering.

"He said he hasn't seen her since their argument."

My brows furrow.

"Why?" Valen asks.

"No, reason. I thought she was visiting him today, is all. How was the council meeting?"

"Dunno, they cancelled last minute, and—"

I pull the phone away from my ear, hearing someone knocking on the door.

"Hang on a second, someone's knocking on the door," I tell Valen.

"Let Dad get it. Also, I need to speak to him, so can you put him on?"

"He isn't here, he left this morning, hasn't been back," I tell him, wandering down the hall.

"But I spoke to him this morning after the school drive. He said he was on his way back to you?"

"He must have got distracted," I tell him as the knocking gets louder and I drag myself back down the damn hallway.

"Hold on, I'm coming!" I yell to whoever it is. Suddenly, I feel my feet get wet as I step into the entrance hallway. I stop, wondering if I imagined it. The knocking gets worse and I hear yelling from the other side of the door, ordering me to open it. Valen is yelling in my ear, asking what's wrong. I don't hear any of it. My eyes are on the huge puddle of water at my feet.

"Everly, who is it?" Valen asks as I stare, stunned.

My mouth opens and closes and I try to answer Valen when I hear the door burst open and smash into the wall. The sound makes me jump and more liquid gushes out of me, covering my feet and the floor—my legs are soaked. I look up to see armed men race down the hall with their guns drawn, straight toward me.

"Valen, get home," I tell him when a man stops in front of me. He holds out a piece of paper, thrusting it toward me before looking down at the puddle I'm standing in and glancing at the men behind him.

"Who are you and what are you doing in my house?" I demand, growling at the man. I can hear Valen yelling through the phone.

"We're looking for Alpha John—we have a warrant for his arrest," the man explains.

"A warrant?" I ask, snatching the paper from his hand a moment before pain ripples through my abdomen. I clutch the hall stand, the paper crumpling in my fist as I hold my stomach with my other hand.

"A warrant for what? And who are you?" I growl through gritted teeth. I look up to see the men in uniforms looking at me warily.

"My name is Deacon. I'm a member of the werewolf council, and your father is under arrest for his experimentation on the rogues and creating the forsaken."

I tried to pay attention to what he's saying, yet pain like a sharp knife tears through my stomach. I groan and grit my teeth, trying to breathe through the contraction.

"Ma'am, are you alright?" the man asks, a little startled. He reaches toward me and I snarl at him, slapping his hand away.

"Of course I'm not alright! My damn water just broke, and you just broke into my damn house!" I snap at him, already feeling Valen getting closer.

"We have a warrant, ma'am," he states.

"FUCK YOUR WARRANT!" I scream at him as another contraction makes my stomach tighten, and more liquid spills onto the floor at my feet. The man jumps back and they all glance at each other as if they've never seen a woman in labor before.

"Ma'am?" the council elder asks. I glare at him.

"Call a fucking ambulance, you idiot!" I snap at him, not in the mood for whatever it is they're doing here or their oblivious faces as they gape at me.

Macey

I pull into the underground parking lot and pull into the space next to Kalen and John before hopping out of the car. Kalen also gets out, and we quickly go over the plans again while John fiddles with my phone and pairs it to his and Kalen's so they can track me.

"We'll be right behind you. John will grab Ava from the meeting spot, and I'll follow. Derrick and Dion are waiting for the call. Once we have your location, we ambush him," Kalen tells me and I nod. My heart is thumping rapidly as nerves kick in; I'm stressing over leaving with Carter, even if only temporarily.

"Here, but just in case this disconnects, take this," John says, handing me something that looks suspiciously like a suppository. He's pulling my leg, right? I hold it up, looking at it.

"And what am I supposed to do with this?" I ask. They both mumble and look away from me. "Oh, hell no! *You* shaft it!" No way is that going up my butt.

"It's just a precaution," John mutters.

"I don't see you shoving anything up your ass! Do I look like a drug mule?" I snap.

"There's always the other—" Kalen starts to say, but I hold up a hand to stop him before he can tell me his suggestion.

"Nope! Definitely not," I growl, annoyed at how easily they're discussing my nether bits.

"Geez, woman, just swallow the damn thing!" John says. I growl but swallow the rubbery device.

"You better hope that comes out. And easily. I am not going to the damn hospital and explaining this shit!" I tell him and John sighs.

"Hey, you wouldn't let us get anyone involved but Derrick and Dion, so we need backup plans. That is the backup plan," Kalen tells me.

I roll my eyes before snatching the water from him and downing some. The damn thing feels like it's lodged in my throat.

Pulling my phone from my pocket, I glance at it, knowing it's getting close to the time. We quickly go over the plans once more. Carter said Ava would be dropped off at the old mine tunnels where he dropped Micah. Once I'm out of the city with him, that's where John will head first.

Kalen will follow behind me to the borders in one of the delivery trucks that came in this morning. Goddess knows how much he had to pay the driver to hand the truck over and wait around, but a random car would look suspicious.

"Okay, where are you meeting Carter again?" John asks.

"The train bridge. Then, once we've left the city limits, he said he'll make a call to whoever has Ava."

I wait for the message to come in. It's the only thing going that we can't plan for because we don't know when he'll call.

Once the message comes in, I drive to the station and we all split up. Kalen goes to pick up the truck; John, to get Ava. As I drive toward the train station, I pass Dion and Derrick. However, when I get there, my phone rings again, but I see no sign of Carter.

"Where are you?" I ask him.

"Get on the train that's waiting," he says, and I look at the train.

"No. We had a deal."

"And the deal stands. If you think I am stupid, Macey, and that I wouldn't know you have a plan, then you are mistaken. Get on the train and catch it to the first stop out of the city," he says, hanging up, and I curse.

Shaking my head, I race to catch the train before it leaves. I have to jump the turnstiles, and I slip through the narrow door gap just in time. Once inside, I start to text Kalen when I notice a teenage girl sitting on one of the seats. She has her earbuds in and I quickly tap her shoulder. She looks up at me, startled. I can tell she's a rogue, and after a sniff of the air, she seems to realize I am, too, and pulls her headphones from her ears.

"Can I borrow your phone to send a message?" I ask her. She looks at my phone in my hand.

"Out of credit," I tell her before she says anything. She hands her phone over, and I quickly message Kalen from it, not trusting my own phone. After handing it back to her with a 'thank you', I wait by the doors as the train passes over the city, watching the buildings slip by.

The train passes Dion and Derrick, parked on the overpass.

I glance down, seeing police cars and black SUVs racing toward the borders before I recognize John's car screeching to a stop as his vehicle is encircled. I try to see what's going on, pressing my face to the glass as I curse, but the train is going too quickly, and I suck in a shaky breath.

The train keeps going.

The girl whose phone I borrowed waves me over. "I, um, think this is for you," she says, showing me the phone screen. Kalen has replied.

'Borders blocked, hang tight. Something is going on'

That's all it says.

"Fuck!" I hiss under my breath. I swallow and quickly thank her. There's no doubt this is Carter's doing.

My phone rings, and I whip it from my pocket.

"I noticed Taylor isn't with you. And you have no suitcase," Carter purrs, and I grit my teeth. He laughs. "Little mate, you won't get one past me, so I don't know why you tried. Never mind, it's alright. I will forgive your dishonesty. Make sure to get off at the next stop. I will be waiting," he says before hanging up.

Even with looking at the train map on the wall, I have no idea what train I'm on, but we passed two stations without stopping. I sit down until I feel the train begin to slow.

Finally getting off the train, I move to the parking lot and spot a black Mercedes waiting. Carter stands leaning against the hood. He looks impeccable in his suit and the bond burns to touch him, but I stamp the urge down.

"What, no hug?" Carter purrs, stalking toward me. I try to side-step him but am swept up in his arms before being pinned against the car.

"Where is Ava?" I growl.

"And where is your phone, love? Hand it over," he growls, feeling my pockets. He finds my phone before dropping it and stomping on it.

"Ava?" I demand. Nothing is going to plan. I'm barely holding myself together.

"In the trunk. Now, I am done playing your little game of cat and mouse, so I will release her the moment I have marked that pretty little neck," he says, pressing closer, and I turn my face to the trunk. I can hear the faint banging and groaning coming from it.

"No. Release her, then we can leave. Let her out, Carter," I tell him.

"I want assurance first. No one will risk your life, so you want her, you will let me mark you," he says, trailing his nose across my neck. I swallow, trying to stamp down the urges of the bond to give in to him.

The crackles of electricity are relentless the longer he touches me, making a moan escape me. Carter chuckles, though I'm seething on the inside that he has this effect. But if it works in distracting him, I'll use it to my advantage.

"Now *there* is the reaction I have been looking for," Carter murmurs, nipping at my neck, and my breath comes in uneven breaths at the sparks as the bond reacts to my mate. Glancing around, I see the girl from the train waiting at the bus stop. If I can just get Carter to release Ava, I know the girl would help her.

"Not here. We have too many observers," I tell him, and he glances around before reaching for the door handle and opening it. I glance at it as he steps away from me and nods to get in.

"You want her back, then get in. Once I have marked you, I will let her go and not a moment before," he says. I bite my lip and reluctantly get in.

"You'll let her out?" I ask worriedly. What if all of this is some ploy? Carter leans in, clipping in my seat belt. When he pulls back, he smirks.

"Of course," he purrs, pressing his lips to mine.

Instead of fighting the bond, I allow it, answering his kiss and internally cringing the entire time. Yet, this insane man seems to think the feeling is reciprocated and cups the back of my neck, deepening it. His lips trail down my neck hungrily, and I offer it to him. Tears burn my eyes at what I'm about to allow him to do. I just hope I'm strong enough to fight the bond afterward.

"Do it," I whisper, and he pulls away to look at me.

"Ava can catch the train home from here. Do it, so you know I'm yours," I tell him.

He observes my face for a few seconds before glancing around the parking lot, and I notice it beginning to empty. The girl is gone— she was by the bus stop, but now I can't see her.

"Carter?" I ask, turning my attention back to him.

"And you'll mark me?" he asks, pecking my lips.

"You'll let her out?" I ask, and he nods.

"Then yes, but–"

"I will let her out," he repeats.

I suck in a breath and quickly nod. Carter kisses me and I kiss him back, playing along until he pulls me to the side edge of the seat so my feet are hanging out the door; the seat belt feels as if it will strangle me. He crouches in front of me, his hands trailing up my thighs when he turns his head, offering me his neck.

"You want me to go first?" I ask.

"Well, unless you can fight an Alpha mark, Love, you first. Because you won't be awake long once I mark you," he says, and my heart beats like a drum in my chest as panic kicks in.

Carter grips my face in his hands. "I promised, didn't I?" he says. He offers me his neck, and I hesitate before leaning closer. I feel my canines tear from my gums as his scent overwhelms me, the bond flaring to life, and I sink my teeth into his neck.

The bond surges as my chest tightens and my heart swells, letting his soul intertwine with mine. Carter grunts, tugging me against him, holding me closer until the bond forges. When my canines retract, I run my tongue over his mark, sealing it. My body feels traitorous, and I try to remind myself I still have control.

"Good girl," Carter purrs, pecking my lips before he yanks my head to the side and sinks his teeth in my neck. I clench my eyes shut as pain rips through my shoulder before pleasure makes my entire body tingle; I submit to the bond and let it forge. Yet as the bond forms and blossoms, I feel my body become increasingly heavy, and I sag back against the seat.

Carter turns me after sealing his mark, pushing me back in my seat and untangling the belt that's caught around my torso.

"Ava," I murmur, fighting the overwhelming exhaustion.

"I will release her. Sleep," he says, kissing my head and shutting the door. As my head hits the glass and I slump to the side, I watch in the side mirror as Carter pops the trunk. He rummages around, then I see Ava stagger forward before falling on the ground as her legs give out from under her. Moments later, Carter climbs in the driver's door while Ava undoes the gag from her mouth and tries to get up.

In a fight I'm never going to win, my eyes flutter as I try to force them to stay open. I manage long enough to see the girl rush from the bus station toward Ava while Carter speaks soft words to me and starts the car. As he pulls onto the highway, relief floods me when I see she's alright.

I smile sleepily.

She's safe.

Me, not so much.

"You won't regret this, Macey; I will take good care of you," I hear Carter's voice.

No, but you will regret ever meeting me, I think before the oblivion of the mate bond sweeps me under.

FORTY-THREE

Valen

The phone temporarily cuts out as it goes through my Bluetooth, and I can hear Everly giving the council a mouthful.

"Valen!" she groans through gritted teeth. Pain courses through the bond as I race to get to her.

"Nearly there. Hold on," I tell her, tearing through the streets. This explains the council canceling at the last minute, but *why* is another question? Yet right now, I have a one-track mind: get to my mate.

"Touch me again, and I will gut you!" I hear Everly growl at someone. "Grab my bag! Over there, you idiot! Now move! Unless you want to deliver my babies, get out of my way," she snarls, groaning as another contraction hits her.

I press my foot harder on the accelerator when I hear her panting as she breathes through another. Marcus white-knuckles his seat as we skid around another corner, the car sliding out and narrowly missing some parked cars before I pull it back.

"It's too early! It's too early, Valen!" I hear Everly cry out. It's early, yes, but we had hoped she would make it to this point—sure, we would have preferred her to go full term, but Doc expected this, and Marcus assures me the hospital is getting prepared and an ambulance is on its way to her.

Now, I just need to get there.

Both the tires and Marcus scream around the next corner when we find a roadblock. Cops are everywhere up the main street, blocking both sides of the road, and I see my father get pulled from a truck while John has his hands in the air.

Both of them are surrounded by the council and half the police force. The car screeches to a stop and Marcus is thrown forward in his seat as we come to an abrupt stop. Then suddenly, all guns are turned and pointed at us.

"FUCK!" I curse as the car becomes surrounded. I growl.

"Valen? Valen, the ambulance is here. Where are you?" Everly cries as pain ripples through the bond, along with her panic. She's scared—scared she'll have to do this on her own, scared for our babies, and overall, just scared for herself.

"Just a detour, love. I'll meet you at the hospital," I tell her, watching as the car becomes surrounded.

"You're coming, though? I can't do this again, Valen!" Everly cries.

"I promise I will be there. Just go with the ambulance," I tell her before tossing my door open.

"Hands where we can see the Alpha," comes a voice, and I turn my head to see John's Beta smiling and walking toward me. John is pinned to the ground, being handcuffed. My father still stands with his hands in the air, and I wonder what's going on a second before I feel Everly's panic through the bond.

'Breathe, love! I'm coming. I'll be there soon. Just gotta take care of something first,' I mind-link her. We've been avoiding the mind link for weeks, worried about the strain it puts on Everly, but seeing as it's baby time, I don't think she could become more stressed than she already is.

"Well, this is a fun turn of events now, isn't it, Alpha?" Beta Clarke says when I see his brother Deacon pull up and get out of his car. I knew he was with Everly, so if he's here, the ambulance has already gotten Everly.

"Valen, my daughter? Clarke said she's in labor," John says, and I nod to him as he struggles on the ground.

"Trying to get to her, John. Give me a moment," I call back to him. A scuffle breaks out and my father shifts abruptly, taking off for the borders. I have no idea where he's going, but the moment he started fighting, so did John before everyone rushes to contain him. My father's huge, black wolf takes out two of the men and effectively escapes. However, Marcus and I are surrounded.

"Well, gentleman, you either shoot or drop your weapons. Because I made a promise, and I don't intend to break it," I tell Deacon as I start undoing my cufflinks.

"You are under suspicion for your involvement in the forsaken and rogue murders," Deacon tells me, and my brows raise. No doubt Carter and Nixon are up to something.

"Is that so?" I ask him while removing my blazer. I toss it on the hood of my car before I start unbuttoning my shirt, and they start backing up.

"Y-yes... Alpha Valen, we have—" Deacon stutters, but I ignore him. Of all days they could have picked to piss me off, today wasn't one of them.

"Now, I have a mate who, as you know, Deacon, is in labor," I tell him, tugging my tie off. I toss it on the hood with my blazer, mindful of everyone watching me as I size them up and count how many surround us.

"We can't let you go, Alpha Valen. Not until–" Deacon begins to say when I cut him off.

"The hard way it is, then," I finish for him as I remove my shirt, dropping it to the side with my other things. I hear Marcus growl behind me, but I pay no attention to him. I know he has my back.

Stepping forward, I smile when they back up. They know the

grave danger they are in if they try to stop me from getting to my mate.

What I never would have expected, however, is for Alpha Nixon's wife to step out of the black SUV behind them. My eyes zero in on her. Of course, Nixon had something to do with this, and looking at Beta Clarke, we now know who the other informant is.

"We have all the evidence we need to prove this was Alpha John's and your doing, Alpha Valen. It would be best if you came with us," Deacon says, while Nixon's Luna saunters over with a smug smile on her wrinkling, made-up face.

"And what evidence is that?" I ask, curious about what I will have to prove myself innocent of.

"For one, the facility being in yours and John's name," Deacon answers.

"What facility?"

"The one hidden in the mining mountains. We have all the evidence needed to prove our case. Both your signature and John's are on it. Also, the amount of incriminating evidence of patient zero, of course—the patient used to create the poison and the vaccine; to use his own wife for his sick misdoings is purely vile. And you helped them all to drive my husband from the city. I won't let my husband take the fall for this," she growls.

"And where did this supposed evidence come from? You? Nixon himself?" I ask her, knowing it did. The other council members look around at each other, while Deacon looks between the elders and me. "Now, I am going to give you one last chance, Deacon, to correct this mistake. If not, you will find out why they call me the Blood Alpha," I tell him.

If they want a fight, they will get one, because no one is stopping me from getting to my mate.

"So, I suggest you choose wisely, because your shitty wolfsbane bullets won't stop me. And if I have to run through all of you to get to my mate, so be it," I tell them, feeling the ripple of the shift as it hovers under the surface, ready to take over.

CHAPTER
FORTY-FOUR

V alen

Deacon shuffles uncomfortably on the spot, looking at Clarke while the other council members glance at Deacon, making me wonder if Deacon is only doing this as a favor to his brother, whom we are now aware is a traitor.

"We found evidence at John's packhouse," Deacon declares and I laugh because it even *sounds* ridiculous.

"Before or after the forsaken attack? Or during?" I ask Deacon, but he says nothing. I see Clarke step forward and John growls and snarls from where he's pinned when we hear the sound of screeching tires across the intersection and a car comes to an abrupt halt. Glancing over, I see Slasher pack's Alpha climb out of the car.

Alpha Daxon and I are on good terms, however, he doesn't have the best relationship with my father, seeing as, reportedly, my father killed his son Preston. Preston himself hadn't had a stellar relationship with his own father, who had threatened to remove his title for misdoings and the negative attention he constantly got from the media. Alpha Daxon is a good Alpha, a little old school like my father, but good. It makes me wonder why he's come here. Is he helping Nixon too?

"Fucking bastard, you found nothing! Your men turned the place upside down, and nothing. I know this is for Amber, Clarke, you prick!" John growls.

Clarke nods to the main officer pinning him before one of the other officers smashes his baton across the back of John's head. I press my lips in a line, and one of the older council members glares at Clarke, who gave the order.

Turning my attention back to Deacon, I fight back a growl. "I don't remember you fighting on the front lines, Deacon. So, while patient 'zero', or Luna Claire, was dying protecting the city, were you planting evidence? Or was it your brother?" I ask him, wondering what Daxon is doing here, as I feel his aura getting closer.

"And where was Nixon?" I ask his Luna, turning my attention to her.

"Fleeing—that is where the scum was. Does it upset you that he left you behind with his psychotic son?" Alpha Daxon says, coming up behind me.

"Dax," I acknowledge as he comes to stand by me.

"I lost over a hundred of my men in that forsaken attack, and not once did I see one of Nixon's men step out to protect our city. In fact, half of them were fucking forsaken, so how can you believe this bullshit? Now let John up," Alpha Daxon growls.

"We have evidence that this was all thought out and Nixon was framed," one of the older council members says, stepping forward with documents, and Alpha Daxon growls again.

"Go. I will handle this," Alpha Daxon nods to me. "Give Everly my best," he adds, making me wonder if that's why he's here. Because of her?

Yet when I start to move toward my car, a gun is lifted at me. I growl furiously, only to feel Deacon's daring hand grip my shoulder. My reaction is instantaneous as I reach back, gripping his shoulder and letting my claws hook into the thick band of muscle along his shoulder and neck before flipping him over my shoulder and onto the hood of my car.

The bang of his body as the air expels from his lungs on impact is audible as I remove my claws and grip his forearm, giving it a quick twist and popping his shoulder out. That's when I feel the first dart hit between my shoulder blades. Reaching back, I yank it out—the toxin burns, but it will take a lot more than one to drop me.

Big mistake.

Daxon howls with laughter. "Oh, you foolish pup," he chuckles at the young officer. I spin so quickly that the officer only has time to gasp—he had come up behind me. Instantly gripping the barrel of his dart gun, I slam it into his face and disarm him. He clutches his face and bleeding nose and I turn the gun on him, letting off three shots in his chest. He staggers back, and the rest of the officers lift their weapons, pointing them at us.

"Uh uh, I would advise you, doing that isn't a wise decision," Alpha Daxon states. The shift pushes harder to take over while Alpha Daxon just leans casually against the hood of my car with his arms folded. Deacon groans behind me and scrambles off my hood, only for Alpha Daxon to shove him away.

"Unless you want to take on an entire city, I suggest you step down and let this man get to his mate," Alpha Daxon says.

Somewhat confused, I look at him. He nods over his shoulder, and I see hundreds of people stepping out from between the buildings and cutting across the roads.

"It appears your council holds no power here; not against my people," I tell the council members when I see Everly's rogues coming to our aid along with Slasher pack. The council looks around nervously at all the enraged faces coming toward them.

"Seems you've found yourself in a predicament. I suggest you leave my city. They will fight for my Luna," I tell the council, knowing full well they are here for her.

"And Alpha," Alpha Daxon says behind me before baring his neck to me. I press my lips together and give him a nod, glad for once that our city will stand and fight together as one, all because of the woman who would fight for them.

"You earned that position when you stood beside me to fight for my people, our people, and my pack will stand with you now," Alpha Daxon says. I smirk, turning back to the council, who glance around nervously when they find themselves completely surrounded.

"Let him go," Deacon gasps, clutching his arm.

"What are you doing? We–" Clarke goes to say, but one growl from his brother shuts him up and Deacon nods to Alpha Daxon, just as John is let up. I wave for him to come to me, but he shakes his head.

"I have somewhere else I'm needed. Take care of my daughter until I return," he says, confusing me, but I shake my head. I don't have time to ask what's going on. I need to get to my mate, whose panic is bleeding into me through the bond. However, the roads are blocked with cars, which is taking time, so I shift. I trust Alpha Daxon will handle things. My bones realign and snap, then I'm off in the direction of the hospital. People scatter, getting out of my way.

'Marcus?' I mind-link.

'Yep, I got the school pickup. Get to your mate,' he says, and I cut the link, my paws scraping concrete as I cut up alleyways and tear through my territory. The sight of the huge hospital building coming into sight makes me run harder, knowing she's just there.

'Where are you?' I ask her, feeling her worry.

'They rushed me in for a c-section. Where are you, Valen? You aren't here,' she cries through the mind-link as I smash through the front doors. The people in the foyer shriek and scramble away, and one of my nurses points down the corridor.

"Second floor, Alpha," she says, and I tear off for the stairs. Buzzers go off in the distance and I find the doors opening by security while people flurry everywhere as I get to the floor.

My heart pounds in my chest as I shift back, racing down the hall to find the surgical ward, following the directions of my pack as they point out which way to go. Just as I come to a set of double doors, a nurse grips my arm and tugs me to a small room beside them before I can shove through to find Everly. It's a washroom. I wash my hands and arms while the nurse thrusts a hair net down over my head before handing me a mask.

There isn't much more than that I can do before she shoves a gown at me. I quickly yank it on and rush to the room next door to find Everly lying on a table while nurses pull up a tent-looking thing, preventing us from seeing as they cut into her. I scoot around behind them to my terrified mate with her eyes closed, muttering to herself.

An anesthesiologist stands by her head to monitor her, and they step aside for me while a nurse sets a chair by her head for me. I nod to the nurse and they move off somewhere as I sit down. Focusing on Everly, I place my hands on the side of her face and lean down, pulling my mask from my face briefly to kiss her forehead.

"I don't break my promises," I whisper to her as her eyes fly open and her lips quiver.

"You made it," she breathes while staring up at me.

"Yes, I made it. Always for you," I tell her. Doc and the nurses hurry around while also explaining what they're doing, yet all my attention is on Everly, trusting they know what they're doing. *She* is my focus.

"Valarian?" Everly asks.

"Marcus will get him for us," I assure her.

"And my father?"

"Will be here when he can," I tell her while brushing my thumbs down the sides of her face.

"Everly, you may feel some pressure, but you shouldn't feel any pain," Doc tells her, and I suck in a breath. Doc explains that the steroids Everly was put on should have helped the baby's lungs develop, and she's past thirty-three weeks, so the fact she carried them this long is good.

We all hold our breath when he declares the first baby is out and briefly holds her above the curtain so quickly I miss it. Everly stares wide-eyed in panic when they rush off with the baby.

"Why wasn't our first one crying?" Everly worries when Doc declares baby two is out and she instantly starts screaming. Moments later, the first one gives a screech and I let out a breath, all panic leaving along with the breath I hadn't realized I was holding.

"Baby just needed some suctioning to clear the airways," a nurse tells us.

Doc talks through what he's doing as he searches for baby number three, and before we know it, she's out, too. At the same time, the nurse comes to place babies one and two in my arms. A moment later, we hear baby three's mighty scream as it fills the room.

I am amazed and awestruck at the two little bundles in my arms, unable to tear my gaze from the little creatures we created. The nurse brings baby three over, bundled up in a hospital blanket and Everly coos as she tries to see. I lean down so she can see better and the nurse places baby three on her chest for a few moments.

All Everly's panic slips away the moment she does, and the bond blooms with love and tenderness. Never in my life have I ever felt so complete. After the nurse checks Everly and they're stitching her up, the nurse awkwardly places baby three in my arms, and I stare down at our three perfect little girls. I can't wait for Valarian to meet his little sisters.

CHAPTER
FORTY-FIVE

Macey

I awake to fingertips brushing up and down my arm. The chill in the air makes me inhale deeply as tingles spread up my skin where his fingertips caress. I pretend to remain asleep when the vibration of a phone ringing beside my head buzzes and vibrates against the wooden table it's sitting on.

My mate growls, and where I'm lying dips, so I know I'm on a bed—the jostling movement as he climbs off reinforces that. Eyes fluttering open, I squint, remembering to remain calm and keep my heart rate down as I try to take in my surroundings.

Brown wall paneling covers the walls and is the first thing I notice in the dimly lit room. The old-fashioned lamp with a floral shade makes very little light in the room, and the smell of burning wood reaches my nose—it smells somewhat damp, making the scent a little too strong, reminding me of pine needles. The crackling sound reaches my ears at the same time his voice does.

"What is it, Father?" Carter asks. At least I know who he's on the phone with.

"Not my problem. I did my part. I am done now. Find your own way into the city to enact your revenge. I want no part of it anymore," he growls into the phone.

"I have better things to entertain myself with, but I left half the money in the mining tunnels for you. It should tide you over for a while."

Momentary silence has me lifting my head, which is a mistake on my behalf.

In my drowsy state, he sounded further away. Turns out, he's only a couple of feet away, and as I turn, I catch his eye. Carter smirks at me, turning away, and I glance around to find I'm in some small cabin.

"Contact Clarke; he may help you," Carter tells his father before I hear yelling through the handset. My eyes flick to Carter to see him pull the phone from his ear and glare at it before he lets out a growl.

"Well, I told you he was a moron. If he has gotten himself locked up, what do you expect me to do about it? Figure it out. This is no longer my problem," he snaps back before hanging up.

I swallow when I watch him set his phone down and I quickly wiggle up on the bed, only to find I have nothing on but my bra and panties. I tug the itchy, brown blanket higher, and Carter purrs before stepping closer and crawling onto the bed.

I watch him. He's a predator, and I refuse to be his prey. Bond or not, he's not my Alpha, and I will never be his Luna.

"Did you rest well, Love?" he asks and I nod, watching him as he moves closer before I turn my head, looking out the window. I'm met with total darkness, my own face reflecting at me in the window. The place, as far as I can tell, is somewhere deep in the woods. I can hear owls and night creatures outside.

"Where are we?" I ask, turning to look at Carter again.

"In the woods," he purrs, and I lift my knees, drawing the blanket closer.

"Yes, but *where*?" I ask him.

"My mother's place. She built it with the forsaken," he says.

"She built this place?"

"Yes, they aren't all crazed. Some still hold some sense. Though she was too far gone by the time I found her," Carter tells me.

"The rest of the forsaken?" I ask.

"Dead. I killed them, and those that I didn't kill, your rogues did in the attack. It is perfectly safe out here," he tells me. I continued to watch him carefully, not liking the sparkle of excitement in his eyes.

"Safe enough to bring Taylor here when I go back for her," he says, and I have to fight back a snarl. "I know it isn't what you expected, but it is only temporary until the heat dies down, and then we will flee the country," he tells me, gripping the blanket and tugging it down.

"I need to use the bathroom," I tell him abruptly.

"There is an outhouse," he says, and I quickly get out of bed. The floorboards creak under my feet, and he watches me.

I try to take in my surroundings, yet when I move off the bed, the clang of chains makes me notice the thing around my ankle.

"Just precautionary, my love. I wasn't sure how you would wake," he tells me as I stare down at the chain from my leg to the bed.

He climbs off the bed before pulling a key from his pocket and bending down, undoing the chain attached to the foot of the bed. How did I not notice that before? Now that I've seen it, the weight of it is all I can feel.

Carter grips the chain before pointing at the door. I look at it as he steps behind me.

"I'll take you," he whispers.

"That is unnecessary," I tell him.

"The feeling through the bond tells me it is," he whispers before giving me a nudge, and I clench my teeth but move toward the door.

"It is an adjustment; one you will get used to. One thing about rogues is we adapt," he says as I grip the door. Ain't that the truth, but I won't be getting accustomed to this place.

Stepping outside, I'm smashed by the harsh coldness of the wind. I rub my arms before spotting the small outhouse. I didn't really need to use the bathroom, or whatever the heck that ice age contraption is, but the moment the wind touches me, I suddenly need to pee.

The steps creak as I step off the tiny porch, and I can see nothing but darkness and trees, showing how utterly alone I truly am out here. The grass is wet from dew; I wonder what time it is. Kalen will come for me. I know he won't abandon me out here, or he'll alert Everly and Valen. They'll be wondering where I am by now. They have to be.

"Ava?" I ask.

"I left her at the train station. I haven't heard any reports on what happened to her. My plans didn't go as expected in the city and my men were arrested," Carter tells me with a growl as I make my way to the outhouse.

The door creaks as I open it and I frown. I would rather piss in the woods or ruin my panties; it seems more hygienic than this shit box—quite literally a box or trough to shit in.

"Door stays open," Carter says, gripping the swinging door before it can shut.

"Where exactly do you expect me to go when you're holding the chain you shackled me with?" I ask, trying to keep the anger from my tone. He huffs and clicks his tongue.

"Good point," he says, letting the door swing closed. I'm plunged into darkness.

I roll my eyes before letting out a breath and pushing the door open again; I sure as shit don't want to fall into the damn thing, and there's no light in here.

Carter gives me a crooked smile.

"There's no light," I tell him, and he holds the door open.

"Yeah, I never rigged the solar panels on that thing. I hardly stayed out here long enough to warrant using it," he tells me as I notice the solar panels on the cabin. We appear to be on some huge mountain, and the wind up here whistles and howls between the trees.

"Don't fall in. The only bath you'll find here is the stream," he laughs, and I look down at the makeshift toilet.

"Can you at least turn away?" I ask him, and he does, keeping one hand on the door, the chain in the other.

I squat over the damn thing and quickly pee, not wanting to touch it in case my ass develops ringworm or I get Tetanus.

"Are you done?" he asks when I pull my panties up. "Or do you want to suss out the woods a little, so you know you can't escape?"

"I'll take your word for it," I tell him as I step out, letting the door swing shut.

I follow him back to the cabin, wondering how far out of the city we are; I can't even see any lights, and I briefly wonder if Kalen and John's tracker I swallowed has a maximum distance.

Stepping inside the cabin, the air is a little warmer thanks to the fireplace. Carter moves toward the bed and locks the chain around the foot of it again. I sit on the edge, watching as he undresses, removing his shirt and moving toward the small kitchenette in only his jeans.

"Are you hungry?" he asks and I nod, keeping an eye on him while looking around the small space. A round table sits off to the side with some stumps for chairs.

A bearskin rug is sprawled on the floor beside the fireplace, and above it is a set of huge antlers. It reminds me a little of a hunter's cabin. There are even a few taxidermy pieces. One is an owl.

"You hunt?" I ask him, wondering if there are any guns kept here. He shrugs, not bothering to answer as he grabs a steel camping kettle and fills it with bottled water from a box on the floor, then sets it on a hook inside the fireplace.

"How did we get here? I didn't see your car or the road," I ask him.

"I carried you. I had this place set up already. I was never staying in the city," he tells me.

"So you didn't want to take over the city?" I ask him.

"No, that was my father's plan. I have no future there, and he

306

won't forgive me for killing my sister. We tolerate each other, nothing more and nothing less," he states.

"You killed her?" I ask, a little shocked.

"I put her out of her misery. That is no life for anyone—lying in a bed covered in bedsores, being pumped full of drugs with a tube breathing for you is cruelty, not a life. My father would have let her rot like that, so yes, I killed her," he says while stoking the fire. "I have packets of noodles; not much fresh stuff, mostly canned food. It isn't much, but I will get more supplies tomorrow, or I can go hunt something if you like?" he says. I shake my head.

"No, noodles are fine," I tell him. When he hands me the water bottle, I start to gulp the liquid down rather thirstily, but when I crane my neck back, I hiss and choke a little at the stinging sensation from his mark on my neck.

I lift my hand to it before he's suddenly in front of me and his hand is sweeping mine away as he grips my chin, turning my head away to examine it. I flinch at his fast movement, not expecting it.

"It's just my venom. It will probably be a little tender," he says, dipping his head before I feel his breath sweep over my skin, making it tingle. His tongue runs across it, making my entire body shudder as the bond flares to life.

He chuckles, pulling back. "I was afraid the bond wouldn't have the same effects, but I am glad it does."

"What do you mean?" I ask. My neck is now burning fiercely, developing its own pulsing throb.

"You didn't hear the rumors?" he asks, moving back to the fire; he grabs a kitchen towel and pulls the camp kettle from the fire.

"I was bitten years ago by my mother and attacked by the other forsaken, nearly killing me. My father spent years getting me treatment to lessen the effects. It prevented me from becoming crazed like the others, but I still developed the venom glands. I wasn't sure if marking you would kill you, though I am glad to see the marking gives you some form of immunity," Carter tells me.

What will that mean when we kill him? Assuming Kalen and John can actually find me out here.

"How far are we from the city?" I ask, changing the subject.

"Four hours, roughly," Carter tells me, pouring the hot water into a saucepan and dropping the dried noodles in it. I try not to let that bother me. Information is vital, and right now, I need to bide my time. I just hope the tracker can lead them to me.

CHAPTER
FORTY-SIX

Zoe

I've been waiting with Marcus at Everly's place for hours since Marcus brought me here after getting the kids from school, yet Macey still hasn't returned home, and I'm beginning to worry. She hates leaving me alone and has always stuck to her times. One thing about Macey is she's never tardy, and her not being here when she said she would only adds to my anxiety.

Marcus pecks my temple as he passes me where I'm cutting up vegetables. We're making the kids dinner when Taylor came over, looking out of place without her mother; I feel out of place without her or Everly here.

"Can you try Mom again?" she asks, pulling a stool from the counter and climbing up on it. I glance at Marcus, who chews his lip, before I smile and nod to her.

"Of course, sweetie," I tell her, about to retrieve my phone when Marcus slides his to me.

'Have you notified Valen?' I mind-link him, and I see him nod out of the corner of my eyes as I dial her number.

'*Any word from Kalen?*' I ask him via the mind-link, making sure Taylor doesn't overhear our conversation. He shakes his head.

The worry on Taylor's face tells me she knows something is amiss. Her mother rarely leaves her unless she's with us, but she had said nothing of the sort to Taylor or any of us that she would be running late. Her phone—which I know she would have had on full charge—goes straight to voicemail.

Valen said his father is unreachable too, and none of us have heard from John either. All we get is radio silence when we try their pack tethers, making me believe they can't be in the city or they would be able to be reached via mind-link.

"She might have gotten caught up with work," I tell Taylor, trying to reassure her. Taylor nods sadly before going off back to Valarian and Casey, who are drawing happily at the table and discussing potential baby names. Everly and Valen are still in the hospital, and I know Valen called earlier to say he was going to collect Valarian after dinner to bring him to meet his sisters and mother.

Opening the mind link, I tug on Valen's tether and he opens it straight away. '*How is Eve?*' I ask him.

'*Good. She's trying to breastfeed. One baby has a tongue-tie so she's having trouble nursing,*' he tells me.

'*Any news from your father?*' I ask him.

'*No, and I can't reach John either, but he seems close. I can feel his tether—it came back about 20 minutes ago. Something is going on.*'

'*Everly can't contact him or Macey?*'

'*I'm not adding extra stress to her by asking her. I know if she finds out, she'll go looking for Macey, and Doc said she can't shift for at least a week.*'

'*Okay, well—*' My words cut off when I hear Valarian shriek.

"Pop, Pop!" he calls, rushing toward the hall when I get a whiff of John's scent.

'*Hang on. John is here. I'll speak to you in a second,*' I tell Valen.

'*Thank the Goddess, ask him where my father is,*' Valen says quickly.

'*Yep, will do,*' I tell him before cutting the link. I move around the counter toward the hall when Valarian suddenly backs up. His head turns to me and a frightened expression moves across his face, and I freeze in my tracks when I see John carrying Ava through the doors.

"Ava?" I gasp, rushing over to help him, throwing toys and the kids' blankets from the couch so he can set her down while Marcus races over. I'm too shocked to properly get my bearings, yet the relief I feel upon seeing her nearly makes me sob as John sets her down before looking at us.

Marcus runs off again, returning with a bottle of water and handing it to Ava.

"My old pack doctor is on his way to check her over. Zoe, you need to watch Ava for me," John says before turning to Marcus. "And you are coming with me."

I look up at him from where I'm crouched beside Ava, helping her hold the bottle to her lips when John turns his attention to Marcus. Marcus stares at him and I see his eyes glaze over, obviously speaking to John through the mind-link. Trusting Marcus to keep me in the loop, I ignore them; right now, Ava needs me and I have to calm the kids down.

"Auntie Ava?" Valarian whispers and crushes her in a hug.

"I'm alright, I got lost," she tells him, not realizing the kids knew or had some understanding of what had been going on. When Valarian lets her go, her hand weakly grips my arms and tears well in her eyes before flicking to the kids, who stand nearby, horrified; Valarian is crying and I see John rub his back and give him a kiss on the head.

"You're okay," she chokes out at me.

"I'm alive," I tell her. I'm far from okay, but I will be one day. I have my village, and our village is family.

"Go get Auntie Ava a pillow and some blankets," John tells Valarian, who runs off to get them. Ava smiles sadly when I feel the mind-link open up.

'What's going on?' I ask Marcus.

'I need to help John and Kalen,' he says, and I watch as he and John leave the room and head up the hall.

'Where are you going?' I ask him.

'To find Macey,' Marcus tells me, and I gasp, looking at Taylor over my shoulder.

'What do you mean?' I ask him, but he doesn't reply. I stand up when he comes back out pulling on a jacket and his boots.

'Where is Macey, Marcus?' I growl through the mind-link, and he lifts his head, looking at me. I start to open my mouth and demand he tell me when Marcus points to Taylor behind me and I close my mouth, trying not to panic and scare her daughter.

"Marcus?" I ask him.

Marcus doesn't answer right away; the silence makes the skin on the back of my neck prickle, and my entire body breaks out in goosebumps as every fiber of my being tells me something is seriously wrong.

'Carter has her,' Marcus tells me, and I feel my legs wobble as I try to make sense of his words. Tears prick my eyes and he comes over and kisses my cheek.

Why would Carter have her?

"I'll bring her home," he whispers, and I nod my head. John comes out in a change of clothes and stops in the hall.

"Marcus?" he calls.

"Yep," Marcus says before Casey rushes over to him with her arms up; he bends down, scooping her up.

"Where are you going, Dad? Can I come?" she asks.

"Not this time. I'll be back soon," he says, pecking her cheek, and setting her down before following John out. All I can do is stare in shock, trying to figure out what is going on and how everything got so out of hand. Casey comes over and climbs in my lap.

"Where's he going, Mom?"

"To work, he'll be back soon," Ava tells her while worry gnaws at me.

J ohn

"Where are we going?" Marcus asks me, and I glance over at him as I pull out of the garage and onto the street. We're going to meet Kalen outside the city.

"To meet up with Kalen," I tell him.

"I just don't get why Carter would take Macey. We should be telling Valen. He'll find out, and he won't be happy we kept this from him," Marcus tells me, and I chew the inside of my lip.

Everly has enough on her plate, and I don't want to ruin what should be a joyous moment for her and Valen with this news. Kalen believes the same thing and doesn't want to taint the day even more for them at this time. We can handle this, assuming Kalen is able to pick up her location. That's the concerning part. We lost her, and her phone was switched off, so we can't even track it with the cell towers.

"John, either you tell me what's going on, or I'm contacting Valen," Marcus snarls at me, and I turn the radio down as we leave the city limits.

"Carter is Macey's mate. She bargained herself to get Ava back.

We were supposed to ambush him, but then the council interfered, as you know, and ruined our plans. We thought we had it under control," I tell him.

"Wait, what? And you kept this from us? FROM THE PACK?" he yells, and I glare out the windscreen.

"Yes, because Macey asked us to! Think about it, Marcus. Think about what I just said," I snap back at him. Marcus falls quiet before he gasps, my words finally sinking in.

"Everly and Zoe wouldn't have allowed us to kill him," he murmurs, looking at me, and I nod. Macey knows that, and she's right.

"Did Macey ask you to keep this from them?" Marcus asks, and I nod again.

"Fuck! So what now?" he asks with a growl.

"We find Macey and Carter and–"

"You kill him, and it will kill Macey! We have to figure out something else. Everly will never forgive either of you for this," Marcus says, sitting back in his chair and clutching his hair.

"And you will keep it to yourself. Valen will tell Everly, and—"

Marcus growls at me. "And he should!" he snaps, and I glare at him before pressing my lips in a line.

"I asked for your help, not your judgment! Either keep quiet, or I will leave you on the side of the road," I tell him. Marcus curses and shakes his head.

"So, where are we headed?"

"To meet Kalen. We put a tracker on Macey, but we lost the signal. Kalen said you're good with tech. We need you to up the frequency, expand it," I tell him, pulling into a gas station just outside the city limits. I jump out, popping the cap and filling the car up.

"What sort of tracker is it?" Marcus asks, climbing out of the car before I see his eyes glaze over. I keep filling the car up, knowing he's being mind-linked. He sighs and shakes his head.

"Zoe?" I ask him, and he nods, scratching the back of his neck and glancing around.

"Yeah, she wants to know what's going on," he tells me.

"What did you tell her?"

"The same thing; that I'm helping you, that we're looking for Carter. But she's suspicious. For one, she knows Macey would never leave Taylor, and two, she wouldn't not answer her calls. She also doesn't understand why Carter would take her," Marcus says when the pump clicks, telling me the tank is full.

"And you won't tell her. She hasn't contacted Valen or Everly?" I ask him, and he growls, not happy about lying to his mate.

"No, she said she would wait until I know what's going on," Marcus tells me, and I let out a breath of relief. The last thing we need is Everly out here looking for Macey after having a C-Section.

"Explains why she had us sign all those documents. I can't believe this. We need to find her! I come back without her, Zoe will fucking kill me."

"We will. And Zoe won't. Besides, you're her mate," I tell him, and he laughs.

"Idiot. There's a reason Macey didn't tell them. She knew what their reaction would be and that Zoe and Everly wouldn't allow it. She knew Zoe would sacrifice her own mental health by allowing him to live so Macey could. Those girls are a package deal, John. Their bond outweighs any mate bond," Marcus tells me, and I nod.

I swallow as I go in to pay for the fuel. He's right; I can't return home to my daughters without Macy. I owe them both this much.

I owe my Claire to fix what I broke, owe her for destroying our family—and her; something I will live with for the rest of my life—but I will not live with knowing I destroyed Everly more.

Macey isn't just a rogue friend. She's as much a sister to my daughter as Ava is. Therefore, she's mine, too. And I won't make the same mistakes of the past. I protect what's mine.

As I head back to the car, the weight of the situation sits heavily on me. We can't fail. I have to bring her home to her daughter—to mine.

Starting my car again, I pull onto the old highway heading for the defunct power station where we're meeting up with Kalen.

"If we can't pick up her location by the end of the weekend, we tell Valen. Just give them the weekend. They don't need this stress right now."

"No, you have twenty-four hours, or I'm going to Valen with this myself. I can hold Zoe off for a day or so, but after that, she'll go to Everly," Marcus says, and I suck in a breath before nodding. Kalen will be angry, but it's looking like we have no choice. We need to find Macey and bring her home.

Macey didn't have to fight for me and save me in the forsaken attack, yet she did. I owe her my life, and I will lay it down for her if needed, just like I would give my last breath if it meant bringing my Claire back. Now we just need to find her.

CHAPTER
FORTY-EIGHT

Macey

The following morning, I wake to a pinch in my neck. I hardly slept all night as I fought the urge, yet my attempts to stay awake were unsuccessful; exhaustion eventually took me.

"Shh, my love, it is just a sedative," Carter murmurs as he pulls the syringe from my neck. My fingertips touch the spot. He handcuffed me to him during the night. I had tried to shift out of my restraints, yet he pounced on me before I even made it a step from the bed, which earned me the handcuffs for my efforts. He had also drugged me the moment he wrestled me back into the restraints. I cursed myself all night. I should have held out longer, earned his trust. All night I had stared at the ceiling, completely paralyzed. Panic courses through me as he stabs me again.

"It's just a precaution. This won't paralyze you completely, only stop you from shifting mostly and is more of a muscle relaxant. My father's invention; shitty man, but a smart one," he says.

There's so much I could say about his father's intelligence, or lack thereof, yet, I hold my tongue.

Carter waits for the drug to start taking effect, watching me as he gets changed. My limbs become heavy, though I still have feeling in them. He sets a bucket by the bed and my brows furrow.

"In case you need to use the bathroom. It should start to wear off just before I get back," he says. I growl at him, disgusted that he would even think I would use it. If that fucker thinks I'm using that, he is sorely mistaken. I would rather shit my pants and watch him clean me with no working water here; payback for keeping me locked up like a dog.

"I know it isn't ideal, but it's just in case. I won't be long."

My tongue feels thick in my mouth, so I smile at him, cursing him to the Goddess. He leans over the bed as if he sees nothing wrong with the entire scenario and pecks my lips.

I hate how the bond reacts to his affections. The Goddess really fucked up when she created us. No matter how vile and despicable our mates are, our bonds flourish and get excited from any form of attention. All I know is when I meet her in the afterlife, I have a few choice words for her about this entire mate bond bullshit.

One thing I've always envied the humans; they seriously have no idea how lucky they are to be able to choose their own destiny and who they allow in it. But no! We shun our fated mate and are punished with death, unless you're an Alpha and pack tethered. What a crock of shit that is. You really fucked that up, Moon Goddess! Shouldn't the Goddess be a feminist? She is a woman, after all!

"I won't be long. There's a town about an hour away, so try to rest, because tonight we complete the mate bond," he tells me, brushing his knuckles down my cheek. I turn my head away from him and he growls.

"We will complete the mate bond, Macey. I would prefer if you willingly accept that, but if not, I will make you submit," he says, and I turn back to look at him. He growls at me, forcing his aura out to show he is perfectly capable of what he threatened.

"Choose wisely, Macey. Sometimes it is better to give in," he says before walking out.

Yep, well, he just solidified it now. If I can't find a way out of these restraints, I am shitting myself. Let's see how willing he is then!

Whatever he gave me works pretty quickly. I find even lifting my head difficult, yet I can move a little, so that's something. After several tries, I manage to roll off the bed and hit the floor with a hard thump. I groan; the floor is harder than it looks, or maybe it's because I feel like dead weight. Once on the ground, I try to sit up, managing to prop myself up against the bedside table. Man, I feel so heavy, and my body tingles like it has pins and needles.

I glance around the room for the hundredth time, yet I know it's pointless. There's nothing here that would break the thick chain. And then what? Even if I could break the damn thing, I can't walk. I could try to roll my way out of here, or army crawl? I would be lucky to make it off the porch.

I stare at the plastic bucket before growling and smacking it with my hand and it skids across the floor by the fire. That took far too much effort for such a small movement.

Minutes pass as I look around the room before I finally give up and rest my head back on the bedside table, the angle making me stare off at the ceiling and fireplace. My mind wanders to Taylor.

What's she doing? What did she have for breakfast? Was it Everly or Zoe who tucked her in last night and kissed her forehead? Gosh I miss her.

Time slips by as I stare at the roof.

My eyes move to the huge antlers above the fireplace. I wonder what they're from and if the poor creature suffered?

I'm running out of time. He'll be back soon; I'm no closer to escaping, and I have no idea if Kalen and John are looking for me. The girls will be questioning my absence. They know I would never leave Taylor.

For some reason, my eyes keep going back to those hideous antlers.

I just need to hold out a little longer, I think to myself. Carter's words come back to me about having to mate with him and my entire body shudders with revulsion. A tear slips down my cheek. I want to go home—back to my daughter and back to my idiot boyfriend who thinks I don't want him because he has a bad leg. Fool of a man; what use is his leg to me? I don't care for his leg! Only his damn heart!

Once again, my attention is drawn to those antlers. But will they work?

I blink, my senses coming to me after my little pity party. How much time did I waste being a cry baby? How much longer do I have left? I'm not sure, but I have to try. So, with every bit of strength I have, I pull myself to my feet. My legs are feeling a little better, though the pins-and-needles sensation makes each step agony, and my muscles keep locking up, not wanting to cooperate.

I stagger to the fireplace, gripping the mantle to hold myself up. Reaching one arm up, I tug on the antlers, trying to unhook the damn things from the wall. I finally manage it, but I'm not expecting the weight, and it crashes to the ground with a loud a bang. I collapse along with it; the exertion was far too much. Yet now I have it down, how will I get it back up there? I'm getting more movement in my limbs, but nowhere near fast enough.

Shaking my head, I decide to figure that out later. For now, I need to find a way to break a piece off of this thing; this place has no knives, not even a damn spoon—it was terrible eating noodles with my fingers last night! Gritting my teeth, I use the fireplace to help stand before grabbing one side of the antlers and stomping on the end over and over, trying to crack one of the spikes off.

What feels like forever later, I manage to break off a chunk about the length from my elbow to wrist. As long as he doesn't look too hard at it, he won't notice I broke a piece off. I glance up at the tiny hook with a sigh. Now to get it back up there.

Getting it back on is another mission that leaves me staggering back to the bed covered in sweat. When I've caught my breath, I stare at the piece I broke off. It's pretty blunt, so I could definitely brandish it as a weapon, but only in this state; I would never get enough force behind it while sedated. At least it's something, and something is better than nothing. I tuck it down between the mattress and the headboard just in time, because it's roughly ten minutes later that I hear noise from outside. I hold my breath as the door creaks open and Carter steps in with a backpack over one shoulder. He toes off his shoes and leaves them at the door.

"Did you rest?" he asks as he walks through the cabin to the small kitchen. He sets some stuff down before rummaging through the bags.

"I need to use the luxury bathroom we have here," I tell him, and he glances over his shoulder at me.

"I see you are still in a mood," he states, and I look away.

"How about we go to the stream where you can bathe before the sun goes down? I bought toiletries," he says.

"Sounds splendid," I drawl.

"Tone, Macey or I will wash your mouth out with soap, so don't tempt me. I am being nice. I don't have to be," he growls, and I swallow nervously. He's right. I have to keep the bitch from my tone. It will do me no favors here.

Macey

"I'm sorry," I tell him, yet those words taste like poison on my tongue. He smirks before turning back to rummage through the backpack. He pulls out a silky, slip dress and tosses it at me; it lands on the bed. I grab it and hold it up. Hardly practical, but better than a bra and underwear.

"Don't suppose you bought underwear?" I ask him.

"You don't need them," he says, and I chew my lip. I suddenly wish I had a period. I bet he would change his tune then.

Carter comes over to me and passes me a granola bar. I try to unwrap it, however, my fingers are not cooperating properly. I have a good chunk of my mobility left, though I'm a little worried about trekking in the woods like this.

Carter takes it from me and opens it, peeling back the wrapper before handing it back to me.

"You should have all your feeling back soon," he tells me as he kneels next to the bed. He pulls my legs to the edge, rubbing the sides of them before gripping my foot. After taking the key from around his neck, he undoes the padlock before rubbing my ankle as I watch.

If only he wasn't a psycho, I could get used to the tingles from the mate bond—the way my heart races when he's close, his intoxicating scent. If only he wasn't responsible for destroying so many lives, I could have come to love him. The bond yearns for him, calling out for him despite my mind knowing I can't keep him. That doesn't stop me wishing things were different, so I could have my mate.

"Can you wiggle your toes?" he asks, and I try. They move to his satisfaction, and he smiles before leaning down and kissing the top of my foot.

"I can carry you. It isn't far," he tells me, placing my foot down before walking over and grabbing the backpack. After placing two towels and the bag of toiletries in it, he tosses it over his shoulder, then scoops me up and heads for the door.

Carter is right, it isn't far. The moment he sets me down, though, he rummages through the bag and produces the handcuffs. I didn't see him slip them in the bag.

I growl and fold my arms.

"Macey!" he snaps, and I glare daggers at him. Carter sighs and glances around at the river that flows slowly. "Macey, give me your hand."

"I won't run; you would catch me if I did," I tell him, and he seems to think for a second. I lean forward and grab the bag at his feet, rummage through it, and pull out a bar of soap and some shampoo. Carter sighs loudly above me before crouching down next to the bag.

"You hold my hand then, and I won't cuff you," he says. "Deal?"

At least I won't be handcuffed. I nod my head. Carter starts removing his clothes and I can't help but admire his toned body, at least until he removes his pants and I know he plans on using that thing between his legs on me, which makes me look away. I don't remove my bra and underwear.

He offers me his hand and leads me to the river before walking into the water. I follow and he sits down. The water isn't that deep, and even sitting, it only comes up to his chest. I sit next to him, my hand still in his when he pulls me into his lap.

Instead of becoming angry and trying to shove him away, I allow it; hoping to gain a little trust. The last thing I want is to be drugged while he has his way with me. Carter takes the shampoo that was tucked under my arm.

"Since I'm sitting on you, can I at least have my hand back?"

"Will you run?"

I shake my head, and he lets my hand go. I start lathering my skin with the soap when Carter grips my hair and turns me sideways on his lap.

"Dip your head back." he says softly, and I do, letting him wet it. He turns me back before pouring the shampoo in his hand and setting the bottle between my thighs. He washes my hair and rinses it out while I sit there awkwardly.

"I won't hurt you, Macey, relax," he says. Won't hurt me, but making me submit doesn't fall into that category?

When he unclasps my bra, however, I growl at him, clutching the front and losing the soap.

"Almost lost it," Carter says, producing the soap I dropped. He tugs on my arm covering myself. "You have nothing to be shy about," he says, and I fight the urge to tell him to go fuck himself. He tosses my bra to the grass beside the river before insisting on washing me. Despite me not wanting him to, I have to admit I love the feel of his hands on my body. The bond makes his touch pleasurable, sensual, yet I do my best to ignore it. All too soon, though, we head back to the cabin. Carter lets me walk but keeps a strong grip on my hand, as if he thinks I'll run. Though I know that would be a stupid thing on my part.

"I have a surprise for you," he says, tucking me under his arm as we climb the last incline to the cabin. The sun is going down now, and I look out above all the trees—no one would hear me scream, no one would know I'm out here if he killed me, there's no place to run to, and I'm not even sure where I am.

Carter leads me back inside before chaining me back to the damn bed. I move to the front of the fireplace, trying to warm up. The temperature has significantly dropped, and this thin nightdress is hardly warm. Carter, noticing me shivering, grabs the blanket from the bed and drapes it over me before going to the kitchen. He returns with a block of chocolate. I blink at him; yep, chocolate will really take my mind off being kidnapped, held against my will, marked, and all the other shit he's done.

"Thanks," I tell him, trying to muster as much excitement as possible. He chuffs before going to cook dinner. Tonight's dinner consists of Irish stew in the can, though it tastes better than the noodles and is more filling.

As darkness swallows the place, my nervousness amps up exponentially and I can see he's getting impatient with my excuses of saying 'I'm warmer by the fire' or the constant 'I need to pee'. He even went so far as not allowing me water after the third time of claiming I needed to pee.

"Macey," Carter says, patting the bed. I open my mouth.

"I know you're stalling, and I know you don't need to pee, or go for a walk, and it isn't cold in here," he pats the bed and I look back at the fire, earning a growl from him. "One," he snarls, and I look at him.

"My patience is running very thin, Macey," he growls, and I feel his aura slip out. The hair on my body stands on end but I'm not completely defenseless against it now he's marked me. Nevertheless, it still hurts like a bitch.

"Two," he growls, forcing the crushing pain down on me. I grit my teeth, trying to feel for my own nonexistent aura in an attempt to push back against him when he pummels me with his aura, making me scream and double over. Sweat coats my skin and I glare at him.

"Your choice, Macey. Get here or find out what happens next, but it won't be pleasant. You will submit to me. You have been rogue for too long and are no match for me yet," he snaps, and his eyes flicker to the monster that lives inside him. Carter growls and goes to get up when I raise my hand.

"Fine, fine," I tell him, and he drops his aura while I catch my breath. I finally climb to my feet and make my way over to the bed. The entire time, he watches me as if he's getting ready to strike the moment I make a move wrong. The moment I'm close enough, he reaches over and yanks me onto the bed.

"See, that wasn't so hard," he purrs before kissing me. His kiss is gentle, his touch is gentle, yet my skin crawls and he growls. I can feel his frustration through the bond.

"Why are you being difficult? We are mates, Macey, it is inevitable," he purrs, nipping at my chin and working his way to my mark. He sucks on it and tingles flood my body, and an involuntary moan escapes my lips.

"I know you hate me, but we can get past that," he says.

"I can't have kids," I blurt. I don't know why I blurted it, maybe hoping he would run like every other man, yet all he does is look down at me.

"I'm aware, and I don't care. You are my mate."

"You don't care that I can't give you an heir?" I ask, a little shocked.

"No, and we will have Taylor once my father finds a way back into the city to retrieve her for us," he says, dipping his head down to capture my lips. Yet, his words make me fight harder to block the bond. All I can think is his father was going to take my daughter. Over my dead body, he would touch my daughter.

Carter, not realizing I shut down at his words, continues tasting my skin while all I do is stare. My mind is all over the place until I feel him slide the dress up over my hips, snapping me out of my troubled thoughts. I grip his hands and he growls, but I push on his shoulder and he looks at it. I suck in a breath and push him to roll onto his back, which he does reluctantly, it's clear he doesn't trust me. He leans against the headboard, watching me cautiously.

"What are you playing at?" he asks. I figured he would find my abrupt change of mind suspicious.

"You're right, it *is* inevitable. But that doesn't mean it has to be unpleasant, right?" I ask before climbing between his legs. His eyes weigh heavily on me as I reach for the waistband of his pants.

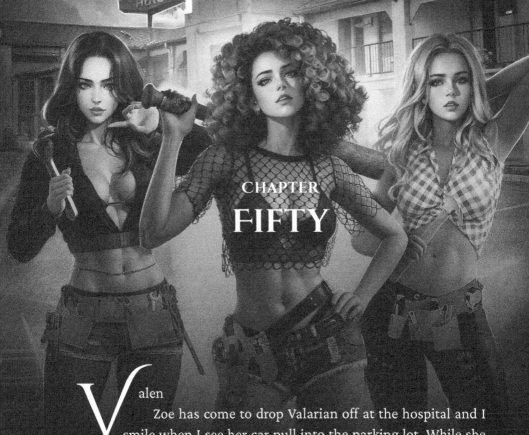

CHAPTER
FIFTY

Valen

Zoe has come to drop Valarian off at the hospital and I smile when I see her car pull into the parking lot. While she parks the car, I make my way over to her before opening the back door. Quickly unclipping his seatbelt, he hops out of the car excitedly, wanting to see his sisters; he brought the plushies he helped pick out with him. I glance in the car and notice Taylor and Casey are both in their car seats too, which is a little odd; it's pretty late at night.

"Where are Marcus and Macey? Also, have you heard from my father?" I ask Zoe, who chews her lip nervously.

She glances in the back at the girls before climbing out of the car and ushering me to the rear of the vehicle. Valarian climbs up onto the hood of the car and waits for me while clutching the blue and green plushies; Zoe glances at him as if to make sure he's out of earshot.

"John returned home with Ava," Zoe whispers, and I blink at her, dumbfounded because nobody told me Ava was found or handed back. Why had no one told me? This is good news, assuming she's alright, and Everly will be relieved to know her sister is okay.

"What do you mean? Is she okay?"

"She's fine. She was a little dehydrated. John had his old pack doctor check her over," Zoe tells me.

"And no one thought to tell me?" I whisper-yell.

"No, because your father and John didn't want to ruin your first night with your babies. But there's more. Macey cut a deal with Carter; she swapped places with Ava."

My brows furrow at this information. Why would she swap places with her? It makes no sense. And what would Carter want with Macey? I open my mouth to say something when Zoe speaks first.

"John and Marcus went to help your father look for her. That's why you can't get a hold of anyone. They told me not to tell you."

"I'll send men out to help them search. Whereabouts in the city are they looking for her? I can send scouts out to help."

"I'm not supposed to tell you, but Macey isn't in the city. They have a tracker on her; Marcus called me just before you did. They picked up a signal, but it's weak and not giving them an exact location," Zoe tells me, and I curse, shaking my head.

"Just go take Valarian in to see his sisters and tell Everly her sister is fine. As soon as I know what's going on, I'll let you know. I told Marcus he should call you."

I growl, knowing they were doing this behind my back. "Please do, because apparently, no one thought to inform me!" I snap, and she cringes.

"They didn't want to ruin yours and Everly's day."

"It has been nearly forty-eight hours since they were born. Someone should have fucking told me by now! Get hold of Marcus and get him to fucking call me! He's been ignoring my calls," I snarl at her, and she nods her head before climbing back into the car.

My head is all over the place. They didn't tell me, and now they are Goddess knows where and could be walking into an ambush for all they know. But it explains the silence through the pack link and why everyone was ignoring my calls. Even Everly has been worried because she was expecting her father and mine to be here by now, especially with how excited they were.

"Is everything okay, Dad?" Valarian asks as he rushes over to grab my hand.

"Everything is fine. Are you excited about meeting your sisters?" I ask him.

"Yes, and Mom. I don't like being away from Mom. I brought the plushies," he says, showing me.

"The girls will love them," I tell him, giving his hand a squeeze before we navigate our way to the maternity ward. As we get closer, I can hear them crying and I pick up my pace.

Everly still can't shift to heal for a few more days and struggles with moving much. The moment I open the door, she beams when she lays eyes on Valarian. He rushes toward her excitedly, where she's trying to get one baby to latch, while one cries in the bassinet. The third is lying between her thighs asleep, having just been fed.

"Can you grab her?" she nods toward the bassinet, and I wander over, plucking her bundled-up little form out of the crib.

All three babies inherited my genetic mutation. All three girls have amber eyes and dark hair. We still haven't picked out names yet. I have an idea for one name, but I have yet to run it by Everly. So, for now, they're still babies A, B, and C.

Moving to the chair beside the bed, I rock baby B in my arms while Valarian drags a chair over to the other side of Everly so he can kneel on it next to the her. He places his hands on the side of the bed, peering at baby A sleeping on her legs, sucking on her fingers.

"They're so small," Valarian whispers, stroking Baby C's foot while Everly attempts to breastfeed. She's finding it harder to nurse this time with three babies and no supply. We've been supplementing with formula, yet she's still determined to try to give them as much breast milk as possible.

"Are you being good for Auntie Zoe, Auntie Macey, and Pop?" Everly asks Valarian, sweeping his hair from his face. I need to cut it; it's getting too long, and he's been complaining his hair is messy. Zoe had tried to cut it for him last night, but he refused to let her touch it. Valarian looks at me. I swear that boy is too smart for his own good. The look he gives me is far too knowledgeable for a five year old. I wait to see if he mentions Macey being gone.

"Yep! Pop brought Auntie Ava home," he says before showing the baby the dinosaur plushie. Everly's head whips to the side to look at me.

"Ava's back?" she stammers the words out, and I nod.

"Carter gave her back. But we'll talk later when Valarian isn't listening," I tell her. Her eyes well with tears, and she swallows but nods her head, turning her attention back to Valarian and the girls.

"Can I hold one?" Valarian asks excitedly, reaching for the baby on her legs.

"Wait! Wait, you need to be careful. Come here," I tell him, and he climbs down off the chair and rushes over as I stand holding baby B in my arms.

"Sit in the chair, and I'll help you hold her," I tell him.

Valarian does, holding his arms out. I place her in his arms but keep a firm grip under her bundled butt and head in case he drops his arms. Valarian looks down at her in awe and sniffs her little head.

"She smells like Mom," he says before kissing her little head. The baby squirms in my hands and opens her eyes, and Valarian gasps.

"She has our eyes, Dad!" he squeals, inspecting them before smiling brightly.

"They all do," I tell him, leaning closer to kiss his head. Valarian plays with her tiny fingers before he leans down and kisses her nose.

I kneel while holding her—my back hurting from the hard, blue hospital chairs—while Valarian coos and makes babbling noises. When my phone starts to ring in my pocket, the vibration makes me stand, and Valarian pouts when I take his sister away, setting her in the bassinet.

"Go sit with Mom; I'll be back in a minute," I tell him while I pull my phone from my pocket.

Everly shuffles over on the bed carefully and he climbs up next to her with my help. Once I see all the kids and my mate are secure, I walk out of the room. It was Marcus calling me when I saw the screen.

Shutting the door behind me, I quickly answer it. "Forget to tell me something?" I snap at him.

"I know. I know. You can kill me later. We need your help," Marcus says, and I growl at him through the phone.

"Did you find her?"

"We think so. We have an approximate area. But the search area's too big. We need men out here. And we're in the forsaken territory. It would be good to have someone who has immunity besides your father out here to go in first," Marcus tells me.

Fuck, my father and I both have some strange immunity to forsaken bites from the mutation handed down, which I kind of hope is handed down to our children. Few people know about it, and it isn't something that we publicize. Though with how many bites we both had after the forsaken attack, they probably figured it out when we didn't get sick. Alphas have a little more immunity to the venom in general, but the forsaken bites had no effect on me and my father at all besides a burning sensation.

"Send me the coordinates and I'll send scouts and warriors out. I'm on my way," I tell him, hanging up. Everly is already staring at the door when I walk back into the room, and I know she would have been straining to listen, which is why I shut the door. I could feel her curiosity while I was on the phone.

'What is going on?' she asks through the mind-link while glancing down at Valarian. I know she can feel my worry and anger through the bond; I should be out there with my men.

'Carter has Macey,' I tell her, and she purses her lips. The look of fury on her face is as angry as I feel.

'So, why are you still standing there?' she replies, and I smirk before moving toward the bed. I lean over Valarian and peck her lips.

"Come on, Valarian, I need to drop you off at home," I tell him, and his lip quivers, not wanting to leave his mother and sisters. I hate to be the one to break his heart.

"He's fine here. You can help me with your sisters, right?" Everly asks him, and he nods excitedly.

"I want to stay. I can look after Mom," he smiles.

'You should tell Tatum,' she mind-links, and I know she's right. Tatum had managed to use his crutches earlier and walked down to see us. I think he thought he would find Macey here because he looked pretty disappointed when he asked where she was and I had no answer for him. He had stayed for an hour or so and said he wanted to apologize to her and that he didn't mean what he said.

I get it; he feels useless not being able to walk properly and doesn't want to be a burden on her. The nurses scolded him for walking down because he has an infection in his leg that requires extra surgery to clean it out and they forced him back to his room.

"I'll tell him before I leave," I tell her, gripping Valarian's face.

"Behave for your mother and stay in this room. Don't leave. Your mother can't chase after you right now," I warn him, and he nods his little head.

"He'll be fine. I'll see you soon," Everly says. I nod to her, kissing each of the kids quickly.

'Make sure you come home to me. You are not leaving me with four babies to raise by myself,' she says through the mind-link.

'Not even the devil himself would stop me from coming home to you. Or them,' I tell her, and she nods, yet I can tell she's trying not to cry. She doesn't want me to go but knows I have to if we want to find Macey and have everyone come home safely.

My father and hers can handle themselves, but we aren't sure what they're walking into, and each new Alpha is stronger than their father; it means Carter is stronger than them, plus he was forsaken once, so we aren't sure what it means in terms of his bite.

As I leave, I swing by Tatum's room, stopping at the door. I don't know how to tell him Macey is in trouble, yet he has a right to know. He loves her and Taylor, and after seeing him today, I know he wants her back. Swallowing guiltily, I push the door open to find a nurse in there checking his vitals while another is redressing his leg—the room smells sterile, and I can smell antiseptic strongly in here. He looks up at me.

"Late-night visit, Alpha," he states, and I nod.

The nurse checks his dressings once more before smiling gently.

"I'll come back and finish up," she tells him. I wait for her and the other nurse to leave, and Tatum pulls himself up higher on the bed.

"Everything alright?" he asks.

I sigh and shake my head, moving closer to the bed. "It's Macey," I tell him, and he instantly perks up at her name.

"Is she here? Did she bring Taylor?" he asks.

"Carter has her, Tatum."

His eyes widen and he instantly tosses the blanket back. I grip his shoulder.

"Everly wanted me to tell you. I'm going after her, but you are in no state to travel," I tell him, trying to shove him back onto the bed.

"If it were Everly, would you be sitting around?" he growls at me, and I press my lips in a line.

"The doctor has told you, you can't shift."

"Fuck the doctors," he growls, standing, and I grip his arm. "I'm coming, Valen. That's my girl and my daughter's mother. You don't get to tell me something like this and expect me to sit around and wait for you to return," he snaps. I curse.

"Fine, but we're leaving now, and you are to hang back when we get there," I tell him, and he nods, though I have a feeling him hanging back with patrols isn't happening.

"Let's go," he growls, shaking my arm off and moving toward the door. When we step out, the nurse's eyes widen.

"Tatum, you should–"

"Leave him," I tell her, and she backs up as he moves past her, ignoring the worried look of the nurse. Nothing anyone could say is going to stop him from shifting to get to her if he needs to—not even the risk of losing his leg.

Kalen

"What did he say?" I ask Marcus as he hangs up the phone. I start unfolding the new map we bought from the gas station on the hood of the car.

"He's sending scouts and is on his way," Marcus tells me as we shine the flashlight on the map—we're trying to find any sort of trail. Though her signal is weak and keeps blinking out, we know roughly where she is, but the forest is so dense that navigating through unfamiliar terrain, even for us, could end up with us becoming lost or walking straight past her without seeing her.

John is walking along the forest edge, trying to pick up any tracks or scents, but we are at a standstill for now. We need help.

No doubt my son is furious with us. We had hoped to have found and brought her back before he found out, yet the hours ticked by, the day turned to night, and we found nothing. We had to ask for help.

Macey's life is the priority, and we don't want to take unnecessary risks more than we already have. This area is known as forsaken territory, yet we have yet to come across any.

"What about this track? It leads toward the river?" I ask, finding a tourist trail.

"Too small for access by car—hiking trail?" Marcus suggests. It cuts off before it gets to the river, but it is the only trail we have found.

"Over here," John calls out, and I look down along the road, the wind whipping my face as I turn in his direction. I can just make out his head and arm waving for us to come to him. It is bloody freezing out here. And the grass is ridiculously high along this road.

"Wait here," I tell Marcus, and he nods, putting his head down to go over the maps again with his flashlight as I walk toward John. One is a tourist map—though why anyone would take a tour out here is beyond me—the other is just an ordinary road map.

I stop beside John, but he immediately starts walking toward the truck stop about a quarter of a mile down the road; we had passed it on the way here, but it was empty.

"What is it?" I ask him, jogging to catch up with him when he turns on his heel.

"I think I found Carter's car," John tells me, and I pick up my pace to follow him. We walk to the far back of the truck stop, but all I see are a bathroom and some dumpsters; the place is entirely empty. Then John disappears into the long grass, which is angled wrong—bent toward the forest slightly. I follow him. Barely a couple of yards off the road, covered by branches and obscured by the grass, is a car.

"That's definitely his car," I tell John while trying to peer in the windows, but the tint is too dark, and with the lack of light, I can't make anything out.

The breeze picks up from the brewing storm—we will be racing the storm once the scouts and Valen arrive on the scene. Lightning has been streaking the sky for the past half hour, and the thunder is growing louder as it gets closer. The trees sway, bending in the wind whipping through the mountains, making it howl and whistle like something possessed.

"He can't be too far, surely. That's dense forest," John mutters, his eyes scanning the area.

"Yes. Unless Macey was knocked out, he would struggle to drag her through it; she would have fought."

"Not necessarily. Macey is smart. She would bide her time and wait, knowing we would search for her," Johns says, turning and staring at the ground and looking for tracks.

"What do you want to do?" I ask. He glances back toward the road.

"Valen will be hours away," John mutters, peering back into the forest's darkness.

"Not with the way my son drives," I tell him, knowing Valen doesn't seem to understand speed limits or how to abide by them. My son seems to have a lead foot. Even so, it would take him time to get here.

"I'm going in and taking a look around," John says, walking around the car.

"Wait, let me tell Marcus. And I will come with you. Marcus can hang back for Valen and the others to arrive," I tell him before walking out of the long grass and back to the road.

I make my way back to Marcus and let him know, and he fiddles with my phone, linking it to his. Walking around the back of my car, I pop the trunk and grab some flashlights before returning to John, who is stripping his clothes off.

"You're shifting?" I ask, and he nods.

"One of us should. Besides, I didn't bring my glasses, and my eyesight is better shifted," he laughs. I nod. Best to be a little prepared. Goddess knows what we will run into out there.

"You got the app open?" he asks, and I nod, holding up my phone to see her name blinking on and off. It will not give us a direct location though—it just flashes in general on the screen, but not in one spot, as if the signal is being blown around and bounced off things.

John sets his clothes on the car's roof and then shifts, and I turn the flashlight on before stepping into the forest after him. The darkness under the canopy of trees swallows us instantly. The place is silent, all noise dying out when it senses John, a predator, stalking through with his nose to the ground, tracking. Not even the crickets chirp. We move a little deeper, and after ten minutes or so, John starts sniffing a large fern under a tree.

"What have you found?" I ask him.

'Blood,' John mind-links back, and I shine the flashlight on the fern he was sniffing to see speckles of blood on the stalks. It has dried, and I pluck a leaf off and sniff it.

"Macey's," I tell John, and he nods, peering into the darkness. A soft growl escapes him and he lowers his head, moving through the trees silently, with me following behind.

CHAPTER
FIFTY-TWO

Macey

"You're right, it *is* inevitable. But that doesn't mean it has to be unpleasant, right?" I ask before climbing between his legs. His eyes weigh heavily on me as I reach for the waistband of his pants.

My fingers tremble as I grip them and slide them down his legs, only for him to grab my shoulders and haul me up his body. He crushes me against his body, and rolls on top of me, his hips sliding between my legs and pressing against me as he purrs.

His hands reach for the thin slip dress and he bunches it before slipping it over my head. Tossing it aside, his lips go to my chest. My skin buzzes and comes alive at his touch, tingles spreading every-where as he captures my nipple in his mouth.

After a moment, his lips trail down my ribs, nipping and grazing my flesh with his teeth. I swallow, trying to ignore our bond that's telling me to give myself to him; despite not wanting his hands pawing over me or his lips tasting me, the sensations are over-whelming. At least down there, he'll be distracted.

He nips at my hip, shoving my legs apart, and I feel beneath my pillow to the edge of the bed just before his mouth is suddenly on me; I cry out at the pleasurable sensation as his tongue sweeps over me even as my fingers search for the piece of the antler I broke off.

The chain on my ankle seems to annoy him when he shoves my leg higher and spreads me wider for him. I need to move closer to my side of the bed, knowing the antler is at the very edge of the mattress by the headboard, but the moment he sucks my clit, an involuntary moan escapes my lips and my hand fists the sheet. I hate that he can play my body like a damn instrument, thanks to the bond we share.

"You seem distracted," Carter murmurs against my lower lips, and my hand freezes in its search. I glance down at him to find him watching me, and his eyes flicker to that of his wolf side. It's eerie staring into them and seeing my face reflected back at me.

"No, I'm just worried about Taylor," I tell him, which isn't a lie. I'm terrified for her. I don't want Nixon anywhere near her, and if I don't tell him the truth, he would feel it through the bond and know I'm up to something. Carter sits up on his elbows and kisses my knee before he looks at me, his eyes scrutinizing my face.

"You will be reunited with your daughter soon enough, but for now, we complete the bond, Macey," he says, dipping his head and running his tongue along my thigh. He grips my hips, his hands going beneath my ass so he can lift me to his mouth. His hot lips cover me, and I squirm, using the movement to wiggle closer to the side I need.

While he's distracted, I slowly move my arm above my head again, placing my other hand on his head and fisting his hair while my fingertips search the edge of the bed. Carter growls against my clit, the vibration sending shock waves through me before I brush the edge of the antler.

I gently pull it out, knowing it isn't a hundred percent straight, and if it bangs on the wood, he'll be alerted; I leave it beneath my pillow within easy reach before tugging on his hair and moving my hips. He growls at me, trying to hold me still when I jerk his head back by his hair; he lifts his face in surprise, then crawls up my body, settling his weight between my legs. I wrap my arms around his neck, hugging him closer to kiss him.

My tongue delves between his lips and he kisses me back hungrily when I feel his erection pressing against me. I wrap my legs around his waist, rolling my hips against him, and arousal floods me. It helps me keep my plan concealed, yet also clouds my mind as my body decides it wants to overtake all rational thought. Carter groans against my lips, his tongue tangling with mine as he tastes every inch of my mouth.

Tears spring to my eyes at what I'm about to do.

I'm about to kill the one person whose soul should be linked to mine, my twin flame. I'm about to extinguish the fire and replace it with his blood—and death, including my own.

He's my mate. Carter is willing to love me despite me not being able to give him kids, despite me being rogue. It saddens me that the one person who actually wants me is toxic. I can't have him.

Though I hate the man, I still want him, just like I want Tatum, yet the bond pulls me to Carter so strongly. Some rational part of me knows it's just the bond making me feel this way but it's hard to focus on that part. If only Carter hadn't done what he had, no doubt I could have loved him. But I also love Tatum, and that love is pure, not tainted by death and anguish.

Carter rocks his hips against me, his hand going between our bodies as he positions himself at my entrance as his lips travel down to my mark on my right side. He sucks on it, nipping at my flesh, and I run my fingers through his hair.

My throat suddenly develops a lump as I choke back emotion, and I kiss his cheek before he thrusts himself inside me. He groans, and I roll my hips against him while he buries his face in my neck and breathes against my skin.

My hand leaves his side, slipping beneath the pillow beside me. I can't get his heart from this angle, yet still, I wrap my hand around the piece of antler.

His tongue traces over my mark. I'll miss that feeling. Tears stream down my face as he moves slowly, rocking his hips against me. I twine my fingers through his hair, getting a good hold and locking my legs around his waist. His hand grips my thigh.

Before I can stop it, sob tears from my lips as I plunge the antler into his neck.

He stills and gasps, startled, and I can feel the pain through the bond, the betrayal he feels at what I just did. The sobs grow harder and my heart aches with agony.

I grip him harder when he tries to push off the mattress, and I jerk the antler out, only to plunge it back in. Blood spurts across my face and gushes out of him, and his hand tries to pry free my hand holding the antler in my fist.

"Macey," he gasps, and I choke at the sound. Even so, I twist it, causing more blood to pour out. I feel it give as it goes through his windpipe, and I hear him gurgle.

"I could have loved you, and I would have loved you!" I cry as I clutch him. "But you hurt my sister," I breathe.

Carter gurgles, trying to lift up, but my legs are wrapped around his waist, my feet locked behind him at the ankles, keeping him trapped, keeping him inside me. I hold on to him as he struggles to breathe.

"No mate bond is stronger than the bond I have with my sisters," I tell him as he chokes on his own blood. It spews out of his mouth and coats my shoulder, face, and neck with its warmth.

His last breath beside my ear will always haunt me.

As will the pain that slices through my chest as sharp as a razor edge; it cuts right through my heart and makes my soul bleed as a coldness settles over me—so cold, it feels like death.

His.

And mine.

I feel the part of me that was connected to him die along with him. The bond tether snaps and agony tears through me, and I hiccup a sob.

Kalen said killing your own mate would have consequences, and it feels like I'm rotting from the inside out. I feel blood trickle from my nose instantly.

I sniffle, feeling his dead weight crushing me as his body goes limp, and it takes every ounce of strength I have left to crawl out from under him.

I'm drenched in his blood, and I look at his body, face down on the bed, before my shaky hands tuck the blanket up, as if I can somehow pretend I'm tucking him in instead of being unable to look at what I did. As I do, my legs crumple from under me, and I fall heavily beside the bed.

I killed him.

I killed my mate.

And knowing that only kills me even more.

FIFTY-THREE

Valen

We're all the way on the other side of the mountain from where we're meeting with my father. We're still about an hour away because the storm is making visibility a real bitch.

Dion and a few other men are traveling in the cars behind us as we try to get to my father. When the mind-link opens up, Marcus comes through. Stupidly, I open it, allowing Tatum in on the link, not expecting the news we get.

'How far away are you?' Marcus asks.

'About an hour away still, this storm is fucking terrible,' I tell him. My windscreen wipers are going a hundred miles an hour, and the road is barely visible, even to my enhanced eyesight. We're going to have a hell of a time finding anything out there if it doesn't blow over soon.

'Your father and John have headed in,' Marcus tells us.

'They were supposed to wait for us,' I growl, annoyed they would be so reckless and enter forsaken territory without backup. My father, at least, should know better. I know John isn't in the right headspace at the moment because of Claire, but even he should know better than to be this foolish.

'Yeah, well, your father found Carter's car and apparently some dried blood not far from it and decided he was sick of waiting,' Marcus says. *'That was the last contact I had with him via the mind-link. I can feel them through the tether, but it's as if they're both ignoring me now.'*

"Pull over," Tatum snarls. I glance at him out of the corner of my eyes, ignoring him.

'Okay, have they got their phones?' I ask Marcus.

'Yep, but there's some sort of interference. After ten minutes, I lost them on the app,' Marcus says.

"Valen, pull over!" Tatum snarls, punching my dash when I continue to ignore him. We're still an hour away. What use would pulling over be right now?

"Settle down. We're nearly there," I tell Tatum, shoving him out of the mind-link, so I can focus on what Marcus is trying to say to me. I know Tatum is scared for Macey, but I would never have expected his next reaction when I don't do as he asks.

"Let me out! It's quicker to go over the damn mountain than around it. PULL THE CAR OVER, VALEN!" Tatum yellS at me.

'Send–' My words are cut off when Tatum throws his door open beside me, and I jam both feet on the brake. The car locks up, and I grit my teeth, trying to hang onto the steering wheel as he tosses himself out of the car.

Horror washes over me at the speed I was going. I had barely slowed down much before he threw himself out. The screeching of the tires on the wet road is loud as I try not to slide out and into a ditch. My eyes go to the rear vision mirror to see those behind us slamming on their brakes while Tatum's body skids and rolls across the road. One of them has to swerve to miss him, and for a few heart-beats, I think he's a goner.

My heart races in my chest as the car comes to a stop and I toss my door open. Climbing out, I hear him groan as he gets to his hands and knees.

"Tatum!" I yell, running toward him. All I can smell is burned rubber from my tires.

My warriors pull over when he stands and staggers toward the opposite side of the road. Blood drenches him from where he all but skinned himself alive, as his clothes were torn from his body. He snarls, and my eyes widened in horror when I see he's about to try to shift.

If he manages it, it will either help him heal or kill him, I'm not sure, but his leg!

"Tatum!" I yell, about to Command him, but I suddenly hear his bones snapping and he screams. Each pop and crunch of bone is loud even over the raging storm, and my men start jumping out of their cars to try to stop him.

His skin is replaced with bloody fur, and his hands turn to claws as he tries to change, only to collapse to his knees. He forced the shift. It won't work properly.

I feel bile rise in my throat when he roars in furious anger as his body tries to refuse him, his bad leg not cooperating. His claws rake across the wet road as he drops his head and snarls.

His leg is dragging; it's the oddest, most gruesome thing I've ever seen in my life. He's going to rip off his own leg if he doesn't stop! Every part of him shifts slowly, except for his leg.

Moments pass, which feels like hours, before I see his knee bend the wrong way. His shin pops and fur runs along his busted leg. The scream of agony that tears from him makes me want to throw up when his femur finally snaps and his leg twists and shifts with him just as Dion and I reach him.

We reach him at the same time and I start to tackle him, but instead, I hit the cold, wet ground with a thud when he takes off running for the forest surrounding the mountain. Dion grabs my arm, yanking me up, and I curse, looking at the forest to see Tatum disappear into the long grass and trees.

"Shit!"

"What do you wanna do, Alpha?" Dion asks.

"Get back in your cars. I won't risk anyone else," I tell him. I hate it, but Tatum is on his own out there. This place is full of forsaken, and I have to look out for my men. Marcus said the other side had been scoped out pretty well and they hadn't seen any forsaken. On this side, however, we have no idea what's out there.

We race back to our cars, and I shake my head, cursing myself for being so stupid and allowing him into the mind-link. Yet, I never expected him to jump from a moving car!

M acey

I stare at Carter's body for Goddess knows how long before I come back to my senses. I glance around the room, and it suddenly looks a lot different. It was depressing before, but now it's as cold and dead as I feel inside.

My nose still hasn't stopped bleeding, and vertigo washes over me as I stand up. I stagger, moving toward the bag Carter had brought back with him. Undoing the zip, I rummage through it, looking for the key to the padlock before remembering it's around his neck, and I glance at his body, tucked in bed as if he were sleeping.

Hesitantly, I move toward him and pull the blanket back. My hand shakes as I reach forward, grab the chain around his neck, and yank it. The gold links snap, and I quickly shove the blanket back up to cover him. Tears spill over, and I blink and wipe my eyes, trying to clear them before my vision turns red. I rub at them furiously, only to vaguely manage to see my hands come back bloody, making me gape at them. I knew it would be harmful to kill a mate, yet I didn't consider myself dying beside him.

I don't want to die here! I want to see my little girl one last time —to at least tell her I love her, to see her face one more time. However, looking at my hands, I don't want her to remember me this way.

Something feels like it's decaying me from the inside out; as if my soul is rotting as quickly as my body. I feel sickly, and I know this is the consequence of me killing my mate.

I choke back a sob and undo the chain around my ankle as a crack of thunder makes the world seem like it's ending. The cabin rattles and the floor shakes with its violent tremor. It's pouring with rain now, and I know I'll be walking blindly out there, especially since I'm not sure I can shift.

But I have to try.

I may not be able to go home and see Taylor, but I need to get somewhere my body can be found. I don't want her to grow up not knowing if I abandoned her or if I'm dead. No, I will at least give her a body to bury.

Glancing at Carter, so much anger suddenly boils within me.

"I HATE YOU!" I scream at him before collapsing to the floor.

I punch the ground, my fist slamming into the shitty wood as I scream my anguish, frustration, and pain. My knuckles bleed as they split, and I clutch my hair, ripping at it. I want to hurt something, anything—myself—for feeling so weak.

I hate him. Hate him. The man took everything from me. Everything and everyone he touched was destroyed. He destroyed Zoe. He destroyed me.

But more than anything else, I hate him for destroying my baby, because she will have to grow up without the one person who loves her most.

I know Everly and Zoe will look after her, and I know they won't stop looking until they find what's left of me. I won't be able to raise her—they will for me.

But no one could ever love her the way I do.

I choke on a sob, cursing at how fucked up this is. How cruel life is that I not only lost a mate but my daughter too.

That saying, 'you don't know what you have until you lose it,' seems to laugh at me, because I never pictured finding my mate and losing him. Never pictured having my daughter and not being able to raise her. Never thought I would die without watching her become the woman she is destined to be. I would have been content to be mateless as long as I served my purpose—to see her through to adulthood when she didn't need me anymore.

That was my life's purpose, to raise my baby, and now the only part of that purpose I have left is to get to a road so my body can be found, so she has something to bury. I can't die peacefully knowing she'll always wonder if I left her, abandoned her.

When I'm done destroying myself, I look at the handfuls of hair and my bloody fists. Numbness spreads over me, cold and uncaring, as I inhale a shaky breath. The air thickens with the storm as it pelts the tin roof.

All my fight is gone. It's empty. And I'm as dead inside as the bond I shared with him.

Deep down, I know I have to move, I need to get up.

Dragging myself to my feet, I stare at the door, swallowing down my sadness as I take a step toward it just as it bursts open, making me jump.

I stare at the darkness outside before a low, deep growl vibrates throughout the cabin as an enormous wolf I recognize, not only by scent but by his fur, to be John. His paws make the floorboards creak as he steps inside.

My legs give out from under me, realizing I won't have to die alone. More footsteps on the stairs outside reach my ears when John spots me.

"He's dead," I whisper. His body relaxes, and Kalen steps in behind him, pushing the door open more as John shifts back. I turn my gaze away, knowing he's naked. John moves toward the bed and I hear the blanket get yanked back.

"That he is," John states. I look at Kalen, who nods at John's words.

"Good. Now, what are you doing on the floor?" Kalen asks, and I blink at him.

"Dying!" I laugh, rolling my eyes at him. Great, now I'm numb—I can joke about my own death.

"Nonsense, *that's* what death looks like," Kalen says as he points to Carter.

"Is that an antler?" John asks curiously, holding up the bloody piece of bone. Kalen shakes his head at John before turning his attention back to me.

"Well, time to clean this mess up," he says, moving toward me, and I snort. He crouches in front of me.

"I killed my mate," I tell him.

"So did I," Kalen whispers, but I shake my head.

"Maybe not the same way, but I killed my Val. You know it, and I know it. What you did was brave. What I did was cowardly," Kalen tells me, gripping my face in his hands. "Now get up. You have a little girl to get home to, and I got grandbabies to meet."

"I can't go back like this. I won't force Taylor to watch me die. She will not remember me this way," I tell him.

"No. Taylor won't have to remember you, Macey because you are not dying. Now get up!" John says, and I look over at him to see he's stolen a pair of Carter's shorts from the bag and slipped them on.

"What about him? Even if I miraculously survive, I killed someone in cold blood. He was no threat to me," I tell them.

"Sadly, Carter won't be missed," Kalen says, and to me, that truly *is* sad, because despite everything, I know he was just broken and twisted. He wasn't a complete monster—I saw parts of him that proved that.

"Yeah, but the courts and council won't see it that way," I tell them before coughing.

"If that's the case, you never killed him. Just like you didn't kill Preston—I did," Kalen states, and I look at him before I heave.

Blood splatters the floor and covers Kalen's already drenched shirt. John steps forward as I choke on my blood. When I finally stop coughing, my throat feels extremely itchy. I know it's pointless to worry, because I'll be dead long before I get home.

"Suppose it doesn't matter," I tell them, holding up my hand, drenched in my blood. Kalen looks at John, who nods. Kalen's eyes turn glassy and he clears his throat before shaking his head and John stalks toward me almost angrily as he hauls me to my feet.

"You are not dying on us! So choose. Me or Kalen? Choose. Because I am not going home without you!" John growls.

I look between them as Kalen grabs a makeshift chair and John shoves me down in it.

"You will choose, Macey. Neither one of us wants the job of telling your daughter their mother is dead when we could have saved you," Kalen says.

I swallow, glancing between them and saying nothing. If I choose one, either way, I would be Valen's new stepmother or Everly's. That thought disgusts me. I love these two old fossils, but not in that sense, and after feeling the bond with Carter, I know what marking one of them would make me feel towards them. It was inevitable and so gross!

Yet, I also have no choice. This is my chance to go home to my baby.

"Fine, rock, paper, scissors?" Kalen says, turning to John.

"You won't choose, we'll choose for you," John adds.

I look at my dead mate on the bed, his body cold, and the two men who are old enough to be my damn father. I know Valen or Everly would forgive me for marking one of their dads, yet it feels wrong. The one person I *want* as a mate, I can't have, and my true mate is dead because I killed him.

Panic courses through me as I watch them repeatedly tie, both of them becoming frustrated as they shake their fists and both go scissors.

"This is ridiculous," I mutter at the stupid situation I'm stuck in.

Of course, not only did the Moon Goddess give me a shitty mate, she had to make two old guys be the ones to find me and is now forcing me to choose between them to save my life.

Kalen curses when they both choose paper this time.

"You're just going to have to choose, Macey. John or me? Which one is marking you?" Kalen says as they look at me expectantly. My lips part as I glance between them.

"So, who's it going to be?" John asks.

"Me!" comes a voice I never thought I would hear again. Kalen and John turn toward the door where the voice came from and so do I, to see Tatum walk up to the door. He's drenched and naked, and I have no idea how he got here, but there he is and I'm in disbelief.

"And you better say yes because neither of their dusty old lips are touching my mate!" Tatum says, stepping into the cabin.

Emotion chokes me and makes me speechless, and my body is moving toward him long before my brain comprehends it. I crash into him and my arms wrap around his neck as my legs circle his waist. Tatum stumbles back, clinging to me, his fingers tangling in my hair as he grips me like I'm his life jacket.

"I'm here now. I'm so sorry," Tatum whispers, kissing my face before tugging my head back, but I can't even form words, stunned he's here.

"I choose you, Macey. You are far more than I deserve, but I won't let them mark you," Tatum whispers, his eyes going to my neck and Carter's mark on it. He glances at the bed where Carter's body lies, then swallows and turns back to face me.

Tatum sweeps my hair over my shoulder that's caked in blood and Goddess knows what else before he snarls and sinks his teeth into my neck. Pain ripples through me as his teeth slice through my flesh, tearing Carter's mark to pieces and forcing Tatum's in its place.

The tingles start out slow as I feel the bond start sewing its way through me, ridding me of Carter's essence and replacing it with his. It burns like acid, but the pain is excruciating bliss as he sinks deeper before his canines hit bone. I feel his saliva move through my veins, feel his soul binding itself to mine and forcing mine to stay.

A sob escapes me and tears slip down my face as I turn my face into his neck. His bond strengthens me, allowing my canines to extend. Not an ounce of hesitation runs through me as I sink them into his neck, and fireworks explode in my head. Tingles make my skin vibrate as our souls entwine and bleed into each other when the bond snaps into place.

Tatum gasps, pulling his teeth from my neck. Gently, he runs his tongue along his mark, sealing it just as I pull my teeth from his. He presses his forehead against mine.

"Let's go home," he whispers, and I nod. Immense relief slivers through every atom in my body.

I can go home.

And I can go home to Taylor with the man I love as my mate.

E verly

Hours Later

All night I panicked. I felt useless, sick with worry and guilt that I was just sitting here waiting for them to return. I knew I would have just gotten in the way or become a constant worry for Valen and sometimes, you need to sit back and allow someone else to take over.

But for me, that's easier said than done. However, Valen had proven to me that he could be relied on. Even when we didn't see eye to eye, he still showed up and still kept his promises.

And this time was no different. Valen said he would bring Macey home, and he did. Earlier in the night, not long after Valen left, Zoe couldn't bear being home alone and Ava felt unsafe at home with just Zoe; or maybe it was her guilt about what happened to Zoe that she struggled to be alone with her, I don't know; I was just relieved to have them here.

So my room in the maternity ward had turned into a drop-in center. We sought comfort from each other's presence. Zoe had some warriors bring in blow-up mattresses for the kids to sleep on and the nurses had also found two extra beds and brought them in.

Macey had caused quite a fuss when she got here. She refused to be checked over until she saw Taylor.

Valen, Tatum, and Marcus almost immediately went off to deal with pack dramas, council members, and officials, and Ava had gone home with Dad and Kalen. After they all left, I felt wired and overly emotional.

Maybe it's because of everything that's gone on recently, or perhaps it's my fluctuating hormones from having the girls, but as I look around the room, I'm brought back to the day I met these two women—two women who became my sisters.

Macey lies beside me in the hospital bed, an IV in her hand, while she holds one of my girls with Taylor tucked against her side, asleep. Zoe sits by my feet, holding my other daughter, while I breastfeed the third one in my arms.

Zoe, feeling my gaze on her, looks over at me, placing my daughter over her shoulder to burp her.

"Don't you start. You cry, we all freaking cry," she chuckles with a sniffle. Shaking her head, she glances at Casey and Valarian asleep on the blow-up mattress in the room's corner.

She turns back to me and smiles sadly, then stares off at Macey, who's watching us. Zoe's guilt is clear on her face; she feels terrible Macey killed her mate for her—for all of us.

"Man, this is like a dose of déjà vu," Macey mutters, and it's clear she's thinking the same thing as me.

"Only thing missing is our rumbling bellies and the rude nurses and midwives," Zoe chuckles darkly.

"And the sneers and mutters, let's not forget those," Macey says, and I swallow.

"This hospital is a little nicer, too," I snicker, peering down at my daughter attached to my breast.

"It feels like a lifetime ago," Zoe mutters, and I nod, looking around at our kids, at my sisters.

357

"That's because none of us are those girls anymore," I tell them, and it's true. All of us came from nothing and built ourselves up in our own images. We raised our children together, and we did it through blood, sweat, and tears. We did it despite not believing we could at the start, until we showed ourselves what we were capable of—showed ourselves we didn't need anyone because we had each other.

"We aren't alone this time. It's not the same. We aren't scared little rogue women with no names, no identities, and no chance. It's different because *we* are. It's different because we know our worth; back then, we didn't," I tell them.

Macey nods, wiping a stray tear that escapes, and Zoe, I see, bites her lip to stop it from trembling.

"I know, it's just, I hate maternity wards," Macey says, and I understand that fear; understand what it's like seeing families gushing excitedly while we're tucked away, not to be seen; understood the trauma that's left behind from that experience. I know the feeling of walking out the hospital doors with a newborn in your arms and not knowing what you're doing or whom to turn to; not knowing how to provide for the baby in your arms when you can't provide for yourself.

"We'll get through this," Zoe says, pursing her lips, a faraway look in her eyes, and I brush her lower back with my feet through the blanket, bringing her back from where her mind took her.

We all know that feeling of being so low we thought we would drown in our despair and fear—it's what brought us together. It's also what drove us to prove everyone wrong. We would be heard, seen, and prove to them and ourselves that we didn't need anyone. And we did just that. So I know Zoe is right—this is just another obstacle we'll get through.

Because despite everything going wrong and finding ourselves back where we started, in a sense, it's not the same. We're far from that place, facing new challenges, but now we have the knowledge and drive backing us to overcome them. And most of all, we have each other and the village we built—the village we watched get destroyed and then rebuilt again.

Brick by bloody brick, we will rebuild the fractured parts of us. We won't bleed anymore. We'll patch those walls, repaint, readjust, adapt, and rebuild ourselves. We will morph into the next phase of life because life will continue, and we will continue showing it we aren't to be beaten.

We will show life that all our flaws and scars, the peeling paint and cracked crumbling pieces, don't mean we're broken or condemned. No, those broken pieces, once put together again, restore and strengthen us, and just add character. They show the rough edges, but still, it comes together beautifully, just like I know we will again. Only this time, we have our mates behind us to help.

For so long, we relied only on each other and the routines we had built. We lived and breathed each other, leaned on each other or ourselves so much that it feels good to let go of some of that weight on our shoulders and breathe without restraint. And by the looks on the girl's faces as our mates walk in, they feel the same.

Gone is the fear of loneliness, burden, and responsibility, because we now have others willing to share it. And not out of obligation or expectation, but because they want to.

"Did you sort everything out?" I ask Valen as he comes over to me. He leans down, kissing my forehead and brushing baby's cheek. Marcus is trying to steal the baby from Zoe's arms, while Tatum watches Macey hold Baby C, resting his head on her shoulder as he sits on her other side.

"Yes," Valen whispers.

"What about Carter?" Macey whispers, her glistening eyes flicking to Zoe and then Tatum. He pecks her cheek.

"I'll help you organize the funeral," Zoe says, and Macey chokes.

"I'm sorry. I know—"

"He was your mate," Zoe says simply, glancing at Tatum.

"And as much as I wish I was your fated mate, I understand you need to put this behind you," Tatum whispers to her.

"I doubt anyone will go, but it didn't feel right leaving him there to rot," Macey states, looking down at my daughter.

"You don't have to explain yourself, Macey. You know this," Zoe tells her.

"I know it's just—"

"It's because you're not a monster like he was. And I don't expect you to pretend not to care, Macey, just because of what happened. We will be standing right beside you," Zoe tells her with finality in her voice.

"That leads to another question I have for you, Zoe?" Valen says beside me. Marcus growls, the sound threatening, and Valen presses his lips in a line.

Zoe looks at Valen questioningly before sighing loudly.

"Let's hear it, then," she states. I see her walls go up as if she's about to take a blow. I had hoped Valen would hold off, but I supposed it needs to be taken care of.

"Amber handed over the location her new mate was hiding out at. Derrick has him in the cells. He's the last one; we found out Carter killed the other. But—"

"Amber and he marked each other when she left Micah," Zoe finishes for him, and Valen nods his head.

"We want to know what you want to do? The council supports any decision you make. Well, what's left of the council," Valen tells her, and she sucks in a breath.

"Amber?"

"She wasn't in on the plans, but she was made rogue. And obviously, she was the motivator for her father."

Zoe nods her head at his words.

"I let you kill him, and Amber dies." She sighs.

"It's your decision," Valen tells her, but what Marcus wants her to say is clear.

"There's been enough death. Please ensure he isn't jailed in the city," Zoe answers.

"Zoe?" Marcus says.

"No, it's my decision, and I won't kill her because of what he did. She can live with it just like he will have to live with his mistake, the same way I have to live with the memory of it," she says.

Marcus nods to Valen, his free arm slipping around her waist as he pulls her to his side.

"What about Nixon's pack?" I ask.

"It will be dismantled. Those pack members still alive can decide where they go, or remain and live as a rogue," Valen states, and I nod.

"We still have no idea of Nixon's whereabouts. His mate is being questioned, but the werewolf council is trying to find something to charge her with. Besides her trying to get us arrested, we don't really have any charges against her," Valen tells us.

"And if they can't charge her with anything?"

"She'll be made rogue and watched until she slips up," Valen states.

Well, it's better than nothing. I don't like the idea of her being in the city, but she can only be charged with what we can prove.

Valen holds his hands out, wanting to take baby A, and I hand her over to him, my arms suddenly feeling empty.

"She'll need burping," I tell him, and he nods, placing her over his shoulder while I tuck my boob away.

"Thought of any names yet?" Macey asks.

"Yeah, I wanted to ask about that actually," Valen states. I'm glad he has names because I have nothing.

"So let's hear them," Macey says.

"I'm still stuck on one. And if it's okay with you, I was wondering if I could pick the names?"

"You want to name all three?" I ask him worriedly. What if he names them something strange, or all their names start with V?

"I promise I won't fill out the paperwork until you agree," he states. I chew my lip but sigh.

"I swear if you name them after a car or something strange that they won't be able to pronounce, I will kick your ass. And don't name any Everly!" I tell him.

"Promise. But you have to wait until tomorrow. Dion is engraving their bracelets."

"Wait, you already went ahead?" I chuckle.

"I knew you would say yes. He's just waiting for the final name," he shrugs.

"What if I'd said no?"

"You could have named the last one, but we would need to make it match my chosen middle name. That's what I'm having trouble with-a name to go with the middle name," Valen tells me, and I narrow my eyes at him accusingly.

"You'll like the names, I promise," he says, smiling slyly.

V alen

We're finally going home, and I'm beside myself with panic. I think this is the slowest I've ever driven in my life. Cars are honking their horns behind me and I glare at the driver in my mirror. Does he not see the 'baby on board' sticker?

"Valen 45 miles per hour is already too slow for this strip. You're doing 20 under," Everly hisses at me as cars overtake me.

"We have fragile cargo in the car. What if their little heads wobble?" Just saying that has me reducing my speed more. It isn't worth the risk!

"We're more likely to get hit with you going this slow," Everly scolds, and I sigh. "I'm serious, Valen. Speed up or let me drive. They're more durable than you think."

"They're newborns!" I catch Everly rolling her eyes.

"I get this is your first newborn and you want to wrap them in cotton wool, but seriously, they're durable, geez. Valarian fell off the bed once, screamed his damn head off, but he's perfectly fine,"

"You dropped him off the bed?" I ask, horrified.

"No! Of course not! He rolled off. Damn near had a heart attack." She laughs.

"Why are you laughing?" I ask, outraged. She's not holding them if she's going to drop them.

"Nothing. Just something your mother said when she raced to our room because I was screaming like a banshee thinking I killed him."

"What did she say?" I asked, curious.

"I told her what happened, and her reply was 'He's screaming, he's fine. It's when they don't make noise that you worry'."

I raise an eyebrow at her. "How old was he?"

"Six months old. Don't even get me started on how many times I smacked the kid's head on the door frame lifting him into his car seat. He turned out perfectly fine," she states, while all I can think is how the heck my son is still alive? He should have brain damage with all these bumps to the head.

"Perfectly fine? The kid has OCD. See what dropping him did?"

Everly sighs and shakes her head. "I wonder where he gets that from. I bet the entire house is baby proofed," she taunts.

"OCD is not genetic," I tell her.

"I would debate otherwise," she retorts.

"And I don't have OCD," I argue.

"So you didn't babyproof the entire place?" she scoffs, and I swallow.

"Of course not!" I tell her, opening the mind-link. She shakes her head and peers out the window.

'What's up?' Marcus asks. He's watching Valarian for me since I couldn't fit everyone in the car.

'All the baby proofing stuff—hide it. Undo it. I need to prove to Everly I don't have OCD. She thinks I'm OCD,' I scoff.

'Ah, but you do have OCD,' Marcus replies and I bite back the urge to growl at him.

'No, I don't! Just do as I ask, damn it. I'm five minutes out.'

'On it,' Marcus says, and I cut the link.

"So, are you going to tell me the names you picked?" Everly asks, leaning over to check the babies, then hisses, clutching her stomach as she turns back to face the front.

"You'll find out tomorrow when I pick up the bracelets," I tell her. "And sit still before you hurt yourself."

"I'm fine," she says as I pull into the parking garage. "That was the slowest damn drive of my life. Next time, I'm driving!" she states, shoving the door open.

Now, to master these carseat carriers. They were a real bitch to get in. I had to get my father to show me, who was just as useless, and he then enlisted John to help, but he was no help either. So we all gave up and let Zoe and Macey handle it.

Everly plucks the first carrier out, then the middle one, while I'm still struggling to undo the one I'm in charge of.

"Squeeze the handle, the red button on the side, and lift!"

"I am squeezing and pressing. It's faulty," I tell her, becoming flustered. Everly clicks her tongue and walks around to my side, one carrier in each hand. She sets them down and pushes me out of the way with her hip. I glare at her when it takes her two seconds to do it. Now she's just showing off!

"You'll get the hang of it," she says, walking toward the elevator while I grab the baby bags. Man, these tiny creatures own some shit. I feel like a mule carting it all up. When the elevator doors open, Marcus opens the mind-link as I step inside.

'How do I get the toilet things off? I can't even open the lid,' Marcus tells me.

'What? How am I supposed to know? I didn't install them. Maintenance did just before you got there.'

'Not even Valarian can open it. I had to piss off your balcony earlier because of this contraption,' he growls. *'Valarian is pulling down the gates. I don't get it. Why do you have gates up when they can't even lift their own heads, let alone walk?'*

Everly presses the button impatiently, crossing her legs.

"Are you okay?" I ask her.

365

"Yeah, I need to pee," she says, and I blink.

'Get the damn toilet thing off! Break it for all I care!' I scream at Marcus through the link.

'I'm trying! What do you think I'm doing?' Marcus snarls as the door opens up.

Everly waddles like a duck to the door and shoves the key in the lock. She twists frantically and growls before the door opens and she rushes inside. I trail behind her to see her set the babies down next to the couch before darting off up the hall. Then I hear a crash.

"Valen!" she groans. I set baby C down and rush up the hall to find she's tripped over a safety gate. She hauls herself up to run to the bathroom. Marcus rushes out just before she enters, slamming the door behind her. I look at Marcus, who shakes his head. The next minute, I hear her scream.

"Valen!" she snarls as she tries to undo the toilet trap. I cringe and wait for the door to open.

"Not OCD, huh?" she mutters when she steps out.

I smile awkwardly as she folds her arms across her chest, her overfull boobs giving me a delicious sight; those puppies are huge, and I can't wait to touch them.

"Eyes are up here!" Everly says, while I lick my lips, imagining them jiggling above me as she rides my cock.

"And now you get to clean the bathtub because I just had to pee in it," she growls, pushing past me.

Damn it!

E verly
Watching Valen is rather amusing. He treats those girls like they're made of glass.

"Should she be crying like that?" he asks, watching baby C

scream her head off. She's struggling to latch on this side so I switch boobs and Valen passes me Baby A. I'm getting better at tandem feeding.

"She is fine," I tell him, though I'm getting sick of calling them the baby alphabet. I want to know the names he chose, but he's remaining tight-lipped. Baby B is asleep. Or was until a few minutes into the feeding.

"Can you grab her?" I ask him, although he's already walking to her bassinet. He leans over, cooing and pulling faces at her and I watch him lift her. He subtly sniffs the air before holding her at arm's length, his fingers behind her little head as she stretches and farts.

"You need to change her," Valen demands, and I raise an eyebrow at him. "Please!" he offers.

"No, you need to change her. I'm feeding these two," I tell him with a smirk. I know he can change a diaper. I've seen him change wet ones; now he gets to change a shitty one.

Valen purses his lips, determined. I try not to smile and laugh as he sets her down on the end of the bed, gathering what he needs just as Valarian walks in.

"Ew, what's that smell?"

"That would be dynamite-butt," Valen says, pointing to her squirming on the bed. He takes her onesie off, undoes the diaper, and heaves instantly. "Nope!" he says.

"Yep! You have to get used to it," I tell him. He heaves again, which makes Valarian heave while I watch, amused. I'm not helping. He needs to get used to it. I am not being in charge of diaper duty for all three babies!

"I'll swap ya?" he pleads, giving me puppy dog eyes.

"Oh, you figured out how to breastfeed?" I ask and he mutters something, tugging his shirt over half his face.

"Why is it black like tar?" he chokes out. He cleans and wipes, heaving the entire time, his face turning red. When he's finally done, he dresses her.

"Run this to the garbage for me," he tells Valarian, dumping the diaper in his little hand. Valarian stares at it, horrified and I watch as he pales just as Valen picks up the baby.

"Valarian?" I ask a little too late because he throws up all over Valen's pants. I watch Valen's eyes widen, and he blinks a few times before quickly glancing down at his pant leg.

"Sorry, Dad," Valarian says, gripping his father's shirt to wipe his mouth on. I press my lips in a line, trying to stifle my laugh as Valen sets the baby down before he gags, runs for the toilet, and throws up himself. I sigh.

Yep, this will be interesting, I think to myself.

V alen

"You need to take the batteries out. Why doesn't she stop crying?" I whine, hearing baby C scream for the hundredth time since we got her home. *Either that one's faulty, or she needs to be placed back on demo mode,* I think as I roll over with my sandpaper eyes to retrieve her from her bassinet.

"Babies cry," is all Everly offers as she shuffles up the bed and yawns. I peer at the clock. She wasn't even asleep for forty-five minutes this time. It's 2:20 a.m.!

"You need to get that one checked. Something's wrong with her," I tell Everly as I hand her over. Everly flops out a boob while the baby opens her mouth like a fish, enjoying *my* fun bags. And Everly won't let me touch them either! I eye the baby with jealousy.

My balls are so blue they ache, and I know I'm never getting laid again at this rate, and here Everly is, flopping those big, juicy titties out in front of me every two seconds. Does she not know how full my balls are? They need emptying. Everly's eyes go to me for a second. I wonder if she knows what I'm thinking.

I lie back down and just shut my eyes when another starts

screaming. Oh, how I took sleep for granted! It's our first night at home, and I'm already exhausted. No way I can survive this for... Wait, how many years do babies cry for?

I groan, and Everly snickers, and I swear if she says one more time, 'you'll get the hang of it', I will... I will... I will do absolutely nothing because I can't!

"Go to sleep, please! I need sleep," I whine, pulling the pillow over my head. Everly nudges me with her knee and I sigh, rolling back out of bed to retrieve baby A this time.

I hand her over, and Everly tries to get her to latch. I watch my fun bags deflate as the baby gulps down the goodness.

"You may need to make a bottle. My supply isn't very good," Everly tells me, and I nod while walking toward the door.

"Can you make me a cup of tea too, please?"

I yawn, and plod to the kitchen. My eyes are so blurry I have to squint at the formula can, checking the scoops and ounces before fixing a bottle. Just as I'm about to walk out of the kitchen, Baby B wakes with a loud scream. Then I remember I still haven't made the tea.

Torn, I look between the kettle and the hallway when Everly calls out. "She's fine. It won't hurt her to cry for a minute or so."

I'm halfway through making the tea when the crying stops. A sigh of relief leaves me. This is my life now; it will be filled with bottles and diapers, and the smell of dirty diapers in the air is getting on my nerves. It's torture. Blissful torture, but still, torture.

By the time I get back into the room, Baby B has fallen back asleep in the bassinet, Baby A and C have fallen asleep in her arms, and Everly has her head back, resting on the headboard, also asleep.

"Looks like I made myself tea," I whisper, walking into the room. I place the mug down, propping more pillows under her arms so they don't slip out. Everly has become a baby pacifier, and I'm not waking any of them.

Lying down, I close my eyes, but paranoia has me opening them every two seconds and flicking the lamp on, worried one will slip out of her arms. Giving up, I drink the tea and watch them sleep, sticking my finger under Baby B's nose every two seconds to check she's still breathing.

Again I try to sleep, yet that nagging voice in my head has me flicking the lamp on and I decide to try to detach them from her. I unlatch one, only for Everly's eyes to fly open.

"Did you make my tea?" she asks, glancing around before spotting the empty mug.

Midday
Marcus is on his way to come to get me. I finally figured out the name to go with the middle name I chose. I just hope Everly likes the names I picked. When he texts to tell me he's here, I climb off the couch, passing Baby C to Everly and kissing her and the baby's head.

"Everyone should be here soon for the baby's name reveal. I'm hoping to get back before they get here," I tell her, and she nods.

Everything seems to come so naturally to Everly, and despite the chaos our lives have been of late, she holds it together well.

We have so much to do and to get ready. The hotel is opening up soon. Everly has the council meeting next week, and she's officially changing the laws on the rogues. Court cases and investigations are still ongoing, and I spent half the morning on the phone or checking emails. Until Nixon is caught, I don't want to be away unless necessary, so John came over early this morning to sit with her.

Everly and I discussed briefly this morning the need for a bigger place, so Dad is getting the packhouse ready. Everly wants an extra room so our fathers and Ava can remain with us to help with the kids, and I'm not saying no to any help. One night has taught me this is going to be exhausting.

I press the elevator button, and lean against the wall as soon as the doors shut, closing my eyes. I'm nodding off when the doors open up to the underground garage. Marcus is leaning against the hood, waiting for me. He wasn't happy about not being able to kill the other one responsible for hurting Zoe, yet he understands it's her choice. I don't know if I would have made the same decision as her, though; I would have wanted revenge.

But it shows what sort of person she is. Despite hurting herself, she didn't want to hurt another or kill Amber, though death, I believe, is too kind even for that girl.

"You look like shit," Marcus comments as I open the car door and slide into the passenger seat. He moves to the driver's side and hops in.

"Thanks for taking me. I didn't trust myself to drive." I yawn while covering my mouth. He nods, starting the car and driving toward Dion's jeweler's.

"Derrick had Clarke removed from the city, and the other scumbag, Deacon, is also under investigation for corruption within the council," Marcus tells me.

"Good. I spoke with Alpha Daxon earlier. He doesn't want Nixon's land, so we decided to leave it as neutral territory," I told him.

"More housing for the rogues, then," Marcus says while navigating a roundabout.

"How is Zoe?" I ask him.

"She says she's okay," Marcus says with a sigh.

"Nightmares?" I ask.

"No, guilt. She feels bad for Macey having to kill Carter. Even though Macey told her it wasn't just because of her, I think Zoe knows it was," Marcus tells me.

"Macey loves Tatum, and they're good together," I tell him, but yeah, I could not imagine being in her shoes and killing my mate; that would be torture.

"Think it's just knowing Macey did it for her. Anyway, hopefully today will take her mind off it. I have to pick them up after I drop you back, home" Marcus tells me.

We pull up along the sidewalk and climb out. I'm excited to see the bracelets engraved though I'm nervous about the names. Marcus knows two of the names and even tried to help me pick a name suited to the middle name I was stumped on. It's not usually a middle name, and nothing seemed to go with it until I finally found something perfect.

The bell rings as we step inside, and Dion looks up.

"Just waiting on that last name. The other two are done," he tells me, getting to his feet and pushing his glasses up his nose.

"Summer," I tell him, and he nods, walking out the back to do the last engraving.

"Summer?" Marcus asks.

"Everly's mother's maiden name. It's also the name she used to go by before I found her. It seemed to go with the other," I tell him, and Marcus smiles.

"I can't wait to see her face when she hears them," Marcus chokes up. He knows the meaning behind each name. Each one has a link to someone special to us, inspired by the strongest women I have ever met or wish I could meet, names from women I find inspiring. Each holds a special meaning not only I will hold dear, but Everly, too.

Dion takes about twenty minutes before he returns, using the polishing cloth on the last one. He sets them in little boxes and bags them for me after I check them. Satisfied, we leave and head back home, yet the trip is taking way too damn long. I'm excited to show Everly, but these damn roundabouts!

"Seriously, why do they have so many roundabouts along this straight? Someone needs to complain to the council," I growl.

Marcus raises an eyebrow at me. "You designed this road to stop the street racers and hooligans. You *are* the damn council; complain to yourself," Marcus laughs, and I roll my eyes.

Everly

    I anxiously wait for Valen to return while going over bridal magazines with Ava. Dad is making me coffee while I sit and ponder what names he chose. Valarian's on the floor, watching his sisters squirm in their swings. Every noise they make has him jumping to give them their pacifiers or soothing them. All morning he's been passing diapers and following me around, wanting to help, wanting to cuddle, and wanting to touch them. They're his prized possessions—until the diaper changes. Then, he's nowhere to be seen.

Dad has just set my coffee down on the coffee table when the door opens and Valen walks in. I eagerly look over the back of the couch toward the entry.

"Evie," Valen says, leaning over the couch. He pecks my lips, looking down at the magazine sitting open in my lap.

"Finally going to start planning?" he asks, and I nod.

"Show me," I tell him, reaching for the bag in his hands. He shakes his head.

"Grab the girls and bring them into the room first, then you can see," he tells me, and I pout before hauling my ass off the couch and over to the baby swings. I grab baby A, and Ava passes me Baby B while Valen grabs Baby C.

I'm just glad to be rid of the baby alphabet and can't care less what he names them at this point, as long as they have names. Real names.

I follow Valen into the room, and he places the baby on the bed. I place the other two beside her, peering over his shoulder as he rummages through the jewelry bag.

"Away. You will see in a minute," he says, shooing me.

I growl at him and sit near the head of the bed, watching as he clasps each one in place. When he's done, he glances at me nervously.

"Come on, they can't be that bad. Now let me look," I whine at him. Valen moves aside and motions to them. I hop up, going over to examine the tiny gold bracelets on their wrists. My lip quivers as I pick up the first one's little wrist. I blink back tears, moving to the next. And the last one damn near breaks me.

"You like them?" Valen asks nervously, and I gaze up at him.

"Love them," I whisper, and he smiles, stepping closer and wrapping his arms around me. I squeeze him tight, resting my head against his chest. "Their names are perfect," I tell him, looking up at him. He kisses my nose.

Hearing the door moments later, I smile as voices come echoing throughout the place. Macey, Tatum, and Taylor have arrived, along with Zoe, Marcus, Casey, and Kalen. Scooping the girls up, Valen takes two while I grab baby C.

"I think her name is fitting. She is definitely a troublemaker with all her crying," Valen comments as he walks out to greet everyone. They all chat excitedly while Dad makes himself handy in the kitchen.

"Dad!" I call to him, and he looks over at me. "Come sit," I tell him. He stops what he's doing and goes to sit with Kalen on the ottoman.

"No, next to Macey," I tell him. Valen moves across to where Zoey is sitting with Marcus and hands her one baby.

"Can I look?" she asks all excitedly, clapping her hands before taking her from Valen.

"You can look," Valen confirms. Zoe does and falls quiet for a second, then nods, choking a little before looking up with tears in her eyes.

"Well, what does it say?" Macey asks impatiently while trying to peer over my father's shoulder.

"Summer Zoey Solace," Zoey chokes as I hand the next baby to Kalen. He smiles as he looks at her bracelet.

"Now, I said I wouldn't name her after you, but I added a spin on it," Valen whispers to me.

"Everlyn Valarie Solace," Kalen states before leaning down and kissing the top of her little head.

Valen turns to my father before passing her over, while Dad shakes his head, tears streaming down his face. He already knows before even looking.

"Your mate sacrificed herself for her grandchildren, and none of them would exist if she didn't," Valen tells him.

Macey peers down at the bracelet, softly brushing her thumb over the back of the tiny hand.

"Five remarkable women, and I couldn't think of any better way to honor them," Valen tells them.

"Well?" Zoe asks, and Macey sniffles.

"Claire Macey Solace," she stammers, and Tatum grips her shoulders.

"Our village," I tell them.

"Our family," Valen adds.

CHAPTER
FIFTY-EIGHT

E verly
6 Weeks Later

The two of us have pretty much settled into a routine by this point. Everything seems to be going smoothly. We finally moved into the packhouse, and the extra room is very welcome. Dad and Ava are currently living with us to help with the girls, though he and Kalen are quite busy during the day; they're now the heads of the council, and as a result, the laws against rogues have been removed completely.

Clarke, along with the others, pleaded guilty to their charges and are now rotting away in prison cells. We still have no idea where Nixon is, and though they're watching his wife, she almost never leaves the house; when she does, she never leaves her old pack territory.

Unfortunately, the hotel had a plumbing hiccup and still isn't open. Dad and Kalen are stuck helping Valen deal with that today while I'm at my dress fitting. Valen is meeting me afterward so we can go grocery shopping.

"Valarian, can you pass Evelyn her pacifier?" I ask him while the lady finishes pinning my dress. Zoe and Macey were supposed to come to the fitting with me and help me pick out my dress with Ava, but all of them are busy today. It was quite the mission to haul all the kids in the car by myself, so I brought Valarian along instead of sending him to school.

The three of them chose violet bridesmaid dresses, and I chose an off-white dress. I'm still dropping weight, and now my boobs have gone back to normal, the dress needs taking in even more. I have one more fitting after this one to retake my measurements.

The dress fitting feels like it takes forever, and I'm looking forward to getting home. I'm exhausted, and the girls are sick of sitting in the stroller, which barely fits in the back of my car. Slipping the dress off, I quickly get changed and decide to call Valen to find out how far away he is.

I kind of hoped he would volunteer to do the grocery shopping himself. Though I know he wants me to come with him so that I can go to the reserve and finally shift on the way home.

I still haven't. Time is always against me, or I'm far too tired, and knowing how it usually exhausts me, I'm not all that tempted to shift.

Valen answers the phone on the second ring, and I can tell he's in the car by the echo.

"Where are you?" I ask, coming back out of the dressing room. I thank the ladies that work here and kick off the brakes on the stroller.

"About fifteen minutes away," Valen tells me.

"Okay, I'll start getting the kids in the car," I tell him, pushing the stroller out the door as Valarian holds it open for me.

"Yep, I'll follow you home. Dad is meeting us there. He said he would watch the kids for us while we go grocery shopping and out for a run," he tells me. I sigh but say nothing. We hardly spend any alone time together, and I know he's craving that. I can tolerate being exhausted if it makes him happy.

"Okay, see you in a few minutes," I tell him, stepping into the hot sun and squinting at the brightness.

"That you will. I love you."

"Love you too," I tell him before hanging up.

It's scorching hot today, the sun high in the sky. Valarian and I make our way across the parking lot and I hit the fob, unlocking the doors as we approach. Valarian climbs into the back and sits on the center console so he can help do up the seatbelts. He's my little helper and loves being able to assist in any way he can; he adores his sisters. And we worried he would be upset about not having a brother! But he seems to have all but forgotten that now.

I place Claire in the middle seat, and Valarian starts entertaining her while I get the next one out. We clip all three of them in and I ask him to play with them while I fold the stroller down. His car seat is in the front, which isn't ideal, but Valen is getting a van next week for me. We're just waiting for it to arrive.

As I'm trying to collapse the stroller, movement near the bakery down from the bridal store catches my eye and I see Amber walking out looking terrible. It's the first time I've seen her. She glances at me before dropping her head and rushing toward her car. I sigh, going back to my task.

After finally getting the stroller down, I pop the trunk and jam all the crap in it. I definitely need that bigger car; I push all my weight on the trunk just to close it. I can see Valarian shaking the rattle for the girls excitedly and I smile, watching him for a second. He waves to me, and I wave back when a strange expression crosses his face. My brows furrow when he suddenly shouts.

"Mom, behind you!" he cries with the most blood-curdling scream, it sends instant chills through my whole body. Almost instantly, I feel someone grab my hair and hear the sound of my head smashing into the trunk before everything goes black.

The sun shining behind my eyelids confuses me and my head is pounding. I sit up, wondering why I'm on the ground. My keys that were clutched in my hands are now gone.

"Unlock the door, you little shit!" I hear a woman snarl. I blink when I hear my kids screaming and sit up with a groan.

"Stop that!" she yells as I hear my car doors unlocking and locking.

Clutching the trunk, I pull myself to my feet and my eyes widen when I see Nixon's wife hit the fob. The doors unlock and she yanks the door open before Valarian can push the lock back down. The girls are crying and Valarian screams for me, petrified.

My heart races when I see her go to get in the driver's seat; all I can think is she's trying to take my babies. I run at her, tackling her, and we both smash into the open driver's side door. I hear a snarl somewhere behind me but I'm focusing on her when she drops the keys, and we both scramble to get them just as I hear Valarian slam the door shut.

We wrestle for the keys while I scream for help; when fingers grip my hair again, yanking my head back, I toss my elbow back, connecting with someone behind me before diving back onto Nixon's wife as her outstretched hand reaches for the keys. I land on top of her, snatching them before she can and hitting the lock button just as I'm hauled off.

"Get the damn keys, you useless woman," I hear Nixon's voice growl as I'm ripped off his wife. My blood runs cold and I do the first thing I can think of—I toss the keys toward the store's roof as hard as I can. They hit their mark and stay.

Valarian is screaming his head off inside the car, while I kick at Nixon's wife as she tries to get close to me.

"Just take her. Hurry!" she screams at Nixon. I twist in his grip, my hair ripping out painfully before punching him in the balls from my bent position. He lets go with a grunt just as she punches me in the chest. Ribs break and I gasp for air before she knees me in the head.

Once again, I see black momentarily as I hit the ground, coming around to Valen's voice screaming in my head and asking what's happening just as Nixon punches the window.

The snarl that leaves me is more of a roar as I shift, my body smashing his against the car and denting the door before I'm dragged off by claws sinking into my rump. I twist, swiping at Nixon's wife, who has shifted into a murky brown wolf. My claws slash down her face as Nixon's teeth sink into the back of my neck.

'Valen!' I scream through the mind-link as the woman in the store, hearing the commotion, races out, only to pause as I square off with the Alpha while trying to keep my eyes on his wife.

The car is off and it's stinking hot—it has to be heating up like a damn oven inside. Nixon lunges at me, and I duck, sinking my teeth into his hind leg, as his wife grabs my tail, ripping me backward. The screeching of tires in the distance tells me Valen is close; I just need to hold them off a little longer.

I can see the woman from the store finally on the phone to the police—I will slap her for standing there if I survive long enough.

"Why are you just standing there!" I hear a voice snarl at the woman on the phone.

Nixon's jaws grab my front leg and he shakes his head, which leaves his neck wide open, and I chomp down on the back of it. My spine feels like it's breaking as his wife yanks on my tail, trying to get me off him, but I'm not letting go. They aren't taking my babies—they'll have to kill me first.

That's when something unexpected happens. One minute, I'm being ripped apart by them, the next Amber attacks Nixon, her malt colored wolf latching its jaws around his back leg and shaking viciously. I thought she left. Then I realize it was her voice I heard yelling at the shop assistant. With Nixon distracted, I turn on his wife.

Everly

My instincts are running feral. She shouldn't have tried to touch my babies! Nixon's wife backs up, almost tripping over her own tail as she tries to get away from my teeth. Pouncing on her, I rip into her neck and my claws sink into her sides. She wails loudly while thrashing.

I start tearing at her neck, rending the flesh from her bones, spraying her blood everywhere and drenching myself. When I hear a whimper behind me, I know I only have moments before Nixon is on me.

His wife bucks wildly, trying to throw me off as her skin peels back. I let go before chomping down again, only this time on the side of her neck, curling my claws under her ribs and shaking my head. My vision turns red with her blood gets in my eyes. As she rears up on her hind legs, my claws slash down her sides when I'm thrown back.

I hit the ground on my side, my chin hitting the concrete, and I spit out the chunk of fur and skin in my jaws, trying to keep her blood from molesting my taste buds too much. Getting to my feet, I turn to attack her again when I'm slammed into the car. The thud is loud and the windows smash at the impact. My children's screams ring out loudly behind me as Nixon's teeth rip into my chest.

He manages to latch onto my front paw and flings me to the side. As I get up, I'm smashed by his wife again. Amber's naked form, bruised and bloody, lies a few feet away. Before I can really process that, I hear claws on metal and see Nixon trying to get to my kids. I thrash, kicking his wife off before wrapping my jaws around her neck. The sickening crack as her neck breaks in my jaws when I lift her and slam her down makes my teeth ache.

I turn to charge at Nixon, but before I reach him, I'm forced to skid across the ground as Valen appears in front of me. He grabs the scruff of Nixon's neck in his bare hands and rips him back. Nixon goes flying before Valen turns on him again, preparing to shift.

My focus turns to checking on my kids. My paws hit the side of the car and the broken glass cuts into me as I peer in to find them okay, though Valarian has a scratch on his hand—it looks like he tried to shove Nixon's head out of the car.

"Dad!" he screams, looking past me, and I turn to find Valen and Nixon fighting. Valen hasn't shifted, not having the chance when Nixon lunged at him. But watching him, I find he doesn't need to— he dodges him easily, landing blows against the enormous wolf.

Despite Valen's impressive skill, my heart nearly stops as I watch Nixon's wolf launch across the air straight at him. I suck in a gasp, about to help when they collide, Nixon's jaws snapping at his face as Valen is thrown backward. The move would have worked, except that Valen pivoted at the last second, grabbed Nixon's fur, and Nixon was pulled under him. His arms wrap around Nixon's neck as they hit the ground.

Nixon is no match for Valen—he's stronger and faster. My mate wraps his legs around the beast's torso and Nixon's ribs crack under the pressure. As his arms wrap around the wolf's neck, Valen squeezes his legs. Nixon thrashes, his jaws snapping wildly, close to Valen's face, then suddenly shrieks.

One minute, he's writhing under Valen's grip, the next, Valen has grabbed Nixon's bottom jaw with one hand and the top with the other. My stomach heaves when he pries Nixon's jaw wide, snapping it. Blood sprays everywhere and the beast's bottom jaw hangs limply. Yet still, Valen doesn't let him go, even as Nixon's screaming howls cut out.

The Blood Alpha's canines slip out in his rage as Nixon loses the fight, his body moving slower as he bleeds out. Valen's claws slip free before he thrusts his hand straight down Nixon's throat, and I can hear his insides being torn to pieces by my mate's powerful, razor-sharp claws. Blood gushes and spews out of Nixon's mouth as Valen forces his arm down his throat to the elbow before ripping it out along with Nixon's heart.

He drops it and stands. His entire body is drenched from head to toe in Nixon's blood and his eyes move to Amber, who's trying to sit up. It's at that moment I realize he's going to kill her, thinking she was involved.

'*Valen! She tried to help!*' I scream through the mind-link as his hand reaches for her. He stops, glancing over his shoulder just as police cars scream toward us with their sirens blaring loudly. The moment he stands up, relief floods me. Amber drops her head, but she looks terrible. He turns to face me, and suddenly, I feel woozy.

Valen

I'm furious. They tried to attack my kids! My mate!

'*Valen! She tried to help!*' Everly screams through the link as I'm reaching for Amber. My hand pauses before I grab her and I peer over my shoulder at Everly. When I got here, all I saw was my mate fighting for her life and our kids, but now, turning to face her, I'm slapped with shock.

Her wolf is magnificent, strong, and rivals my own in size. Her gunmetal gray fur is covered in blood and she sways on her feet. I can feel poison spreading through my system and my lips part in dismay when I see she's covered in bites; I have no doubt that the poison running through my veins is forsaken venom. Looking at Amber, I can tell she's feeling its effects too.

"Everly?" I stammer as cop cars flood the parking lot. She sways again before running at me. I catch her wolf as she pounces and her tongue licks every inch of my face as I land on my ass.

Relief floods me when I feel through the bond to find the venom not affecting her. My DNA in her veins must be enough to give her some immunity, and though I can tell she still feels a little queasy, her relief upon seeing me and the adrenaline override the effects.

"You're beautiful," I tell her, pulling her furry head back and stopping her mauling tongue. I look past her at the car to see Valarian talking to his sisters as the police start pulling them from their seats.

I suck in a breath. Seeing them thrashing and screaming in the officer's arms, I know they're alright. I've never been so terrified as when I saw Nixon's wolf's head inside the window.

Everly shifts in my arms, and I rip my shirt off as she does, yanking it over her head to cover her nude body before she's even fully shifted back. The moment she is, she rushes toward our kids, but I tug her back.

"I can feel the forsaken venom. Can't you feel it?" I ask her, and she whimpers, wanting to go to the kids. But we can't risk them getting the blood on them; we have no idea if it will affect them.

I wrap my arms around her waist, knowing I'm the only thing keeping her from snatching them out of the officer's arm just as ambulances finally get on the scene. Amber is rushed off in an ambulance and disappears while Valarian is checked over by an EMT. Nixon only appears to have scratched his arm, not actually bitten him.

"It's over, love. It's finally over," I whisper to her, and she inhales deeply, watching our kids being fussed over.

My car had run into another parked car—I hadn't turned it off when I slammed on the brakes and jumped out the moment I pulled in. However, I can't care less about the damage; the main thing is my family is okay. Guilt gnaws at me. What if I didn't get here in time? What if they had succeeded in taking them or killed them all?

Despite all those rampant thoughts, I feel an immense relief flood the bond. I know this was something that had been an endless worry for her. Not knowing where Nixon was had the entire city on edge. And now we know. Dead at our feet.

Now, hopefully, we can finally move on with our lives.

CHAPTER
SIXTY

E verly

Another Four weeks later.

"Keep your eyes closed," Valen says as I walk blindly with my hands out in front of me.

"Is that Zoe and Macey?" I gasp when I hear their voices and try to lift Valen's blindfold off my eyes. He slaps my hand away, and I reach out again, accidentally slapping someone.

"Ouch! That you, Everly?" Macey asks. "Valen blindfolded me before we left and refused to tell me where he was taking me."

"Oops, sorry," I tell her. "Wait, are you blindfolded too?" I ask her.

"Yeah, and Tatum sucks with directions. I tripped over the gutter back there," Macey growls. "My knee is killing," she growls.

"Kids, slow down and away from the paint; it's still wet!" Marcus screeches just as the sound of their voices reaches my ears. A hand grips my arm.

"Glad I'm not the only blind one around. I was becoming paranoid he's walking me off a cliff," Zoe says. Her hand on my arm slides down to grip my hand and give me a squeeze just as my hand finds Macey's.

"Those pricks conspired against us!" Macey hisses.

With them here, I have a good idea of where I am, which is surprising. Valen said the hotel wouldn't be ready. He had used every excuse to keep us away from this place, from gas leaks to plumbing issues to electrical faults.

"I swear, if they have ruined our hotel," Zoe hisses, and I chuckle, knowing there would definitely be blood.

"Maybe the cliff was a better idea," Marcus mutters, and Valen laughs behind me.

"Okay, can we take these off? We figured out where we are," Macey says.

"One second; you have to lift your legs and step up onto the wall," Valen says.

"Wall?" I ask, shuffling my feet, not wanting to trip.

"Shouldn't be an issue for you, Macey. You're good at lifting your legs around your ears," Tatum snickers, and she growls.

"Language, you brute! Or I will jam *your* legs behind your head and test *your* flexibility," she growls at him.

My feet hits something—obviously the wall Valen mentioned.

"You couldn't have walked around the wall?"

"Nah, too much entertainment watching you all trying to lift your legs high enough," Marcus laughs. The other two join in the laughter behind us, earning growls from us.

Valen grips my hips and places me on the little wall. It isn't very high, though I still wobbled before I caught my balance. I felt the girls wobbling on their feet too.

"Now stay there. And don't fall or you'll ruin the garden bed beneath you," Valen says. I sigh impatiently, wanting to take the blindfold off.

"Okay, you can all remove them now," Marcus calls, and I rip mine off at the same time the girls do. I untangle my hair from it before looking up.

We all gasp simultaneously at the sight before us. Our hotel has been restored to its former glory, but that isn't what made me gasp; I knew what the plans looked like. No, I was shocked that the old fountain that sat in the center of the driveway is gone. In its place is a huge statue.

Zoe cups her hands over her mouth in awe, and Macey squeezes my hand as we look up at...

...ourselves!

The statue is amazing. They must have used an old photo I have of Valarie. She's standing up at the top, but instead of the banner she held in that photo, she's holding the sign for our new hotel:

'Village Retreat'

Beneath her is a statue of Macey, Me, and Zoe, all standing at the bottom on a pile of tools and rubble and all three of us have a baby cradled in our arms. I know they represent Taylor, Valarian, and Casey, and our struggles to get this place up and running.

"This is amazing," Macey whispers, her arm sliding around my waist as she rests her head on my shoulder. Zoe does the same.

"It's perfect," Zoe whispers as I stare up at the woman who inspired us all. Valarie would have loved it, and I know she's watching, I know we made her proud, because *I'm* proud of what we built. We had *built* something. Something extraordinary. Something that made all our hardships so worth it.

Zoe snorts, choking on a sob, and I rub her back, looking at her when she points toward the massive statue.

"Look at the shirts," she says, pointing at our uniforms. The detail is magnificent. No wonder Valen was putting it off for so long; it would have taken ages to have commissioned. Even the little features like our name tags on our shirts are included, and I read the tiny details on them. Instead of our names, they have something else.

'Watch me'

"We watched," Tatum says.

"We saw," Marcus adds.

"And we loved you all more," Valen finishes.

Macey snickers, and Zoe and I laughed at them.

"Shall we go inside?" Marcus asks, and we all nod eagerly.

Walking into the restaurant, we find all our old staff waiting, dressed in their uniforms, the place decorated, and food on all the tables.

"Welcome home," Valen whispers behind me, and I see Ava walk across the restaurant with the girls in the stroller, a huge grin on her face.

"Wait, who's having a baby?" Macey asks, pointing toward the back of the room, where a baby bunting hangs along the wall. Cakes and candy decorate the tables in that corner.

"We decided to kill two birds with one stone, the grand reopening, and..." Valen says, and I gape, looking at my sister, but she shakes her head.

"You said we would wait," Zoey hisses at Marcus.

My eyes widen, and so do Macey's. Zoe glances at her nervously, and I know she must have been worried about telling her from the look on her face. She blushes as Macey's mouth opens and closes like a fish in her shock.

"You're pregnant?" she whispers before rushing over and cupping Zoe's non-existent belly.

"Yes, I was trying to hold off telling everyone until I was showing," she mumbles.

"You're pregnant!" Macey gushes excitedly before the smile falls off her face completely.

"Wait, you're pregnant, and *they* knew before *us*?" she says in outrage, pointing to Tatum and Valen.

"Marcus wasn't supposed to tell," Zoe growls at him, and he smirks.

"Oh, I bet it's gonna be–" Macey starts to predict when Marcus clamps a hand over her mouth.

"You be quiet with your witchy voodoo. It will be one baby. One!"

Marcus says before shrieking and ripping his hand away from her mouth.

"Ew, you licked me!" he complains, wiping his hand on his jeans. Zoe and I laugh.

"Oh, let me help you open all your presents," Macey gushes excitedly, steering Zoe toward the table at the back.

I watch them wander off when an arm drops across my shoulders. Looking up, I see it's my father.

"Your mother would have loved this," he whispers as I rest my head on his shoulder.

"Mothers; you were as much Val's as Valen is," Kalen says, gripping my shoulder and leaning down to peck my head. I nod, wiping a stray tear at their words.

"Yes, they would have," I whisper, then curse. "Damn dust."

"Terrible isn't it?" Kalen mutters, passing me a handkerchief.

"Pop, Pop!" Valarian screeches, wanting Kalen's attention.

"I have been summoned," he says, wandering off.

Dad sniffles and I look up to find his nose all red and his eyes puffy as he looks around the place. I offer him the handkerchief and he dabs his eyes before clearing his throat.

"You really showed them, bub; showed me," he says, and I nod, unable to form words.

"I'm proud of you—proud of what you built and the Alpha you have become. Most of all, I am proud that you're my daughter," he says, pressing his lips to the side of my head and wrapping his arms around my shoulders.

"I love you, kiddo."

"I love you too," I tell him, squeezing him back. We stand there for a bit, watching everyone.

"So, what's next?" Dad asks. I look up at him, resting my chin on his chest. This man was once my hero, then my rival, but now he's just my dad.

"What's next is you walk me down the aisle," I tell him and he chokes, nodding his head and crushing me against him.

"I'd be honored," he whispers, squeezing me tight.

CHAPTER
SIXTY-ONE

E verly

4 months later

It's scorching hot today, and Macey, Ava, Zoe, and I have just left from the final dress fitting. This time, it wasn't my dress that needed altering, but Zoe's; her growing baby bump is getting bigger every day.

"I just need to grab bread and milk. I don't feel like stopping after getting Valarian from school," I tell the girls as we step out of the bridal store.

"I'll come; I need to grab a few things too," Macey says, slipping her sunglasses on. Zoe pulls the sunshade over the stroller and we walk the short distance to the shopping center. It's easier to walk than wrangle all three girls from the stroller to the car and back in again.

Walking into the store, I sigh as the cold air conditioning sweeps over us. We're wandering through the shopping center when Macey shrieks, making us all nearly jump out of our skin as she takes off toward a store.

"Man, this baby has more clothes than I do at this point," Zoe whines as Macey bounces on her heels, holding up a blue, Winnie The Pooh onesie.

"No, Macey, please! I'm running out of places to put all his clothes," Zoe complains, but Macey isn't hearing it and simply wanders further into the store. Zoe and Ava reluctantly follow her in and I wait out the front, since the store is much too small for me to navigate the stroller around. When Macey comes out, she's holding two bags full of baby boy clothes.

"You're impossible," Zoe tells her, but she thanks her anyway.

"So, have you and Tatum had any luck yet?" Ava asks her, nudging me aside and taking over the pushing of the stroller.

"No. We met one surrogate the other week, but Doc said the chances of finding a she-wolf to donate her eggs is near impossible. So, we thought of adopting," she sighs, and I nibble my lip. Tatum and Macey want a child, and Macey wants to give Tatum his *own* child, but her options are limited. And besides human donor eggs, she's had no luck.

"The surrogate?" Zoe asks.

"A little cooky, and Tatum worries she isn't of sound mind to carry to term *and* hand the child over at the end," Macey says. "Some things aren't meant to be," she states as we walk into the grocery store to do our shopping.

I'm looking forward to getting home, and poor Zoe's feet are so swollen from standing all day, I know she wants to get home too.

We're at the checkout, and I've just set my basket down when Zoe nudges me with her elbow toward the self-checkout across from us. Looking up, I see Amber.

I tried to find her after the attack from Nixon, but as soon as she was better, she left the hospital. I have no idea where she's even living, though we hear rumors that she's homeless. We constantly check the homeless shelter to see if she shows up, but never find any sign of her.

"Is it weird that I feel terrible for her?" Zoe whispers as she scans her minimal items.

Macey leans against the register and peers over at her.

"No, she lost everything; her family, her pack. We've been where she is. That's probably why," I tell her. Ava smiles sadly. Amber was our friend growing up, so seeing her down in the dumps bothers me.

This is not the Amber we were accustomed to. The clerk bags our items when I hear her self-checkout register go off, saying her card was declined.

My stomach sinks and I peer over to see what she's buying, only to find canned food and toilet paper. Is she really struggling that bad?

"Evie," Zoe whispers, nudging me and nodding toward her. Zoe is too kindhearted. Most in her position wouldn't care for the girl after all the heartache she sat by and kept tight-lipped about. But we know exactly what it's like to be in her shoes.

"So who's going over there?" Macey sighs, looking at us expectantly. A smile slips onto my face, and Zoe nods to me.

As I cross over to the self-checkout area, she tries her card again, only for it to decline once again. The girl watching the registers asks her to remove some items.

"Leave it," I tell the woman, waving her off. Amber jumps as I approach her. She's wary of me as I pull my card from my wallet.

"No, no. It's fine," Amber hurried to say as she tries to stop me from tapping my card on the card reader. Her cheeks flame as I pay for the few things she has.

"You didn't have to do that," she whispers.

"Yeah, I did. Everyone needs help, Amber. Maybe not always financially, but no one can say they have never struggled. And those that claim they never have, are liars," I tell her. I feel someone brush up against me; Amber steps back, and I notice it's Zoe. She holds her hand out to Amber, one of our business cards in her hand.

"If you're looking for work, we need kitchen staff and cleaners," Zoe tells her. Amber takes the card and looks at it.

"You would hire me?" she asks, clearly shocked. "Why?" she says while looking between Zoe and me. However, it's Macey that answers as she comes up behind us.

"Because we've been where you are," Macey tells her. I see Ava waiting off to the side with the girls in the stroller.

"You made poor choices but did the right thing in the end," I tell her. Zoe wanders off over to Ava and I turn to follow Macey.

"Everly?" Amber asks, and I stop.

"Thank you," she says, holding up the card and motioning toward her groceries. I nod before walking off. Well, we tried and offered; it is up to her now if she accepts our help or not.

V alen
A week later
I watch her from where I'm seated at the bridal table while I twist the ring around my finger. A smile appears on my lips and I slip it off, staring down at the engraving on the inside. At last, she has given herself to me, and now she will always be able to remind me how fortunate I am to have her in my life.

'My love, My mate, My Alpha.' the engraving reads. I'm complete with my Luna by my side, I'm complete with my family, and I'm complete with myself—content with the life we've built.

My feeling of completeness when I watch her dance with the girls and the children is something I've never experienced before.

This was the last piece to put everything together, and she looks stunning. It's the perfect finish to everything. Her hair is pinned back from her face, cascading down her back in soft, dark curls with small flowers pinned into it. She looks like some sort of princess in a fairy tale. I can't wait to mess it up, to see those curls turn wild and damp as I slam into her from behind.

She's wearing an off-white and ivory lace dress that hugs every smooth line of her body, the pale silk flaring out at her hips and seeming to subtly enhance her every curve—curves I can't wait to trace with my hands and mouth.

Since her arms are covered with pale lace, glimpses of flesh are visible, leaving me with a desire to press my lips to them and taste her milky skin. The back is open, revealing skin that I know will later be covered in marks from the brutal way that I'm going to fuck her.

I can't wait for the night to be over so I can take her back to the suite and tangle my fingers into her dress as I strip it from her. The perfect vision that she is now has me anticipating the night's end— to see the meticulously done mascara smeared across her cheeks as tears stream down her face and she loses herself to me again .

She is mine now, in every way possible, and I want that skin to be marked up for the world to see that.

I watch her as she turns her head towards me and waves for me to dance with her. A bigger smile spreads across my face as I get up from my seat and make my way across the dance floor, where she's spent the majority of the night.

When I walk up behind her, my hands fall onto her hips and I glance down at her. She's tipsy, her cheeks flushed, her skin shimmering under the fairy lights. She turns in my arms, wrapping her own around my neck, and I lean down, brushing my lips against her softly.

Although the music is too fast for the way we stand, I couldn't care less as everyone, and everything, slips away; it's as if there is only us here alone, as if nothing else matters.

Through months of chasing her, I managed to regain her love and trust. There was a time when I thought she would be the biggest regret in my life.

As it turned out, she was my redemption.

SIXTY-TWO

E verly

A year later

Zoe and I sit with Valen and Marcus as we wait for Doc to tell me how many viable eggs they were able to extract.

"Man, I have never been so nervous in all my life!" I whisper to Zoe.

"I know! My hands are shaking," she whispers.

"What if she says no?" Zoe worries as she bounces her son, Noah, on her lap. Macey was unable to find a surrogate or an egg donor. Zoe had come to me and told me she wanted to offer to carry a baby for Macey, yet she wasn't sure she was comfortable carrying a baby that was biologically hers. When I had spoken with Valen and told him what Zoe wanted to do and that we just needed an egg donor, he had sighed heavily.

"You want to donate your eggs?"

I nodded my head. I needed his blessing because it was a big ask for him, knowing biologically the child would be mine and Tatum's, though I wouldn't be carrying this child, and it was just eggs I had no intention of using—this was not my child but theirs, and Zoe was the vessel.

"As if I would say no," Valen had said.

So Zoe and I had gone to all the appointments, made sure everything was safe and would work out before deciding to present it to Macey. We didn't want to get her hopes up only for them to crash down again.

We had all witnessed her heartache when she couldn't find a donor or a surrogate. She desperately wanted to give Tatum a baby, though we all knew he was content with Taylor, but in Macey's eyes, their little family wasn't complete. We wanted to help her complete it.

The door opens and Doc walks out, and I think all four of us suddenly forget how to breathe as we stare at his desk as he sits down and goes over his notes.

"Seven viable eggs. Now, you just have to ask," Doc tells us, and we all let out a breath simultaneously.

I squeeze Zoe's hand excitedly and she squeezes mine back. We have it all planned on how we'll ask her. A little corny, but we're excited to see their faces.

"We'll ask at the barbecue tonight," I tell Zoe, and she smiles. Noah babbles on her lap excitedly, eating his hands with no idea what's going on.

The packhouse is full of family.

Kalen and Dad are wrangling the girls. Ava is chasing the kids around the huge climbing frame while they pretend the grass is lava—apparently Ava is the lava monster.

Tatum is with Marcus and Valen as they man the meat; the smell of sausage and steak on the barbecue makes my mouth water as I carry a salad bowl out and place it on the table. Zoe is giving Noah his bottle and talking to Macey about the upcoming event at the hotel and arrangements that need to be made.

"Zoe!" I sing out, and she looks over at me, her lips curling up at the edges as she stands.

She passes Noah to Macey. "Can you give him to Marcus? I just have to help Everly for a second," Zoe says.

"Sure," she replies, taking him while Zoe makes her way over to me. Macey sets her beer down, eyeing us as we disappear back inside.

We walk into the kitchen and I grab a boiled egg from the fridge, chuckling at the silliness of it, while Zoe finds the little plastic medical diagram of a womb she bought off eBay.

"Ready?" I ask her, grabbing the paperwork showing she has seven viable eggs available, if she wants to use them.

Macey is talking to Marcus with Noah perched on her hip when we come back out. Marcus, spotting us coming out, nudges Valen, who places the tongs down.

"Tatum?" he calls out and waves him over.

Tatum raises an eyebrow at us as we stand with our hands behind our backs, but Macey is far too distracted talking to Marcus, who swiftly steals Noah from her arms just as we stop behind her.

We both fall to one knee in some strange proposal position, making us giggle. She still doesn't turn around. Tatum looks at us as if we have lost our minds before clearing his throat loudly and sipping his beer. Still, Macey is absorbed with lecturing Marcus about Goddess knows what.

I sigh and reach up, tugging the back of her shirt. When she spins around and looks down, I hold up the boiled egg and chuckle. She stares at us amused as she takes the egg—it's obvious she thinks we're just being silly.

"If we are having an egg and spoon race, I am totally winning that shit!" she states.

"Macey, will you let me be your egg donor?" I ask her and her smile slips off her face as she gapes at me, at the same Zoe offers her the little plastic gyno-womb model.

"Macey will you put your baby in me?" she asks and Macey takes the plastic womb.

Valen reaches down, plucking the doctor's paperwork from my hands and passing it to her.

"Wait? Are you joking?" she asks, staring between us. Valen taps the paper, showing her the number of viable eggs she has, and Tatum reads over her shoulder.

"Wait, you're both okay with this?" Tatum asks, looking between Marcus and Valen.

"Of course!" they both say simultaneously.

"We can have a baby?" Macey asks, stunned, her hands shaking as she stares at the boiled egg and little womb.

"Is that a yes? Because my knees are killing me kneeling like this," Zoe whines.

"Are you sure?" Macey asks, tears glistening in her eyes, and we both nod.

"Positive! Let us do this for you," Zoe tells her, and she sniffles but nods.

"So that's a yes?" I ask, my knees also aching at the position. All she does is nod her head again, unable to form words.

"Yes!" she finally croaks out, and Zoe and I beam with excitement for her.

"We're going to have a baby!" she suddenly shrieks, hauling us up and into her arms and—since she's taller than us both—crushing us against her breasts. Tatum, Marcus and Valen join in on our group hug.

As we all separate, Tatum screams out, "We're having a baby!" while hugging Macey and kissing her head.

"You're having a baby!" I laugh as the kids all scream excitedly, rushing over to join in the celebrations of our little village growing larger.

CHAPTER
SIXTY-THREE

Macey

Seven eggs later and one finally stuck! The joy I felt when we found out our baby made it past what they considered the safe date was overwhelming. Zoe was devastated each time; just as devastated as me. Some part of my mind thought it just wasn't meant to be, that Carter had ruined every chance I had once he marked me—the venom of his bite had serious ramifications. I can't even try to use my own eggs.

The city scientists managed to scramble and find a safe vaccine, thanks to Valen's genetic mutation—he's an anomaly and so is Valarian, entirely immune to the effects of the venom—yet for me, the damage is done. Every year for the rest of my life I will need the vaccine to keep from turning forsaken. Things could have been worse, I suppose; I could be dead, just like Emily, and all the others who were infected. Tatum is also subjected to yearly vaccinations too.

Last year, our lives were turned upside down, but one thing we're good at is rebuilding; and each time we do, our foundations are stronger, reinforced with love and family.

Our tribe has grown, our city united, and for once, we aren't separated by borders, rules, or stereotypes; the name 'rogue whore' is long forgotten. No, those are things of the past—a past I hope will never be repeated.

Instead, the Slasher pack Alpha stood down and submitted to Everly and Valen, and the entire city is now one pack; just people, co-existing together peacefully, choice given freely and everyone united. Valarie's dream has come true, and for that, I am grateful. It shows all our hard work and sacrifice paid off.

"Here we are," Doc says, pointing at the screen. Zoe grips my hand as Doc moves the device over her rounded belly. He turns the screen so I can see better. Zoe gazes up at me with a smile on her lips and Everly drops her chin on my shoulder, looking at the screen from behind me. Crammed in the small space like sardines in a tin can, we all watch as Doc finishes the ultrasound.

"You're having a little boy," Doc confirms, and Tatum does a happy dance and fist pumps the air. He didn't really care; Doc could say the kid had three heads and he would be just as excited.

Excitement bubbles within me, and Zoe, I can tell, is just as ecstatic. On the way back to the packhouse, Zoe and I discuss going baby shopping.

Valen and Marcus are at home on baby duty, and tonight we're doing a gender reveal at the packhouse, but as the car pulls up out front, we hear utter chaos inside. Everly groans, resting her head back on the headrest beside me.

"If we're quick, we can back out of the driveway before anyone notices," she chuckles.

"Nope, we've been spotted," Zoe says, and Everly and I lean forward to look out the windowshield. Valen is frantically scrubbing the second floor window, a peg on his nose and wearing gloves.

"Is that—" Zoe looks at Everly.

"Yep. That is poop. Definitely back up, I am not dealing with that today," she whines, but Valen points angrily at the window. Tatum winds down the window and sticks his head out.

"Are you good, Alpha?" he calls out and Valen shakes his head, trying to open the window, mouthing something, or maybe he's yelling, it's hard to tell because he can't seem to open the window.

"What? We should come back later?" Tatum taunts.

"Yes, that is what he is saying, come back later," Everly says, tapping his shoulder. "Quick, let's escape. I hear a bottle of wine and eight hours of sleep calling from the hotel," she says, and Tatum chuckles at her, not realizing she's dead serious.

"Do you need help?" he yells out. Valen nods his head viciously, pointing and motioning for us to come help.

"What? I can't hear you?" Tatum yells out the window. Valen presses his lips in a line and facepalms himself before he starts pointing angrily while Everly continues to block the mind-link.

She giggles; Valen hasn't realized that when he facepalmed himself, he smeared shit down his face.

"Oi, shitface, we'll come back at a better time," Tatum hollers, and Valen glares at him, pointing angrily and tapping the window.

"Yes, now let's go," Everly says, tapping Tatum's shoulder. "Quick!" she snaps at him.

Zoe giggles and I lean a little closer, peering out.

"He still hasn't noticed," Zoe laughs. No sooner than she says it, Valen removes the peg, then sniffs the air before looking at his hand like he suddenly grew extra fingers. He blinks, ripping a glove off and wiping his face on the back of his hand.

"Go! Go, now!" Everly squeals, then groans when he loses his stomach on the window he was trying to clean. Valarian wanders over to his father standing at the huge bay windows, holding his sister out like she's contagious, a peg on his nose too—she's naked, legs kicking, and we realize who the poopy culprit is that removed her diaper and decided it would be fun to paint in it.

"Darn it," Everly groans, tossing her door open. I follow, climbing out after her while cackling my head off when she stops abruptly. She points up at the window. "No, Valarian! Hold–"

He doesn't hold it in. Turning green at seeing his father puke, he just adds to the muck on the window as he, too, loses his stomach. Little Claire just cackles, clapping excitedly and patting Valarian on his head.

"You would think he would have a stronger stomach by now," I tell Everly with a shake of my head as we head inside.

Everlyn and Summer are sitting on the mat with building blocks while Marcus—with Noah over his shoulder—tries to stop Taylor and Casey, who are playing tug-o-war as they fight over a book.

"Geez, we're gone for an hour and the place is in chaos," I mutter.

The girls freeze from their fighting, hearing my voice, and I narrow my eyes, giving them both the look. They straighten up, turning into perfect little angels and batting their eyelashes, knowing I don't mess around when it comes to the naughty corner.

"Thank the Goddess!" Marcus says as Everly rushes up the steps to sort her out her kids and Valen.

Zoe waddles in and collapses on the couch, Tatum coming in behind her and passing her some cushions as she lies down.

Suddenly, Tatum claps his hands loudly, drawing all the kids' attention. They immediately stop and stare at him.

"Time to play a game," he cries out and they jump excitedly, "called, find the house!" he continues.

They groan, though Casey and Taylor start cleaning up the mess they had made. Everlyn and Summer plop back on their bottoms, tossing their blocks back in the bucket, just as the doorbell rings and I peer over my shoulder to see a figure through the stained-glass. Wandering over to the door, I pull it open to see Alpha Daxon, John, Derrick, and Kalen.

"Grandpa!" Taylor squeals behind me and rushes over to her grandfather. He scoops her up, propping her on his hip and stepping inside just as Valen comes down the stairs, drying his face with a towel.

"Dad! Great, you're just in time," Valen exclaims.

"I am?" Kalen asks.

"Yep, shit explosion upstairs. I nominate you to take my place," Valen says, and Kalen looks at John.

"Rock, paper, scissors?" he asks John.

"He's your son," John says.

"He's your son-in-law!"

John raises an eyebrow at him and I watch as Daxon steps closer and pecks my cheek.

"Afternoon, love," he chuckles, moving to help the girls clean up. Just as I'm about to close the door, I see Ava's car pull into the driveway and step aside to wait for her, too.

Ava wanders in, a bottle of wine clutched in her hand, and stops in her tracks, watching her father and Kalen argue over who is helping Everly upstairs. They stop as she enters, both turning to face her.

"Ava! My favorite-est daughter," John exclaims with exaggerated delight.

"What?" she groans.

"I'll give you—"

Kalen sifts through his pockets as Ava pops her hip and places a hand on it. He pulls out some cash—a few fives and a ten. "$25?"

"Nope! Whatever it is, no!" she says and Kalen nudges her father, who starts fishing in his own pockets. He pulls out a twenty.

"I'll add $20 and a peppermint," John says.

"Have I told you why you're my favorite sister-in-law?" Valen says, reaching for her and leading her upstairs.

"I'm your only sister-in-law!"

"Exactly! And that's why you never have to compete for that special spot."

I clear my throat and raise an eyebrow when the mind-link opens up.

'You know you're my favorite, just don't tell the others,' Valen says, and I shake my head while closing the door.

CHAPTER
SIXTY-FOUR

E verly

Four Years Later

"I don't like it," Valen growls, pacing the living room. I sigh, trying to work through the backlog of paperwork I've been avoiding. If he paces any more, I'll need to replace the damn carpet.

Valen stops next to the coffee table. "Do you hear it? Does it not bother you?" he demands.

I raise an eyebrow and shake my head, turning back to the paperwork resting on my lap until my pen suddenly disappears from my hand. Annoyed, I huff, pinning him with a glare.

"Can you hear it? It's driving me damn insane!"

"Hear what?" I ask, shaking my head and holding my hand out expectantly for my pen.

"Exactly!" Valen hisses, passing my pen back. "It's so quiet," he mutters to himself.

I roll my eyes. Is he seriously still carrying on over this?

"Yep, it's great! I can now scratch my ass without one of them being up it."

Valen glares at me.

"I'm going to get them." He snatches up his keys, and I groan and rest my head back on the couch.

"They have been at school for not even two hours. This is part of life; kids grow up. They need to go to school, Valen!"

"Then we homeschool! Simple. Problem solved."

I blink at him before pursing my lips. "And who would be doing this homeschooling?"

"You, of course. I have to work."

Uh, uh, no fricking way. I finally have six hours of freedom; I am not giving that up.

"Nope, if you want to pull the girls from school to 'homeschool,' you are doing the damn homeschooling," I growl at him.

"I have a city to run, I can't homeschool; you'll have to quit and do it," Valen tells me.

"Exactly why am I homeschooling if you aren't going to be here?" I ask him. He grumbles, pacing some more.

"I can't take the damn silence. It's too quiet, too fricking quiet, Everly. How does it not disturb you?"

I don't even bother answering.

He's being irrational. The man hates mess, hates loud noise, and suddenly the girls start school and he's on the verge of a nervous breakdown. He cleaned the house frantically in an hour, and the next hour, he's paced the floor so much I swear I see tracks.

Valen stops again, and I wait for his tirade when he jumps. "I got it!"

I toss my paperwork aside. Clearly, I'm getting no work done today. I glance at my mate, his tailored suit ruffled from his stress, the top two buttons on his shirt undone. He stands with his hands on his hips like he has a solution to the problem I didn't know we apparently had.

My eyes skim over his face, and his lips tug up into a smirk before I meet his dazzling amber eyes. I'm ogling. I do that too much these days, but when my eyes go to his, I don't like the look on his face.

He's too upbeat, like there's some joke I'm not in on. His smile grows devious.

Before I can demand to know what he's on about now, he slowly, methodically walks around the coffee table as if he's stalking prey and not his mate and wife. He stops in front of me and I raise an eyebrow at him. There's something sinister about that smirk on his face that makes my ovaries shrivel up and die instantly.

I shake my head, and he nods, licking his lips.

"Nope, out of the question, not happening," I snap at him. Before I can give him a list of reasons for why we have too many children and more is not an option, he grabs me and tosses me over his shoulder.

I beat his back as my paperwork goes everywhere, scattering on the floor.

"I am putting another bun in this oven," Valen declares, stalking off toward the stairs.

"Like hell you are!" I growl, biting his damn back and thumping my fist against his ass.

"It's the only solution. Problem solved," Valen tells me while I grip the handrail on the stairs. He is brought to a stop, but twists, prying my fingers off.

That's it, the bastard asked for it. I open the mind-link, pulling out the big guns. I search for his father.

'Hey, Evie. What's up?'

'I am about to kill your son. So, I will need someone to help bury the body,' I growl at him.

'Very intriguing. I'm listening.'

'Bring a shovel.'

'Man, that is a big hole to dig. I will ask your father to come help and tell him to bring an extra shovel,' Kalen tells me.

I grip the wall cornice with my fingertips while Valen cackles his head off like a madman as I hang on for dear life and for the sake of my womb.

'Exactly why are we plotting to kill my son?' Kalen asks.

'*The bastard is trying to impregnate me!*' I snap at him, as if it's his fault. Well, he spawned him, he can deal with him.

'*Like right now? I really think this is hardly the time for a mind-link. I love you, Everly, but there are just some images of my daughter-in-law I don't want in my head.*'

'*Not now, now! He's trying to kidnap me. Bring a big fucking shovel, so I can beat him with it.*'

'*So this act hasn't been performed yet...... Oh.... If it is a boy, can we name this one Kalen? Oh, or maybe Kal?*'

'*You're supposed to be on my side!*' I screech at him.

'*There are sides?*'

I growl at him through the link as Valen turns onto the third-floor stairwell.

'*Yes, there are sides. Now pick one! Either you sort out your son, or you help me bury the body,*' I snap at Kalen. He sighs.

'*So, back to this name situation; Kal would be fitting for a girl too.*'

'*Dad!*' I snarl at him.

'*Fine, fine.*' He sighs, shoving the mind-link open and including Valen.

'*Oh, you want to do this telepathically? I can whisper sweet nothings in your head instead of your ear,*' Valen purrs.

'*Please don't—not while I am here,*" Kalen quips.

Valen stops and I feel his hand come down on my ass over my skirt. I jump and yelp.

'*That's damn cheating, and you know it—they always take your side,*' Valen growls.

'*Because I'm his favorite!*' I snap at Valen, gripping a door handle for a moment before my fingers slide off.

'*I am his son! This is some bullshit!*' he huffs, stopping outside our bedroom, though still not putting me down.

'*Valen, put the Luna down and step away from your mate.*'

'*No!*' Valen huffs defiantly.

'*We have plotted your death and organized the location for your body,*' Kalen warns him.

'Is it at least a nice resting spot, and will you visit regularly and clean it?' Valen taunts.

'Put the Luna down, son,' Kalen argues. I snicker to myself, listening to them bicker.

'Nope! I'll cut you a deal—if it's a boy, I'll name it Kal,' Valen states triumphantly.

Kalen falls silent for a second. "Oh, really?"

I growl and Kalen chuckles awkwardly.

"Such a strong name—your counteroffer, Evie?"

His poor father gets dragged into all our arguments, playing mediator. I think hard about my offer.

'Valen will mow your lawns for the next year,' I declare through the link. Valen scoffs, his hand coming down on my ass again.

'Now, that is a nice offer. Backyard too?'

'Yep, even weed the gardens,' I assure him.

'You can't offer me!' Valen growls.

'As Luna, I think she can,' Kalen adds. *'So many choices,'* he taunts, but we all know who he's going to pick— me! I could shit on that man's lawn right in front of him, and he would say it was the neighbor's cat.

'Put the Luna down, Valen. Don't make me cover up your murder,' Kalen tells him, and Valen growls.

'Fine!' He huffs and I go flying. A shriek leaves me as he dumps me on the bed and I bounce. Valen smirks down at me with his hands folded and I feel the mind-link dissolve.

"You always cheat and play dirty," he accuses.

"I don't want any more kids," I tell him.

"Two more?" Valen pleads, crawling onto the bed. I shake my head, finding his pleading amusing.

"Fine, if you want two more kids, then I want a Ferrari," I tell him, knowing damn well he wouldn't waste money on one. He's more frugal than me these days.

Valen jumps off the bed and rushes from the room. A moment later, he returns and jumps on the bed, dropping something between my cleavage peeking out of my blouse. I grab it, giving him a deadpan look.

"There, I got you a Ferrari!" he declares and I shake my head. A toy one.

"One more?" he begs.

Nope, I am not changing my mind. He gently cups my face in his hands.

"Three more?" he offers.

"How did we go from one to three?"

He laughs. "So one it is!" he declares.

"Definitely not. I'll buy you a puppy," I tell him.

Valen pulls a face at me. "I am not having a dog shit on my floor."

"But a baby can?" I deadpan.

"They wear diapers. Please, please, just one? I'll look after it." He gives me his best puppy dog eyes, but I am not falling for it. I shake my head.

He groans, dropping his head against my shoulder.

"Fine, I'll take the puppy," he whines before lifting his head. "But can we at least still pretend to make a baby?" he asks, his amber eyes glinting back at me as he rocks his hips against me.

I grab his head, pushing him down.

"I can be persuaded," I chuckle.

E verly

        Six months later.

        "Frankie, get back here with my damn shoe!" I shout, chasing the damn dog through the house. He races up the stairs, my heel in his mouth, while I try to catch the little turd. His short, stumpy legs run a million miles an hour as he tries to evade me.

"Frankie!" I screech as he darts into one of the kid's rooms. He peeks over his tiny shoulder, giving me a challenging look before hiding under Valarian's bed.

"Come here, puppy, puppy; give me my damn shoe, or I will make one out of you," I growl at him.

I reach for the squirming beast and grip the heel, and it becomes a game of tug-o-war.

"Give me my damn shoe!"

"Should have chosen the baby," Valen says behind me, and I jump, bumping my head before I wiggle out from under the bed.

"We have a meeting, and your dog stole my heel!" I snap at him.

Valen whistles, and Frankie yelps excitedly.

"Now, Frankie," Valen calls. I see his little head poke out from

413

under the bed with my slobber-covered heel in his mouth, then slink his way out. I eye the little Frenchie. Does he not realize I could shift and eat him? The rotten little sod still tries my patience. He races over to Valen, dropping my heel at his feet.

"Who's a good boy," Valen says while crouching down and patting his little head.

"Good boy?" I snap, snatching my heel that is now not only covered in slobber but also chewed on.

"Leave his shoe fetish alone. He gets it from his momma," Valen chuckles, scratching his belly while Frankie's tongue lolls out the side.

Valarian comes in to see what all the commotion is. He scoops Frankie up, taking him from his father.

"Is Momma being mean, Frankie?" he coos, pulling faces at him. If anything, the dog has done wonders for their OCD. It's practically nonexistent, though Valarian and Valen still have a thing about coasters.

"Who would have thought that breed of dog is so damn naughty," I scold the cute little squashed-face dog. He licks frantically at Valarian's face.

"Don't listen to her, Frankie. You're a good boy, and I know where she keeps her favorite shoes," he whispers.

"Valarian, don't you dare," I scold him, and he snickers, walking off. While trying to fix my clothes for my meeting across town, I look down and groan. I'm covered in his fur. No! Now I need to find something else to wear.

Walking out of the room, Valen follows me back to our room so I can change quickly. Once dressed and semi-presentable again, he then follows me downstairs. Macey and her son are playing blocks with Taylor and Casey. It's the middle of summer vacation, and everywhere I look, I'm stepping on children or playing Russian roulette with toys. Yet, I wouldn't have it any other way. It's chaotic and messy, but so worth it.

"Are you going to meet this new Alpha coming into the city?" Macey asks.

"Yes, we're just waiting for my father to get here to help with the kids," I tell her, and she nods. Zoe is working, covering my shift at the hotel today, while Valen, Marcus, and I go to check out this new Alpha wanting to move into the city.

We value our way of life here and won't accept just anyone who might ruin that peace. But werewolf cities are becoming fewer since the new human government regulations and seizures of land and there is nowhere to house everyone. Since werewolves are centered around pack communities, we've had no choice but to accept two new packs.

The first one was easily dismantled and spread out, and Alpha Daxon, Taylor's grandfather, decided to reunite his pack. Years ago, he had stepped down and given us ultimate control, and we still have it, but with the city's growing numbers, and pack members growing antsy with so many strangers, they feel more comfortable in their own packs.

No matter what, though—whether or not they ultimately decide to join one of our packs or remain as rogues—the old laws on rogues will never be accepted in our city again.

So far, we've had no issues, and most of the pack members that did come here either joined ours or Alpha Daxon's. The Alphas didn't care for titles and land as long as their packs could stay together, so the city is more council-run now; everyone equal, everyone gets a say.

Yet, we have qualms about this new pack. Slowly we've extended the city borders all the way out to the mountains; subdivisions have gone in, and even a new railway. But this new Alpha doesn't want to join another pack—he wants his own, and that's what this meeting is about. He wants to buy half my land—he wants the forsaken territory.

We had no plans for it, so I am considering it, but before we agree, I want to meet him—sus out exactly who he is and any intentions he has. We won't allow disruption to the peace we finally have here.

Hearing the door open, a chorus of 'grandpa' rings out as the kids rush toward him and I smile.

"Love you, Dad. Bye!" I call over the chaos while grabbing Valen's hand to escape for a moment's peace by ourselves.

CHAPTER
SIXTY-SIX

Everly

The meeting with the new Alpha goes off without a hitch.

Alpha Lee is around the same age as Valen, perhaps a few months plus or minus, though not as clean-cut. The new Alpha is more of a rough-around-the-edges type of guy.

He also has a son around Valarian's age. We learned he's a single father and had built his pack from nothing—all on his own. He didn't mention any family besides his son, so we take it as a sign that the man has no one who helped him after his wife passed.

His story is very similar to mine; his pack is originally a pack of rogues who had lived in Lake City but were forced out by the human councils who took over.

After meeting him, we decide to invite him back home for dinner. We think it's a nice gesture and could help us to get to know him better. Everyone knows how wrong trusting strangers is, and this guy technically is just that—a stranger—so although we're friendly and nice, we're also still slightly cautious.

Until his pack settles in, we've decided to give him Nixon's old pack lands, which have been pretty much abandoned. We'll give him time to use the land until he builds out the land he's purchasing and extends his borders out.

Checking my phone, I sigh. Valen is still talking to Alpha Lee, while I'm watching and waiting in the damn car. I want to get home —the comfort and warmth is calling me back. It pulls on my heart like a magnet as the odd feeling of missing the kids overwhelms me. They drive me up the wall, but there is no place I would rather be.

Besides, we still need to tidy up before the Alpha and his son arrive in two hours. We can't let them think we're slobs, and with the way I left the house, with toys scattered everywhere, it will look like it. People judge others when they enter houses, and I would be damned if I allowed anyone to judge me, especially the new Alpha.

I know that Macey and Zoe are already tidying up, and my father is setting up the tables out back, but I still want to get home and freshen up before his arrival.

Plus, I want out of these damn heels. They're fucking killing me.

The urge to beep the horn at him is strong as I watched him happily chatting away to Alpha Lee on the steps. However, something seems off. Valen is super excited about something; I can see it from here. Not that I don't want to see him happy or excited, but damn, it makes me a little suspicious about their conversation.

I arch an eyebrow and focus on them as I try to figure out what they're discussing. The feeling through the bond is almost giddy, yet I can feel the hint of nervousness about something.

I'm just about to actually go through with beeping the horn when I see them shaking hands.

"Finally!" I mutter to myself as Valen strolls over to the car.

He climbs into the driver's seat but I don't give him time to settle in before I turn my entire body to him.

"What are you so excited about?" I demand while he unbuttons his suit jacket and shrugs it off.

My suspicions about his out-of-character behavior grows when he tosses the jacket in the back seat. Usually, he hangs it up and ensures it stays neat for the next time he might need it. I watch as he plugs in his seatbelt, then shrugs again.

I raise an eyebrow at him.

"What? I can't be excited about a new pack coming to the city?" he asks, while turning the key in the ignition.

I shake my head; I just want to get home to shower. If that means that I have to miss out on some answers, so be it.

"Alpha Lee will be at our house in three hours instead of two, he just needs to duck home real quick," he adds as his eyes focus on the road ahead.

Lake City is on the other side of the mountains. Before the bypass went in it would have been a four-hour round trip. The new road and tunnels cutting through the mountain lessened that time by more than half.

"Sounds good; gives us more time to get everything ready." I speak right as a yawn escapes me. To minimize the awful sound, I cover my mouth with my hand.

Valen hums as he drums his fingers on the steering wheel. There has to be something he's hiding from me. There just has to. I can see how much more weird he's getting with each passing second—feel it through the bond like alarm bells going off. He can barely sit still in his seat.

Once we arrive home, I see that my father and Valen's have recruited help in setting up because the street is lined with cars. The barbecue is open to whoever wants to attend to meet the new Alpha. Just for that fact alone, I'm not surprised by the number of people here.

They have a chance to meet someone new and get free food. I mean, who wouldn't take up on an offer like that? I would fall for the free food offer alone if it meant I didn't have to cook—screw everything else.

Valarian comes rushing out of the house the moment our car pulls into the driveway. I feel as if every time I close my eyes, that boy somehow manages to grow. Literally by the second, I swear. And now, he's getting so tall that he's nearly as tall as me.

Not to mention that every day he looks more and more like his father. He's a carbon copy of him, just a little smaller. Well, he's smaller for now.

"Where are the girls?" I ask him as his father scoops him up, hanging him over his shoulder.

Valarian laughs and giggles as he dangles half upside down. "Out the back with Pop," he answers while he's trying to wrestle out of his father's grip.

"Is Marcus home?" Valen asks him as he finally sets our son on the ground.

"Yep, just got home," Valarian tells him. "So Alpha Lee has a son?" he asks excitedly.

"Yep, his name is Sam," I tell him as I smile at my son and grab the last of the files from the back seat along with my purse and Valen's discarded suit jacket.

I roll my eyes at the piece of clothing. Our son might have distracted me when we pulled up, but this once again reminds me of how suspicious my mate is acting. Which, in turn, annoys me, since I both want to know and drop the matter at the same time.

Valarian and Valen move toward the door and I huff at them; like father, like son, for fuck's sake! *No, no, guys, don't you mind me, I'm all good being the damn donkey of this family and carrying everything,* I think to myself.

"Thanks for your help!" I call after Valen and he stops in midstep.

His brows furrow, then his eyes widen when he finally sees how much I'm struggling as I try to juggle everything I'm carrying. Valarian laughs as his father quickly rushes back to help.

"What's gotten into you?" I snapped at him. He isn't usually this distracted. Once again, he gives me a vague answer of being excited about the new Alpha coming to the City.

As soon as I've dropped everything inside the downstairs office, I spend the next two hours helping to set everything up for the barbecue, making some salads, and getting the kids' table set up. When I'm done, I check on the triplets and go upstairs to shower.

I'm just stripping off my clothes when I hear scratching on the bathroom door before it's nudged open by Frankie. I pat his little head as he lies down on the bathroom floor mat, though I eye the Frenchie suspiciously as I finish getting undressed. He still isn't forgiven for his earlier stunt of eating my heels.

"You better not be in here to cause mischief," I warn him. He cocks his head to the side and his tongue lolls out of his mouth. My wild guess is that the little shit actually thinks he's winning and will earn himself some extra pats by being cute. I shake my head at him as I toss my heels off next to the door and climb into the shower.

Halfway through my shower, I glance out to find Frankie licking the shower door. His big eyes are watching me as he tries to open the glass and climb in with me. He is a terror.

I snap it shut as he nudges it with his squished nose.

"No, go harass Valarian or the girls!" I tell him as I squeeze some shampoo in my hand and start washing my hair.

Rinsing it out, I open my eyes to find Frankie is eyeing me through the glass, only this time he has my *designer* high heels in his mouth.

I point at him. "Don't you dare."

He drops it, and I'm just about to go back to showering when he grabs it again and darts for the door.

I try to slam the door shut before the little mutt takes off out the door, but he weaseles his chunky body out the door just in the nick of time.

I growl as I shut the water off and jump out of the shower. Angrily, I snatch my towel off the rail and wrap it around my body as I dart out after him. He's standing by the bedroom door, looking in at me. These are my only heels he hasn't slobbered on.

"Here, puppy, give me the shoe," I try to coo like Valen does when he's calling the dog spawn of Satan. I creep forward as I hold my hand outstretched, but he takes off again.

"Little fucker!" I curse, chasing after him. "Frankie, get back here!" I snarl at the pint-sized dog. I'm going to skin it and turn it into slippers!

He darts for the stairs and I snap at Valen through the mind-link to help me, but get no answer. The mutt moves to the second floor and turns for the last set of steps.

"Get back here!" I order the half-a-dog.

He stops briefly—the little bastard is taunting me. I slow down, trying not to spook him as he adjusts his grip on my $1,000 heels he's drooling all over.

I'm nearly beside him when I try to snatch the shoe, but he takes off down the next set of steps. I must sound like a stampede of elephants coming down the stairs as I chase the mongrel, then see Valen heading toward the stairs out of the corner of my eye.

Just as I'm taking the next step, my foot slides out from under me. My scream is visceral as I step on a Hot Wheels car and start somersaulting down the steps. Everything slows down—time, everything. My stomach flops and I go ass-up just as Valen opens the front door. Valen shrieks, and I feel his panic as I land on my back, butt naked, my towel having unraveled and disappeared.

"Crap, are you alright?" Valen asks, helping me sit up to find Alpha Lee standing at the front door.

I blink at him and his son.

"Dad, I see her boobies!" the boy whispers, tugging on his dad's jacket while pointing at me.

The Alpha shakes his head, coming out of his shock, and his hand covers his son's eyes as he gapes at me.

I shriek, yanking Valen in front of me to cover my nude body. Frankie is definitely becoming my next set of slippers.

Alpha Lee clears his throat, looking up at the ceiling. "We'll go around the back way," he says, rushing off.

I grit my teeth and look at Valen. "Where is he!" I growl, my eyes scanning the area. I find Frankie chomping away on my heel by the fireplace.

"I'm sure it was an accident," Valen defends his thief of a dog.

"It dies! I kill it!" I scream at him, absolutely livid. That dog is my nemesis, and now he is my next set of slippers.

"How about you go get dressed, and I will go speak with the Alpha?" Valen offers, edging closer to his devil dog. He scoops him up before I can wring its neck. "Besides, I have a surprise for you later that'll cheer you up," he adds.

Valen steps closer to me, quickly pecking my cheek before darting off with his shoe goblin. I growl as I start stalking back to the room to get dressed.

CHAPTER
SIXTY-SEVEN

E verly

As I walk back down to the barbecue, I feel like I'm doing a damn walk of shame. After the adventure that shoe-shredder of a half-dog pulled me into, this sure feels like one of the most embarrassing things I've ever experienced.

The new Alpha's son saw me butt naked! Well, so did the Alpha, but at least he didn't say anything. The little guy, oh yeah, he went full on and pointed at me with his finger just to tell his dad he could see my breasts. I'm sure he's already told the story to the entire party, which, by no means, makes me feel any better.

Yet, as I join everyone, I notice Alpha Lee seems to have brushed off his unfortunate introduction to the packhouse. His son and Valerian have become quick friends—way faster than I imagined, but that makes me feel a little better about everything.

As I scan the crowd, I notice that Taylor and Casey also seem to get along with Sam pretty well, and the boy doesn't seem to be traumatized by meeting my breasts before he met *me*.

My cheeks heat up again as I recall the incident. That fucking mutt is so darn gone; he has no idea what's coming for him. Oh, I've got a better idea—how about I make a damn hat out of his skin and gift it to the very man who brought the menace into my life?

For the time being, I focus back on the barbecue. We have guests, many of them, and it's already enough that two of them witnessed me at my worst. The others won't see how far I'm willing to go for revenge.

Just like the meeting, it goes off without a hitch, everyone enjoys themselves. As the night comes to an end, Valen's excitement becomes almost uncontrollable when we all hear the sound of an engine revving out the front.

"Ah, finally arrived!" Alpha Lee says as he slaps Valen's chest. Valen nods for me to follow him and Alpha Lee.

"Who is it?" I ask him, but he remains tight-lipped.

As we pass Zoe, she chuckles, and once again, I grow suspicious of her odd behavior.

"What?" I ask her.

"Nothing, congratulations," she snickers, covering her giggling with her hand. My eyes narrow on her. I'm about to ask her what she means when Valen grabs my hand and tugs me after him. He leads me up the side of the house, stopping just before we round the corner to cover my eyes with his hands.

Yeah, nothing to bloody worry about—just a shoe shredder, my mate keeping secrets, and an entire pack of people who seem to know something I don't.

"Valen, what are you doing?" I hiss at him as I feel sidewalk turn to driveway under my feet. I keep tugging at his hands, but he doesn't release me, so I give up on trying. Just a second later, he stops me again.

"Thanks, Cole," I hear Alpha Lee tell someone when Valen's lips kiss the side of my neck.

"Remember when you said if I wanted another baby, you wanted a Ferrari?" Valen purrs in my ear.

My face drops. What the hell does he mean by those words. And I don't like the cocky tone of his voice. What has my mate done now?

He finally lifts his hands from my eyes.

"Ta-da" Valen cries out triumphantly.

I blink at the Ferrari in the driveway.

I said that because I knew he would never get me one! It was nothing but an excuse to get out of the damn baby talk!

And yet, here it is, a bright canary yellow Ferrari sitting in my damn driveway. Alpha Lee tosses me the keys and I barely catch them before they hit the ground.

I stare at them, only to hear laughing from the side of the house as Macey and Zoe peer around the corner at my horror. How is my worst nightmare amusing them? Had they lost the last remnants of their minds? They know I have goals to accomplish—they even helped me plan!

I shake my head as I finally reach the understanding of what Zoe's 'congratulations' were for. Valen thinks he's spitting another litter out of me. Heck no!

"No, we have the future-slippers dog!" I tell him.

"A deal is a deal!" Valen huffs as he plucks the keys from my hands. I shake my head and glare at Alpha Lee. I know he owns the most car dealerships in the country, but.... No!

Alpha Lee puts his hands up in surrender.

"He asked, I delivered." He laughs.

"And for half the price!" Valen chirps in a stupidly happy tone.

I turn slowly and clench my teeth. "We have my slippers," I tell him, pointing to Frankie, who's excitedly watching from the front window.

"Now, I need a robe—your pelt will do just fine!" I growl at him.

Valen's face falls and he backs up. "Hey, I delivered on my end, a deal is a deal!" he says as he folds his arms across his chest.

By now, both our fathers and those who remain are in the driveway, getting ready to leave or just watching us.

"He has a point, Evie. A deal is a deal," Macey chimes in and I shoot her a glare, to which she just laughs.

"And about the name? Is Kalen or Kal still on the table?" Kalen asks.

I press my lips in a line, shooting my father-in-law a look to 'shut it'. He shrugs as my father wanders over with Ava, both ready to leave. He stops, giving me a hug and kiss.

"Congratulations sweetheart. Hopefully, this one is a boy." I slap his arm and he laughs, rushing off before I can kick him too.

Valen smirks, thinking he's won. He may have won this one. But he has to sleep sometime.

We bid our farewells to everyone and head back up the side of the house to clean up when Macey speaks up.

"I predict this time it will be quadr–"

I clamp my hands over her mouth.

"Shut it! You jinxed me last time," I snarl at her, and she laughs, swatting my hands away.

"Hey, that reminds me. Valen, you still owe me that foot rub!" she calls after him.

He peeks over his shoulder. "I am not touching those Neanderthal feet!" he says, and she growls.

"You'll be rubbing my feet!" she snaps as she darts after him. I shake my head and Tatum laughs as she gives chase.

SIXTY-EIGHT

Later that night.

I knew from the beginning that it was a bad idea to agree to Valen's deal, although I know, undoubtedly, he will not be letting me get out of it. I'd started it myself, of course, by saying I wanted a damn Ferrari if he wanted a baby. I underestimated him and his eagerness. He had laughed at me and said he would take the puppy. I thought that would be the end of it. Apparently not!

"How about some fish?" I offer and Valen smirks.

"Not a chance, you're paying up!" he purrs as he climbs onto the bed.

"A guinea pig?" I ask.

"Not a chance. You're not getting out of it," he growls, nipping at my thighs as he crawls up my body. He pushes my night dress up, then kisses my stomach. "I am filling this womb—a deal is a deal," he growls, nipping at my flesh.

"You got a Frankie!" I retort.

"And now a warm womb to house another pup!" he chuckles.

"That's double-dipping!" I snap.

"No, but I don't mind double-dipping tonight to ensure you are filled with my seed," he laughs. I roll my eyes at him. I should have asked for a jet.

I shake my head and start to protest some more—try to talk my way out of it—when he silences me with his lips as he settles between my legs. I moan into his mouth as his tongue invades mine, his hard, muscled body pressing against me; sparks spread across my flesh. Every inch of my skin is covered in goosebumps, and my breath hitches as he devours my lips in a soul–sucking kiss.

I feel like I'm on some sort of high, which makes it hard to see straight. I can't concentrate. It's all too much, and Valen knows exactly how to get what he wants—how to get me to comply. And I know he'll get what he wants because he's not going to give me a chance to back out. Yet, some small part of me doesn't want to anyway and is coming around to the idea.

Valen breaks the kiss, then tugs off his shirt with one hand, tossing it aside. A smirk dances on his lips as he sits back on his knees. I raise an eyebrow at him as he reaches for my night dress again. A gasp of surprise leaves my lips when he yanks on it, ripping it straight up the middle.

"Valen!" I hiss at the sting. "I just bought that one," I pout.

He chuckles, uncaring, eyes solely on the prize he thinks he won.

"You owe me a–"

He forces my mouth open with his tongue, and I have no choice but to oblige as he presses his weight against me, cutting off my words once more.

I shiver, the pool of arousal in my panties only growing more prominent as my heart beats out of my chest. I want more. I want so much more. And so I allow him to explore my mouth with his tongue in a rhythm so fast I can barely keep up with it. His claws rake my hip as he shreds my panties, earning another growl from me, which he ignores. Yet, I feel the hint of a smile on his lips as he kisses me.

My hands roam across the hard muscle of his chest as I surrender, allowing him what he wants. Reaching down, I push his boxers down.

"Hmm, somebody changed their mind," he hums.

"Just shut up before one of the kids barges in," I tell him.

At my words, he wastes no time—he slips inside of me. I feel every inch of him as he penetrates me, making me gasp.

"Fuck," I groan, leaning up and nipping at his mark. Valen shivers and a deep purr rumbles from his chest. My breath hitches when he pulls out, then thrusts back in, shooting electricity through me. I can feel the sparks everywhere, making me tingle. My body is warm, my heart flutters, and my stomach swirls. The sensations are overwhelming, and he's savage as he continues to pound into me the way he knows I like.

The moan that leaves my lips sounds like a shout. Every sound falls quiet in my ecstasy straight after, my body freezing beneath him.

It shoots down between my legs now, making my body quiver as I reach my orgasm. Everything is so bright and so sensitive. I can't take it. It's too good. Too much. My muscles spasming around his cock draw a growling sound from his lips.

I've already come embarrassingly quickly, but this entire thing is only starting for him now. He leans down and his mouth brutally attacks my throat. His teeth dig into my skin, biting just to deal with the pleasure he's feeling himself. He's purring into my skin, fucking me relentlessly and rocking my body so hard I start to lose my mind.

A smile spreads across my lips as he picks up his rhythm and I moan, taking whatever his body has to offer. He thrusts harder, his movements crashing against my body and making my breasts bounce along with the thrusts. I love the feel of his hunger, pushing inside of me and making him moan. I love knowing that it's my body that's making him feel utterly blissful, and I love the feeling through the bond—his desires melding with mine.

When he angles himself more, I feel my walls clench and I gasp, my eyes opening again. There's a hazy look in his eyes and he smiles down at me as he fucks me with force and urgency. We're both breathing heavily, moaning and groaning. It's all so in sync as he chases to finish it.

He moves faster and harder, squeezing his eyes shut as he focuses on the feelings that shoot through his body, and his lips crash against my own. The sensations build between my legs, and before I know it, there's a sudden wave of bliss that crashes down on me, making me moan.

Valen's movements slow as my pussy grips him, my inner walls pulsating as my orgasm washes through me—he slows with a groan and he falls quiet for just a second, until a loud growl escapes his throat. He thrusts forward, then stills, his cock pulsing, filling me with his cum before he collapses on top of me.

My fingers trail up his sides while he catches his breath, and I hold mine under his crushing weight until he rolls, pulling me with him.

I rest my hands on his chest, propping my chin on them as I watch him. Valen leans forward, a devious smile on his lips as he grips my hips and drags me higher. He bumps my nose with his before kissing me and letting me rest on top of him.

"Give me a minute," he growls, and I raise an eyebrow at him.

"No, I need sleep," I whine.

"You can sleep once you're knocked up," he laughs.

"I have plans, Mr. Solace," I growl at him.

"So do I—to fill this womb." he chuckles.

I shake my head. Now is not the best time to get pregnant, but is there ever a right time? We'll see what happens, I guess.

Valen sweeps my hair behind my ear and groans.

"You don't want any more," he sighs like he was hoping I changed my mind. In a sense, I have, but the timing... I have big plans, goals to reach.

"No, that's not really it," I admit, and he smiles.

"Then what is it?"

"The state meeting. I can't be pregnant for that—I'll be run off my feet."

"I'll rub them," he offers, and I roll my eyes.

"How am I going to look after a baby while running for state?" I ask him. For the first time, humans are allowing us in office and I want to rid us of the rogue laws for good—win our cities back and fight for equal rights.

"With my help. Always with my help," he promises. I chew my lip and his fingers trail up my sides.

"So you decided you're going to run for it then?"

I sigh and nod my head.

"Are you sure, Mrs. Solace?"

I tilt my head, watching as his lips tug in the corners.

"I don't know about that. I have my doubts. What you're planning is unachievable—you'll never do it," he taunts.

I sit up, straddling his hips as I raise an eyebrow. "Is that right?"

He shrugs. "Impossible. You can't run for office," he growls, and I grip his face, then nip at his lips, feeling his tug up into a smile.

"Watch me!" I growl.

Valen grips the back of my neck and his lips press against mine as he rolls me onto my back, crushing me into the mattress.

"Always," he promises, leaning down and recapturing my lips.

The End

About the Author

Join my Facebook group to connect with me

https://www.facebook.com/jessicahall91

Enjoy all of my series

https://www.amazon.com/Jessica-Hall/e/B09TSM8RZ7

FB: Jessica Hall Author Page
Website: jessicahallauthor.com
Insta: Jessica.hall.author
Goodreads: Jessica_Hall

ALSO BY JESSICA HALL

Authors I Recommend

Jane Knight

Want books with an immersive story that sucks you in until you're left wanting more? Queen of spice, Jane Knight has got you covered with her mix of paranormal and contemporary romance stories. She's a master of heat, but not all of her characters are nice. They're dark and controlling and not afraid to take their mates over their knees for a good spanking that will leave you just as shaken as the leading ladies. Or if you'd prefer the daddy-do type, she writes those too just so they can tell you that you are a good girl before growling in you ear. Her writing is dark and erotic. Her reverse-harems will leave you craving more and the kinks will have you wondering if you'll call the safe word or keep going for that happily every after.]

Follow her on facebook.com/janeknightwrites

Check out her books on https://www.amazon.com/stores/Jane-Knight/author/B08B1M8WD8

Moonlight Muse

Looking for a storyline that will have you on the edge of your seat? The spice levels are high with a plot that will keep you flipping to the next page and ready for more. You won't be disappointed with Moonlight Muse.

Her women as sassy and her men are possessive alpha-holes with high tensions and tons of steam. She'll draw you into her taboo tales, breaking your heart before giving you the happily ever after.

Follow her on facebook.com/author.moonlight.muse

Check out her books on https://www.amazon.com/stores/Moonlight-Muse/author/B0B1CKZFHQ

T.C. Kraven

Looking for a steamy retelling of your favorite Greek myths like Hades and Persephone? Then you'll love T.C.'s works, she's even dipped her toes into the paranormal romance genre giving a new twist to a Cajun legend that I absolutely adore.

Follow her on https://www.facebook.com/profile.php?id=100090445042285

Check out her books on https://www.amazon.com/stores/T.C.-Kraven/author/B0BKGQ33BP

Made in the USA
Coppell, TX
30 March 2024

30711134R00260